As it was freed, the thing freed Kyellan, and he staggered back with a cry. It rose in a mist, dripping the blood of sacrifices. A demon-shape twice the height of a man, with huge, serrated teeth and claws, and crimson eyes that commanded worship.

"*Abarath . . .*" hissed wan voices from the shadows. Doubtless the thing's name. Kyellan held up his dagger like a shield, but the Power of that crimson gaze drove him to his knees. The dagger began to heat with orange fire. He had to drop it, but in the same moment he drew his sword and leaped at the demon with a war cry that sounded puny against the echo of the thing's triumphant wail.

Mask Of The Wizard

Mask Of The Wizard

Catherine Cooke

TOR

A TOM DOHERTY ASSOCIATES BOOK

MASK OF THE WIZARD

Copyright © 1985 by Catherine Cooke

First printing: March 1985

A TOR Book

Published by Tom Doherty Associates
8-10 West 36 Street
New York, N.Y. 10018

Cover art by Victoria Poyser

ISBN: 0-812-53384-4
CAN. ED.: 0-812-53385-2

Printed in the United States of America

To my father, William Peyton Cooke,
in answer to a challenge.

The Sanctuary

LORIN

THE TARNSEA

CHELM

Khymer

ISHAR

Laenar

CAERLIN

MAER CUNIN

AHN

CAVERNON CITY

Erinon

Cavernon Bay

SYRYN

THE KINGDOMS

Chapter One

The wind howling across the Atolan bay slammed another choppy wave against the dock pylons, sending up a bone-chilling spray that drenched Kyellan where he stood. Stamping and swearing, he backed another few feet from the edge of the pier and turned to eye the bay with suspicion. It seemed quieter. The great two-masted ship moored there no longer bucked and pulled against its ropes like a newly caught S'tari horse. Sodden laborers appeared again to take out part of the railing and lower the heavy gangplank; Kyellan moved slowly to help anchor the walkway to the pier. His fingers were numb on the ropes, and the knots were slow in forming.

At last he stood back and watched as another heavy four-wheeled cart, its gay paint beginning to run, was pulled down the unsteady plank by four stocky, pale, red-haired men in place of horses. Others staggered after it bearing great loads of baggage wrapped in soft hides. No longer feeling helpful, Kyellan merely waved his doubtless frostbitten hand in the direction they were to go. Why in Shilemat's name had he decided to supervise the last of the unloading? One of his lieutenants would have done as well. But he had sent them with the horses to see that the stable was warm enough; when they were done, he had said, they could take the rest of the night. By now they were settled in some friendly tavern over a mug of steaming ale, while their commander was becoming a statue of ice.

The score of Atolani laborers he had hired that morning did not seem to feel the cold. Kyellan wished he had some of the layers of fat they bore over their bulky muscles. Better still, he wished he had never achieved the honor of commanding the thirty-man detachment of the Royal Guard accompanying His Highness the Crown Prince Arel and his sister on this idiotic pilgrimage. To become the heir to the vast Caerlin Empire, Arel had to receive the blessing of the Goddess from the hands of the First Priestess. The First Priestess and her Sanctuary were in the hills of Garith, the northernmost Kingdom; thus the journey. Kyellan did not believe in either the Goddess or her priestesses. And he particularly disliked the Prince, though he had never met him. The new rule that prevented a commoner in the Royal Guard from rising past the rank of lieutenant was attributed to Arel. Kyellan was lucky to have already been a captain when the orders came through.

At this time of day in Cavernon City, five hundred miles to the south on the map and twice that by ship, the sun would just be touching the tallest temple domes. The high wailing of the Tarish criers would be calling the faithful to evening prayer. The day watch would come in from the outer walls to the barracks behind the ivory-towered palace, to eat or sleep or change their clothes for a night in the taverns and brothels of the Lower City. The heat of the day would have lessened, and the street people would be emerging from the quiet houses and alleys where they had slept. If Kyellan was there, he would be ready to discard a day of defending the mighty Caerlin Empire from invisible enemies for a night of laughter and lovemaking with his

usual companion Alaira, a thief and dancer he had known
from his childhood in Rahan Quarter.

Kyellan pulled his cloak an impossible inch closer around
him. Two weeks ago he had thought his uniform oppres-
sively hot; now the Garithian wind cut through it like a
knife in cheese. He glowered at the thick sky where it met
the sea horizon before him, hiding the sun as effectively as
a veil over the face of a pretty girl.

"My lord?" One of the pale laborers shuffled across the
dock, speaking the harsh tongue of the North. "We are
finished, my lord."

"Everything is unloaded?" the Guardsman asked, stumbling over one of the strange Garithian vowels.

"All but the second cabin of the underdeck, lord. You
told us to avoid it."

"Good. How much?" Kyellan was no man's lord, but
he did not correct the potato-faced Atolani.

"Fifteen denas."

"You had the help of my men. Ten denas is too much."

"We are poor men, lord, with large families. Shall it be
told in Atolan that the Captain of the Royal Guard of
Caerlin, protector of that land's Prince, would cheat an
honest dock worker?"

Kyellan laughed softly and countered, "Shall it be told
in the Kingdoms that Atolan's people charge foreigners
thrice the worth of their services? There are other ports in
the North." The man reminded him of the S'tari horse
traders, who were the best bargainers in Cavernon bazaars.

They argued amiably. Finally, Kyellan dug a shivering
hand into the kidskin purse at his swordbelt and paid the
Atolani twelve golden denas. The Guardsman thought it a
low price, but the laborer ran from the pier to the clustered
knot of his fellows waving the coins gleefully over his
head. Kyellan realized then that what would be a low fare

in Cavernon's bustling port was a fortune in this bleak, windy place where only one ship was docked. That was why he had never become a merchant.

His work was almost done. As soon as he finished, he could find a warm place for the night. Perhaps he could seduce some pale Atolani tavern maid. In Cavernon, at least, women thought him very handsome and called him honey-tongued. But he was unsure of the effect of romantic talk in the torturous Northern language. If worse came to worst, he supposed money would be language enough.

The rough planks of the dock echoed hollowly under his boots as he strode briskly toward the huddled mass of Guardsmen on the waterfront. They groaned collectively when they saw him.

"Everything in the warehouse?" Kyellan growled. "Good. Behn, supervise the loading of the carts. You have the list of where everything goes. Erlin, see that the horses are fed and watered, and try to find them some blankets. Half of you men with each, and as soon as you're done you'll be free until morning." Satisfied with the sluggish response, he turned and started back toward the ship. It was chillier now, if that was possible, and an icy sleet was falling with the wind.

His second-in-command, Tobas, met him at the top of the long gangway. The curly-headed youth, already a captain at twenty because of his noble birth, had been supervising the work on board.

"You look like a drowned cat, sir," he said cheerfully. "Did you fall in?"

"I might as well have. How did you keep so dry?"

"I sent Janos topside and directed them from the hold. Really, Ky, you should have done the same. Are those ice crystals on your cloak?"

The ship's deck was slick and glittering. The sailors

were all Southerners, and apparently they were all below; it seemed more a ghost ship than the proudest vessel of the royal fleet. The two Guardsmen walked carefully across the slippery deck toward the mainmast. Kyellan tripped once on a frozen cable and nearly fell.

"I was never meant to be a sailor," he muttered. Tobas chuckled. Kyellan grasped the iron ring set in the top of the hatch, cursing at its temperature. He pulled up the heavy oak cover, his frozen limbs creaking, and revealed the dark shaft with its wooden ladder. Tobas began to climb down, and Kyellan followed, shutting the hatch overhead. The short ladder ended in a long, narrow hall, dimly lit by a single smoking torch. The underdeck of the huge ship smelled overwhelmingly of the long voyage, of people and horses, smoke and the sea, but it was warmer than the outside.

Coughing a little, Kyellan followed the younger officer, thinking how strange their friendship was. The second son of the Earl of Laenar, Tobas had risen to captain in only three years. He was a fair swordsman and had a quick grasp of strategy, but the only reason he had come so far was that his father was one of the King's close advisers.

Kyellan, in contrast, could look forward to nothing better than he had now. He had joined the Guard at sixteen, at the beginning of the S'tari campaign, and at its end four years later he was a lieutenant. Now he was twenty-two years old, at the highest rank he could hope to achieve. Drunk, he was sometimes bitterly jealous of Tobas. Sober, he knew he should feel fortunate. Most nameless, fatherless sons of tavern girls never made it off the streets of Rahan Quarter.

The passage ended in a heavily carved wooden door, flanked on either side by torches in wall niches. The floor swayed suddenly and violently, and something stirred in front of the door. It was a small boy, dressed in a rich blue tunic embroidered with the tiger rampant of the Caerlin crest. He was asleep.

Kyellan stuck a toe in the child's ribs. The boy woke with a start and jumped to his feet like a rabbit. Peering uncertainly at the two Guardsmen, he wiped his eyes with his sleeve.

"Captain Kyellan! My lord Captain Tobas! I swear I only slept for a moment!" His ten-year-old voice shrilled upward with fear.

"No matter," Tobas said gently. "Go tell the Prince and Princess we're here." He pushed the page boy toward the door, which opened only enough to admit him, then shut again.

"The Princess," Kyellan repeated, intrigued. "I'd forgotten she was along. She never came out of her rooms during the voyage. Is it true what they say about her, Tobas?"

The youth shrugged. "I played with Valahtia when we were children, but I haven't spoken with her in years. She was a spoiled, intelligent little girl. Probably won't have changed much."

"They say she's beautiful."

"Yes. She'll make a good marriage for the Empire."

Kyellan leaned against the smoke-begrimed wall. "Strange, to be in the Royal Guard, but never have seen any royalty. I've always been assigned to guard the walls, or escort caravans to Khymer, or shadow suspected nobles. Why haven't they given me palace duty?"

"They probably weren't sure what courtesy you'd show," Tobas suggested with a slight smile. "A lot of people heard your opinion of the royal family when the new rules for advancement were posted."

"That was damned unfair of them. Was I supposed to

be happy that I'm going to be a captain for the rest of my life? That someday all of our higher officers will be incompetent fools with titles? I don't mean you, Tobas,'' he added hastily.

His friend looked uncomfortable. This was slippery ground between them, and usually avoided.

"All right," Kyellan admitted. "Maybe they're right. I might not be the best choice for the palace, but still . . ."

The door suddenly swung open. The page looked out and said formally, ''Their Royal Highnesses request your presence, Captains of the Guard. You may enter.'' He held the door for them, then resumed his post outside.

There was no one in the room. Pots of scented smoke stood in each corner, perfuming the air heavily and masking some of the odors of the voyage. Kyellan fought to keep from sneezing. The cabin was richly furnished, with ornate cedarwood chairs and a deep carpeting of desert-cat fur. Bright cushions were scattered, and the walls were hung with elaborate tapestries. Kyellan had rarely seen such expensive-looking luxury in Cavernon City, much less aboard a ship.

Curtains parted at the back of the room. Kyellan squared his shoulders, determined not to show the resentment that was growing inside him. The Crown Prince sauntered in with his sister on his arm; he had a youthful, arrogant face, curried shoulder-length hair, and elaborately brocaded clothes, but Kyellan barely noticed him.

Valahtia was the most beautiful girl he had ever seen. Her skin was pale olive, her figure slim and tall but sensual. Her hair was ebony, piled on her head in an intricate pattern of braids interlaced with light-catching gold thread. Her face was high-boned and flawless, with huge brown eyes rimmed with kohl and a soft red mouth whose promise was belied by her distant, regal bearing.

Such beauty might provoke a hundred years' war, Kyellan thought, as Maira's did in the familiar story.

The Guardsmen knelt quickly, barely touching the plush fur that covered the cabin floor. "You may rise," said the Prince remotely. "Tobas of Laenar, old friend, your rank becomes you. My sister and I have watched your rapid advancement with pleasure."

"I am honored, Your Highness."

"Of course. Now tell us, if you will, what preparations have been made for our comfort on the journey."

Tobas began to recount the details. The Prince seemed to be ignoring Kyellan, so he felt no obligation to listen. Used as he was to demure, veiled, highborn women who surveyed the world from beneath downcast lashes, Kyellan was unnerved by the bold gaze of the Princess. She was measuring him as frankly, as admiringly, as would the dancer Alaira. Was he mistaken, or was there an invitation in those not-so-innocent eyes? He broke his gaze and became very interested in the pattern of a hanging tapestry. It depicted a mailed warrior protecting a scantily clad girl from a horde of demons. He did not recognize the story, but then he was no lore-master.

She spoke. Her voice was low and musical. "Tobas, darling, you have not introduced your silent companion. Surely he is difficult to overlook? Pray tell me his name."

Tobas stopped his monologue with the Prince and grinned at Kyellan. "I beg forgiveness, Your Highness. This is Captain Kyellan, my friend and superior officer."

"Your Highness." He bowed deeply, thankful for the opportunity to escape those brown eyes. But the Princess smiled radiantly as he rose again and held out a slim, jeweled hand for him to kiss. He complied as gracefully as he could.

"Valahtia," the Prince said quietly but dagger-sharp,

"please go to the other room while I conclude this business."

Disappointment clouded her young face. "Do I have to, Ari?"

"I wish it." He pointed her toward the curtains. She hesitated, then tossed her head and flounced away in an imitation of her brother's mannered walk that brought an involuntary smile to Kyellan's lips.

Arel glanced at him and back to Tobas. "Your superior officer?"

"Yes, Your Highness."

"There is no house crest on his tunic. Nothing like the proud Boar of Laenar you wear. He is a commoner, then? A houseless man?"

Kyellan's shoulders knotted in anger. He felt his face flushing as he stood at attention. The memory of Valahtia's beauty was fading.

"Yes, Your Highness," Tobas answered reluctantly.

"And you are in line for the throne succession. You should not be commanded by such a man. The new laws should prevent it."

"Kyellan became a captain the year before your laws. He's one of the best commanders in the Guard, twice decorated by the regiment—"

"Enough," Arel interrupted. "Your loyalty is commendable, my friend, but you need not keep up the fiction here. Does it not shame you to be commanded by a peasant?"

"N-no, Your Highness," Tobas stammered. "I . . ."

"It should. If you are your father's son, it should." Arel glanced again at Kyellan, who kept his face set and expressionless. "You will command the Guard in Garith, Lord Tobas. You will consider yourself the senior officer in all matters. No, do not protest. Those are my orders." He turned on his heel and stalked through the curtain.

Kyellan watched the cloth swing and billow for a moment, then whirled and jerked the heavy door open. The small boy on guard shrank back from the anger on his face as he strode down the passage, boots pounding, echoing off the narrow walls. He swung up the ladder and out into the frozen air, barely noticing the stumbling sounds behind him as Tobas tried to match his speed. As he began to shut the latch again, he remembered and waited until the youth's curly head appeared in the opening.

Tobas appeared to be in shock. He pulled himself out and helped Kyellan replace the cover before he spoke. "Why did he do that? Why? I don't want to command."

"He doesn't want his Guardsmen taking orders from a peasant," said the other with a harsh laugh. "A peasant! I never saw a farm until I was sixteen. There are a lot of things he could have called me that would have been true. Thief, bastard, tavern brawler . . ."

"That was only his excuse." Tobas shivered and muffled his hands in his cloak. "He knew from the beginning you were in command, but chose to ignore it."

"Then why? My lord?" Kyellan bowed sarcastically.

"I think it was his sister."

"The Princess?"

"The way she looked at you. Asking your name, offering you her hand to kiss. That's what angered him." Tobas chuckled dryly. "If you weren't so damned attractive . . ."

Kyellan had to laugh. "So if I hadn't smiled at the Princess, I might still have my command?"

"He would have just ignored you."

"There are things a man can't control," he said philosophically. Then he started across the deck at a swift, long-legged stride that Tobas had to half run to match.

"Where are you going?"

"To a tavern, of course. If the Princess of Caerlin let me kiss her hand, think what a Garithian tavern girl might let me do!"

Tobas groaned and followed him into the sleet-fogged night.

Behind the heavy curtains in the cabin was a larger room, hung in green and gold, brightly lit with many candles. The ladies-in-waiting of the Princess sat together on the overstuffed couches, trying to appear uninterested in the scene before them.

"Why did you send me away like a child, unfit to hear the speech of adults? Ari, answer me!" She stamped her slippered foot ineffectually.

"Because you behaved like one," her brother answered, absently adjusting one of the pleats of his tunic. "Valahtia, you must stop so openly admiring every pretty man you see. People will think you are a spoiled little girl who lives only for pleasure. They will be right, of course."

"They should not think of me at all, except as their Princess. I behave as I please, Arel. You have no right to lecture me."

"It is not that simple. You're supposed to be a virgin, the Goddess help you, when you marry whichever foreign prince Father chooses. At least you should not have a reputation that will make it difficult for Father to make an alliance for you."

It was a familiar, hateful argument. Valahtia wanted to end it the usual way, by screaming or bursting into tears, but she held back in the presence of her ladies. Besides, tears rarely affected Arel. At home, they only brought concerned servants to take her away from her upsetting sibling.

She smiled instead. "You're just jealous of that hand-some captain, Arel."

The Prince snorted in disbelief.

"What would you do if he became my lover?"

"I would kill him."

"That might be difficult. I know something of this man. One of my ladies at home has a brother in his command and speaks of him often. He fought in the S'tari campaign and has won several duels with members of the court. He is considered the finest swordsman in the Guard."

"You mistake me, little sister. If you seduced him, I would hardly challenge him to fight me in the streets. I would either have him quietly assassinated, or arrest him and hang him without a trial."

Valahtia giggled. "You are jealous. But I will do as I like."

"Any man with intelligence will know what it means to be your lover. He will refuse."

"Do not underestimate me," she said softly, pulling a fur cape around her shoulders against the chill. The Prince bowed and retreated to his own bedchamber. The wind outside was howling like a banshee mourning. Valahtia shivered.

She looked out the porthole of the cabin, west over the grey, darkening sea. The last glimmer of cloud-shrouded daylight had gone. Perhaps this pilgrimage would not be as boring as she had expected. With a hint of a smile, she beckoned her ladies to help her dress for bed.

The Sea Serpent was crowded that cold night. Its main room was hazy with smoke that rose thick from the central firepit and from the fragrant Syryni pipes in the hands of its customers. Only a few streets from the docks, the inn attracted mostly fur-clad laborers and unemployed sailors, along with a few quiet fishermen and several of the Royal Guard of Caerlin.

Kyellan and Tobas ordered hot ale from the buxom, freckled waitress. The atmosphere of the tavern was pleasantly boisterous, and they tried to relax, not wanting to think about what had happened.

"Shall we bet on who gets her?" Tobas leaned across the table with a slightly forced leer.

"The waitress?" Kyellan was scornful. "No contest. I'm looking for something more interesting tonight."

Tobas looked around and laughed. "Good luck. She's the only woman in the place."

The woman in question arrived with their drinks, set them down with a fetching wiggle, and left before Tobas thought of anything to say. Kyellan shook his head sadly, taking a welcome sip and feeling the strong drink burn a path to his stomach.

"Not so. You haven't noticed the girl in the corner. Over there, by herself on that bench."

The figure he indicated was indistinct, wrapped tightly in a greenish shawl, sipping something steaming. The face was in shadow.

"She's skinny as a desert ape, and probably twice as ugly, if you could see through the smoke. Could even be a boy."

"With your waitress, nothing is left to the imagination," Kyellan protested.

"Nothing," Tobas echoed fondly.

"Shh." Kyellan leaned forward. "She's doing something."

The girl had uncurled from her huddled position, pulled back her shawl, and knotted her long, beet-red hair, revealing a lean figure and a pretty, snub-nosed face. She reached under a table and brought out a large bundle which proved to be a harp, then stood up and threaded her way between the tables. Three men rose to give her a bench by the central fire. She sat gracefully and played a few experimental runs like the music of waterfall. The room quieted to a low rumble.

"A minstrel, by Shilemat. I told you she looked interesting."

"Well, she's still skinny," Tobas retorted quietly. He caught the eye of the full-figured waitress, who smiled coyly and disappeared into the back room.

The girl began to sing a soft sea ballad that seemed well known to her audience. Her voice was low and expressive, her fingers expert on the harp strings. Kyellan stretched back in his chair, swinging his long legs onto the table, and watched her intently. She made even the ugly Garithian language sound musical as she performed in the quiet tavern, the music rising with the curling, salt-scented smoke to the firehole in the roof. She was good. Kyellan had rarely heard better, even among men who had played at the King's court and sung for the soldiers sometimes. What was she doing in a dockside tavern in Atolan?

He was so intent on the minstrel that he hardly noticed when the waitress came up to the table and whispered something to Tobas that made him grin widely. She giggled, pulling him from his seat, and they went quickly to the door that led upstairs.

The music went on for nearly an hour, and Kyellan suddenly realized that the red-haired girl was watching him as she sang. She met his eyes and faltered in her lively tale of a Garithian fisherman and a mermaid. Beginning the verse again, she finished the song, but her voice quavered a little. Her audience began to shift restlessly.

The minstrel paused, a long, slow beat in which the crackling of the fire seemed to echo her music. Suddenly she struck a weird minor chord and began to hum softly, a strange, urgent, disturbing melody that sent a quick chill to raise the hair on Kyellan's neck. She added words, very softly, in what seemed more a harsh whisper than a singing voice:

> "Death stalks the highlands:
> In from the seashore the
> Death-wielding dark ones with
> Bright banners flying
> And spears in the light.
> Run, O Rhiannion, run
> Swiftly, run along, oh
> Escape, do not fight!
> (Thus spake Ayetra, the
> Child in the night.)"

The last line was barely audible. The minstrel stopped, her thin face confused and frightened. There was some grumbling from the audience. Kyellan realized that she had sung in the Caer language, not in Garithian, though some of the words were too obscure for his neglected education. The girl picked up her harp, shaking, and ran like a startled doe between crowded tables, out the door, and into the darkness. There was a heartbeat of strained silence, which dissolved into head-shaking and laughter. Kyellan's chair slammed to the floor as he swung his legs from their perch and followed her, attracting curious stares as he passed.

The wind hit like a stone wall outside the door of The Sea Serpent. He pulled his cloak tightly closed, which was very little help, and squinted into the sleet and darkness. The girl stood not far away, stone still, clutching her harp, the light shawl slipping from her shoulders. Unsure of why he had come after her, Kyellan approached carefully. She seemed not to notice, even as he wrapped his own cloak around both of them, slipped an arm about her waist, and propelled her toward another light that shone dim through the whirling sleet.

As he had hoped, it was another inn. The Sailor's Rest was smaller and quieter than The Sea Serpent. A few patrons played Hounds near the firepit, rolling dice and scratching scores on a slate. They glared as Kyellan entered in an icy swirl of sleet. He ignored them and led the girl to a seat by the fire. She made no sound. Her eyes were empty, but their soft shade of green contrasted prettily with the strong beet-red of her hair, and her tiny waist was firm under his hand. He wondered if she was mad. Musicians often were.

"Are you all right?" he asked gingerly, taking the harp from her limp hands.

She suddenly recoiled from him and threw up an arm as if to guard against a blow. "Rhiannion!" she hissed.

"What's wrong?" He tried to sooth her with his voice. "What happened back there?"

She shook like the last leaf on a winter tree, but her eyes were losing their empty glaze. She soon answered softly, "I'm sorry. It was something that happens sometimes. Don't concern yourself."

"You sang in Caer."

She seemed to gain strength as she warmed her hands by the fire. Her hands were long-fingered, callused, with short, thick nails; Kyellan thought they might feel hard and soft at the same time.

"That's where you're from, isn't it? Caerlin? I'd never seen a Southerner before. Most of the oldest lays were written there, and I was never able to picture their heroes. Until I saw you."

He laughed.

"Really! 'Dark skin, dark eyes, hair like raven's wing,' just as the songs say. I was thinking that, and it happened again. You wouldn't understand, you're a soldier."

"Tell me anyway." He liked her voice. It had music in it.

"Very well." She smiled, gaining confidence. "I saw you as Rhiannion in the old story. You know the tale? 'Rhiannion and Ayetra'? The fragment I sang came from it. It isn't a song I'd have chosen for that audience. Myrthym made it, a songsmith of Targeln's court in Cavernon almost a thousand years ago."

"I don't know the story," Kyellan said gently. "But I'd like to hear it later. Do you have to go back to The Sea Serpent tonight?"

She gazed somberly at him for a moment, then smiled again. "No. Bring my harp, will you?" And she headed for the stairway at the back of the room.

The tale was forgotten for some time. They lay quietly in an upper room of The Sailor's Rest, listening to the wind moaning around the eaves of the inn. He had finally learned her name; it was Melana. Now she ran her hands lightly over him, as if to memorize his body, until she reached the small, lumpy leather pouch that hung sweat-stained from a slender thong around his neck.

"What is it?"

Kyellan chuckled. "Take it off and see."

She fumbled with the knot at the back of his neck until she loosened it. The pouch fell into her hand, and she pulled open the drawstring with an amusing look of anticipation. The contents spilled out into her palm.

"Jewels!" she exclaimed. Five sparkling stones reflected the candlelight.

"Not really." He was sorry to disappoint her. "An old witch in the bazaar gave them to me, for catching an eight-year-old pickpocket who had stolen costume jewelry from her stall. She called them luck-stones. Said no warrior should be without them."

"What are they for?"

He picked them up, one by one. "Brown agate for victory in battle, jade for the same purpose. Jasper, she said, would help heal a wound. A bloodstone to protect against harm and turn dull when danger nears. And amber for luck."

"Do you believe in them?"

"I don't know. I haven't been wounded since I've worn them."

"If you believe in them, they'll work for you," Melana said with assurance as she replaced the stones in the bag and tied the bag once more around Kyellan's neck.

"Now tell me the story," he suggested.

"Oh!" She snuggled deeper into his arms, pulling the blankets around them both against the cold. "Rhiannion was a famous Caer warrior long ago. He was nineteen when he first saw Ayetra, who was twelve years old and an Earl's daughter, and promised to the Temple of the Goddess. So of course he could not have her. He fought the pirates that were raiding from the North, and after more than a hundred stanzas' worth of adventures, he died in battle with the Hoab Wizard. Ayetra defeated the wizard and became First Priestess. It's a sad story, and not one of my favorites."

"And you saw me as Rhiannion?"

"I have the Sight," she said defensively. "It was a true vision. I can't say what it means; your fates may be similar."

"Every soldier faces death." He shrugged.

"You can interpret it as well as I. But there are so many more interesting things to do this night. Let's leave the reading of visions to your bazaar witch-woman and go on to something better."

Kyellan laughed and drew her closer. "Exactly what I was going to say. Maybe you read it from my mind. Something the old witch would give all her wares to do."

He left her in the murky hour before dawn, easing out of the bed and into his uniform in catlike silence. Melana watched him through slitted eyes, studying the shadowed hollows under his cheekbones, the slight arch of his thick black brows, the lean hardness of his body. When she had every detail she closed her eyes again and listened to the soft click as the door shut that led from the tiny room.

She would not cry. She had that much command of herself, though she was sure she would never see him again. Later she found solace in her harp, and those below in the tavern listened into the morning to her sweet, piercing laments.

Chapter Two

"The First Priestess sends for you!" gasped the young white-robed novice, leaning against the cold stone wall of the Dances Room.

Briana was startled out of her critical scrutiny of the six straining, awkward girls who struggled through the opening of the Sixth Cycle Dance. She had been trying to convince herself that in the courtyard, with the giddy smoke of the incense pots and the power of the moonlight, these Candidates would somehow capture the true meaning of the movements. It would be embarrassing both for her and the Order if the dancers performed as they were rehearsing in front of the Southern Crown Prince. If the First Priestess could see them, she might regret her command that they show the foreigner one of the Great Rituals five days hence.

Perhaps that was the reason for the summons. Briana nodded to the breathless messenger. With a sigh of annoyance, she twisted her long auburn hair up behind her head, pushing the unruly mass of it into the silver filigree net that depended from her headband of Third Ranking. The sun was barely peering over the sills of the east-facing windows in the Dances Room; she had hardly begun her day's lesson. The line of Candidates waited their turns in the Sixth Cycle, whispering and giggling, a particularly untalented group of seventeen- and eighteen-year-old girls who seemed far younger than Briana's twenty years. And two of them still had not appeared.

She frowned. "Darwa!" The flutist stopped in mid-measure; the dancers halted in confusion. "I've been called away. Please take them through the opening a few more times, and try to put some emotion into it. Remember this is a Dance of thanksgiving and supplication. And it wouldn't hurt to think of the Goddess occasionally, between steps."

A pretty brown-haired Kerisian trotted into the room; instead of joining the line inconspicuously, she came directly to Briana. "I'm sorry I'm late, Priestess. Gemon is sick again. I couldn't convince her to come to class."

"All right, Pima. Join the others. I'll be back as soon as I can." She walked away from them, shaking her head. Gemon was almost always sick. A frail, visionary girl with unquestioned Power, she was prone to hysteria and fits of weakness. She would have to pass up with the other Candidates later in the spring, but she would not be a priestess long. One of the Goddess's Chosen, she would return to Her soon.

There was an atmosphere of tension in the other rooms of the Teaching House. The Fourth Rank teachers were still there, Briana noticed, but some of the older Third Rankings must have been summoned as well. It no longer seemed that a routine discussion of student dancers awaited her. There was something wrong.

Priestesses who had been working outside, taking advantage of the rare mildness of weather, were clustered in tight, worried groups. Some called to Briana, but she could not tell them what was happening. The wind was rising from the west, a breath of darkness, whipping her heavy robe around her legs and threatening to tug her hair from its net. It chilled her. She walked faster. The wind seemed more than wind, and she slowly became aware of a vague sense of danger borne with it. A threat. Out of the northwest.

Suddenly afraid, she broke into a run toward the Great House, holding the skirt of her robe up from the gravel that was kicked from the path by her pounding feet. Her heart thudded in an odd, offset rhythm to her running. Northwest. There lay that abode of Darkness, the Wizards' College at Akesh on the Small Sea. She could always, if she tried, feel the evil from that place. But never this tangible or immediate. Perhaps the wizards were tampering with the Otherworld again. Someday they would summon a demon beyond their power to control.

The tall doors of the Great House were ajar. She slipped between them and ran down the dim stone corridors. The air tasted of age. The mortared cracks of its walls held dust that could have been there when the builders of the Great House had walked to morning tasks in the grey time before written history. The halls were low and close, lit by widely spaced, guttering torches. Briana had feared them when she had come to the Sanctuary as a seven-year-old novice; now they were warm and comforting.

She passed the unmarked, doorless hole that was the entrance to her tiny cell and glanced inside. The Goddess's Flame still burned steadily, twelve inches high and a hand's breadth wide, as she had set it at dawn. The pattern she had drawn in the air to bring the flame still hung pale and glowing.

Ahead was the inner courtyard, open to the sky. She ran across worn, patterned paths made by the feet of priestesses over years of walking and dancing in the same places. The stones beneath her sandals seemed to quiver with expectation. On the other side stood the archway that led to the quarters of the First Priestess. Inlays of ivory on

the walls glinted in the light of the two white flames that
flanked the entrance of tall pillars. A novice stood ceremonial guard and waved her into the outer room.

An uneasy crowd of women filled the small space. Most
were black-robed Second Rank priestesses, still half-asleep
from their night's work. A few wore the grey robes of
Third Ranking, but none were less than twenty years older
than Briana. She seemed a child eavesdropping on the conversation of her elders. One venerable old Second Ranking
glanced at her, and Briana smiled; the woman turned away
with an offended air. The girl wished she had not been
summoned. She hoped the First Priestess could dispel the
cloud of fear and foreboding that seemed to hang above
their heads.

Briana made the Sign of the Goddess with the others:
hands crossed at the chest, then brought out open, palms
up; the woolen rustling of their robes was like a breeze
through autumn leaves. The First Priestess entered. Her
proud, hawklike face was pale under the coiled white hair,
and there were dark circles below her hooded green eyes.
Her veined, brown-blotched hands were shaking, transparent,
the hands of a ghost. She was not wearing her silver
headdress, and her feet were bare beneath her black robe.

"Daughters, forgive me for summoning you from your
beds," she said softly. Her voice was thin and tired. "I
had reason. I have dreamed."

Anticipation whispered through the room. Briana's skin
prickled. The dreams of the First Priestess came from the
Goddess.

"Those of you who work the night rituals know that for
the past several weeks there has been a curb on the free
range of our Power. At first it seemed a neutral shield, but
it soon resolved itself as a menace. We lost contact with
the Temples in Chelm and Ishar, and with the hermit

priestesses of the northeastern mountains. We were troubled, but unsure what we were facing. The Goddess has shown me.''

Briana had heard nothing of this. They must not have wanted to alarm the lesser ranks until they were certain. Perhaps this explained the danger she had felt that morning.

''My vision was unclear, confused, many images in quick succession,'' continued the First Priestess. ''I saw a faceless specter of unnatural death striding over rivers and oceans, and its companion was a shadow hand of deepest Darkness that overcast the land like a storm cloud. This hand reached into the heart of the Kingdoms, and grasped the hidden place, the Seat of the Goddess. Then I knew night would be eternal. I saw every high place torn down, every flame go out. And I cried out in my dream as I flew over the devastation. I cried, 'Must this come to pass?' And I was answered.'' She paused and looked out over them. Her eyes met Briana's, and the girl felt herself weighed in a balance.

''We can prevent this horror. We can find the Goddess's Seat before the Darkness does. I do not know how difficult the task will be. When they found it necessary thousands of years ago to conceal the Focus of Power, they did not trust its location to written records. It was passed from First Priestess to First Priestess. But five hundred years ago, the Order was forced to accept Hailema, the Unholy One, as their Mother, by the arrogant King of Garith. In fear she might misuse the Seat's Power, Hailema was not told its hiding place. She reigned long, and we have lost what we knew. We are sure only that it was hidden somewhere in Caerlin.

''Each of you in this room will accompany me. The most powerful of us must combine our strength in the search. To assist us, we will take most of the older novices.

There is no time to waste. The Crown Prince of Caerlin will arrive in five days, and we will enlist his aid to escort us to Atolan port. There, we can find ships for the bulk of the journey.''

The First Priestess spoke gently. "I am sorry to take you by surprise this way. Most of you need not concern yourselves with the preparations for departure; such work will require daylight and falls to the Third Rankings among us. The girl who teaches the Dances will be in charge of those tasks; she is strong and untiring. The rest of you may be dismissed.''

Briana heard herself named in stunned amazement. She watched as the other women filed out of the room and left her alone with the First Priestess, and she felt as nervous as a child on her first day at the Sanctuary. The old woman smiled at her.

"Come sit beside me, daughter.''

Briana accepted the proffered stool. "Mother, I don't mean to question you . . . but why did you choose me for this?''

"The others will grow tired enough on the journey. You are healthy and young.''

"Too young. That's what they'll say. They always do.''

"I am aware of their jealousy, and it is hard for you, but they will soon accept that you are of the Chosen.'' The First Priestess sat heavily in her chair behind a polished desk.

"We will need carts from the caves under the plateau, food and warm clothing, and enough of the valuable offerings in the vault to pay for our passage. The rest I leave to you. You have the authority to take novices or priestesses for the work, and the responsibility to have it finished before the arrival of the Southern Prince. No more argument, child. You have my trust, and that should be enough.''

Briana rose and bowed deeply. "I won't disappoint you." The old woman waved dismissal, and she turned and walked quickly out into the courtyard.

The next five days would be difficult, but that was the will of the Goddess. And there would be a journey. . . . Briana paused in the center of the stone floor, seeing the worn lines that were the steps of the Sixth Cycle Dance. Suddenly she leaped into its wild, whirling final movements, as such unexpected joy filled her that the only recourse was dance. Finally. Finally to see the places she had always dreamed of, those faraway, exotic lands of legend. To see the places she had made herself forget when she had come as a child of seven behind the high wall of the Sanctuary of the Goddess.

Garith was a land of dust and wind and a few rocks. So Kyellan had decided from beneath the layer of grit he had acquired riding the rearguard of a long, slow cavalcade of dusty men, dusty horses, and creaking caravan wagons that sank to their hubs in dust on the poorly kept road. He had developed an annoying cough, though he kept a kerchief tied over his nose and mouth. Every few miles, he had to dismount, soak a rag in water from his saddle flask, and clean his horse's eyes and nostrils of the gritty, clinging stuff.

His opinion of the priestesses of the Goddess had never been lower. They had to be crazy to choose this place of all the Kingdoms for their Sanctuary. He had never seen such a Goddess-forsaken country. So why did Caerlin have to go to all this trouble to get Arel blessed by the First Priestess, who had to be the maddest of the lot?

Kyellan had never considered believing in the Goddess, even after he had taken his oath of loyalty to the state, which included an affirmation of faith. He did not believe in the supernatural, or in anything he could not see or touch. He swore by the Goddess sometimes, but more often by Shilemat, the god of thieves in the unofficial Cavernon City pantheon. Shilemat had no temples or worshippers, but most of Rahan Quarter followed his moral teachings.

"Why does the Prince need to be blessed by some crazy female, anyway? Can't the old King just make him his heir?" he grumbled to his riding companion.

Cathan, a youthful follower of the Goddess who was in the Guard because of a highly placed father and through no fault of his own, did not know how to respond. To call the First Priestess a "crazy female" was blasphemy, but he could not challenge his captain to a duel over it.

"Sir," he began, "I wouldn't call the First Priestess that, sir. She's the Voice of the Goddess on earth!"

Kyellan saw that the youngster was serious. He immediately dissembled. "Of course. I don't know what made me say such a thing."

"Probably the Dark, sir." Cathan shivered. "They would be strong here, so far from civilized lands."

"Doubtless."

A rider approached from the column, muffled so well into his cloak that he halted before Kyellan recognized him. Erlin, a short, muscular, talented boy who was being groomed to replace the old Royal Huntsman. For now he was a corporal in the Guard. He saluted briskly.

"Morning, sir. Captain Tobas sent me to relieve you. He wants to see you right away."

"You'll soon wish he sent someone else." Kyellan grinned with no real sympathy. He had been riding rearguard long enough.

Erlin cleared his throat, shifted in his saddle, and finally blurted, "I wish you were doing the sending, sir. It wasn't right to take your command like that. The Prince is being foolish. Tobas has no experience, and—''

''Captain Tobas,'' Kyellan corrected sharply. ''He deserves your respect.''

''But you deserve our loyalty.'' The boy's square face was stubborn.

Kyellan did not reprimand him again. He nodded thanks and put spurs to his horse. It gave a halfhearted lunge of protest, then broke into a reluctant trot. He spoke sharply to it and finally urged it to a quick canter. The wind was loaded with eye-smarting particles that made him duck into the collar of his cloak. Damn. That blunt little corporal had opened the wound again, when he had thought he had it plastered over with grime and joking. And it was true. That was the worst of it. He had fought his way up in the ranks, reckless in battle and always seizing the chance for leadership. He had forced the generals to notice him, had made it impossible for them not to promote him. And Tobas had it handed to him as his birthright.

A flash of color from one of the carts caught his attention. He bowed low over the horse's neck, smiling brilliantly; the Princess Valahtia waved her bright scarf again, her beautiful face enigmatic under its daintily wrapped turban. She sat beside her driver, escaping the stifling atmosphere of the caravan's interior. Kyellan remembered the feel of her soft brown hand against his lips. Judging from the dislike Arel had taken to him, perhaps the Princess really had been interested. It was unlikely to go further, but if it did . . . what better way to get revenge on the Prince than to go to bed with his sister?

Tobas rode back to meet him from his place in front of the column. Kyellan tried to greet the younger man cheerfully, but he could not keep sarcasm from his voice. ''Good morning, my lord. I've just been having an amusing conversation with the dust. Hated to leave in the middle.''

Tobas looked properly embarrassed. "I'm sorry, Ky. Arel's orders. He wants us as far apart as possible; thinks you want your command back.''

"I do.'' He had thought of telling his friend that discipline was lax, a least with one young corporal, but something decided him against it. After all, Erlin had only voiced Kyellan's own thoughts.

Two unfamiliar riders flanked them a little distance from the trail. Tobas nodded in their direction. "Those men claim to have seen some tracks in a gully up ahead. Looks like a large force passed this way, maybe a few weeks ago. An army, they said.''

"The Atolani said no one uses this road this time of year. And Garith barely has an army.''

"I think we need to check their story. But I can't leave the column.''

"I'll go.'' He was glad to have something to do. Tobas looked immensely relieved; Kyellan realized that his young friend had doubted he would volunteer for anything in his bitterness and anger. It was true that though they had camped together as always the night before, Kyellan had barely spoken. He would have to be more careful. There was no reason to take it out on Tobas. "I'll report back in a few hours at most.'' He snapped an uncharacteristic salute. Tobas returned it with a slow smile.

The two riders were not Guardsmen, but they were Caer. One was short and bearded, the other taller and very dark. Kyellan reined his horse in beside them, and they greeted him eagerly.

"We were scouting,'' began the tall one.

"Scouting? On whose orders?''

"The Prince's,'' answered the other man. "We're part

of his personal bodyguard. Neither of us has much experience reading tracks, but we know what we saw. A lot of people walked in that gully. Will you come look?''

He followed them away from the road. The land was broken and rough, covered with stones, pocked with the treacherous holes of small animals. Kyellan had to concentrate on guiding his nervous horse slowly around obstacles. Amusing, he thought, that members of Arel's personal bodyguard might prove to be useful. He had argued against them, saying that with thirty Royal Guardsmen the Prince was well protected, but he had been overruled. He had rarely seen Arel's men afterward. No doubt they had kept out of his way.

They climbed a difficult slope and halted. ''The horses can't get down here,'' said the taller man. ''I'll hold them. Ishoam will take you to the tracks.''

Kyellan dismounted, still more curious. The cleft was far below, between high ridges. It was narrow, but it might have made a decent road for someone who did not want to be observed. He followed the scout. The hill was steep, covered with jagged boulders scattered atop each other like the dice left from a giant game of Hounds. It was a difficult descent, but he almost enjoyed it. The ridges cut off the Garithian wind, and he had never tried to climb on such a hill before. The smooth-soled riding boots he wore made the footing insecure, which added to the challenge.

They descended into a scrub-brush notch and turned to follow the bottom of the narrow valley. The ground was dry and sandy, crunching under their boots in the still, clear air. Kyellan breathed deeply, glad not to have his lungs coated with dust.

''A little farther, Captain,'' said Ishoam over his shoulder.

Something halted Kyellan then. A sound that should not

have existed, a scraping in the rocks at the sides of the gully. A sudden chill brushed him, and he cursed his stupidity when he realized what he had walked into.

With yells meant to freeze their victim in terror, four men leaped from the rocks. The steel of their drawn swords glittered coldly in the midday sun. Kyellan launched himself rolling to the ground, feeling the breeze from the sweep of blades where he had stood, and came up in a fighting crouch, sword drawn. They had expected to cut him down unarmed, and their faces showed it was a different thing to face a Guard captain with sword in hand.

City assassins, Kyellan judged, not swordsmen. Yet they were confident in their numbers, warily closing in, circling him. They would know his reputation for swordplay. He grinned suddenly and made a move they would not expect from a noted fencer.

With a wild, berserker yell, he grasped his curved sword in two hands and whistled it around in a dervish whirl. The steel connected and sliced through tissue, once, twice, and two of the men fell, clutching crimson, bad-smelling stomachs. The other bravos quickly moved out of range of his madness.

The odds lessened, the circle broken, Kyellan halted in a more conventional defensive stance. He was a little dizzy, but the elation of battle possessed him, and his death's-head grin and low laugh unnerved his opponents more than any bladework would have done.

"Come on," he snarled. "I hope the Prince was generous."

The remaining men moved forward again, grim and determined. Kyellan laughed at them, and with a barely perceptible movement of his left hand at his belt, he threw his dagger into the chest of the man who had been his guide to ambush. With pleasure, he watched Ishoam go down.

Two swarthy bravos closed with a flurry of steel. He parried desperately, sending up a whistling fence of sword around him. One of the assassins was a better swordsman than he would have guessed. And he had thrown away his dagger, so he could not fight two-handed. His opponents were fresh and rested. They had not just climbed down a hill of boulders. He held off the skilled bravo, but the other was sidling around behind him.

Close to panic, Kyellan locked hilts with the assassin and leaped toward him. The man had to turn with his sword, until he was on the same side as his fellow. But the assassin not caught in the duel closed in. Kyellan lunged to the side, but the man's sword sliced hot into his upper left arm, numbing it. Not yet in pain, the Guardsman broke the hilt-lock and slashed downward in one motion, half severing the swordsman's head and killing him instantly.

He stumbled back from the remaining bravo, feeling the blood warm and sticky on his side, unsure how deep the wound was. The man attacked but had little finesse. In no more than a few flurries Kyellan found an opening and drove the sword between ribs and into a quickly stilled heart.

Breathing in aching gasps, covered with sweat, Kyellan leaned on his upright sword, still stuck in the last assassin's chest. He had done it. Wonder gave way to pride. He still had that talent for killing which had given him his rank, taken him out of the squalor of Rahan Quarter. The barren gully reminded him of the desert rocks of the S'tari campaign, his first battles as a soldier. He could almost see a band of turbaned S'tari warriors rising from cover to take him captive, as they had so many years before.

Kyellan shook his head, trying to clear the dizziness.

His arm was beginning to burn with a fierce flame, consuming his weary body. He was in no condition for such work; two years of guard duty with an occasional duel or tavern brawl were not enough. He straightened and pulled the weapon from its place. It came free with a rush of the dark blood of the dead man. He wiped it clean on the assassin's cloak.

The horses and the tall men were gone from the top of the ridge. He was going to have to walk. If he moved quickly, he could intercept the column on the road, since he had ridden ahead of them; if he missed them, he would have to follow until they camped for the night, which could be many miles. The flow of blood from the gash in his arm was alarming. He stooped over the least bloody of the dead bravos, retrieved his belt knife from the man's chest, and used it to cut a strip of cloth from his cloak. Awkwardly, he bound it as tightly as he could over the wound and fashioned a sling from the ends.

A glint of gold winked at him from the sliced-open belt pouch of one of the first men to fall. The man was not quite dead, but Kyellan gathered the money and did the same to the rest. Arel had paid them in advance, to avoid being seen with them afterward. None of the men bore a badge or token of the Prince's. It was too bad. He could have shown something like that to the First Priestess; surely a cloistered holy woman would refuse to give her blessing to a man who hired killers.

It took nearly an hour to climb back up the hill; rocks that had been interesting on the way down were insurmountable on the way up. His boots were wet from the bloody ground of the notch and slipped dangerously again and again. Once he fell nearly eight feet and lay half-stunned for some time before he resumed his climb. The wind rose as he got higher, bringing the Garithian dust.

The smell of blood, his own and others', filled his nostrils, and the roaring of weakness pounded in his ears.

Damn them all, he thought. He had planned to try his luck with one of the Princess's prettier ladies that night, hoping for a pathway to Valahtia herself. Arel with his righteous jealousy had spoiled his chance. The noon sun brought little heat as he topped the ridge and pulled himself shuddering into a near upright position. He did not allow himself to rest but began plodding over the broken ground back to the road. He was light-headed and in pain, and he wondered what the Prince would do when he saw him. And perhaps more importantly, what he would do when he saw the Prince.

Tobas found him at sunset—half-conscious in the dust of the road, less than two miles from the campsite of the caravan. Kyellan was vaguely aware of being lifted and felt the peculiar, jolting rhythm of a horse being led. He heard Tobas's explanation: the tall bodyguard had returned a half hour ago, with several horses and a tale of ambush by the force whose tracks they had seen.

The Guardsman did not come to full awareness until he woke to find his wound being stitched together by a veiled woman with quick, strong hands. He turned his head the other way. The cart was luxurious, and bending over him was the dark-eyed Princess Valahtia. She grew and shrank and doubled, until his head finally cleared, and he realized the danger he was in.

"My woman tells me your wound will heal cleanly," Arel's sister whispered. "No great damage was done, but you lost blood."

The quiet servant finished and eased his arm into an embroidered sling. She withdrew at Valahtia's signal. Kyellan found that his clothing had been removed, and he was nude under the blankets that covered him from the waist down. He was still as weak as a baby and saw no sign of his sword or his clothes: helpless, if Arel wanted to finish the job his hirelings had failed to do.

"Your brother . . ." he began urgently.

"Arel cannot know," she murmured. "He went to bed early, and in a good mood." She wore a bed-gown of filmy, sheer weave that concealed nothing.

"He tried to have me killed today."

"He is a fool and a coward, or he would not hire assassins to do his work."

Her coolness was fascinating. "But he's your brother. If I'm his enemy, should I be here with you?"

She giggled girlishly. He remembered she was only eighteen. "He's your enemy because of me. He gets so jealous. He saw that I admired you, that day on the ship."

"You did?" He sounded eager, but he could not help it.

"Arel is a fool to forbid me what I want. He would have that power if he was King, but he isn't."

"He has the power to have me killed."

"You can take care of yourself. And tonight he cannot know. He thinks you're dead." She leaned across him and kissed his forehead.

"But I'll reappear alive tomorrow." He was trying very hard to think clearly.

"Forget tomorrow," she whispered, lowering herself to the soft bedding beside him. In the dim light of the covered lantern, Kyellan watched her remove the bed-gown with a lithe shudder. Gods, she was beautiful. Her skin was soft, evenly brown all over, like a seal's.

"I'm exhausted," he said faintly into her lush black hair. "And my arm hurts."

"It doesn't matter."

He pulled her close with his good arm and found that she was right.

Chapter Three

Kyellan dropped lightly out of the back of the cart into the still, frozen darkness. The cold sank into his wounded arm like an icy knife after the warmth of the night, but he smiled up at the sleepy Princess, who leaned through the open half door.

"Come again tomorrow night, when everyone is asleep," she murmured. "Without fail."

"I will." He hurried away, sidestepping the bodies of sleeping soldiers on the ground. The stars were fading into pinpoints with the approaching dawn, and the ridges of rock on either side of the road stood out in stark relief. It was very beautiful, he thought, though the bitter cold made his breath come in gasps that puffed white in the frigid air.

It had been a good night. His wound had bothered him, but the Princess had been so beautiful and inventive he had not cared. She had even outdone Alaira in the variety and complexity of her desires.

He found Tobas asleep at the western edge of the camp. Shivering, Kyellan stooped over the dead fire and poked through it with numb fingers. A faintly glowing coal was buried deep in the ashes; he pulled it to the top, protecting it with his hand, and blew it into life. Tobas had piled tinder beside the fire the night before, and he fed the coal patiently until he had a small, warming blaze.

The yoke of his tunic was open to the air. He reached up to lace it and touched the pouch that held his luck-stones. An amusing find; they had done nothing for him this time. He supposed the Atolani minstrel of several nights before would say he did not believe in them enough.

Tobas was stirring in his bedroll. Kyellan grinned and picked up the cloak his friend had discarded on the ground the night before. It was stiff and cold. Tobas poked his curly head out, like a wary turtle, and with a gasp pulled it back inside. Kyellan chuckled and threw him the cloak. The younger man sighed and wriggled out of his shell. He pulled on the garment, his teeth chattering loudly, and put his hands almost into the flames of the small fire.

"Are you all right?" He seemed to speak to the blaze.

"Nothing serious."

"Valahtia's women wouldn't tell me. What happened?"

"Her brother hired six men to kill me. I killed five, and the sixth you saw last night. One of them gave me this." He scowled at his arm, then laughed. "All of them gave me these." His belt pouch produced five heavy gold pieces.

Tobas did not laugh. "He ordered you killed before you'd done anything? That's like Arel. And now that you've slept with her, he's lost his best assassins."

"He won't find out."

"Of course he will. He has to have spies among Valahtia's ladies."

"Let him try again. I'm not easily killed."

"They'll come in your sleep. You don't realize what you've done. It's death for a commoner to seduce a member of the royal family. Arel can legally kill you just on suspicion of it."

"Death for a commoner," Kyellan repeated. "Tobas,

what would they do to you if they caught you with
Valahtia?''

"Exile me, take my title," the youth said impatiently.
"That isn't important. Promise you won't see her again."

Kyellan shook his head, stood, and walked away. The
familiar anger was building inside him, but it was not
Tobas's fault. He would not take it out on him. It made
him even more determined to keep seeing the Princess.

The grey sun of dawn promised little warmth that day.
In civilized countries, it would be early spring. He walked
past Arel's cart, and his hand ached for his sword when he
saw the Prince coming outside in his fur-trimmed night
robe. But he had vowed to protect the royal family. Arel's
face tightened with anger, yet he did not look surprised.
Kyellan suddenly grinned, unaccountably cheerful, and
saluted mockingly. Then he went to see if he could find
his horse.

The wide, flat plateau that surrounded the walled Sanctuary afforded an excellent view of the land around for
miles. An easily defensible place, Kyellan thought idly. It
would be simple to pick off attackers making the climb up
the steep, winding road. The hill had cost the caravan one
baggage cart; the axle had broken, and there were no trees
for a hundred miles to repair it. It seemed that after going
to all that trouble, the priestesses might at least acknowledge their presence. He and Tobas had been sitting on
their horses before the silent gate for an hour. The rest of
the company was already making camp on a fallow
wheatfield.

Arel was sulking in his cart, Kyellan supposed. He had
not come out since the day before, when he had made still
another offer to one of the veteran Guardsmen: two ranks'
promotion for the death of Kyellan. The man had laughed

in his face and gone off to tell his captain. Kyellan had stopped worrying about another attempt. No one would accept Arel's proposition.

"Ky!" Tobas hissed sharply. The stone slabs of the gate were being pushed open by white-robed adolescent girls whose faces were shadowed beneath voluminous hoods. A slim young woman in a grey robe walked through the opening, her pace slow and measured.

Somehow, Kyellan had not expected any of the priestesses to be pretty. This one was beautiful, pale and high-boned, with a serenity and confidence in her face that was rare in his experience. Her hood was pushed back from bright auburn hair caught in some kind of sparkling net, and the folds of her heavy robe did not hide her shapely figure. Her eyes were large and sea green.

"Welcome." There was no warmth in her clear voice. "We will allow the Prince and four men of his choosing within our walls tomorrow night. Until then, only the Princess and her women may enter. They will be housed plainly, but they may find it better than the open road. The Goddess keep you safe in Her land."

"Thank you," Tobas said with courtly gravity. "A day of rest will be welcome."

The young priestess turned away stiffly. Kyellan revised his initial judgment. No woman without feeling could be beautiful, and this one had a wall around her as thick as that of the Sanctuary.

One of the white-robed girls relieved the driver of Valahtia's wagon. It started in at the gate, followed by the second cart that housed most of her ladies. Kyellan watched closely and finally saw a familiar face lift a curtain and mouth the words, "Do not fail me." He bowed in assent as the gates closed.

"What did she say?" Tobas asked sourly.

"She wants me to come to her tonight." He turned his horse toward the camp.

"In the Sanctuary?" Tobas followed him, his voice an angry whisper. "Haven't you courted death enough? You've been with her the past three nights. And you'll be doubly condemned for entering the Sanctuary uninvited."

"But I was invited." He grinned. "Don't worry. I won't get caught."

Night settled over the plateau. One by one the fires of the soldiers went out. Kyellan doused his own and began creeping toward the wall. Tobas was at his heels, a nervous puppy.

"You can't change my mind," Kyellan reminded him.

"If you must kill yourself," Tobas muttered, "at least wait until after you've been with the Princess. How were you going to get over a twelve-foot wall with only one arm?"

A good question. Kyellan laughed, grateful for his friend's loyalty. It was obvious the young nobleman had never broken a rule in his life, and this was hard for him. But Kyellan's childhood had been outside the law. Things were more desirable if they were forbidden.

Supported precariously on Tobas's shoulders, beside a shadowed portion of wall between torches and girl guards, Kyellan pulled himself to the top with one arm. It was more difficult than he remembered. As a boy, he could scramble over gates with bags of stolen treasures in one hand and snarling dogs close behind. But that was years ago. He strained to get his elbow over the parapet, then his chin, and after that his left leg swung up and the rest of him followed. He waved Tobas away and looked into the yard of the Sanctuary.

Buildings cast eerie shadows, but nothing moved. The

huge central structure looked older than anything Kyellan had seen. Two caravan wagons stood deserted nearby. The Princess was probably inside the forbidding edifice, but the place was so big he wondered if he could find her. Footsteps thudded, muffled, on the wall, and he squirmed over the edge and dropped, buckling his knees and rolling on impact. He shrank against the wall as the guard passed overhead. His left arm had jolted from its sling and throbbed angrily as he replaced it.

When the wall was quiet again, he started across the shadowed yard between the tall, domed temple and a long, low building of unknown purpose. Increasingly confident, he padded across the loose gravel with the grace of a shaggy-maned desert cat. Nothing challenged him, nothing moved, nothing sounded but the crunch of his boots. A half-moon shone dimly overhead.

The doors to the ancient central building were cavernously open. The entrance seemed the dark mouth of a giant, taller by at least five feet than Kyellan's six feet two. He moved cautiously inside. A single door led from the small antechamber. Beyond it, he found a low, cavelike corridor with the roof a bare four inches above his head. He closed the door behind him. Blackness swam, thick as water. The air smelled dry and dead, like old bones.

His outspread hands touched both walls as he walked. The stone beneath his fingers was not smooth; it seemed covered with strange small carvings. His imagination transformed them into grotesque, weird faces with bulging eyes from nightmares he had known as a child. A shudder gripped him, but he pressed on.

His ears began to register sounds. Rappings, footsteps that began behind him and abruptly stopped. Holes began to interrupt the walls. He supposed they were the entrances to doorless rooms, and he had to force himself to pass them, imagining horrible things snatching at him from their depths. Once, a flickering, bobbing light came toward him in the passage, disappearing just as he shrank against the wall in the vain hope of escaping notice.

He grew angrier as his heart beat faster. Even as a child, he had never been frightened by tales of ghosts and monsters. He had never seen a magician's trick work as promised; stones did not disappear, balls of pitch did not light magically, ropes did not rise in the air. Men who claimed to have seen those things were deluded. There could be nothing here but stone.

Through the thick walls, he began to hear an unmelodious chanting. It modulated from key to key with a weird effect that grated against Kyellan's skin. The priestesses were conducting some ritual under the moon. That would explain the emptiness around him. A little less wary, he kept on through the dark maze, until he heard voices speaking the Caer tongue.

The room had a door, which alone could have told him it was what he sought. He knocked quietly. A chubby middle-aged woman opened it and gave a startled squeal before he clapped a hand over her mouth and entered the room.

"Do you want me killed and your lady dishonored?"

She shook her head, wide-eyed. He released her, and she cowered away from him and called softly at another door, "Your Highness . . . Captain Kyellan is here."

"Send him in," Valahtia called back happily.

The Princess's room was plainly furnished. The bed was narrow. One of them would probably fall off it during the night, Kyellan thought in amusement.

She ran to him like an eager child, her sheer red robe delightfully inappropriate to the severity of her surroundings.

Her hair was elaborately done, and a smooth ruby hung at her throat.

"I knew you would come." She sighed. "This is an awful place. Everyone is so solemn and quiet and boring. I won't be sorry to get back to the road again. . . ."

Kyellan smothered her chattering with a long kiss, loosening the ties of her robe as he did so. She made a small sound of happiness and returned his kiss expertly as her hands moved slowly on the lacings of his tunic. Soon they moved to the narrow bed.

"I wonder if anyone has ever loved within these walls before?" Valahtia sounded awed and slightly frightened.

"We'll show them what they missed."

"Is that a challenge? I don't suppose the Goddess would really mind . . . after all, she is the Mother of Mankind, she must have done it sometimes. . . . Where shall we begin?"

Kyellan left the Sanctuary long before dawn, retracing his steps without a stirring of fear. One of the girls' ladders provided an easy way up the wall. He dropped quietly to the ground and ran back to the campfire where Tobas had fallen asleep, sitting cross-legged, waiting for him to return.

Briana woke uneasy in the early hours of morning. The handsome, arrogant face of one of the men at the gate haunted her. She fancied she heard his sure steps in the hall outside her cell, but when she looked there was no one. It was ridiculous, but she thought the dark soldier who had looked at her so admiringly had been inside the Sanctuary that night. She slept only fitfully before the dawn bell.

In the early afternoon, she was called from her tasks to

the rooms of the First Priestess. Filthy from helping to load the last ancient cart for the journey, she washed hastily under the hand pump in the yard and followed the messenger.

"Sit down, child," said the old woman absently. She was reading a brown-edged scroll that looked about to fall apart. Her small, thin hands held it reverently.

"You called me, Mother?"

"You have done well in preparing for the journey, Briana. I wish to commend you, and to tell you I will not be requiring the Candidates to dance the Sixth Cycle tonight."

"Not dance? Mother, they have worked hard . . . they are ready!"

"You are skilled at spell-binding an audience. The older women say they have not seen your equal."

Briana was confused. "I've only been dancing five years. Trialh was better than I."

"Your teacher has not danced since she hurt her leg in the fields. You are more than she ever was." The First Priestess sighed, replacing the scroll into its wooden tube and tamping in the cork. "Listen. The Prince of Caerlin has much of the Dark in him. Yet I must give him the blessing, for the Ardavan line has been unbroken since the first King, and he is the only son of Chaeris."

"He is in Darkness?" Briana felt sudden fear. "Then will he guide us to Atolan?"

"It seems unlikely. That is why I sent for you. You will change his decision before I ask. You will dance for him tonight, and you will dance the Binding."

Briana knocked over her stool in her haste to rise. "It is forbidden!"

"I see no choice if we are to reach the Goddess's Seat before our enemies. I must have him Bound to my will for one night. Arel will certainly refuse otherwise. He has little love for the Goddess.'' She sighed deeply. "It is a terrible thing to ask of you. The times are evil indeed, that we must resort to such means.''

Briana was silent, looking at her feet, shocked and frightened.

"Daughter?''

"I will if I must,'' she whispered. "But I believe it to be wrong.''

The First Priestess inclined her head in acknowledgment. "It may well be. Go and rest, Briana. You will need strength.''

The girl hurried back to her cell, numb with the task that faced her. She had seen the Binding only as a diagram of steps drawn on the floor of the Teaching House and quickly erased. She had not forgotten it, but she had never practiced it. It was one of the great Patternings, which could disturb the balance of many things if performed. Control of others' minds was an art of the Dark. It could be bent to serve the Goddess only with great difficulty. She felt a horrified pity for the Southern Prince and his people. They would never know what had been done to them.

The corridors of the Great House were well lit as the Prince and his party of four men were led toward the courtyard by three hooded, grey-robed priestesses. Kyellan saw that the walls were not carven, as he had thought, but crumbling and weathered into strange relief designs. He walked slowly at the rear of the group, not wanting to draw attention; he did not believe the rumors that the priestesses could read thoughts, yet neither could he believe they were as unaware as it had seemed in the deserted compound the night before.

Arel had not wanted him along, but Tobas had insisted;

Kyellan suspected the Prince meant to keep Tobas in his debt by continuing to grant him favors after giving him command. Perhaps Arel was succeeding. The young Earl's son was becoming distant at times, and disapproving, but apparently his first loyalty was still to Kyellan.

The courtyard was crowded with rank upon rank of hooded and robed priestesses. It was stone-floored and torchlit. The smell from the torches' smoke was sweet and dizzying; the Guardsman wondered what kind of wood they used. The women watched silently with shadowed eyes as the five men were seated on a long bench of woven brushwood. Kyellan was not eager to trust his weight to the seat, but it seemed sturdy enough. Across the circular arena, he saw Valahtia standing with a tall, black-robed old woman on a narrow raised dais. The Princess had taken pains with her hair and clothes, but somehow her beauty faded against her companion's regal bearing. The old woman was not hooded. She wore a rich, elaborate headdress inset with a moon of ivory and stars of silver. If the pale ornamentation was really what it appeared, the tall helmet would be worth more than Kyellan could figure.

A slim, grey-robed priestess stepped forward. Though her hood covered her hair, her pale features leaped into sharp focus as she faced them. It was the young woman who had greeted them the day before, and she was still more beautiful in the gathering darkness.

"Welcome, Your Highness," she said as if to an equal. "We will perform our usual evensong ritual tonight, as well as a special Dance in your honor. The blessing of the Goddess will be given when the moon is high."

"Very well." Arel sounded annoyed. He had probably expected to be able to march in, be blessed, and go out again in time for drinking and one of the Princess's ladies before he slept. Kyellan was amused. Surely the Prince could wait a few hours more; he would have to wait years to become King. His father was only in his midforties and unlikely to die young.

The ceremony began. Priestesses swayed and chanted, swinging incense-filled globes on long chains until the air was hazy and thick, and Kyellan's eyes stung. The women moved in slow patterns, pausing and holding somber postures. Their hoods blanked their faces, as high and low voices interwove with inharmonious music. The Guardsman grew steadily more uneasy and uncomfortable. It did not help that Tobas and Arel to either side of him appeared rapt, enthralled, half-stupefied by the mingling smokes and voices; the same things were giving Kyellan an angry headache.

The moon rose at its usual stately, imperceptible pace, though he urged it to hurry. He longed to finish with this, to breathe the clear, high air of the plateau again. The worship of the Goddess in Caerlin was a mystery to him, but he did not think that even the weird calls of the Tarish criers approached the eerie, unhuman sound these priestesses were making.

Kyellan studied the decaying stones of the courtyard morosely. The building that surrounded it was in no better repair; nor were the other buildings, if his quick judgments of them had any value. The place had the look and feel of poverty. Yet he was certain there were more treasures where that headdress had come from—probably buried in a vault somewhere, gathering mold. It was strange that the thieves' legends in Cavernon City had never spoken of the Sanctuary.

Finally, the chorus of banshees seemed to reach a climactic chord, and the priestesses' movements slowed. Soon they had resumed their silent vigil at the edges of the courtyard. The young woman who had greeted them stood alone in the center. Her hood had been removed, and her bright auburn hair hung unbound to her waist. A simple fillet of silver wrapped her forehead. Kyellan had to remind himself that this was part of the priestesses' rituals; it would probably be equally boring. And if the girl was beautiful, she was also as cold and remote as a living statue.

Muffled drums sounded, and she began to dance. First she stretched in supplication to each of the four directions, then bowed like a graceful reed to the Prince. Arel smiled thinly. The Dance moved slowly at first, but gained in speed and complexity until it was impossible to say where one step ended and another began. She seemed more a creature of air than of the earth, as she twirled and leaped with incredible agility and suppleness, her long red hair blowing wildly in the wind she made.

There was something about the Dance that unnerved Kyellan. At first he attributed it to the lingering uneasiness from the first rituals and glanced back over his shoulder at the somber, shadowed faces of the priestesses behind him. But the feeling did not fade as the Dance continued. It grew stronger. There was something here beyond the movements themselves, some underlying meaning, something he almost understood.

The drums stopped. His eyes were riveted by the frenzied figure of the dancer as he tried to grasp what eluded him. A watching priestess moaned and fell. No one seemed to notice. There was no sound but the soft rustling and footsteps of the red-haired girl. Tobas, Arel, the two lieutenants Janos and Marben, all sat like corpses of men with flickering eyes. They could see nothing but the dancer. Horror began to replace Kyellan's disbelief. He was being pressured to become one of them. To surrender, to throw down his arms against the power of the Dance. It was so beautiful, one could easily be lost in it.

No. It was wrong. Evil, dark, something that fought against a barrier in Kyellan's mind until his head was afire with pain. He struggled to rise against invisible chains. He had to stop it.

The dancer wilted like a storm-battered seedling, exhausted, and three women hurried out to support her limp body. She was half carried from the courtyard, but as she passed Kyellan, she looked at him with strange intensity, almost with fear. Then she was gone, and the other men on the woven bench began to move and whisper in appreciation.

"Wasn't that beautiful, sir?" Lieutenant Marben leaned across Tobas to Kyellan, who was sweating and breathing heavily. "Sir? What's wrong?"

"Nothing." He attempted a smile. "My wound is bothering me a little. It will pass."

They looked normal enough now. He wondered if anything had really happened. Imagination could be powerful. But it had seemed so real. His head was still awash with waves of pain.

"The moon is high." The regal woman in the headdress spoke. Her voice rang clearly out over the courtyard. "Come before me, Prince of Caerlin."

Arel rose and walked to the dais. The others followed at a respectful distance.

"Welcome, Arel den Ardavan, first son of Chaeris den Ardavan who is King in Caerlin. Your father, young Prince, stood before me as you do now, and swore the oaths I required of him without hesitation."

"I will do the same." He seemed eager.

"Will you, as King, obey the laws of the Goddess and do Her will?"

"I will."

"Will you protect those who serve Her, and raise your children in obedience to Her commands?"

"I will."

"Will your reign be one of justice and peace?"

"I swear it," he said fervently.

"Arel den Ardavan, you have the blessing of the Goddess, who is Wiolai the Maiden, who is Cianya the Mother, who is Rahshaiya the Death-Bringer. May your reign be long and your country prosper, through the Power of She-Who-Guides. And now I have a request to make of you."

This could not be part of the formula, Kyellan thought. The half-sick feeling of the Dance was still strong in him.

"If it is in my power." Arel was uncharacteristically courteous.

"The Goddess has willed that some of my priestesses and I must travel to your land in the South. We ask an escort to the port of Atolan, and help in finding ships there to Cavernon City."

"I am honored, Priestess," said the Prince. "Should I leave my commander here to discuss the arrangements to be made?"

"I thank you. Yes, we would speak to your commander. There is much to be done."

Arel bowed deeply and followed a thick-set priestess out of the courtyard. Kyellan watched in astonishment. Did the Prince know what he was agreeing to? Surely this was the reason for the Dance.

"You should stay, Ky," Tobas said distractedly. "You know our capabilities better." The young captain's eyes were still glazed and drugged-looking.

Kyellan was about to agree, seeing Tobas's condition, but the First Priestess descended from the dais and spoke sharply.

"No."

"Why not?" Kyellan measured her with his eyes. This was a woman who could rule the Eleven Kingdoms if she desired. She had Power, whether it was supernatural in origin or not.

"You were in some discomfort during the ceremonies, Captain. In pain from your wound, perhaps? You should rest." Her thin, lined face was properly concerned.

"No doubt." He bowed low, with a flicker of a smile. Neither was fooled. Somehow their Dance trick had gone wrong, and he had not been taken in as the others were.

He hoped Tobas still had the sense to deal intelligently with the First Priestess, after falling neatly into their trap.

"Good night, then," he said with unfeigned respect.

One of the older grey-robed women beckoned him to follow. With Janos and Marben, he obeyed. He would not attempt to see the Princess that night, though Valahtia followed him pleadingly with her pretty eyes. Though his weariness was not from his wound, the First Priestess was right; he could use the sleep.

Chapter Four

Kyellan cursed steadily as he harnessed his horse to the ancient, rotting cart. It was wrong to turn fine S'tari animals into carthorses, and worse for cavalry soldiers to become drivers. He doubted Tobas had cared, the night before. Teams of straining girls had pulled the wagons out of the gates that morning; the design of the carts was centuries old, arched and scalloped, with a small door at the rear and another that opened onto the narrow driver's board. The wheels were fixed to plain axles, with none of the shock-absorbing suspension that enabled Valahtia and her brother to ride in such comfort. The wood they were constructed with must have been older than the giant trees of Parahn's Elandi Hills. It was rotted with years of damp; apparently the priestesses had stored their thirty carts in caves at the base of the plateau and had not needed them for the past two hundred years.

Murmuring gentle-sounding threats to his restive, frightened horse, Kyellan pulled the straps tight. It would be interesting driving an animal that had never been under harness. He hoped the two priestesses he was to transport would not be much longer; the more his horse had to stand still, the worse it would be.

Idly, he counted the women who trudged past him on the way to their assigned carts. Twenty-eight novices and twenty-eight older priestesses ignored him as they passed. Finally, the remaining four emerged from the Sanctuary. The gates closed behind them. Two were white-robed girls, each of whom supported a woman who walked with the steps of great age or infirmity. One was grey-robed and hooded. The other was the First Priestess.

She wore the same black robe as the night before; her headdress was absent, but the power of her presence was not lessened. Kyellan found himself drawing to attention as she approached, as if for review by a superior officer. The old woman nodded to him and stopped, leaning on the shoulder of a frail, pinch-faced girl.

"Captain Kyellan?" she said, her voice trembling with age, no longer clear and ringing. "After I spoke with young Tobas, I wished I had asked you to remain. It appears he is only the nominal commander of your soldiers, and does not have their trust. I suspect matters will be easier if you understand the need for haste in this journey; then we will reach Atolan more quickly."

Kyellan was flattered, but he doubted she would say anything he could believe. He was uncomfortable under the hostile gaze of the young novice, whose eyes glittered at him with obvious disdain.

"Your Goddess told you to go"—he shrugged—"so you're going."

"We must save the Kingdoms from destruction!" shrilled the white-robed girl.

"Gemon," admonished the First Priestess, "it is not your place to speak here."

"Destruction?" Kyellan repeated. "We've been pretty much at peace for the last three centuries."

"That peace is breaking. I do not yet know the face of the enemy, but I know they will attempt to reach our

destination before us. A great Focus of Power was hidden
in Caerlin long ago, and they would turn its force against
us.''

"A weapon?" He humored her.

"If you like. One whose use you could not imagine. Yet
we must have it, and the time is short."

"My help was pledged last night," Kyellan muttered.
"We'll get you there, Priestess. But don't expect me to
believe any of it."

"That will have to do." The First Priestess moved
away. She was to ride with Tobas, Kyellan remembered.
Perhaps the youngster could make something of her
conversation.

The other two women approached him now. Both were
hooded. The white robe of the girl promised a pleasantly
rounded figure beneath; the grey-robed one was so bent
and shuffled so painfully that he could make out little of
her form. They had to be his passengers.

"The Priestess Briana is not well, sir," said the novice
in a softly feminine voice. "Can you give her a smooth
ride?"

"I'll try." He smiled. "The horse may not cooperate."

The girl bowed her head and half carried her companion
around to the rear of the cart. Kyellan heard the small door
creak open and the warped floorboards moan at the added
weight. He climbed to the driver's seat, a splintery board
with a thin plank footrest and an empty whipstock. The
call came from Tobas's horn. With a soft oath, he flicked
the reins over the confused horse's back.

Seeing the cart ahead begin to move, the S'tari warhorse
followed but found itself pulling a heavy, slow-moving
weight. It reared screaming in the traces. The front wheels
of the cart left the ground. Kyellan cursed the animal in

several languages and whipped it with the reins, wishing he knew anything of driving.

"Let me help," said the small voice of the hooded novice. Her head appeared through the front door of the caravan.

"Stay back there. You'll just be in the way."

She crawled up onto the seat, awkward in her long woolen robe. He reluctantly made room for her. She called to the horse in a strange, soothing, musical language. Kyellan watched in disbelief as the angry animal stopped leaping about and stood shivering on the road. The girl spoke again, and it followed the cart in front with the docility of a peddler's beast.

"Animals like me," she said shyly. "I can persuade them sometimes. One of the few Powers I have."

"What did you do?" He sighed. "Whatever it was, thanks."

"Now the ride will be smoother for the Priestess Briana. It will still be too hot back there. . . . Captain, do you suppose I could ride with you for a while? It would give her more room."

"I'd be glad of the company, if your priestess doesn't mind."

The young novice opened the door again and spoke quietly. A weary voice answered. She looked back at Kyellan, and he caught a glimpse of a pretty chin inside her hood. "I can't."

Kyellan concentrated on guiding his strangely docile horse as the girl climbed back through the small door. Obviously the old woman in the back did not want the novice to enjoy the journey. It was a pity; the girl was quite attractive. At least he guessed she would be, if he ever got to see her face.

* * *

Briana waited until Pima had latched the little door, then admonished, "Don't be too friendly with him."

The novice blushed as she removed her hood. "I'm sorry, Priestess. I didn't see the harm. He spoke softly to me and smiled."

Briana sighed and tried to find a more comfortable position for her fiery muscles on the few pillows Pima had been able to find in the Sanctuary. Her body was drained of strength from the Binding Dance, but her mind was sharp. She feared for Pima in the world of men. That they would find her appealing was evident; that she would feel the same was all too likely. Pima's father had delayed intolerably in sending her to the Sanctuary. When the girl was twelve, the priestesses had been forced to go to the Kerisian Baron's manor to test his daughter in his presence. He had been forced to give Pima up, but the girl had lived five more years in the world than she should have.

"Be wary," said the priestess finally. "This Kyellan doesn't believe in the Goddess, and has no respect for our vows."

Indeed, she was almost frightened by the hardened young man who was their driver; she had pleaded with the First Priestess to assign him elsewhere, even as they had walked toward his cart. He had resisted the Binding Dance, which should have been impossible. The way he had looked at her at the gate . . . She feared Pima would see only his handsome face, and not the coldness of his eyes.

The First Priestess had dismissed Briana's worries. The old woman had not slept. She had spent the night seeking to make her vision clearer, alone in the Temple of the Altar deep within the Great House. Now she was certain the wizards were part of the threat, and that an old enemy, something called the Shape-Changer that she would not explain, was an even greater danger. Briana supposed it would all be clear enough in time.

Loud voices interrupted her thoughts, and she concentrated her hearing on deciphering them. One was haughty, slightly high-pitched, imperious; the other was low, sharp-edged, the officer driving the cart. Both spoke Caer. The tension in the conversation was obvious. She wished she could see what was going on.

"I don't understand you, Your Highness," said the soldier. The other was the Prince Arel, then.

"You should have refused her. Do you know how little she cares what happens to you? She is young, she finds you exciting, but when she tires of you she will toss you away like yesterday's fashion."

"I don't believe you."

"I give you one chance. If you stay away from her, all is forgotten. If you continue to be a fool, you will return to Cavernon chained in the hold, to die slowly in the dungeons of the Tiranon for your crime. Consider well." Hoofbeats rapidly faded, and the voices were stilled.

Captain Kyellan was someone's lover, then. The knowledge eased Briana's mind considerably. He was unlikely to press any attentions on Pima, if he would risk the wrath of his Prince for another. The novice might even ride with him if she wished. It was certainly uncomfortable inside the cart.

The Guardsman was pleasantly surprised to see the young girl again. The squeaking door swung inward, timidly, and her white hood poked out. Her face was half-visible and extremely pale.

"Captain? May I come up? I'm getting sick back here, and the priestess said it was all right until I feel better."

"Thank her for me." Kyellan grinned. He wrapped the

reins around the whipstock and reached his hand back. The girl took it gingerly and crawled cautiously forward from the jolting cart to the narrow board. Seated, she clutched the side of the plank nervously.

The column's progress was slow and torturous down the steep incline of the Sanctuary road. Weighted brakes dragged behind each vehicle. Kyellan's right arm ached from holding back his inexperienced horse; the animal kept trying to crowd the preceding cart and almost got its hooves tangled in brake lines. It was a welcome diversion to have the ghostly body of a white-shrouded girl to talk to.

"It's almost a warm day," he commented, steering his mind from morose recollections of Arel's threats.

"We've had some nice weather," she said very softly. "But it was a bad winter."

"I'll bet you got too hot," he said. "You'd feel better without that hood."

She did not respond. He imagined the priestess in back filling the youngster's mind with the terrible things that might happen if she let Kyellan see her face. Now she would not even talk. His thoughts ranged unwillingly back to Arel. He did not believe the Prince when he spoke of Valahtia's feelings, but he was certain Arel was not lying when he spoke of prison and torture. It was a hard choice. He did not want to abandon the Princess.

Perhaps he could continue seeing her, then desert his company in Atolan. The Prince would never find him, and there would be other Kingdoms, other troops that could use a man with his talents. It was not an unattractive prospect, especially considering Caerlin's refusal to promote him further. He spoke most of the languages of the bigger countries; his childhood had been spent in a place that harbored criminals and beggars from every land.

"Tell me about Caerlin." The novice's curiosity overcame her fear. "Is it really as beautiful as they say? As green as Keris in the spring?"

He smiled, knowing she could not see him past the edge of her hood. "In the west it is. Especially around Laenar. But beyond the Maer Cunin is desert. The whole eastern half of the Empire."

"I've never seen a desert," she said wistfully.

So Kyellan told her of things he had seen on the S'tari campaign, of the stark beauty of the land and the people. He told her of life in a nomadic S'tari camp, not mentioning that he had gained his detailed knowledge as a prisoner of war. Somehow talk of war did not seem appropriate with this gentle being beside him. It was surprising how much he could recall of customs and legends, leaving out the weary fighting that had seemed the whole of those four years.

The other women he had known would have delighted in bloody tales of skirmishes and raids. Alaira always begged for such stories and hugged him proudly when he told of killing. Valahtia was the same. He pictured the two in his mind: Alaira sitting wide-eyed on the bed in her warm garret in Rahan Quarter, Valahtia reclining on dyed fur cushions in the lantern light. Then he looked at the innocent child at his side. She was totally alien to his experience. Yet he enjoyed the conversation, and time passed pleasantly until the call sounded at nightfall.

The abrasive sounds of chanting and wailing filtered over the hill from the priestesses' camp. Under the deep sky with its clouded stars, the ritual seemed wilder than it had on the distant plateau that reared in the east. Men and horses were restless. Kyellan and Tobas had pulled their ancient carts together to shelter their small fire against the

Garithian wind and made a tasteless meal of warmed-over salt meat and hard biscuits.

"The First Priestess rode with you," Kyellan commented. His curiosity about the impressive old woman had grown. He could not convince himself she was lying; certainly, she believed what she said. "Did you talk to her?"

"No." The younger man grimaced. "She slept most of the day. But that skinny girl Gemon sat with me, and prophesied doom and devastation until I felt like strangling her. Even though I didn't understand half of what she said."

Kyellan chuckled and reached for the hunk of stringy meat at the end of his roasting stick. "She probably didn't want you to. They like mystery. But the First Priestess seems sensible enough. She talked about an enemy, about the peace being broken after hundreds of years. It worried me."

"I thought you didn't put any faith in prophecies," Tobas said grimly. "Not even the ones that are guaranteed to come true."

"What do you mean?" He did not like his friend's expression.

"I spoke with Arel this afternoon."

"And?"

"He told me what he had said to you. He gave you a chance."

Kyellan looked up at the moon. He was waiting for it to descend and intended to go to the Princess when the darkness was absolute. He did not need Tobas's moralizing tonight.

"Damn it, Ky, he told you the truth. She's using you."

"She said she loves me."

"To her, love is just another word for pleasure, and you give her that. And I know you're not in love with her."

"How do you know that?"

Tobas's voice was harsh. "You've never loved anyone. Not even Alaira. I don't think you're capable of it."

Kyellan stood angrily and swept his cloak around him, all thoughts of the First Priestess's words evaporated. "I don't need to listen to this." He hurried from the fire in the waning moonlight, dodging the dim glow of other fires on the way to the Princess's cart.

"You're early," Valahtia said in a half sob, opening the door of her luxurious cart and shutting it after him. She threw herself against his chest and began to cry. He held her, confused, jolted out of his own anger, until she began to speak again.

"Arel knows," she sniffed. "He came and accused me today. I denied it, but he knows. What shall we do?"

Kyellan looked down on the soft darkness of her hair where it spilled across his tunic. He stroked it awkwardly, realizing Tobas had been right. He did not love the Princess. She was beautiful, and an accomplished lover, and the danger of seeing her was like heady wine; but she was a child.

"Don't worry, Valita," he soothed. "Arel won't tell anyone. He wants you to marry well."

"But he'll kill you. I'll never see you again."

Her tear-streaked face turned up to his. He had meant to tell her he did not love her, but she was so near and so desirable that he kissed her instead and pulled her unprotesting down into the nest of furs.

Kyellan sat on the step at the back of his cart, eating a dry midday meal, watching the road that stretched empty and barren behind the caravan. His senses were heightened by the last night's lovemaking; Valahtia had been more demanding and more giving than ever before, and he had promised to return. But now he had the uneasy feeling of being followed, a soldier's instinct he had always trusted. He strained his eyes in the dust and haze, unsure what he was looking for.

The door behind him opened, and he leaped to his feet in surprise. The young novice, whose name he had discovered to be Pima, had already gone to eat with her friends. The grey-robed priestess stood in the doorway. He had not seen her emerge without Pima's shoulder to lean on. Now she disdained his offered hand and leaped lightly to the ground. She showed no signs of infirmity or age.

The Priestess Briana shook off her hood. She was the dancer of that night in the Sanctuary. Now Kyellan understood. The Dance must have sickened her, but she had regained her poise and her austere beauty. Near as they were, her green eyes were startling.

"Good day, Priestess," he ventured when he had recovered from his surprise.

"What are you looking for, Guardsman?" She gazed out over the long, dusty road.

"I'm not sure. I think someone is behind us."

"Or some*thing*," she agreed darkly. "I felt it, but I'm surprised you did. Men have no Power."

"Soldier's intuition."

"Doubtless." She sat wearily on the step. She was not fully recovered, then. Her auburn hair was dull, and there were smudges under her brilliant eyes.

Kyellan stood beside her and finished his inadequate meal. They watched the road intently. Finally, he noticed a moving cloud of dust, and figures within it. He shaded his eyes.

"What do you see, warrior?"

"A rider, two ponies." Soon they could see the young man clearly. He was slim and of medium height, his thick, rough-cut hair lit to a golden-bronze sheen by the sun. He was tanned and well muscled, and carried a short, straight sword at his left side. He rode one of the shaggy ponies. The other followed without a lead, like a great dog.

The rider approached quickly and stopped a few yards from them to raise a hand in greeting. His face was neither handsome nor ugly, sharp-featured, with a hawk nose and wide cheekbones, bushy brows over deep-set eyes. His eyes were unlike any Kyellan had seen: tawny yellow, slit-pupiled, the eyes of a maned desert cat.

Briana drew in a sharp breath of recognition. "Why are you following us? On whose orders?"

"I hoped to join your caravan," said the youth with a slight bow. His voice was pleasant. "You seem to be going to Atolan, and it's safer to travel with others."

The laws of caravan mandated hospitality, and Kyellan was intrigued by the strangeness of the boy. "You're welcome to join us."

Briana scowled. "We'll see what the First Priestess has to say."

"She can say what she likes." Kyellan shrugged. "It makes no difference." Even if Arel had agreed to escort the priestesses, they had no authority over the Royal Court.

The young woman climbed back into the cart and slammed the door angrily. The ancient vehicle shook. Kyellan grinned at the yellow-haired boy and went to tighten the harness on his horse, which he had loosened for the stop. The strange youth dismounted and followed him.

"Why do they mistrust us so?" he said cheerfully, helping Kyellan expertly with the harness. His long, slim fingers moved quickly, adjusting the buckles to the S'tari horse.

"Who? The priestesses?" Kyellan guessed. "I don't even know who you are."

"Gwydion," the boy said promptly. "Of Akesh."

"Captain Kyellan of the Royal Court," he replied. "Why do the priestesses mistrust you?"

"You might call us rivals in the same business."

"You're a priest?"

"He's a wizard," Pima said disdainfully, passing them on her way behind the cart. Kyellan watched her go and tried hard not to laugh. The yellow-eyed boy did not argue with her statement.

"What do I know of wizards?" Kyellan mused. "They live in high castle towers with owls and bats; they're old, bearded, and wear robes with stars on them. And they're a myth."

Gwydion chuckled. "I suppose we are, in Caerlin. But we exist."

The call came to move the caravan again. Kyellan climbed to the driver's seat. The self-proclaimed wizard mounted his shaggy pony again, which had been standing patiently at his shoulder, and rode alongside.

"Prove it to me. Do something magical."

"Sorry. I'm not a wandering conjurer. I don't do tricks."

"No ropes that climb by themselves?" Kyellan recalled the last magician he had seen fail to accomplish that feat.

"No. I suppose the tricksters in Caerlin call themselves wizards, but all the true race is in the North. We're outlawed in Caerlin. I'm surprised you didn't know." A shadow crossed his features briefly. "You'll find us in every other Kingdom. I'm on my way to the island of Altimar. They need a wizard."

"Why?" Kyellan laughed.

"A sea monster has been terrorizing Keor. It's blocked the harbor, won't let anything in or out, and it's destroyed the outlying villages. I intend to stop it before it attacks the city." He frowned up at Kyellan. "Their last wizard died trying to kill it with a couple of beast-hunting spells and an effigy. He was a fool."

"The people of Keor hired a boy to kill a sea monster?"

"I'm seventeen," Gwydion said defensively. "There were lots of older wizards at Akesh when the request came in, but my masters chose to send me. I'm the best apprentice to come through the College for hundreds of years. I'm not worried."

"Did they grade you on humility at this College?" Kyellan grinned.

"No. It takes confidence as well as Power to work a spell."

The Guardsman chuckled. He liked the talkative youngster. If nothing else, Gwydion was the best liar he had ever met.

The camp was dark one moment and torchlit the next. Kyellan finally woke to Tobas's frantic shaking. "What is it?"

"A rider from a village to the north. He wants to talk to the commanding officer. Arel tried to tell him that was me, but he didn't believe it." Tobas shrugged. "You'd better come."

Kyellan shook off the blankets and pulled on his boots. It was cold and frosty, several hours before dawn by the stars. The camp was alive with shouting, and fires were lit. He had not thought anyone lived in the barren Garithian hills, though he had heard of another road north of the one that led to the Sanctuary.

Near Arel's wagon, a middle-aged, copper-haired man

sat exhausted on the ground. A sturdy pony, similar to Gwydion's, was being held nearby. Guardsmen and baggage-cart drivers were crowded around the lonely figure. When Kyellan pushed through the press, the Garithian stood eagerly.

"You're the commander?" He did not await the answer. "Thank the Goddess. You must come. The man who calls himself a Prince says you can't, but you must."

"Where?"

"To my village, if it's still there. If the demon army hasn't razed it already."

"Who?" Kyellan was not sure he was awake. But if this was a dream, it was certainly a cold one.

"The demon army! If you've been on the Sanctuary road, you won't have heard the news. Thousands upon thousands of demons and wild men led by the accursed wizards. Marching through northern Garith like a cyclone, killing people, burning villages and crops. This is how they repay the haven we granted them long ago." He spat. "You must come. My people must leave. They don't believe it, but I have seen it. You must come and convince them to leave."

There was no lie in the man's broad face. Kyellan shivered, remembering the First Priestess's words. An invasion, shattering the peace of centuries.

"Where's the Garithian army?" Tobas wanted to know.

"What army? They run like lemmings to the sea. I don't blame them; they never were much anyway. But you can help me. My people are sheep. If someone tells them what to do firmly enough, they will do it."

"We'll go," Kyellan assured him.

"No. We will not." Arel strode from the shadows, indignant.

"You can continue on to Atolan without us, if you

wish,'' Kyellan said. "We cannot refuse to help these people, Your Highness.'' To refuse a direct order from his sworn lord meant he could never think of returning to Caerlin; however, he had already made that decision by continuing to see the Princess. It made little difference now.

He turned back to the Garithian, curious about the army the man seemed to fear. Surely they were not demons. Why, then, would the villager call them that? But the copper-haired man was staring past him, into the shadows, and Kyellan looked that direction. Gwydion stepped out of the darkness, his golden eyes glittering in the torchlight.

The man screamed in terror. "A wizard!'' He drew his short sword and charged at the boy. Gwydion leaped back, unarmed, his young face bewildered and sleepy. Kyellan grabbed the Garithian from behind and disarmed him, but the man still struggled to get at Gwydion.

"What do you know of this?'' the Guardsman demanded of the wizard.

The youth shook his head. "Nothing. An invasion led by the wizards? My masters are peaceful men. I left them in conference at Akesh with most of the wizards of the North, but there was no army.''

"He lies!'' shrilled the Garithian. "I swear it on my name, Jarl of the village Poavra. I myself saw the leader of the demon forces. He was yellow-eyed, and there were fifty more like him in the ranks.''

"You're mistaken, sir. Even if there is an army, I can't believe there are wizards involved.''

Kyellan sighed. "Until we know the truth, I don't want either of you out of my sight. Understand?''

Gwydion and Jarl nodded, equally hurt at his mistrust.

"Break camp!'' the Guardsman called. "I want us headed north by daybreak. And someone had better tell the priestesses.'' He heard Tobas begin to relay his orders out of old habit.

Smiling broadly, he strode back to his campsite, followed by two sullen enemies who darted venomous glances at each other. There was a spring in his step that had not been there since Atolan. Maybe the Kingdoms were about to be plunged into war . . . but he had his command back.

Chapter Five

Briana returned from speaking with the Guardsmen's messenger and bowed low to the First Priestess. The old woman sat calmly by the fire. "You were right, Mother. We are asked to be ready for a detour to the north by daybreak."

"As I thought. The young Captain Kyellan is as eager as I am to see the face of our enemy."

"You did not . . . suggest his course to him, did you?" Briana tried not to sound disapproving.

"No. You have not noticed? Kyellan is shielded so well mentally that no suggestion of mine, not even the great Power of your Dance, could reach him. His mind reveals nothing to my strongest probing." The First Priestess sighed as she pulled herself wearily to her feet. Gemon was already finished rolling and tying her sparse bedding.

"Shielded?" Briana said incredulously. "By whom?"

"No one. The wall seems to be innate. I doubt he himself is aware of it. Perhaps it stems from his great disbelief in the supernatural." The old woman chuckled. "Perhaps it causes that disbelief. Since he cannot sense the unknown, he is certain it does not exist." She dismissed further speculation with a wave of her hand.

Briana bowed to greater wisdom. That a man should have such a mind-block was surprising, but the First Priest-

ess did not seem worried about it. Surely that was what
had unnerved her so about the handsome Guardsman when
she had first seen him. She had not received the usual
images and feelings that enabled her to decide whether to
trust a stranger. A shielded person could not be read save
through his actions.

Kyellan drove uncomfortably. The rocky, brush-matted
hill trail that led to Jarl's village threatened to shake the
ancient carts apart with each rut and wind-eroded hole.
The two young women, Pima and Briana, were unable to
ride inside the jolting vehicle without becoming bruised
and battered; they sat on either side of him on the driver's
board. They stiffened whenever his elbows brushed them,
and he tried to drive without moving his arms. That proved
impossible. The priestesses would have to continue being
annoyed.

Since he seemed to have usurped the command the night
before, he had maneuvered his cart to the front of the
column that morning. No one but Arel protested. Tobas
actually seemed relieved and showed no sign of resentment.
The men were openly pleased. He wondered what the
priestesses thought; they had not complained about the
deviation from their route, though they had been so insistent before on the urgency of their mission.

Jarl the Garithian rode with knotted shoulders and head
thrust forward as if to arrive sooner that way. Gwydion
trotted his shaggy pony beside the cart, a sullen, wronged
expression on his downcast face. Even Pima's bright chatter had been stifled by the presence of the grey-robed
priestess. No one had spoken more than a few words since
the morning. It was like a funeral procession, Kyellan
thought, but no one had died.

He could not keep his thoughts from the consequences

of what he was doing. Arel would never forgive this affront to his authority. The prospect of never returning to Caerlin was unpleasant; for all he knew, the other Kingdoms were like Garith, half-empty and uncivilized. Though they might reward his talents with promotions and command, those would be meaningless without some place to enjoy the perquisites of rank.

"How much farther, Jarl?" he called in hope of conversation.

"Not far. Within the hour."

The older man turned back to his riding. Kyellan sighed. He still could not believe anyone could live in these grey hills. The Priestess Briana had mentioned briefly earlier that there were several such villages scattered between the Sanctuary road and the northern steppes. They were not on the official maps, but their people appeared yearly at the Atolan sheep markets with thick, rough wool that made sturdy cloth.

Gwydion suddenly straightened in his furry saddle. His face sharpened.

"Something is wrong," he muttered, and followed with a phrase in a language unknown to Kyellan.

"Yes," agreed the priestess.

"I fear we come too late. Go warily, Captain."

"What is it?" Kyellan saw nothing amiss ahead.

"The army Jarl spoke of has been before us."

The Garithian whirled in his saddle. "Don't listen to that lying son of Darkness. He means for us to turn back, so my people can be destroyed."

"We should hurry," countered the young wizard. "There may be survivors."

Briana spoke accusingly. "Your people are there, boy."

Gwydion's strange face was anguished. "I know."

*   *   *

"The valley is just beyond this rise," Jarl said.

Even Kyellan felt it now. Smoke rose dim against the clouded sky, and there was a faint, unpleasant smell that made the horse prance nervously as they approached. The land was stony and bare. On the ridge top stood a lone juniper tree, mute witness to the devastation below.

Jarl gave a wordless cry of horror and buried his face in his hands. The valley was blackened and smoldering, the houses of the village no more than skeleton frames and piles of wreckage. Vultures and kites circled and dove in a macabre ballet.

"The Goddess protect us," Briana breathed.

Pima's face was white and still with horror. She should go no closer, Kyellan thought. He handed her the reins. The restive S'tari horse quieted immediately. "Tell Tobas to make camp here. We can't get the carts down that trail. Tell him to organize a burial detail and await my return."

The novice nodded mutely as he dropped to the ground. The Garithian villager moaned and spurred his horse down the slope, heedless of danger.

"We must follow him!" Briana leaped down from the seat. "He shouldn't be alone."

Gwydion dismounted, and his shaggy pony watched wistfully as the three of them started quickly down the hill. Gravel and loose shale slid under their feet on the well-worn trail. The opposite ridge, beyond the blackened valley, had been trampled so that it looked like a highroad. Dust and ash rose behind the now distant figure of Jarl's horse, almost at the village.

"He's not a soldier, used to death, for you to speak so casually about it," Briana said angrily.

Kyellan did not answer. The smell that pervaded the still air was burned human flesh. It was true he was familiar with death, but he was sickened. At the bottom of the hill, a pile of slaughtered, half-charred sheep lay in a black, stubbly hayfield.

"A temple of Rahshaiya," Briana muttered.

"Rahshaiya?"

"The aspect of the Goddess that delights in war and killing. The Death-Bringer. You follow Her path, as do the men who did this." Her eyes were bleak and hard. "We do not worship Rahshaiya. We try to placate Her."

Bodies that had once been villagers were strewn in agonized postures on the ground. Some had been tied to the door frames of their huts and still hung there grisly and burned. The village square was the worst. The people there had escaped the flames in death. Some had been hacked to pieces, others tortured for a long time before they died. Babies and small children had been swung against posts, their heads crushed. The only sound was the harsh cries of carrion birds.

Kyellan's gaze roamed the place of death, uneasy, trying to reckon how long ago it had happened. Long enough for the fire to burn itself out, but, judging from the condition of the bodies, not before that morning. The destructive force that had swept through this peaceful place could not be far gone.

Gwydion glanced up at him from where he knelt, next to one of the corpses that had been dismembered. "She was alive for a long time," he said thinly. "They wouldn't let her die. They laughed, when she begged them to kill her. . . ."

"You must not," Briana said gently. "The last thoughts of the dead are not safe to hear."

"Who could do this?" said the boy miserably.

"Your people, wizard." Jarl joined them. His face was like an open wound. He gazed at the bloody head of the woman on the ground. "She was my wife."

"My people?"

"There were wizards here," the priestess said.

"I know . . . but Names of Power, what they did . . ."

"You truly didn't know their plans."

"I didn't know." His face was drawn with grief and horror. "How could they have told me? I would have tried to stop them. They always said I was too weak."

"Where is the army now? Be still, Gwydion, and listen for them."

"Close. No more than five miles away." He rose slowly to his feet. "It is the Kharad. The great war. I thought their talk of it was only rhetoric, only the senile dreaming of a few old men."

Briana turned to Kyellan. "We must be careful. If he can feel their presence, they can feel ours."

Tobas had been sent out three hours ago with a small band to look for survivors. He had not returned. The ancient rites of Garithian burial had been performed, without the usual bonfires, and Kyellan sent the remaining Guardsmen back to the camp with the priestesses. He entered the village for what he hoped was the last time, leaving the silent Jarl standing beside the broad new mound that loomed dark in the approaching twilight. The stench of death clung to him; it had been an unpleasant afternoon's work.

A ring of ruined weapons surrounded Gwydion, who sat in the center of the village square. Kyellan stepped gingerly over crooked swords, a heavy double-bladed axe, and several short spears. The young wizard looked up at his approach. His eyes were unbroken gold; the slit catlike pupils had contracted into thin lines.

"The First Priestess has called a council tonight," Kyellan said uneasily. "We're invited. What were you doing?"

"Trying to backsee with these." His voice was hoarse and weary. "I found a few images, nothing clear. The weapons were borne by men, not demons. The wizards directed the pillaging, but didn't fight. I had more, but it's gone."

"I could have guessed that much without spending hours trying to listen to a bunch of spears. Come on."

The wizard shrugged, brushed the black ash from his tunic, and followed Kyellan slowly across the shadowed fields and up the steep trail to the ridge top. A nervous Guardsman challenged them, spear in hand, then let them pass.

The camp was quiet. No fires burned, by Kyellan's orders, except a small, uncanny white flame in the center of the circle of priestesses. Sixty women in dusty dark robes sat on the ground beyond the circled carts. Valahtia was with them, her legs curled under her on a silken cushion. The Prince had been invited but had not come. Kyellan and Gwydion lowered themselves to the dirt between Briana and the First Priestess.

"The Goddess bind this circle," said the regal old woman. The other priestesses murmured an indecipherable response. The small white flame on the bare ground before them leaped high, then resumed its faint illuminating glow.

The First Priestess turned to Gwydion. "You were right. The army that destroyed Poavra is camped only a few miles from the western ridge." The old woman drew a sign in the air, which hung glittering like captured starlight. "They will not attack us tonight. But they are between us and Atolan, so we cannot go on. Neither can we go back. They are only the vanguard of a larger force."

"How much larger?" Kyellan did not know where she got her information, but he was willing to listen.

"An invasion force. To regain what was taken from the

wizards thousands of years ago. It is the Kharad, and even young Gwydion must admit that it is the work of the Wizards' College. The minds of our enemies are too powerful not to be his masters. Yet the one I hoped to find is not with them. I fear his attack will come from an unexpected quarter.''

''Who?'' Gwydion wondered.

''The Shape-Changer.''

The wizard laughed incredulously. ''That's only a story they tell in the dormitories of Akesh. There is no such person.''

''He exists, though where and in what form I cannot see. His is an ancient Power, and not to be taken lightly.''

Valahtia protested, ''I don't even know who the wizards are. I never heard of them at home. What was taken from them that they want back?''

''The Kingdoms, of course,'' said Briana witheringly.

The First Priestess smiled at the Princess. ''I will try to explain. When our people landed on these shores, the wizards were a nomadic people, not very numerous. We eradicated them through intermarriage and the Power of the Goddess. They were either killed or absorbed into the population. There were a few generations without wizards, but the taint remained in the people's blood, and soon they began to be born to human mothers. Most were killed in infancy. Some survived. Their parents hid them, or fled with them to isolated lands such as Garith. Those children became the founders of the College of Akesh, which is where newborn wizards are now sent to be raised and educated. Only Caerlin still requires them to be killed at birth.''

''I didn't go to Akesh until I was twelve,'' Gwydion said.

''I suspected something like that,'' agreed the old woman.

"If you were raised by parents who cared for you, who did not teach you to hate humankind from your first conscious thoughts, that may explain why you were not asked to join the Kharad. They did not trust you."

"I wouldn't have joined them," the boy flashed. "They're killing people like my parents, harmless farmers and villagers who never hurt them. How can they still be angry over something that happened three thousand years ago? To a race that would probably have been as alien to modern wizards as we are to you?"

"I cannot answer that, young Gwydion. But I am pleased to know your thoughts." She turned her gaze on Kyellan. "Now we must reach Caerlin even more urgently. The wizards will try to find the Goddess's Seat."

"The only road leads to Atolan," he said, "and the wizards seem to be headed that way."

"Then we must do without a road. We will travel south, into Ryasa, and reach the port of Chelm on the Tarnsea. Ships can take us from there to Laenar, the northern city of Caerlin."

"We'll never get that far," Gwydion said. "By now they know the Crown Prince of Caerlin and the First Priestess are with us."

"We have no choice. If we stay here, they are sure to attack," Briana said.

"And if we leave, they are sure to attack."

"We might as well go somewhere." Kyellan shrugged. "I don't want to sit and wait for them to kill me."

"South, then," said the First Priestess decisively. "Before daybreak."

"Good." Kyellan and Gwydion stood and bowed, then returned to their own campsite as the women began a soft chanting in the darkness.

* * *

Tobas still had not returned. Kyellan could not sleep.
He glanced at the wizard curiously. Gwydion was rolling
himself up in a fur wrap that had served as his pony's
saddle earlier.

"Were you really the best apprentice at that College?"
he asked. "Even though the others were there since they
were babies?"

The tawny eyes blinked sleepily. "Yes. They say I
could be incredibly powerful if I wasn't so softhearted."
He looked embarrassed. "I don't like to kill things."

"If they attack us, will you fight?" Kyellan said
pointedly.

"To keep them from killing more people. I don't understand them. They talk about justice, about the innocent
children slaughtered in Caerlin, then they smash babies'
heads against posts."

There was a commotion at the border of the camp. Was
the search party returning? Kyellan leaped up, scattering
his blankets. He ran past the carts, to see Tobas at the head
of a bloodied, limping group. The young officer carried
something that looked like a body.

"Trouble?" he snapped.

"We ran into a patrol. Fifteen men, mercenaries by the
look of them, and badly equipped. They won't be report-
ing back to the wizards."

"Casualties?"

"Just scratches. They were such rabble it was hardly a
challenge." Tobas grinned. One of the searchers slapped
him on the back.

"What about that?" Kyellan indicated the wrapped figure in his friend's arms.

Tobas sobered. "A survivor. The only one we found,
and not in very good condition." He set the bundle down

near Gwydion's baggage packs, while the Guardsmen gathered around curiously.

It was a girl, perhaps thirteen or fourteen years old, small and skinny, with a torn dress and matted red hair. She lay still, her eyes wide and terrified. There was a wicked sword cut across her left calf, and Tobas's cloak around her was soaked with blood.

"She was hidden under the roots of some bushes, in a gully. Tried to run away from us. Hasn't said a word, only whimpers."

The young wizard moved toward the girl, who shrank away from him. Tobas looked dubious. "Shouldn't we take her to the priestesses?"

"Let me see what I can do," said Gwydion softly, laying one hand on the girl's forehead and taking her right hand in his. She lay still, trembling, but quieted a little as Gwydion's brow furrowed in concentration.

"Ky . . ." Tobas began.

"Don't worry. We can trust him. If he can't help her, then we'll take her to the priestesses."

The rest of the men filtered away slowly. Tobas and Kyellan sat together on their blanket rolls, watching the wizard and the girl. Both were motionless now.

"I think she's mad," whispered the younger Guardsman.

"No." Gwydion spoke with an effort. "She's behind a wall. If I can reach her and bring her out . . ."

Kyellan had no idea what the wizard was doing, but the girl seemed less afraid. Her face smoothed into a thoughtful expression. Suddenly, Gwydion laughed and dropped her hand, startled.

"She pushed me out! I reached her mind at last, but I barely had time to find out her name . . . Chela . . . when she shouted, 'Get out of my head!' and pushed me out."

"Shouted?" Kyellan had heard nothing.

"Mentally. Gave me a headache," he said wonderingly. "She has Power!"

The girl sat up slowly, her eyes alive and aware. "I surprised you, wizard."

"You certainly did, Chela." He bowed from the waist as he knelt. "I wouldn't expect to find a girl your age with Power still in her village. Why haven't the priestesses taken you?"

"I wouldn't go with them. I didn't want to live with a bunch of old women. I want to stay at home, and tease the boys, and someday marry the blacksmith's son. . . ." Her voice trailed off as her eyes widened in horror. "But they're all dead, even Dael. I wish I was, too!" Chela flung herself sobbing to the ground.

"She must have felt every pain, every torture, as if she went through them herself," Gwydion muttered. "But her Power saved her, as well."

Kyellan laid one of his blankets on top of the weeping child. "What about her leg?"

"I'll take care of that." Gwydion reached into his smallest pack and brought out an herbal-scented bag and a pot. "I'll need a small fire to boil water, Captain."

Kyellan nodded. Tobas growled, "I still think we should give her to the priestesses."

"Chela," said the wizard gently, "would you like that?"

She shook her head through her tears. "They . . . they'd make me a novice. They wanted me bad when I was little."

"She wouldn't have the strength to resist them." Gwydion selected herbs from his bag and filled the pot, while Kyellan gathered tinder for the fire.

Tobas unbuckled his swordbelt, took off his leather-and-iron helmet, and climbed into his blanket roll. He looked exhausted. Kyellan wondered how hard it had been to ensure that no member of the wizards' patrol returned to their masters. A few were sure to have run at the beginning of the skirmish. The Earl's son may not have earned his promotions, but he was quickly proving his right to his rank.

The priestesses circled the caravan after it was loaded and ready, chanting, waving incense burners, claiming to be laying a spell of silence on the carts. Kyellan was unsure of their methods. He sent Pima around with kerchiefs to tie around the muzzles of the horses, admonishing her to keep them quiet as she did so; her ability, whether it was magic or not, had already been proven. It was perhaps two hours before dawn. Garith had long nights.

The column moved slowly. Chela rode high on the packs of Gwydion's baggage pony, her lower leg thick with bandages, wearing Kyellan's blanket for a cloak. The priestesses had offered her a place in a cart, but she had declined, saying the jolting would hurt her leg. Beside her rode Jarl, and they spoke occasionally.

"She's a strange one," Jarl had told Kyellan earlier. "The young men liked her, pretty as she was, and always laughing, but I had little to do with her." Now he seemed to gain comfort from her presence.

Briana watched the pair from the cart's seat, frowning. She finally muttered to Kyellan, "We told her when she was seven that she was one of the Goddess's Chosen. But her parents gave her the choice, and she chose to marry and lose her Power. Now that she has no one to marry, perhaps she'll reconsider."

"I doubt it." He laughed.

They conversed lightly, watching the hills for the army they were sure would come. The day passed slowly, and in fear.

*   *   *

Around midday, Gwydion noticed that Chela was alone. Jarl had gone off by himself. It would be wise to keep her talking. The youth urged his pony up beside its partner.

"Hello." She turned a little and nodded. He tried again. "Remember me from last night?"

"You . . . you didn't give me to the priestesses."

"No. My name is Gwydion."

"I know." She giggled, her thin face relaxing a little. "I felt you in my mind last night. I found out lots of things."

He wondered if he was blushing. "Why didn't you want to be a priestess?"

Her blue eyes focused thoughtfully. "They said my Power was a gift from the Goddess, and had to be used in Her service. I've never really believed in the Goddess. And they said if I didn't become a priestess, I'd lose my Power when I grew to be a woman. I didn't like them. I made my father's dog chase them away. I'm surprised they still want me."

"I'm not." He winced at the memory of his headache.

"I'm almost grown up." She was silent for a few moments, then pleaded, "Is it true I'll lose my Power?"

"I don't think so. They've never seen raw, untrained Power in a woman. If they'd shut you up in the Sanctuary, they would have convinced you that you could only use your talents in prayers and rituals. After a while, you wouldn't be able to use them any other way. But that doesn't have to happen."

"Sometimes I can do things," she mused. "Other times I try and it doesn't work."

"You don't have the discipline. If it weren't for what's happened, I'd send you to my masters at Akesh. They'd teach you how to control it." He glanced away from her troubled blue eyes, thinking of those masters leading an army that had destroyed her life. They would try to destroy him, too, since he had turned against them.

"You're a wizard," she said slowly. "But I knew last night I could trust you. Could you teach me?"

He laughed at the thought. A boy just out of apprenticeship, who had been fool enough to think his assignment to Altimar was an honor when it had just been a ruse to get him out of the way . . . to teach another what he had not yet learned? But he agreed. It probably would not matter, anyway. The Kharad would soon fall upon them and continue what it had begun in Chela's village.

They had crossed their own tracks on the Sanctuary road hours before. By nightfall they reached the edges of a dense evergreen forest. Kyellan located it on the map; once through it, they would be on the bank of the river Is'nai, the southern border of Garith. But it was impossible to penetrate far into the woods in darkness, and horses and drivers were exhausted from seventeen hours of overland travel.

The heavy carts were turned onto their sides in a tight circle in the center of a hidden glade. Kyellan posted guards at the perimeter and a few scouts at the forest edge. Gwydion set ward-spells at each corner of the clearing, claiming they would warn him of danger.

There were no fires. Kyellan could eat little of the cold salt pork he had distributed to the soldiers and priestesses. He watched Chela munch it contentedly as she struggled to read a book from the wizard's pack by the light of a shrouded lantern. The camp was unnaturally silent. People sat clustered in groups, seeking companionship, but did not speak. The distant thunder of rapids sounded loud; the small stream that ran through the glade probably became a torrent before it reached the Is'nai.

Pima walked by carrying heavy buckets of water for the priestesses. She stopped in astonishment when she saw what Chela was reading.

"That's a forbidden book!"

"For you, maybe. I'm not a novice of the Goddess."

"You should be. Briana says it's wrong to refuse Her Choosing," Pima said. Her words were virtuous, but her tone was half-admiring.

Chela drew in breath for a rebuttal, but she saw Gwydion's upraised hand and the expression on his face. The voices of the wizard and the First Priestess, from opposite sides of the camp, spoke together.

"They are coming."

A short statement, but it was enough.

Chapter Six

They could hear them now, crashing through the woods, calling to each other in a harsh distortion of Garithian. The priestesses swarmed into the center of the circle, with Valahtia and Arel and the ladies-in-waiting. The Guardsmen were deploying on their own initiative behind the overturned carts. The cart driver who had been in charge of the weapons crawled into his vehicle and dragged out the stores of bows and arrows and spears. The other drivers helped him distribute the weapons, keeping some for themselves.

Kyellan strung the powerful longbow and piled arrows within easy reach. He drew his sword and laid it at his side, wishing he had thought to bring shields and mail-coats on the voyage. They had not expected the pilgrimage to be opposed; Garith was a peaceful ally. The only defense of the Guardsmen was their thickly padded leather tunics and reinforced helmets. Their smooth-soled boots were meant for riding, not for footing on a battleground; their cavalry horses, picketed just beyond the fortified circle, were useless in a forest.

The scouts had not returned. They were left with twenty-seven soldiers and ten carters to face a small army. Kyellan did not think much of their chances, yet they had no choice but to fight.

Gwydion settled in beside him. Kyellan nodded a greeting, his muscles as taut as his bowstring. After the wizard crept the girl Chela, the longbow in her hands much too large.

"Get in the middle with the priestesses," Kyellan muttered irritably. "You'll be safer there."

"I can shoot. They killed Dael and my parents. I've never shot a man, but I've hunted with my father. I won't wait for them to come to me."

Kyellan shrugged. It was unlikely the priestesses would be able to protect themselves, much less a half-crippled girl. He watched Gwydion take herbal powders from a pouch, orange and purple and foul-smelling, and dip some of the arrows into them. He wondered if they were poisons.

A flight of small tree birds rustled up from the woods, trilling protest in the moonlight, and the first soldiers of the wizards' army broke through into the open. The archers let fly, taking much of the front line, but the sheer numbers of the horde surpassed their speed. The ranks behind trampled the fallen men, hurling spears and brandishing crooked swords. Some wore mail-shirts and bore shields, but most were worse equipped than the Guardsmen. They were easy to fell.

Gwydion lifted his powder-tipped arrows and handed them to Kyellan. The Guardsman shrugged and shot one off; it hit a man squarely in the chest and exploded into a torch of colored flames. The victim's horrible screams did not deter the charging army. Kyellan quickly shot the rest of the arrows, with equally satisfactory results.

But the enemy was upon the carts, clambering over them like Syryni tree apes. Kyellan threw his bow to the ground and swept up his sword. He leaped with the others to engage the first comers. The crooked swords of the enemy caught at his curved blade and threatened to jerk it from his grasp; he had to modify his usual methods, fencing with them, glancing in and out rather than trying to overpower them with his strength. The crowded camp was very different from the desert battlefields of the S'tari campaign. There, horses and men had room to move. This was more like a tavern brawl, though the results were deadlier and the men he felled were immediately replaced.

Gwydion beat off attackers with his short sword as he pulled Chela toward the center of the clearing. A few of the Guardsmen were posted in front of the priestesses. Gwydion pushed through them and stopped in surprise. There was a protective spell-wall that resisted entry. Taking a deep breath, he plunged into it and pulled Chela through, giving himself a knifing headache and making her cry out in pain. An old priestess took Chela from him, clucking her disapproval that she had ever been elsewhere.

Briana, the First Priestess, and some of the black-robed women stood in a tight circle in the center. Gwydion could feel the concentration of Power radiating from them. He hesitated for a moment, then hurried over, ready to offer assistance. But the circle was breaking up, and he could hear Briana arguing fiercely.

"You know how this will end. What will happen to the Kingdoms if you expend all your Power fighting a doomed battle, and die hundreds of miles from the Goddess's Seat? You must escape. There are too many wizards out there."

"The Power of the Goddess can prevail against them," gasped the First Priestess, but her ashen skin and sunken eyes belied her words.

"With what cost?" Briana demanded.

"I'll take your place in the circle," Gwydion offered. The women turned to him, surprised. "Get out while you can. I saw Captain Tobas just outside your spell-wall; he'll protect you. I can make them think they've killed you."

"Go," Briana pleaded. "Think of your greater mission."

The old woman finally agreed. Taking Gemon, she crept through the invisible wall. Gwydion hurried to patch the breach, using the strongest building-spells he knew. Then he added a binding-spell, attempting to make the wall a single whole. It solidified a little. Briana smiled at him and reached out her hands to draw him into the ring of Power.

Moving without thought, swift and deadly and half-crazed with battle, Kyellan was lost in the melee. It was a swirling mass of blades and men, blood and death cries, the fear and desperation in other men's eyes as his slim, curved sword ended their lives. He was scratched and battered, but unwounded, and seemed to feed on a source of energy unrelated to the weariness of his body.

Dimly, he was aware that the enemy was pressing harder on them, and that he encountered less and less of the Royal Guard. He heard the terrible screams of horses and glancing to the side saw men with axes killing the caravan's animals. Gwydion's shaggy ponies were bloody on the ground, and his beautiful S'tari horse shrieked as it fell. Fresh anger coursed through him, renewing his strength.

Gwydion flinched with recognition as the spell-wall quivered with blows. Four wizards, his kindred, battered it with blasts of Power, crumbling it like a tide against a sand castle. The women were drained and exhausted. Even Briana was fading. Gwydion tried to draw on his deepest reserves of Power and failed, his efforts blocked easily by his opponents.

"Don't be foolish, boy!" The voice of his master, Belaric, rang through the enclosure. "Your Power is no match for ours!"

Gwydion did not answer, shattered by his sudden vision of the tall, handsome Belaric presiding at the torture of Chela's people. As he was distracted, the wall gave way. The priestesses scattered. One old woman fell to an iron-shod spear. He laid a makeshift illusion on her to give her the appearance of the First Priestess and heard a girl shriek that the Mother had died. Perhaps Belaric would believe it. Gwydion caught Briana, who staggered half-conscious with much of her strength gone. He drew his sword and protected her as she struggled to gain her feet. Where was Chela? He looked and sent out weak mental probes, but he could not find her in the madness.

Kyellan now fought next to the stocky corporal Erlin, whose youth and size were no deterrent to his grim bladework. He heard the screaming of priestesses and guessed that however they had been protecting themselves, they could do so no longer. He saw few Guardsmen who remained on their feet. The battle had become a charade.

"To the woods!" he called above the roar. "We cannot fight them all!"

Valahtia appeared, her black hair streaming behind her, fleeing three enemy soldiers. The novice Pima ran with her, her pretty round face contorted with weeping. Kyellan dove through the intervening warriors, followed by young Erlin. The Princess screamed his name. He cut down one of her pursuers and wounded another, while Erlin finished the third. Together, the four of them raced for the forest.

Briana had found a sword and wielded it clumsily, but well enough to defend herself. She could not bring herself to kill the enemy soldiers. Gwydion fought with her as they forced a path to where the wizard had last seen his small apprentice. Chela swung a huge broadsword ineffectually, and an axe-bearing enemy laughed as he ran to cut her down.

Gwydion leaped and pierced Chela's adversary through from behind; the man died not knowing he had been killed. Chela's face was tight with pain and exhaustion, and her bandaged leg was swollen. Gwydion lifted her across his shoulders and ran for the trees. Briana stumbled at his elbow. The wizards' men were scattering, following the caravan survivors into the forest. The battle had become a massacre.

The priestess was overwhelmed with the deaths of her sisters. The keening wails of old women, the high terrified peals of girls, battered her ears and mind. The most powerful of the Goddess's Chosen could not defend themselves against steel. They had never been taught to use their Power for violence, only to heal, to praise, to worship. Yet Briana could feel a force within her for destruction, an angry, outraged force that grew as she ran. She suspected it came from Rahshaiya. It frightened her that she did not know how to release it, how to use it, and it frightened her more that she desired so strongly to do so.

Gwydion kept a swift pace. They outdistanced their pursuers. He boosted Chela into a red-barked, leafy tree and helped Briana to follow, then swung himself up. They climbed as far as they could. The young wizard muttered something about placing an illusion around them so they would appear to be birds or shadows cast by the leaves; Briana never knew if he had succeeded, because soldiers passing beneath them never looked up.

Kyellan led his small command deep into the woods, toward the sound of the swift-running river where the forest stream turned sharply and reached a long slope. The water was deep and white-capped, full of rocks and concealed by thick, tangled bushes. Kyellan held tightly to the whimpering Valahtia and led her into the water, fighting the current and the freezing cold, splashing downstream for nearly a hundred yards into a particularly dense clump of bushes. Erlin and Pima followed. They crouched down, shivering with cold, until their heads showed dimly among the branches, and listened to the distant sounds of the searching enemy.

The wizards' army hunted through half the night, beating the forest with their swords, killing everyone they found, whether soldier, priestess, or lady-in-waiting. Before dawn they marched on toward Atolan, leaving the forest to lick its wounds. The birds returned with protesting chatter, joined by vultures and kites from the plains. Those had a great feast in the clearing, until they were driven off by the survivors.

Cold and stiff in every limb, Kyellan stood silently for a long time, sickened by the carnage that met the soft morning light. The ground was soaked with blood and piled with bodies so thick they were layered three deep in places. Valahtia had found two of her ladies and crouched over them, sobbing hysterically. He picked her up and set her to going through the burned carts for salvageable items. Pima had clung tightly, mindlessly, to the solid form of Erlin all night; now she realized her mistake and broke from him to join the Princess.

Kyellan and Erlin began to search among the dead. Twenty-seven of the Royal Guard had fallen. Even the scouts were there; the wizards' men must have brought the people they had killed in the forest to the clearing for a more accurate tally. Tobas was missing. Kyellan had seen him shepherding the First Priestess and Gemon from the circle early in the battle. They were probably safe, if he knew Tobas.

"Demons of Arigoth! What a mess," commented a familiar voice.

Kyellan whirled to see Gwydion, Chela, and Briana at the edge of the glade. Something leaped inside him. He was even relieved to see the haughty young priestess. They were scratched and filthy, but they did not look as bad as his own small group.

Gwydion clasped hands with the Guardsman and asked, "How many?"

Erlin had been counting. He answered from the center of the dead. "Almost everyone. I can't find one novice, the First Priestess, Tobas, or the Prince. The rest are here. Along with a hundred twenty of the enemy." He allowed a little pride to surface.

"They missed their targets." Gwydion laughed grimly.

"They were in a hurry to get to Atolan," Briana said thoughtfully, joining them. "The wizards didn't even participate in the search. If they had, none of us would be here."

"You didn't find Arel?" Valahtia frowned at Erlin. Her arms were full of half-charred dresses and jewels, which she piled neatly beside her cart.

"No," the boy reassured her gently. "He's probably alive."

"Maybe he drowned," she muttered. "Or got lost in the woods."

But the Prince appeared several hours later, followed by a man Kyellan was astonished to see. It was the taller of the two who had led him into ambush, a man who had taken gold to kill him on the Sanctuary road. Kyellan had thought the assassin would have left the caravan long before. He must have been hiding. Probably in Arel's own cart.

"The Royal Guard!" Arel snorted in disdain. "The elite soldiers of the Kingdom, sworn to protect the royal family. A fine job of it they did."

"Most of my men are dead," Kyellan said, his voice dangerously soft. His hand strayed to his sword hilt. They could always say the Prince had been killed in the battle.

Erlin grabbed Kyellan's sword arm and spoke hastily. "You and your sister are safe, Your Highness. Be grateful for that." The Prince sniffed and walked away, followed by his bodyguard.

"Let go of me, Corporal," Kyellan muttered.

"I'm sorry, sir. I couldn't let you kill him." The boy stepped back, frightened but stubborn. "We swore an oath to defend the royal house of Ardavan."

"Even if it tries to kill us?" Anger uncoiled in him, a snake in his spine, as he watched the nonchalant strolling of the Prince and his bodyguard.

"Hasn't there been enough killing, man of Rahshaiya?" said Briana wearily from behind him. He stiffened. "Whatever your personal feelings, they have no place here. We may need the help of those men to get to Caerlin."

"I don't think they'll be much help," he countered, trying to suppress his anger. She was right, of course. If he meant to command, he had to forego revenge. He had a responsibility to protect them all. Even the Prince.

"Priestess!" Pima shrieked, leaping up and scattering a pile of rope and food and other necessities. "Look!"

"Dear Goddess," the young woman cried. Kyellan followed her gaze. The First Priestess and Tobas walked slowly into the circle of destruction, and the thin novice Gemon hobbled behind them. Briana picked up her skirts and ran like a child to hug the old woman with such force that Kyellan feared she would knock her down.

Tobas grinned widely. Kyellan embraced him with little less emotion than Briana had shown. "Are you all right? You're not hurt?"

"Not much," the youth said. "I got scratched across the ribs by a Parahnese rapier wielded by a Hoabi mercenary. I must have killed someone from each of the Eleven Kingdoms. Those wizards did some widespread recruiting."

"Maybe. But there was something strange about those recruits, Tobas. Something in their eyes." He shook his head.

Gwydion passed nearby with a load of dry wood. "They were spell-bound. No fear of death, mindless loyalty, blind obedience. Belaric is taking no chances."

That would explain it, if Kyellan believed in spells and magic. He did not know what he believed anymore. Certainly it was unheard-of for an army of mercenaries who had been traveling overland without camp followers to murder twenty-eight virgin girls without protest.

Briana shivered as she watched the flames through the trees. There had not been enough stones in the forest to build a cairn for a single body, much less nearly two hundred dead. So they were burning friend and foe alike. Shadowy figures moved against the fire. The three Guardsmen and the wizard kept the blaze hot and contained. They were like black spirits of death, and Briana thought she could see the smoke-formed shape of Rahshaiya above them breathing in the fumes.

They were camped within a tangle of trees near the white-foamed stream. The six women huddled close together for warmth beneath a huge evergreen, some distance from the Prince and his silent servant.

"The wizards move quickly," Pima said. "They might be in Atolan in two days."

"And in Cavernon City in two weeks." The First Priestess sighed. "We can only pray they will not easily find the Seat of the Goddess."

"We could be close behind them," Valahtia said, "if we didn't have to cross the Border Hills of Ryasa to get to Chelm. Why can't we just follow the Is'nai River west to Dallynd? The river is no more than a day distant."

"Dallynd is less than twenty miles from Atolan. The wizards are sure to attack it. We'd be walking into a siege," Briana said.

"I fear what we may find in Chelm," said the First Priestess. "We have not heard from our sisters there in more than three weeks. Yet we have little choice. Dallynd is certainly too dangerous." She looked at Briana thoughtfully. "I only wish I knew where our greatest danger lay."

"You mean the Shape-Changer?" the young priestess guessed. "I wish you'd tell us who he is. Why do you fear him?"

"He could be anyone. That is his Power: to take on any shape as his own. Not as illusion, but as reality. I could not detect his presence if he was beside this stream tonight."

"Is he a wizard?"

"Sometimes. He has not concerned himself with them for the past hundred years."

"How old can he be?" Chela asked. She was wrapped in salvaged blankets but shivered constantly. Briana knew her leg was painful, but the girl would not let anyone but Gwydion see it.

"His spirit is ancient." The First Priestess made a sign of aversion. "It is reborn each generation, through blood descent. Each Shape-Changer fathers the next. So the records tell. The spirit is from the enemy, I think. It has chosen to serve the Light on occasion, but more often serves the Dark. It does not concern itself with petty skirmishes such as this one, but if the wizards succeed in taking the Kingdoms, it may act. I fear it will.''

"It will seek the Goddess's Seat," said Gemon distantly.

Briana yawned. ''If the Seat appeared here tonight, none of us would have the Power to use it. We need to sleep. Tomorrow begins the journey to Chelm, and we need strength.'' She curled up on the rough ground and was pleased to see the others follow her example. She had been afraid the First Priestess would insist on exhaustive rituals for the dead. All of them were too weak as it was, without the added drain of worship.

"There is Darkness in this camp," Gemon's voice keened softly. Briana shuddered at its tone. "In the Guard captain, in the Prince, but most in the man who sits with the Prince and has no name. His mind is closed. I fear him.''

"Sleep, child," soothed the First Priestess.

They trudged through the green forest most of the next day. It was beautiful but treacherous, full of undergrowth, grasping roots, snapping branches, sudden patches of boggy ground. The thick canopy of leaves filtered the sun. They walked slowly but steadily, the stronger bearing heavy packs, the weaker finding their own bodies burden enough. Chela had to be carried, passed from man to man at intervals.

It was late afternoon when they left the shadowed forest for a broad meadowland. The river Is'nai sparkled like a silver ribbon in the distance. The high outlines of the Ryasan Border Hills rose faint and purple beyond. Kyellan winced, surveying his motley company over the tangled red hair of the girl in his arms. Few of them looked capable of crossing the river, much less the mountains between them and Chelm. Of them all, only Erlin, Briana, and Gwydion had not been exhausted by the trek through the woods. The Guardsman eased Chela and his heavy pack to the ground, feeling the protest of muscles that had rarely been used. His recently wounded arm, only released from its sling a few days before, throbbed with a dull, steady pain.

The others dropped wearily into the knee-high, lush grass of the meadow. Kyellan dug into his pack for the dried meat and biscuits he had searched out in the carts. There was not much. The wizards' men had taken most of their stores, as well as the gold and silver that had been meant to pay both soldiers' and priestesses' passage back to Cavernon City. All that was left were the five gold pieces Kyellan had taken from Arel's assassins on the Sanctuary road and a few jewels Arel and Valahtia had retrieved from hidden caches in their carts.

"How long will it take to get to Chelm?" Tobas asked through a mouthful of tough pork.

"Less than a week, with luck and good weather," Kyellan said.

"This food won't last a week."

Erlin unslung the longbow that hung behind him. "This place reminds me of the Dhalen Meadows near Cavernon. The Royal Hunting Preserve. There should be plenty of game."

"Anything would be welcome," Kyellan said, recalling the youth's prowess as an archer.

"How can he have so much energy left?" Pima wondered. Her wide brown eyes followed Erlin's retreating form with admiration. Kyellan almost laughed at Briana's disapproving expression.

"Come, daughters," said the First Priestess, rising with

an obvious effort, preventing Briana's imminent words. "We will give thanks to the Goddess for our deliverance."

The four women were soon established in a nearby hollow, and the soft sounds of chanting and prayer from tired throats wafted faintly over the meadow.

Wildflowers swayed in the early evening breeze, brushing Kyellan's face where he lay prone on the soft, spongy turf, some distance from the others. It was early spring now, everywhere but the high hills of Garith. He had been cold for a long time. White clouds wisped across the sky in a high wind that did not touch the plains. He thought of loss, of waste. They were all dead. All the men he had fought with, drunk with, commanded. He remembered the boy Cathan, who should never have been a soldier. And Jarl, who had survived the destruction of his village only to die the next night. He had failed them.

It was just as well he could not return to Caerlin. They would probably assign him to wall guard for life. The most he could do would be to ensure that the remainder of his command reached Chelm safely and found ships to take them to Laenar. From there, he did not know where he would go.

A shadow blocked the setting sun as the Princess knelt beside him, disheveled from the forest, her dress torn and muddy, her hair trailing wildly from its braids. Her beauty took his breath. She reached over and kissed him.

"I never thanked you for saving my life."

"You just did."

"That isn't enough. I should give you jewels, diamonds, half my father's treasury. I know!" Her eyes sparkled. "I'll make you High Commander of the Armies. Would you like that?"

"Very much. But it's impossible."

"Because you're lowborn? I could give you a manor or two."

Kyellan laughed softly, sitting up beside her. "Valita, you know I can't go back with you. Your brother would kill me."

"I suppose he would," she admitted. "I won't be surprised if he kills our father to become King. It's happened before. He doesn't care about me. Only my virtue, so I can marry some good ally." She looked down at her twisting hands. "I wish he had died in the battle."

"Then you'd be your father's heir."

"That's unlikely. He'd only legitimatize one of his bastard sons. Any of them would be better than Arel, if he had died."

"But he didn't."

"He still might." Her dark eyes blazed at him. "I saw you when he came out of the woods yesterday morning. You wanted to kill him. Why didn't you?"

"I swore to protect him." Kyellan shrugged, his voice bitter.

"Your oath isn't binding. He tried to kill you first."

The Guardsman did not answer.

"It will be a long journey. Anything could happen." She rose gracefully and wandered away.

Kyellan had the first watch that night. Gwydion sat up with him, nervous, unable to sleep. The priestesses were still performing some kind of weird ritual under the slivered moon. A chant for their dead, Kyellan supposed. It was certainly mournful.

"I wish they'd stop," said Gwydion finally. "They're shouting their Power for anyone to hear."

"The wizards, you mean?"

"By now they know they didn't kill the First Priestess.

She frightens them. They don't know how strong she is, or how dangerous. There hasn't been a duel between a wizard and a priestess since Ayetra killed the Hoab Wizard long ago. And that time the wizards lost.''

"She's an old woman.''

"The most powerful woman in the world, and their deadliest enemy. They have to stop her. She's the greatest threat to the Kharad.'' He shivered. "She's sending out a beacon for them to follow. They'll be coming for her. For us all.''

"What do you want us to do?'' Kyellan asked, half-angry. "Give up and wait for them?''

"No,'' Gwydion said quietly. "Just keep your sword in reach.''

Chapter Seven

It would take the heavy wool of Briana's robe a long time to dry after the crossing of the Is'nai. She walked uncomfortably, wishing she had the privacy to remove her robe and dry her skin in the sun. The river crossing had not been difficult; the Is'nai was slow and deep. They had swum across, pushing a makeshift raft of lashed brush laden with the packs and weapons. Briana had helped the First Priestess across, and the wizard had done the same for his young apprentice. Pima, seeming to forget decorum entirely, had raced Erlin, winning by a length because she ducked him under on the way past.

The low, rolling foothills were very different from the barren lands around the Sanctuary. They were covered with short, stiff grass, and budding yellow flowers. Cottonwood trees gave way to pines that towered like ships' masts, bare wood to the top, where they broke into a cap of greenery. The air was dry and cool, fragrant with fresh scents. Deep, still lakes of cobalt blue nested in small bowl-shaped valleys below the distant peaks, like a string of sapphire beads. If Briana had not been so impatient to reach Chelm, she would have delighted in the beauty of the Border Hills that thrust up into the sky like sharp-edged, jagged blades of blue steel. Their summits were cloud-wreathed. But they were frightening obstacles, especially when she thought of the weakened First Priestess.

By late afternoon, they had left the foothills behind for the bare, stony slopes of the first mountains. Briana had to belt her robe nearly to her knees to climb the steep, pathless rocks. She wished she had a staff. They had hoped to find a way through the mountains but found themselves forced to continually ascend. In some places they had to use the ropes that had been salvaged from the burned carts. Briana was reluctant to trust herself to them; they were blackened and frayed every few feet and looked ready to snap. Usually she could scramble up with little of her weight supported by the rope, but the First Priestess and the two girls, Chela and Gemon, had no such option. Briana watched each time with barely suppressed terror as the Guardsmen hauled them in hand over hand.

Her nervousness was increased by the sense of malevolent watchers all about them. None of the wizards could be in the mountains, yet she knew they could see the little company as it struggled like ants on the slippery face. There were so many opportunities for danger. And though it was bright daylight, the Dark crowded strong around them.

The next day's climbing found them in weathered mountains of strangely shaped sandstone and layers of other rock, gouged as if by some erratic sculptor into ledges and bridges of stone that made the traveling deceptively easy until they abruptly ended. Sometimes the ledges were broad highroads, and other times mere shelves a few feet wide. With walls rising on one side and chasms looming on the other, each step set the heart to pounding and the legs to shaking.

The First Priestess walked slowly, head down, hands

resting on Gemon's frail shoulders. Briana followed them.
The foreboding that had haunted her the day before was
like a stifling fog in her mind. She feared for Gemon
especially. The novice would be highly sensitive to supernatural attack. She had insight and vision that were often
frightening, though many times incorrect. For instance, the
girl claimed now that the Dark was strongest in Captain
Kyellan. She seemed to fear him unreasonably. All Briana
could sense from Kyellan was his protective shield; she
was certain Gemon felt nothing more.

The ledge was narrowing. At the front of the company,
Pima pressed fearfully against the cliff wall until Erlin
took her hand. Just behind them, the Prince faltered a
little, but the steady tread of Tobas at his heels kept him
going. The First Priestess and Gemon moved even slower.
Briana glanced behind her. Valahtia was clutching Kyellan
shamelessly, unmindful of others' eyes. The silent man
who was Arel's servant followed them, and behind him
were Gwydion and Chela.

Gemon's head snapped up like a hound scenting the
wind. Her thin brown hair blew around her tense face as
she halted momentarily. Briana heard her soft whisper, "A
breath of Rahshaiya. . . ." and then something cold floated
over Briana's head. Something cold and dark and aware.

She turned in time to catch the reeling Princess. Valahtia
clung to her gasping, her red-nailed hands digging into the
priestess's arms. Briana hardly noticed.

The Prince's bodyguard had gone berserk. His eyes
blazing unnaturally, his hands outstretched claws, he closed
with Kyellan like a wild beast. His growls were savage,
inhuman, as was his apparent strength. The unprepared
Guardsman staggered back toward the edge, straining to
hold the madman from him. Rocks scattered and crashed
over the raised lip of the shelf.

Goddess, his teeth! . . . Briana almost screamed as the attacker, snarling and staring, fought to get close enough to Kyellan's neck to rip it open. The Guardsman, white-faced, the muscles in his arms standing out like braided rope, was forced to one knee.

"Hold him off!" Gwydion shouted, shrugging the heavy pack from his shoulders with Chela's help. Briana and Valahtia flattened against the wall as Tobas ran by them.

The nameless man launched his full weight on Kyellan, gripping his arms to his sides, rolling with him toward the edge. Kyellan struggled wildly, fighting to reach his belt knife, his fingers sliding in the rocks as they scratched for purchase.

Gwydion and Tobas leaped for the battling pair and managed to grasp Kyellan's feet as the madman rolled with him off the edge. Valahtia screamed. The two young men braced themselves desperately against their friend's weight, pulling him backward onto the ledge again. The attacker fell without a sound. Kyellan soon knelt panting on the shelf, battered and scratched, his face the color of ash.

Valahtia ran to him and threw her arms around him. "Are you all right? Did he hurt you?"

Kyellan shook his head and allowed her to help him to his feet. "I'm fine. No thanks to the Prince."

"I had nothing to do with it," Arel called back. "You may think what you like." The young man pointedly avoided looking at his sister.

"You hired him to kill me once before."

"Not this time."

"Believe him," Gwydion said. "I told you the Kharad would follow us. They chose the easiest of the company to incite to evil."

"He was possessed." Briana nodded. "He had to be."

''Possessed by greed,'' Kyellan muttered, but he did not pursue the matter.

They strung out again, on the Guardsman's assurance he was recovered. Briana felt her legs begin to move without conscious command from her. They were like pieces of another creature, unconnected except by a dull ache with each step. She was sure this was only the first blow. The wizards would try again. She wondered if their enemies knew the nature of the priestesses' quest. Perhaps the Kharad already feared them.

They had reached the highest part of the Border Hills, and clouds enveloped them in dark mist. It hung in beads from their clothes and hair. Thunder echoed above them, but there was no rain. A day had passed since the attempt on Kyellan's life, but Gwydion was certain they were not free from danger. It was like an anvil suspended over his head on a thread, waiting for the scissors. A dull, distant hatred. They thought he was a traitor, but it would have been a worse betrayal to have joined the Kharad.

He had only to look at Chela's trusting face where she lay in his arms to know he had made the right choice. Last night, while they had tried to sleep on a narrow ledge, she had clung to him closely. He could feel her budding woman's body through her thin dress. How old was she? Thirteen? Fourteen, perhaps. Three years younger than he. Was that too young? He did not know. There had been no girls at the College at Akesh, only the old women who nursed the wizard babies.

He almost ran into Kyellan, who was stopped a few feet ahead. The narrow trail had turned into an arched, natural bridge over a deep canyon. The roar of a white-water river reached them faintly. They had crossed such bridges before, but none so long or narrow. Erlin and Pima were already halfway across, he saw through the mist. Chela stirred in his arms, and he put her down. She could walk a short distance now, but her leg was healing slowly. Gwydion was trying to minimize the scar she would have.

"Do we have to?" she asked softly.

"Don't worry," Kyellan assured her from ahead. "It's slippery, but wide enough." The Guardsman almost vanished in the clouded air. Gwydion had to squint and peer a few moments before he could see that Kyellan was crossing rapidly, and that most of the company awaited him on the opposite side.

The girl hugged herself and shuddered. Gwydion put an arm around her, but she was stiff and unresponsive. "I don't like it," she whispered.

"I don't blame you. But I'll be right behind you."

"No. I can't." She turned her blue eyes up at him. "There's something wrong."

"Everyone else managed." He sighed. "If I cross first, and you see it's safe, will you try?"

"Don't." She shook uncontrollably.

"I'm sorry, Chela. We have no choice. Promise you'll come after me," he said gently.

"Don't you believe me? There's danger!" Her breath caught in a sob.

Gwydion thought of carrying her across but did not trust his footing with that much extra weight. Surely she would follow him if he crossed safely. He started over the bridge. Halfway, he turned and waved lightheartedly to her through the thick mist. Then he felt a trembling in the rock. There was a creaking noise. He froze for a heartbeat, then began to walk a little faster. A low rumbling came from the chasm. The arch began to vibrate.

Names of Power. He tasted bitter fear. He could feel the malevolence now. The hatred. Caution forgotten, he ran across the narrow arch, as the sides of it crumbled and fell away. Chela screamed. The arch cracked thunderously and gave a vast, monstrous shudder. Gwydion leaped farther than he would have thought possible. Kyellan and Tobas caught him and pulled him scrambling onto the broad ledge as the bridge crashed into the river below with an impact that shook the mountains. Dust rose in a red, choking cloud.

"Chela!" Gwydion could hear the terrified sobs of the slight figure, nearly sixty yards away over a scar of newly sheared rock.

"Thank the Goddess she's alive," the First Priestess whispered.

Gwydion threw down his pack, loosened the straps, and pulled out three coils of rope. Erlin ran to him and helped him tie them together with strong knots. The Guard corporal unslung his longbow, chose a clothyard arrow, and secured an end of the rope just behind the iron-shod head. Gwydion took the other end around a sturdy outcropping of boulders and wrapped it several times before tying it.

"What can she do with a rope if she gets it?" Briana asked helplessly.

"Climb across," Kyellan said grimly. "I'd send one of us after her, but I don't trust the rope with that much weight."

"Come on," Gwydion urged, herding the others back to give Erlin room.

The young Guardsman took a deep breath and stepped to the edge. He planted his feet firmly, fitted the arrow, and drew the string back beyond his ear. The bow creaked in protest. Erlin strained to pull it farther, then let the arrow fly. The bow almost sprang out of his hands. The bolt flew so quickly they could not follow it and hit the far wall above where Chela stood. It bounced back out of her reach.

"Almost." Gwydion pulled in the rope as Erlin put a new string to his bow. The wizard tried his best to clear his mind of fear, tried not to hear the soft whimpering of Chela from across the chasm. He called up all the reserves of Power he could find in his exhausted body. A binding-spell, similar to the one he had used in the forest battle, the one his masters had battered to pieces. To bind the frayed, burned, weakened fibers into a whole. He pulled the rope through his fingers, envisioning it thickening, strengthening, binding together. At last he gave the arrow at the end to Erlin.

The soldier looked at him sympathetically. "We'll do it this time," he promised.

The wizard nodded, drained and light-headed from the effort of the spell. The young Guardsman again drew his bow. He pulled back until the weapon was bent nearly double. The arrow left screaming and fell to the ledge where Chela was waiting. She held it up triumphantly. Gwydion gripped the rope tightly, fighting to maintain his spell, and felt it grow taut as Chela lashed it to a boulder.

Chela fiercely blinked back her tears. The looming danger had not left the canyon; it swam around her senses, seeking entrance, and she knew it would attack once she was out on the thin rope. Yet she could feel Gwydion trying to comfort her, and she had no choice. She took a firm grip on the rough line, her back to the company, pulled her body up, and locked her legs around. It scratched her skin. She began to walk her hands along, sliding her legs on the rope.

She could feel the cold, deep canyon below, the river roaring over the barrier of rocks that had been the arched bridge. The mist enfolded her like a clammy hand. Her dress clung to her damply, and the rope was wet and slippery. Her hands were blistering. She was almost halfway across when the wind began to blow. It gusted at first, tugging at her, then became a gale that howled through the mountains and threatened to pull her from the rope. She stopped. Her terror had become overpowering. The mist was so thick she thought she was breathing water.

It began to rain. She rocked back and forth like a cloak hanging in the breeze. Her arms were losing strength. She forced one hand to let go and grasp again, and then the other, until she was moving once more. The wind spoke to her in a soothing, pleasant voice and urged her to drop. She would never get across. The insides of her legs were raw and bleeding from being pulled along the rope. Her shoulders were numb. It would be peaceful if she gave in to the voice.

No! The shout rang in her head, making it hurt. Gwydion cut through the murmuring of the wind. She was almost there. She could not let go. He needed her. She began the agonizing traverse once more, clinging to the thread of Gwydion's voice in her mind. The rope swung and stretched, trying its best to break, until it seemed she hung from a living thing. She heard a dim, distant whimpering, like a beaten puppy, and realized it was herself.

Then she was gathered into a pair of strong arms and pulled off the rope. A heavy blanket wrapped her shivering body, and the golden-eyed, brown-skinned face of Gwydion smiled down at her. He looked as exhausted as she. Chela tried to smile back.

Briana glared across the chasm. It was quiet now. The rain and the howling wind stopped as suddenly as they came. "Your masters are strong, wizard," she said.

"They'll keep trying to kill us, one by one. This is only the beginning." The tired youth stroked Chela's hair soothingly.

"We must learn to defend ourselves," said the First Priestess thoughtfully. "The Goddess is Cianya, the Mother. What mother does not defend her children? Surely Her Power can be turned to that use."

"We need more than defense." Briana met the sunken eyes of the old woman, frightened by the conviction she felt. "We should fight back. We should call on Rahshaiya."

The First Priestess stared at her. "Do you know what you are saying?"

"I think so." Briana was uncomfortably aware of Gemon's sharp, disapproving eyes. "The Death-Bringer is one of the aspects of the Goddess. As important as the others, if not as pleasant. I think we'll need Rahshaiya's aid to keep the wizards from the Goddess's Seat. Even after we find the Seat, we may have to fight for it."

"But to kill!" Gemon protested. "We are taught to honor life."

"Death is a part of life," Briana argued.

"Do you think you could actually kill someone, child?" asked the First Priestess sadly.

"They killed most of us," she said stubbornly. The question bothered her. She felt the destructive force inside her waiting for release; but if she released it, and killed, how would she feel afterward? Even if it was necessary?

"Do not speak of this again," said the old woman sharply. "But give it serious thought, Briana. The Dark is strong here. Your shields against it may not be as powerful as they should be."

"I'm sorry, Mother," she muttered. "It was only a suggestion."

The First Priestess did not seem appeased. Briana turned

away, near tears, feeling the gaze of almost all the company. Kyellan's dark eyes met hers, full of sympathy. She turned her back on them and sat huddled at the edge of the chasm. She supposed she looked crushed by her disgrace, but instead she was quivering with anger. Would the First Priestess lay down her life as unresistingly as her sisters in the forest? If so, Briana thought, their quest was useless. She knew that what she had said was true. They would be forced to call on the Death-Bringer to defeat their enemies.

Briana had dedicated her life to the service of the Three-Fold Goddess, not two-thirds of Her. Her thoughts of Rahshaiya did not come from the Dark. Yet her disobedience might be the work of the enemy. She resolved to apologize again but to learn to use the force of Rahshaiya that was within her. They would not be helpless against the wizards next time.

They reached the southeastern foothills on the sixth morning after crossing the Is'nai. Chelm could not be more than a day's journey away. Kyellan led his footsore company south across bright green meadows, hoping to strike a road. There were signs of habitation now. A herd of sheep followed them a mile or two; their heavy winter coats were unsheared, and there was no shepherd. By afternoon, the land grew level, parceled into small fields and dotted with farmers' cottages. Yet the fields were fallow and the cottages empty.

Soon they came across a pleasant highroad, shaded by tall hedges and spring-leaved trees. The road was well graded, wide, and silent. Kyellan had thought Ryasa a populous country and hoped to find himself in civilization again. This was worse than Garith. At least there, no one expected to find any people. But the highroad leading to Chelm bore only old tracks, long since blurred in the dust.

They walked east, uneasy, not speaking. The Guardsman guessed that no one wanted to ask the question everyone was thinking.

Where were the Ryasans? The road led through villages with shuttered windows and bolted doors. They knocked at several houses, hoping to gain permission to fill their water flasks at the village wells. No one answered. They drew the water anyway. It was clear and untainted.

Kyellan decided not to worry yet. Obviously the inhabitants had not died of pestilence or plague; they had left in an orderly fashion, taking time to lock their houses. The stables and pastures around the villages were empty save for a few cows and huge, placid farmers' horses.

The rest of his company seemed nervous, but the First Priestess walked slowly with a thoughtful, listening expression on her thin face. He would wait until she spoke before he changed his plans. He did not know the source of the priestesses' Power, whether it was magic or simply the wisdom of age and learning, but he was beginning to believe it was real.

Chela was able to walk on her own now and was eager to learn. She absorbed Gwydion's words like a sponge.

"The easiest magic to sustain is illusion. Do you know what that is?" he asked.

"Making things look like something they're not?" she guessed.

"Good. See that knothole in the biggest oak ahead of us?"

"Yes."

"Fill it in. Make the tree smooth-sided."

Chela screwed up her face in concentration. The knothole remained. Glaring at the tree, she narrowed her eyes and clenched her fists with effort. Suddenly Gwydion,

Briana, and the First Priestess reached for their heads, grimacing in pain. The novice Gemon made a sharp sound. Chela looked up, confused.

"You're not focusing," Gwydion said finally. "You sent Power in every direction but at that tree."

"How do I focus?"

Briana broke in. "Perhaps you could forget the exercises for a while. Just teach her the theory, wizard."

"Practice is important." He grinned. "Chela won't be a priestess. She needs to learn to use her Power effectively."

Briana made a slight bow to the tree, sketched a sign in the air, and the knothole disappeared. The tree bore was as smooth as glass.

Gwydion chuckled and replaced the hole with a wave of his hand. Briana turned away with a slight smile.

"I felt what she did," Chela said eagerly. "But it'll be easier without all that ceremony." She withdrew into herself and sent an arrow of concentrated Power at the tree. The knothole vanished. She cried out in triumph.

Gwydion hugged her. "Good work."

Chela looked so proud of herself that even Briana had to laugh.

By the next evening, the road was still empty, but the high-walled city of Chelm rose before them, with the glisten of the inland Tarnsea behind it. Chelm, unlike its counterpart Dallynd to the west, had only one wall. The turreted edifice was fifteen feet thick and nearly seventy feet high. Its single gate stood open and unguarded. Kyellan strained his eyes upward and saw no evidence of soldiers anywhere along the wide ramparts.

Gwydion stopped him, a hand on his arm. "Let me take a look inside before you bring them in." His voice was low and worried.

Kyellan agreed. He had grown increasingly uneasy as they'd approached the quiet city, the only people on the highroad that led straight through broad farmland between low stone fences.

"It's probably nothing," muttered the wizard as he started in the gate. "There's a shield around the city that shouldn't be there. I won't be long."

"Nothing?" Briana shuddered. "The second largest city in Ryasa, as silent and empty as a tomb. Can you sense anything from it, Mother?"

The First Priestess shook her head. "Only the shield. But that is not necessarily dangerous. Perhaps the reason we have not heard from the Temple in Chelm is that they received the same warnings we did, and they are defending themselves against the wizards' awareness. The Temple has enough power in this land to pull in the people of all the outlying villages, to keep them safe from the Kharad."

"Do you really think so?" Briana brightened.

Kyellan surveyed his surroundings thoughtfully. The fields were not entirely barren. Several herds of dairy cattle grazed unguarded beyond the low stone walls. Eight huge plowhorses watched his company curiously from a nearby field; the animals were as tall as he at the shoulders, shaggy-maned and dappled with colors ranging from gray to dark brown. They wore rope halters and were picketed to individual lines. There had to be someone in the city. The animals looked well cared for.

Gwydion turned back through the gates, his face pale, almost running. "Get off the road!" he hissed. "Quickly!"

They obeyed his urgent tone without question. Kyellan led them to the field where the draft horses stood and waited impatiently as they climbed the fence.

"The city is taken," Gwydion explained. "Full of the

invading army. They felt my presence. We're in great danger."

The Guardsman looked back. A patrol of perhaps thirty men was moving past the gates. Brown uniforms, close, disciplined formation; better organized, better trained than the army they had fought in the Garithian forest. Damn.

Erlin vaulted onto one of the horses before the placid, broad-backed creature could react. He cut the picket rope with his knife, leaning down over the horse's neck, and tied the cut end to the halter, creating makeshift reins.

Tobas and Gwydion soon followed suit, taking Gemon and Chela up behind them. Kyellan hurried to assist the others. Pima had no trouble controlling her huge mount. Briana looked inexperienced but determined. Arel and his sister mounted together and looked capable enough.

The wizards' patrol was unslinging its crossbows at the edge of the field. "Ride!" Kyellan called, hoisting the First Priestess onto one of the two remaining horses and swinging up behind her.

The ponderous beasts broke into a bone-jarring canter. Kyellan held his back and let the others pass. Erlin was the last. The youth rode as if he sat in an archer's port, almost backward on his horse, his shafts finding several marks in the wizards' men.

Crossbow bolts rained around them, powerful but with little accuracy. Kyellan urged his mount to leap the three-foot stone wall after its fellows and had to cling desperately as the horse landed in the meadow beyond. The First Priestess gasped with the impact.

"Are you all right?" he muttered as they galloped across the coastal plains of Ryasa.

"Yes. The Goddess be praised for our deliverance," she said, and dissolved into a soft chanting in some ancient, indecipherable language.

Kyellan supposed he was grateful, too. Some power must have aided their escape. Whether it was luck, or the priestesses' Goddess, or Shilemat, the god of thieves, it had ensured that they were mounted and the wizards' men were not. Although if he had the choice, he would have wished for any horses but these.

Chapter Eight

The tame farmlands and hedge-ringed meadows of Ryasa blurred together in a montage of spring greens and freshly turned dirt. They rode swiftly at first, jolted on the backs of the huge, rough-gaited horses they had taken. After only a few miles, the beasts slowed to a striding walk. They seemed untiring at the new pace.

Kyellan rode rearguard, scanning the flat expanse of empty land behind them. He could see no pursuit, but he could not believe the wizards' men would give up that easily. Surely they would find themselves horses better than these and follow.

"There is no one behind us," the First Priestess said mildly an hour after midday. "I am satisfied of that."

"I'm not." Kyellan continued to watch.

By nightfall they were approaching a blue line of hills that had been a distant shadow that morning. Kyellan had a vague idea of hiding there, in the low ridge of mountains that bisected Ryasa, and trying to find a way south through them to Keris.

Everyone was exhausted. A cavalry officer, Kyellan had never been so tired after a mere day's ride. The First Priestess swayed with the movements of the horse. Her breathing was so ragged and shallow that Kyellan kept one arm around her to prevent her from falling.

Just outside a grove of white-barked, rustling trees, Gwydion halted and called back to the column, "They haven't been following. It's safe to stay here for a while. We need to rest."

Kyellan frowned. "They wouldn't let us go so easily. They could have kept out of sight. They'd be waiting for us to stop for the night."

"No one is following us," Briana said firmly. "One of us would have sensed it if they were. Gwydion's right. We have to rest."

Everyone seemed to agree. Kyellan knew that this was no military command he could force to go on. But he did not like it. "I don't know much about your mind-powers, Priestess. But I've heard you use this term before. What if that wizards' patrol is shielded? They could be a few miles away and you wouldn't know."

Briana nodded wearily. "I did think of that. But I don't see that we have a choice. The First Priestess is sick."

Indeed, the old woman looked terrible. She was slumped over the broad neck of the horse, her thin, pale hands twisted in its mane. She had not spoken for hours. Kyellan sighed. With relief, the others began to dismount and lead their horses into the grove.

The Guardsman swung his leg over the horse's rump and dropped to the spongy ground. He reached up and lifted the priestess from the animal's shoulders. She weighed no more than a child. The rising moon seemed to shine through her skin. He set her down carefully, wondering whether she would survive the journey.

The priestess chuckled softly. "You cannot allow me to die yet, Guardsman. There is much to do." At his annoyed look, she added, "No, I did not read that from your mind, but from your face. Your mind is closed to me. Whoever placed those shields was quite thorough." She hobbled away, supported by Gemon, who did not look much stronger.

Kyellan tore a handful of rough grass from the ground to rub down the sweat-sticky horse. The animal seemed tired, but not as flighty and uncooperative as a S'tari horse would have been after such a day. He worked across its heavily muscled body, easing over scratches it had accumulated since the morning. The horse watched him, its head turned curiously.

After the horses were securely picketed with their halter ropes, Kyellan took the first watch and let the others sleep. He was as tired as they, but he could not relax. He supposed he should believe the priestesses and Gwydion that there was no danger. Their Power had proven itself to be something real, if baffling. Yet he felt a vague threat, a nearby menace; it was the feeling he remembered experiencing in a field tent years ago on the eve of a battle with the elusive S'tari.

He sat with his back to the small fire, his sword drawn and resting across his knees, listening to the labored sleep of the others and the soft noises of the horses. It had been nearly two weeks since they had left the Sanctuary. The wizards must have held Chelm port nearly that long. The Kharad army must have been crossing the Garithian road just before the arrival of the Prince's caravan. Perhaps the two assassins sent by the Prince had actually seen the tracks they had claimed when they had led him from the column. He had never gotten far enough in the gully to see.

Atolan was surely taken. The wizards would have had enough time to stock ships for the voyage to Caerlin. He did not know where they would get the ships, but this invasion had been well planned. Their journey might already have begun.

If he led his people overland, down the spine of mountains into Keris and Parahn, the priestesses would probably be too late for their religious quest once they reached Caerlin. If they ever got that far. Kyellan was not fool enough to believe they had a chance against a wizards' patrol. Five men and a handful of women and girl-children . . . it was foolish to believe they had any chance at all. Yet the First Priestess was confident. She trusted him.

Her skinny novice Gemon certainly did not. She seemed to avoid his gaze, but when their eyes met he shivered at her enmity. What had he done to make her hate him so?

The ground was spongy and moist. He lay back and looked up at the stars through the framework of branches. He did not like the responsibility of protecting so many people. When he commanded a group of men like himself, he could solve any problem with a fist or a sword point or a bribe. It was so much simpler.

Suddenly he sat bolt upright. Something was wrong. The horses. They had been quiet for minutes. The small animal noises of the night had stopped. Silence louder than the clash of arms in battle filled the spring-green wood. Kyellan moved warily to the fire and pulled out a burning branch. He crept to the edge of the camp with the makeshift torch in his left hand and his sword in his right. The small pool of light illuminated only a few feet ahead.

There were glints of metal like stars among the trees. Spear points. A dozen men surrounded him before he could do any of the things that passed through his mind. The soldiers behind the spears were black-clad and scowling under iron cowls. They were soundless shadows in the darkness. Kyellan heard more of them behind him. They were waking the others. The Prince's sleepy protests were loud. One took Kyellan's sword and dagger, and another took the torch and held it up.

Briana stumbled against Kyellan, pushed into the circle of spears along with the others. Kyellan steadied her with a hand on her arm. The soldier with the torch played its light across their faces, revealing their anger and bewilderment, until he reached Gwydion.

"Wizard!" the man cried, thrusting the torch almost into the youth's eyes, forcing him to draw back. Other black-clad soldiers crowded around Gwydion. Three of them seized him while another drew a long knife and put it to his throat. Chela cried out.

"Are you ready to die, demon?" spat the man with the knife. His arm tensed to cut.

"No!" Kyellan stepped forward with a shout of protest. He was thrown back and grabbed by two of the soldiers.

"Quiet, fool, or you'll be next," one hissed.

Kyellan spoke rapidly, trying to project command authority. "He's on your side. We all are. You can't kill him."

"Somebody shut him up," a deep voice growled.

A spear haft crashed down on Kyellan's head, driving him to his knees with dizziness; another, and everything went dark.

Briana watched in horror as Kyellan fell unconscious to the ground. Blood began to seep through his black hair. She forced herself to waken fully and projected Power into her voice.

"Fools!" she cried, stepping into the light with her hood thrown back and anger shining in her face. The man with the knife paused to look, as she had hoped. "If you will not listen to him, then hear me. We are not your enemies."

A scarred veteran stepped forward and bowed a little. "This isn't your concern, Priestess. The wizard is an invader."

"He is a boy," she said scornfully. "An idealistic, harmless boy who has fought the invaders and will do so again. The wizards hunt him as a traitor."

"No wizard would fight another," said the man with the knife. "She lies."

"Hold your tongue, Vras," said the veteran. "She is a priestess of the Goddess. Do not turn your hatred of the wizards into blasphemy."

"She's no priestess. They're all spies."

The older man moved closer to Briana, his face thoughtful. She glared at him with all the righteous indignation she could muster and was glad to see him wince. "We are priestesses of the Goddess," she said, "from the Sanctuary in Garith, and we are on an urgent mission against the wizards. You will order your men to release us at once."

He frowned thoughtfully. "I'd like to believe you," he said at last. "But this is just the sort of trick the wizards would try."

"Do you fear us, then?" Valahtia said in her lilting Caer accent, moving forward so they would all see her. "A group of women and children with an escort of only five men?"

"I will not make the decision," the veteran said firmly. "We will take them to Firelh. All of them. Alive."

Vras, the man with the knife, shot him a venomous look. He moved the blade with a jerk that left a thin trail of blood across Gwydion's neck and disappeared into the trees. Chela ran to the wizard, fighting back tears. Gwydion held her gently, trying to master his own sick relief.

Briana breathed a prayer of thanks in the Old Tongue as she knelt beside the prone Kyellan. She could not feel his presence in her mind, but that was usual and no cause for alarm. Still, it frightened her to see him thus. She had come to rely on him; more than she should, if Gemon's suspicions had any basis. Reaching out a tentative hand to his shoulder, she channeled her Power to wake him.

Kyellan groaned and pulled himself to his knees. His hand went to the back of his head and came away sticky with blood. The pretty face of the Priestess Briana was close to his, concerned, and he let her help him stand. Blinking, trying to clear his blurred vision, he remembered what had happened.

"Gwydion?" he asked painfully.

"Alive," Briana whispered.

"Sorry about the head," said the black-helmed veteran. "We have decided to let Lord Firelh decide your fate. The priestess claims the wizard can be trusted."

Kyellan remembered now where he had seen the black uniform before. These were Ryasan soldiers. "You people should be fighting the wizards," he growled, "not waylaying travelers in the forest."

"It's our job," the Ryasan said in irritation. "We have our orders. I'm going beyond my authority as it is, keeping that one alive."

Kyellan shrugged and turned to see Vras reappear carrying a load of heavy rope.

"Sir, if we can't kill the wizard, can we at least be sure he won't cast any of his demon-spells?" the soldier asked tightly.

"Very well." The commander nodded. "Go ahead, Vras."

"There's no need," Kyellan protested.

"Quiet, young man, or you'll get the same treatment."

Vras and three other men bound Gwydion with ropes pulled cruelly tight, in a strained, unnatural position that Kyellan winced to see. Gwydion was stolid and oblivious to the discomfort, though his lips were drawn and pale.

The Ryasans stuffed rags into his mouth and bound them
with gag strips, then sent him sprawling to the ground with
a heavy push. Chela knelt beside him. Gwydion's tawny
eyes smiled at her reassuringly, but she was not convinced.
With a fluid, angry motion, she leaped to where Vras
stood laughing and kicked his shin as hard as she could
with her bare foot. His expression was a mixture of amusement and annoyance, but he gave her a blow in return that
sent her reeling.

"Control your men," Kyellan snapped. "You'll find
we're telling the truth."

"Every man here has lost someone to the wizards in
these past two weeks," the veteran answered grimly. "You
can't expect us to treat one like an honored guest. But I'll
reprimand Vras for striking the girl." He turned away in
dismissal.

They moved out in the morning. The Ryasan soldiers
rode their horses and led the animals from Chelm, with the
captives walking in the middle of the column. Gwydion
was bound across one of the horses. Kyellan could see that
he was bleeding in several places from cuts and bruises
that had not been there the night before. He was still, his
muscles bunched and corded under the ropes, his hands and
feet white and bloodless. A dark mass of blood was clotted
in his golden hair where someone had struck him. His eyes
were glazed with pain.

The soldiers had not fed them that morning and would
not let them rest. Kyellan cursed methodically under his
breath as he walked. Once again he had failed his command.
He should have trusted his own feelings instead of the
assurances of the others and kept them moving instead of
camping in the grove. Now they could not even consider
escape. His head ached steadily, and he had intermittent

attacks of vertigo and blurred vision. Valahtia was hobbling now, supported by Tobas's arm, her court slippers flapping around her ankles with the soles long since worn away. Arel's feet were lacerated and leaving bloody tracks, but he disdained help. The First Priestess leaned heavily on the sturdy novice Pima, while Gemon stumbled behind like a frail shadow, coughing so that her thin body shook.

Chela limped as near to Gwydion's horse as she dared, her face ashen and full of pain. She walked like one blind. Finally, Kyellan dropped back to where Briana strode steadily and seemingly untiring.

"What's wrong with Chela?" he asked her softly, his eyes straight ahead in hope that their captors would not hear.

The young priestess whispered, "She's attuned herself to Gwydion. She takes some of his pain onto herself; she probably read about the procedure in that book of magic."

"I don't like it."

"No. Gwydion is trying to block her, but he's too weakened." Briana's soft voice was angry. "She shouldn't try this, and she knows it. She can't control the linkage properly, and she has sent too much of her strength into it."

"Could you make her stop?"

"I?" Briana sounded shocked. "No. It is impossible. There is a wizard's spell involved, Dark magic and not the Goddess's Power. I cannot."

Kyellan nodded and moved nearer to Chela so he could at least catch her if she fell. It seemed likely at any moment from her jerky, unseeing motion.

Briana turned it over in her mind. She could not begin to do this thing; it was not part of her training, it was part of the heathen magic she had been taught was heresy.

Blasphemy. Work of the enemy. But Gwydion could do
nothing. He was barely conscious. And Chela was so
eager to help him she might kill herself trying. The First
Priestess had to use all her strength to keep her own body
moving forward. Briana was the only one left.

"I can't," she whispered.

Try. Deep inside her mind, inaudible, anguished.

Gwydion? But the fleeting contact was gone. Briana
took a deep breath, trying to calm her mind. What was
wrong with her? She was vowed to help those in need with
everything in her power. But was this in her power? It
should not be.

Wiolai, Cianya, Rahshaiya, Goddess, she prayed silently,
I hope this is Thy will. Then she began to build a wall in
her mind between Chela and Gwydion. She laid every
stone carefully, mortaring it, chiseling it to fit. A high
wall, thick, topped with jagged ramparts; modeled after
the wall at Chelm, but with embellishments from stories
she had heard.

Briana visualized the linkage between Chela and Gwydion,
creating images and then discarding them until she found
the one she was certain the Garithian girl was using. It was
a stone water pipe, like the one from the pump in her
village square, and through it flowed the strengthening
water of Chela's Power. With an intense effort of will,
Briana raised her mind-built wall and lowered it onto, and
then through, Chela's linkage pipe. The link shattered but
quickly rebuilt itself in a snakelike path around the wall.
Briana gave her wall the power to move at will between
Chela and Gwydion, until no move the girl made was not
countered by the priestess.

Then into Briana's mind came a slim Chela-wraith,
manning a clumsy catapult below the wall. Allowing a
little amusement into her intense concentration, Briana

created defenders on the ramparts who poured boiling oil on the head of the attacker. The Chela-ghost fled her mind, and with an exhausted sense of finality Briana opened her eyes.

Kyellan was picking up Chela's fallen body. The Guardsman settled the girl into his arms and carried her over to Briana.

"You did something," he accused.

"I broke the link," she answered wearily. "I did what you asked."

"They both look worse."

This was true; Chela limp in his grasp, and on the horse Gwydion stiff with renewed pain until his head lolled into senselessness.

"She'll be all right in a little while." Briana tried to keep fear from her voice. "Gwydion feels everything now, without her strength to help combat it. If this journey is over soon, he should be all right. Once the ropes are untied, he should recover in a few hours."

"If this Firelh doesn't have him killed."

"Don't," Briana whispered.

They came at sunset through a narrow, guarded pass into a small mountain valley, barely able to stay on their feet, urged on by the unrelenting spears of the Ryasan soldiers. Before them sprawled a crowded, makeshift village, built of green boards roughly nailed together. The valley was dominated by a gigantic fortress cut into the side of a hill. It looked ancient, rising to huge grey battlements, surrounded by a series of moats, ditches, and earthworks. The land for two hundred yards around the fortress was broken and rough. Terrible footing for siege machines, Kyellan noted. This place would be nearly impregnable.

"Dafir," one of the soldiers said; apparently the name

of the hold. They were herded into the village. Each
rickety shack was large enough to house three or more
families. People turned out to stare at the newcomers.
They had the haunted look of refugees. Some looked noble
born, if Kyellan was any judge. The wizards must have
been very bloody in a short time if so many had fled them.
If Gwydion had walked in here among them, he would
have been torn to pieces. As it was, his golden hair was
dusty brown from the trail, and his face was blood-encrusted.
With his eyes closed, no villager would guess what he was.

They followed a narrow, raised path out of the village
and across the broken land in front of the hold. At last they
reached the tall, spiked main gates, and after an elaborate
exchange of passwords they entered. Inside was a bustling
soldiers' encampment. Crowded, hastily constructed barracks lined the walls, with stables and armories scattered
in the yard. A few of the thin, hungry-looking soldiers
wore Ryasan uniforms. Others were dressed in piecework
of leather and cloth, with ragged black armbands. Kyellan
began to feel a grudging admiration for the lord who had
brought all these people together. Not that they had a
chance against the wizards.

The soldiers ringed them tightly, their faces betraying
nothing. The grizzled commander entered the main hall,
an imposing stone building of several stories that looked
even older than the rest of Dafir.

Chela pressed close to Kyellan. She had been walking a
few hours now, seething with anger at Briana. Now she
looked trustingly up at the Guardsman and asked, "Will
Gwydion be all right?"

He could not meet her blue eyes. "I hope so."

Pima patted Chela awkwardly on the shoulder, trying to
soothe her as she would one of the horses. "Don't worry.
He'll be fine."

The doors opened once more, and the commander returned with a man who had to be Firelh. As tall as Kyellan and twice as broad, he moved like a surly, just waked bear. None of that bulk was fat, Kyellan guessed. His light brown, grey-flecked hair was caught in thick braids at his shoulders, and he wore a short, bristly beard. His clothes were rich embroidered silk under a cloak of brushed fur, but his boots were worn and cracked with much use. An old scar puckered his forehead under a circlet of silver, and his eyes were hard.

Yet he smiled in a friendly way as he approached. The circle of soldiers parted for him, and he stopped in front of Kyellan.

"These are troubled times, Guard Captain." His booming voice hurt Kyellan's head. "The wizards sniff for us in the hills. They've not discovered us yet, but it's only a matter of time. You must forgive my men. I failed to warn the outer guard of your coming. They were a little overzealous."

"You knew we were coming?"

"The Border Hills are not as empty as they look. You were watched, of course, by my men in the north."

Briana frowned sharply but said nothing.

"Well, Wramin?" Firelh said to the veteran. "Untie the wizard. Be quick."

Soldiers moved swiftly to obey. They cut the ropes that bound Gwydion to the farmhorse's back, then undid the others and removed the gag. The youth's eyelids fluttered open. The soldiers helped him to his feet. He walked a few steps before he fainted again.

Firelh sighed. "Wramin, you and two men carry him upstairs to my best guest chamber." He dismissed the other soldiers with a wave.

"We'll go with him," Chela said firmly. She rescued the

wizard's pack from the pile of baggage beside the unloaded horses.

"He'll be well cared for, little one," said the Ryasan
lord. "I hope to make amends for your ill treatment, by
offering you a bath and a dinner. Surely you won't refuse?"

"I'll stay with Gwydion."

"Of course," said Firelh gravely. "But I expect the rest
of you to honor my invitation. Come along."

Kyellan hesitated, watching Chela struggle with the heavy
pack behind the men who bore Gwydion. But Firelh ges-
tured to a liveried house servant standing in the doorway,
and the man took Chela's burden and followed her with it.

"Well?"

This Firelh seemed determined to play the host. Kyellan
glanced at the First Priestess, who nodded. They joined the
Ryasan inside his great hall, a high-beamed place of barbaric splendor, hung with shields, banners, and bright
tapestries. Servants were clearing long tables of the evening meal and banking huge firepits set along the walls.

"Quite an army you've gathered," Kyellan commented.

"Some are the old Ryasan forces," Firelh said conver-
sationally. "Some, merchants and noblemen whose families were broken by the wizards; some, retainers of the old
King, who has fled to Dallynd. The wizards have been
destroying the Tarnsea coast. They wipe out whole villages.
Of course, they'll soon realize that a land without people
to work it is no prize. They'll only kill those who resist."

"Your men aren't very experienced soldiers, then."

"No." The lord of Dafir led them up a massive stair-
case to the second floor of the hall. "Even the Ryasan
soldiers never did much actual fighting. Our country's
been at peace since the Hoabi pirate wars twenty years
back, and those were naval battles. But you're Caer, you
and your men. Have any real experience?"

"The S'tari campaign a few years ago," Kyellan answered. "And we've been fighting the wizards' men these past few weeks."

"But not very successfully," Tobas said wryly, moving up to walk with them.

"Perhaps I can use you," Firelh said. "We'll speak of it." He held a door for them. "There are bathing rooms here on the second level. Come this way."

Beyond the heavy, carven door, the Northern, warlike decorations abruptly ended. A long corridor opened into rooms that were lavishly furnished, like the Tiranon palace in miniature. There were tiny fountains, delicate paintings and mosaics, rich furs and cushions. Valahtia sighed in contentment.

Firelh called more servants and bowed low to the disheveled company. "After you have bathed and rested, perhaps you will join me."

Gwydion woke in a feather bed. The discovery was so surprising that he simply lay there for several minutes, eyes closed, wondering if it was true. The ropes were gone, and his lower legs and arms burned with the pain of their blood returning. But that was the pain of healing. He found the strength to add a quick mending-spell to the salves that had been applied to his cuts and rope burns. Then he opened his eyes.

The ceiling was elaborately hung over the high, pillared bed. Shimmering fabrics, golds and greens, so Southern in style that he wondered if he had been unconscious all the way to Caerlin. But no, the polished shield that hung on the wall as a mirror was the sign of a Northern Kingdom. The home of Firelh, he guessed. He had a vague memory of a crowded, dusty yard and a tall building. This small room was certainly odd.

Chela slept in a chair near the bed. She had bathed and

washed her copper hair, and she was dressed in a clean black gown. Gwydion noted with amusement that his dusty old pack was propped against the wall beside her.

He, too, had been bathed and dressed in a soft black tunic shot through with embroidered threads of gold. Wide-legged trousers of the sort he preferred hung over the end of the bed, along with a tawny, short-haired fur robe and his own wide leather belt and sturdy boots. He swung down off the bed, wincing as the material of the tunic rubbed on his bruised arms. The trousers felt soft but strong. He finished dressing and moved in front of the mirror.

A darkly tanned, serious young man gazed back at him. His bushy golden hair was freshly washed. There was a thin line of pink at his neck where the knife had grazed, and several purple bruises marred his angular face.

Gwydion whirled as someone entered the room.

"You look almost human, wizard," said a huge, richly dressed Ryasan. "My name is Firelh, and I am master of Dafir. Welcome."

Chela woke at the sound of a voice. She leaped up and hugged Gwydion with a force that made him gasp aloud.

The Ryasan laughed. "Come. Join your friends." He turned back into the corridor without awaiting an answer.

"Are you all right?" Chela whispered.

Gwydion nodded. "I think so. But I'm hungry."

"Me too."

They followed Firelh past curtained doors that rang with female laughter; a harem? Most lords of the North considered such customs barbaric. Another indication that Firelh was not merely the gruff soldier he appeared.

"How long have we been here?" Gwydion asked Chela as they walked.

"Only a few hours," she reassured him. "It's just after moonrise."

A brightly decorated room at the end of the corridor held the rest of the company. They were seated on large, plump cushions around low tables piled with venison and greens. They all looked much better. They were bathed and combed, and all except the priestesses wore new black clothing.

"The Goddess be thanked!" Briana exclaimed when she saw him.

"I doubt She was much concerned with me"—Gwydion smiled—"but I'm glad to see you, too."

"The food looks good." Chela pulled him down to a vacant cushion and filled two plates. He ate slowly, savoring the luxury of fresh-cooked meat after subsisting on the salt-cured stores of the journey.

"Now to our business," Firelh said with satisfaction.

"What business?" Kyellan wondered. He had been restless and uncomfortable during the meal and the entertainment, an atrocious song performed by an untalented minstrel. They had dressed him in heavily brocaded black, which looked striking but itched unbearably.

"I think we can help each other, Captain." Firelh settled back into his cushions. "Obviously you can't go to Cavernon City now."

"The wizards' fleet hasn't reached Caerlin yet," Gwydion said. He seemed wary and suspicious, and Kyellan did not blame him.

"A matter of a few days at most. And I don't believe Cavernon's walls will withstand an attack. Kyellan?"

"They won't," he admitted.

"I suggest you all join in the resistance here. No, let me finish. This small outpost has no chance against the wizards, that is true. But messengers have been sent to almost every other Kingdom. They'll be organizing armies of their own. Alone, none of us could defeat them. They've taken most of the lands already. Everyone who can will join me and my people on the island of Altimar to build a force capable of withstanding the Kharad.''

''Why Altimar?'' Tobas asked.

''Our enemies haven't bothered to occupy it. They're content with their monster in Keor harbor. But there's another landing place on the other side of the island, the eastern side, near the Venerin Straits. It has a small natural harbor that will be the base of our operations.''

''Most of us aren't soldiers,'' Arel complained. ''What of us?''

''We'll have uses for all of you. The other Kingdoms' royal families will go to Altimar if they can, for safety. The wizard would be a great help, of course, and we need experienced men. Kyellan, you and the others would be assured positions of command.''

''That is impossible,'' Briana said firmly. ''We must reach Caerlin as soon as we can. You do not know our need.''

Firelh made a half bow from his seat. ''Despite your Power, you couldn't enter Caerlin undetected. And by yourselves you couldn't hold off the wizards' armies. Come with us. Soon you can go where you wish under the protection of our attack. We already plan to liberate Caerlin first. Our goals are the same.''

''That would be too late.''

The First Priestess said weakly, ''He is right. We are too few, child. Our only path is through Altimar.''

Briana bowed her head, unconvinced and angry. ''As you say.''

''You'll join us, then?'' asked the hill lord eagerly.

Kyellan shrugged. ''It seems we have no choice.''

Chapter Nine

On the second morning after their arrival, Gwydion and Chela took horses from one of the many stables and rode out into the pine-covered hills. Gwydion liked Firelh's country. It had a clean, crisp wildness about it, its tall, thick-set evergreens imparting a tangy scent to the dry, cool air. The sky was pale blue and cloudless. Most of all, it was nearly uninhabited. Gwydion much preferred not having people around, crowding him with their thoughts and emotions until his everyday shields strained with the pressure.

He could not teach Chela anything in the hive of activity at Dafir. When he tried to get her to open her mind to thoughts around her, she was overwhelmed and frightened. The grassy, flower carpeted meadow that had opened before them would be better. He dismounted and absently placed a spell of complacency on his horse so it would not stray. When Chela jumped down and skipped over to him, he took her hand and showed her how to do the same for her own horse. Her small hand was warm and soft in his, and he could feel the tingling sensation of contact with a deep, restless well of uncontrolled Power. Sometimes Chela's innate strength frightened him. His own Power, he knew, was greater than most wizards possessed, though it lacked maturity; the bright-faced child who called herself his apprentice would be a match for the masters of the College.

He sat with her in the grass and began the day's lesson, more by rote than by conscious thought, just as it had been taught to him. As he spoke, he let his mind wander over the hills. He could not feel the presence of any wizards in the land of Ryasa, which only meant that they were using a great deal of their Power to stay shielded. Why? Guarding against his probes? They did not need to shield so completely for him. He already knew they were there. Perhaps the effort was being expended for the First Priestess, who rarely spoke now, her mind turned inward or outward far from them.

Slowly, Gwydion disengaged himself from the vain search, allowing his eyes to be distracted by a gleam of sunlight in Chela's red hair. She was very beautiful. More so than the meadow, or the hills, or the flowers that surrounded her.

She was attempting to transform a blade of grass into an illusory dragonfly, with little success. She mumbled words from the spell-books she had seen, she pulled at the blade and tried to make it resemble an insect, she threw it in the air to make it fly. Nothing worked. She held it up at eye level and spoke to it sternly.

"You may think you're a blade of grass, but you're not. You're a dragonfly. Why can't I convince you of that?"

Gwydion chuckled. "You can't convince yourself, Chela. *You* still think it's a blade of grass. No spell will work, no matter how well you draw signs or say incantations, if you don't believe in it."

She scowled. "I just don't see why this is important. Why do I have to learn it? What I want to learn is how to kill the wizards. Please teach me that."

"I can't." He paused, finding words. "Chela, it isn't

difficult to kill. What you're trying to do now, creating, takes much more effort. You must build something before tearing it down. You must know life, to learn death.''

''I've already learned death,'' she said. ''I killed men in the forest.''

''Yes. But killing wizards is much more difficult and dangerous. You have to be able to distinguish between reality and illusion, because some of the things they send against you are very real, though they look like illusions.'' He sighed. ''And I can't teach you that until you learn this.''

She turned back to the long stem in her hand. ''Dragonflies! What's the use of dragonflies?''

''Changing one form of life into another. Plant into animal.''

''But why dragonflies?''

''Because they're easy. Besides, I like them.''

''Plant into animal,'' she repeated dutifully, lowering her head, but not before Gwydion saw the gleam of mischief in her blue eyes. He felt the Power building inside her as she concentrated her energy on the exercise. Good. The blade of grass began to shift, to grow, dragonfly size, then larger and larger, bigger than any insect, bigger than the horses, until it was . . .

A dragon. A real, fire-breathing, jewel-armored dragon that towered over the meadow like an erupting volcano. The horses bolted. Gwydion whistled appreciatively. The dragon looked down at him; the emerald eyes narrowed, sharpened. It opened its cavernous mouth and took a deep, sulphurous breath . . .

And it was a blade of grass again. Chela glared at him and laid the green stem back on the meadow floor.

''Why'd you change it back?''

Gwydion chuckled. ''It would have cooked this meadow.''

"An illusion?"

"It was as real as you could make it, girl, and your Power has depths no one could control. That illusionary fire breath would have burned us to coals."

"I don't like dragonflies." She giggled. "Little flitting things."

"But not dangerous. Next time, please do the exercise the way I tell you."

"Yes, teacher." Then, to Gwydion's surprise and delight, she leaned over and kissed him. A little girl's kiss, he thought objectively as he returned it, but a very promising one. She would learn.

Valahtia was in a sour mood at dinner that evening. The luxury of Firelh's quarters was welcome, but monotonous. Everyone else in the fortress was busy all the time. Arel had spent the day with Firelh's wine cellar. The women behind the curtained doors of the second level were fluttering, mindless sparrows who kept chirping on about her beauty and asking if they could do her hair tomorrow.

Kyellan hardly spoke to her anymore, and though he was still pleasant and flattering when he did, she knew it was over. She felt that she knew now how most of her lovers had felt; she had been an exciting toy, which once attained quickly bored and was soon discarded. Just what she had expected Kyellan to think when she tired of him. But he had beat her to it, and now she was the jilted one. It was a curious sensation, self-pity, a novelty, and she thought she might enjoy it after a while.

The wizard and his pixyish companion had apparently been doing more than magical exercises in the hills that day. They sat close together, lit up with smiles and laughter. Valahtia was saddened watching them. Though she was only one year older than Gwydion, she would never feel what he felt. She had begun to have affairs at thirteen, but she had never been infatuated, never been in love. Though sometimes, remembering the passion of the nights she had spent with Kyellan, she wondered if there had been real feeling in what she counterfeited so well.

A pinch on her thigh jolted her out of her reverie. Arel leered at her like a senile tomcat. Valahtia glared at him, and he grinned drunkenly and turned away. She would have to beat him off that night, the incestuous fool. Sometimes when he had been drinking he behaved that way. He had ignored her throughout the journey, and she had hoped that would continue.

Arel's attention was now arrested by the round-figured novice Pima. He stared as if he had not seen her before. The girl noticed him and flushed a deep red as she picked at her food. The Princess shivered. Better her than me, she told herself fiercely; but she felt sick.

Pima shook as she turned her door handle to lock it. The Prince had frightened her. What if he came to her room in the night? The walls were thick, and the rooms of the company were widely separated. No one would hear her scream, and she had never learned to project her small Power so another could hear. Perhaps she should request a guard at her door. No, that was silly. The lock would keep her safe. She finally slept.

When she woke late that night to the sound of a key turning in the door, it took a moment to remember. Oh, Goddess, make him leave! How had he gotten a key? She had never understood when Briana and the others spoke of Darkness; now, she could feel it through the oak-beam door. Muffled cursing came from the other side. Perhaps he could not enter. Why had she not told anyone of her fears?

The door swung open, revealing a Prince with sleep-mussed hair and a wild, desperate look in his brown eyes. He put the torch he carried in a wall socket and inserted the key into a slot above the regular keyhole. Pima gasped as she heard an outside lock slide into place.

"Waiting for me, darling?" slurred Arel. He reached for her. She rolled out of the bed beneath his lunge and ran to the window. The room was too high above the moonlit, deserted ground in back of the ancient keep. She began to scream.

Valahtia heard her brother leave his room. He did not come to hers. What should I care, she thought, if a pretty little priestess is my brother's companion for the night? A girl so beautiful would not long remain a virgin, whether Arel or another ravished her. But she found that she did care. She rose, put on a dressing gown, and ran out of her room along the corridor until she reached Kyellan's door. Out of breath, she banged on it with her small fists.

He finally appeared, eyes barely open, a short fur robe wrapped loosely around him.

"Come quickly," she gasped. "Arel has gone to Pima's room. He's drunk."

With her help, the sleepy Guardsman pulled on a pair of knee pants, his boots, and his swordbelt. She chafed at his slowness.

"Go back to bed, Valita," he muttered. "I'll take care of it."

As awareness of what the Princess said grew in his mind, Kyellan broke into a run. He had thought Arel looked strange at dinner, but it was obvious the man was drunk. Now his original estimation of the Prince, and his hatred of him, returned in all its force. That sweet, pretty child . . . He followed the dim sound of her screams, unsheathing his sword.

The door was bolted on the outside, but the spring was easy to break, and he slammed into the door with bruising force. It groaned and released, and he staggered into the room. Pima was pinned against the wall, her robe nearly ripped off. Arel was trying to hold on to her and undo his britches at the same time.

"Draw your sword or I'll kill you unarmed," Kyellan snarled.

Arel turned in fuddled surprise. "Sword . . . ? Didn't bring . . . What're you doing here? Get out or I'll call the Guard."

"I am the Guard," Kyellan said, advancing quickly on the Prince. Arel backed away, the strange look in his eyes replaced by terror. He stumbled on a fold of carpet and fell backward. The sword moved to his throat. Gods, it would feel good to kill him.

Pima screamed, a piercing, hysterical sound. Kyellan looked. She was huddled on the floor now, trying to cover herself with her tattered garment. When their eyes met she shrank away. Her face was as terrified as Arel's. She was afraid of him. His violence, his rage. Kyellan withdrew the sword and kicked the Prince lightly.

"Get up," he said, disgusted. "Get out of here."

Arel rose unsteadily, staring; then he ran as quickly as he could from the room, his new slippers pattering.

Hesitantly, the Guardsman pulled off his fur robe and put it around Pima's shoulders. She would not look at him as she wrapped it tightly around her. Her entire body was shaking. Kyellan knelt beside her, feeling helpless. He spoke gruffly.

"Are you all right?"

"I . . . think so," she finally whispered.

He wanted to take her in his arms to comfort her, but instead he asked, "Should I take you to Briana?"

"Would . . . would you? I don't want to stay here alone."

She nearly fell when she tried to rise and finally accepted Kyellan's proffered arm. He wondered if she really was hurt. He helped her slowly out and down the hallway, feeling her grow more relaxed as she walked. No, she was only shaken.

"You've been rescuing me since we met," she said softly when they were almost at Briana's door. "It must be a nuisance. . . ." And she burst into quiet, helpless tears. Kyellan drew her close, meeting no resistance, and held her as she cried.

The door opened, and white light streamed into the hall. Briana cried out in horror. "Pima! You're hurt. . . . What did you do to her, Guardsman?"

"Don't . . . be angry with him," the girl managed to say between sobs. "He rescued me."

"Arel." Kyellan made the name a curse. "He was drunk. But I arrived before any real harm was done."

"Arel?" Briana seemed confused, then she smiled in apology and relief. "I'm sorry, Kyellan. I should not have thought . . . Goddess, how could he have done such a thing? Prince though he is? He may have been more than drunk. Did . . . did you kill him?"

"No. Much as I wanted to."

"I'm glad." She sighed. "Though if ever a man deserved death . . . I would have thought you would have taken the opportunity. I think I've misjudged you."

"I hope Pima will be all right." He gave the girl over to the priestess's arms.

"She should be." Briana turned away with Pima but turned back again. "When you found them, Kyellan . . .

the Prince's eyes . . . could he have been possessed, as the man on the ledge was? The wizards might have tried again.''

''I don't know. It could be. It wasn't the same, but it could be.''

She thanked him again and closed the door behind them. Kyellan stood watching it a moment. That was the first time he had seen the Priestess Briana taken by surprise. She had always seemed so controlled, so prepared for any situation. Somehow tonight she was more human, more real. She had called him Kyellan for the first time, too. Had he noticed before how beautiful she was? Far prettier than Valahtia. . . . He pulled himself away from such thoughts. She was a priestess, even further out of his reach than the Princess had been. Even he could not be such a fool.

The evacuation of Dafir began two weeks after they had arrived. Chela was ready. More and more, Gwydion had been spending his days in council with the soldiers, telling them what he knew of the wizards and helping them formulate strategies of attack. Chela had ridden nearly every horse in the stables, read half the books in Gwydion's pack without understanding them, and swum in the cold waters of the moat for hours with a group of boys who teased her until she beat them all in a race around the keep. Also, though Gwydion and the others did not know this, she had badgered the armorer into giving her a soldier's helm and overlarge leather tunic, and she had stolen a sword and dagger from the storehouses. One of the boys she had beaten swimming was willing to fence with her as long as she liked. She was not going to be dragged into the priestesses' circle in the next battle.

Her soldier's weapons and gear safely wrapped in her pack, she rode at the front of the five-mile column of wagons, horsemen, and refugee families on foot. Firelh was at the head, and just behind him rode Kyellan and Tobas, deep in conversation. Gwydion rode beside her, but she had not succeeded in getting him to talk. All the men were morose and easily angered. Before, they had been that way because they were afraid the wizards would find Dafir before they could leave. Now, Kyellan at least was certain they would have to fight their way to Dallynd, where ships waited to take them to Altimar. The wizards would have armies in the west; they were probably besieging Dallynd by now, and they could not miss a force of this size. Firelh seemed to disagree. It was all very confusing.

After three miles of silence, Chela pulled up and waited for the priestesses' wagon to appear. She had negotiated a sort of friendly truce with the novices and knew at least they would talk to her.

"Good morning," she called cheerfully to Pima, who was driving with Briana beside her. The First Priestess was in the curtained wagon with Gemon.

"Is it?" the girl asked with a wry grin. Her pretty face was coated with dust and sweat. She had apparently recovered from her experience with Arel, though she moved much more warily around all the men.

"No one wanted to talk up there," Chela complained. "Kyellan has them all worried we'll be faced with a wizards' army on the plains."

"Neither Gwydion nor I feel any threat," Briana said mildly.

"He'll be the next to be possessed, you'll see." The startling comment came from Gemon, whose head had appeared through the curtains.

"What?" Pima asked.

"Kyellan. If the wizards keep trying. Now that they

failed with Arel, who had a little Darkness in him, they'll try with Kyellan, who has much more.''

"Oh, you and your Darkness," Pima scoffed. "Why don't you trust him?"

"Just because he saved you from Arel," Gemon countered, "you think he's a hero. So does everyone else. No one listens to me. But do you know what I think?" Her voice lowered and her eyes moved furtively. "I think he's the Shape-Changer. That would explain his shields, and why so many bad things have happened to us since he's led us.''

"You're crazy," Chela said heatedly. "Gwydion trusts him." That, to her, was all that needed to be said.

"Gemon!" The sharp voice from inside the wagon was the First Priestess's.

The novice disappeared again, muttering, "You'll see."

"What will she think of next?" Briana said wearily. "Don't we have enemies enough without looking for them among our friends?"

Chela said a hasty good-bye and rode back farther in the column. Gemon had spoiled her desire to speak with the priestesses. Maybe the Caer youth Erlin would talk to her. He had been given command of a wing of archers who were riding rearguard.

"This will be our path," said the Earl of Dafir, frowning over a map spread on the ground of his small tent. "Through the Yamin Basin, south to the edge of the Llanduhn Forest, and then up the coast."

"Why not straight to Dallynd?" Tobas asked, crowding around with the rest of the commanders.

"We're nearly on the road that runs from Dallynd to Chelm. The wizards will be patrolling it. It'll take a little longer, but this way we'll all make it to those ships in Dallynd harbor.''

"Can we really avoid a battle?" Kyellan was skeptical.

Firelh opened his mouth to answer but shut it again at a knock on the tent post. "My lord! Let me in!" a young voice called.

"Enter."

The scout looked as though he had been running a long way. "My lord, they're waiting for us. Just beyond the hills at the edge of Yamin Basin. No more than three miles away. From the outer guards' talk, they have at least one wizard.''

"So you prove correct, Southerner," Firelh muttered. "No help for it, I suppose. How many?"

"It was hard to tell, my lord. I think they have no more than we do, and they're mostly infantry.''

"Put the camp on alert. See that the tents are struck and loaded, and everyone ready to move at dawn. We'll send the civilians farther back in the hills with Erlin's archers to guard them. The army will be in two groups, one under Kyellan with Wramin his second, one under me with Tobas. Get moving, gentlemen. We have less than half the night remaining.''

The hills were cold and misted over in the hour before dawn. Kyellan watched his breath grow and hang in the still air as he warmed his hands and sword hilt together under his tunic next to the skin. His new command checked and rechecked their saddle girths, reins, spear rests, and weapons. The black of their uniforms was unrelieved, but their eyes glowed like jewels with eagerness. Kyellan wondered if they would hold together on the field as a fighting force or break apart in their excitement like puppies after quail.

Firelh's troops had moved out hours before under the darkness, taking a wide circuit around the flanks of the wizards' army. When the sun first shone full over the hills, Kyellan would attack from the front, while Firelh attacked from the rear. A simple plan, which they hoped was its advantage.

Gwydion rode out of the mist. Briana rode behind him. Kyellan greeted Gwydion softly. "Do you think the wizard down there knows what we're doing?"

"We haven't been probed," the youth said. "The priestesses and I have been shielding. And I think Verasil is concentrating on his own preparations." He shivered noticeably. "We did find out who was down there. Verasil was one of the three we faced in Garith, one of the masters of the College. I don't know if I can defeat him."

"You'll have help." Briana was wearing the black leather of a soldier under a grey hooded cloak. "The First Priestess would be better, but she is ill. I couldn't let her come."

"I can't spare any men to protect you, Priestess," Kyellan said. "Shouldn't you stay back with the wagons?"

"I can protect myself. And Gwydion needs the help."

"I have no authority over you." He shrugged, trying not to let his anger show. "Do as you wish." The sun was rising. "It's time."

They watched the east as light slowly filtered into the hills, softening even the bristling lines of spears with rosy glow. Kyellan raised his arm high. The sun appeared, larger each moment, until it suddenly broke free of the hills. He dropped his arm, and with a great cry the host of soldiers spurred their horses and charged into the plain. The wizards' army waiting below gave an answering shout. Its cavalry moved to meet the Ryasans, followed by rank upon rank of running infantry.

Arrows hailed about Kyellan as he headed the charge,

holding a shield above him. One grazed the left shoulder of his horse, but there was little space for archery as the two armies met. The exhilaration of battle filled Kyellan as he traded blows with a huge enemy soldier with a spiked mace and an overburdened little S'tari horse. If such a weapon once hit where it was aimed, there would be no need for another blow; but it was clumsy to wield since two hands were required. The Guardsman's sword had more range, and his sturdy hill-bred horse darted in and out of the mace's reach until the enemy soldier, goaded into foolishness, put all his strength into one mighty blow. Kyellan barely ducked it and on his recovery killed the man with a quick uppercut.

He could not see beyond his next opponent to tell how the battle was going. The wizards' men were frenzied, almost berserk, caring little for their lives. He wondered if some spell had been used. One enemy soldier, speared through, walked up the spear to its wielder and killed the surprised man with a dagger. It was insane. His joy in battle left him after a few such incidents.

The battlefield ranged over five square miles of flat plains. The two forces were nearly equal, with the slight advantage to Firelh's men since they were all mounted. But the wizard Verasil was a power that shifted the odds. Magical clouds of choking, burning dust drifted through the conflict, seeking out the Ryasans. Some of the wizards' men had poisoned blades that caused near instant death with a scratch. Soldiers would blaze up in a human torch for no apparent reason. Kyellan wished he was facing the S'tari again; at least those fierce desert warriors were men who fought blade to blade.

Gwydion and Briana rode unharmed through the battle, shrouded in clouds of illusion and fear, searching for the

wizard Verasil. He had to be somewhere on the field to be
controlling so many potent spells. Yet he seemed not to
exist. His shield was a distorting wall that seemed to be
everywhere and nowhere at the same time. They finally
narrowed it to the most spell-ridden section of the melee
and rode back and forth through the terror and death with
all their Powers in desperate search.

Kyellan was in trouble. In the midst of his exchange
with a tenacious enemy soldier, three others had killed
their men and turned to Kyellan with deadly single-
mindedness. They pressed in on him with their horses,
leaving him no room to maneuver. He could not break
through their line. They began a slashing, heedless attack
that he was barely able to dodge, much less defend against.
The first volley of strokes broke his shield and killed his
horse. It fell nearly on top of him as he rolled away with
his breath knocked out.

The four soldiers dismounted and closed in on him. He
staggered to his feet and prepared for a final stand, drawing his dagger to fight two-handed, daring them to come
for him with such desperate fury that the wizards' men
hesitated. Suddenly, a black-clad rider galloped into the
deadly circle with a high-pitched, screeching cry. Two
surprised Kharad soldiers fell to a swinging sword. Kyellan
made a running leap, caught the back of the soldier's
saddle, and pulled himself up behind.

The Ryasan wheeled the horse and found a lull in the
fighting, halting the heaving, foam-coated animal.

"Thanks," Kyellan panted. "You saved my life."

A slight figure in an ill-fitting uniform, the soldier was
silent for a moment. Then a giggle came from the leather
helm.

"I did, didn't I." It was Chela. She turned with a

proud, defiant grin on her face. She was splashed with blood but seemed unharmed, and her skin almost glowed. Kyellan stared in shock, then began to laugh himself.

"I thought we left you back in the hills."

"Gwydion will need my help to kill that wizard. He knows it, but he ordered me to stay behind so I wouldn't get hurt. But he'll get hurt himself if he tries to kill Verasil without me. I have to find him."

Kyellan saw the determination in her young face and nodded. "You wouldn't go back if I commanded it, so I won't. All right. Let's try to find your wizard."

"Yes, sir." She spurred the horse into the fray, crouching low over its neck as Kyellan swung his long, curved sword to cut a path. Whether it was his fighting skill or her Power, they easily made their way toward a low knoll on the prairie that was surrounded by thick clouds of mist and smoke. Taking deep breaths, they plunged into it. It burned eyes and nostrils, and they had to breathe again before they were on top of the hill.

Choking, they pulled to a stop in the center of the mist, a clear area perhaps ten feet in diameter. Gwydion and Briana were sitting there on the ground, drawing patterns in the dirt and scattering weird-colored powders over the shapes. They looked up in surprise. Gwydion jumped to pull Chela from the horse, anger and gladness in his face. Kyellan dismounted more slowly. The horse reared, bolted, and disappeared into the mist.

"We found Verasil," Gwydion said as he and Chela clasped hands and formed a circle with Briana. "He's somewhere near. We're almost ready. Captain, when we enter the trance, the clouds will disappear. You'll have to defend the hill somehow. It's vital that we're not disturbed."

"I'll do my best." Kyellan watched curiously as the three on the ground began a low, ominous chanting. The mists wavered like heat shimmers in the desert and were gone, trailing off over the battlefield in wispy clouds. Some of the wizards' men turned toward the hill and began to climb.

"Ryasans! To me!" Kyellan shouted in a ringing voice that carried over the roar of battle. He killed the first few enemy soldiers that made it to the top, but more were coming. Black-clad Ryasans were fighting their way toward him.

Firelh rode up the hill on his huge, well-muscled horse, carrying a torn and bloody banner with his house crest. "There you are, lad," he cried. "A good place for a stand." He dismounted and plunged the end of the standard into the ground.

"They're trying to kill the wizard," Kyellan said uncertainly. "We have to defend them. We shouldn't call too much attention to the hill."

Firelh laughed. "We'll defend them better if we regroup. Need to turn this around somehow." He went off to greet the Ryasan soldiers who had made it up the knoll. There were about three dozen of them.

Kyellan looked out at the battlefield. The clouds of Verasil's magic were everywhere, and his army was winning. But the focus of both sides had become the hill on which he stood. The chanting of Gwydion, Briana, and Chela rose to a terrible shrieking, a howling wind, inhuman, uncanny. They sat rigid with clasped hands as storm clouds gathered. Lightning flashed dangerously close. Kyellan smelled smoke and thought he saw a nightmarish female face in the clouds, a hag with claws outstretched.

Other mists swirled on the hill, orange and crimson, foul-smelling. Shapes began to form, demon shapes. Not illusions, as Kyellan discovered when one leaped at him and locked viselike talons around his neck. It burned like

hot irons. Kyellan cried out in pain and horror as he thrust
upward with his sword and ran the creature through. Purple blood steamed over him, but the demon's grip relaxed
and it fell at his feet. The creatures grappled with the
Ryasans on the hill; little more than four feet high, but
their long claws and teeth, their bodies that burned like
molten lead, made them deadly foes. Kyellan had no time
to wonder what they were or where they were from, as
another leaped at him with open mouth and grasping claws.

"Watch for that next cloud!" Firelh called, holding one
off with his iron-shod spear. "There are more of them in
it!"

Below, the battle eddied and flowed, as on the hill the
soldiers fought to keep the demon-creatures from getting to
the three in the center. Five Ryasans had already fallen in
death, and another was losing his battle with two demons,
when suddenly a terrible sound rose from the plains. A
great, agonized, numbing scream, growing louder and
louder, filling the ears, filling the mind, stopping the battle
cold as soldiers of both sides cringed with hands over their
ears. It covered the basin, and then it was gone.

"The wizard is dead!" Kyellan shouted. The mists faded,
and the demons disappeared. Verasil's army faltered as if
it had no guidance.

The Ryasan soldiers sent up a cheer and attacked their
frightened opponents with renewed confidence. Firelh leaped
onto his horse, pulled his banner from the ground, and led
a charge down into the melee. Soon Kyellan was left
alone, the only one standing on the hilltop.

Gwydion, Briana, and Chela lay unconscious in their
circle, hands still tightly clasped. Kyellan knelt and felt
their wrists; weak and irregular pulses, but they still lived.
He remained with them, fending off the occasional stray
enemy soldier who saw the hill as a refuge from the

carnage below. The wizards' men were like children without direction. They had lost their will to fight, but in their madness they had not the sense to surrender. No prisoners could be taken. Every wizards' man either was killed or fled.

Gwydion was the first to waken. "Did we do it?" he whispered.

"You won it for us. He's dead."

"Naturally." Gwydion grinned. "Was there ever any doubt? He didn't have a chance against me."

"Go back to sleep," Kyellan growled. "I like you better that way."

Chapter Ten

"Lord Firelh knows what he is doing." Gemon tied off a bloody bandage on a delirious soldier who had been caught at the edge of a wizards' fireball during the battle.

"I'm not so certain," Tobas said, assisting Valahtia with another wounded man in the makeshift hospital they had set up beside the rocky coast. "The army of the Kharad is camped all around Dallynd."

"And two men will get through them easier than an army." Valahtia wiped her already smudged brow with a bloody hand. "Those two men in particular."

"We can't afford to lose either Kyellan or Firelh, and they were fools to go themselves. Any two men could have found a way through the wizards' camps to Dallynd," Briana said.

"Firelh had to go, since he knows the city commander, and he took someone he trusts," Gwydion said.

Gemon's head came up like a dog's with a scent. "His trust is misplaced. Do you feel it now, Briana? Darkness, deepest Darkness, in and around the blank in your awareness that is Kyellan."

Briana reached out with her mind and touched what the novice spoke of. The meaning was different, though. "He is in great danger."

"Firelh?"

"No. Kyellan."

"You idiot," Gemon said harshly. Her hands shook. "That's nothing human. And if it's near Kyellan, then he's in trouble."

The ruin was curiously compelling. Not large, it had once been a domed building of smooth stone. Now it was black, fire-gutted. An attempt had apparently been made to pull down its walls, but they stood nearly intact, stubborn against the dim moonlit sky. Another relic of the passing of the Kharad, like the ravaged villages and trampled fields they had crossed on their way up the coast to Dallynd. Yet it was different, alone on this rocky hill overlooking the troubled sea.

They had stopped to rest the horses and could take a few more minutes. "I'm going to have a look," Kyellan said. Firelh took his horse's reins without comment, staring out toward the ocean lost in thought.

"I'll be right back," said the Guardsman, and he walked toward the ruined building over a rough path of unshaped small stones. It did not look as if many people ever came here, even when the place was intact. No wonder, if the wind was always this biting. He pulled up the collar of his cloak and wished he had not left his leather helm on his saddle.

The black stones grew immense and threatening as he approached. The moon was waning that night and gave little light. Where was the beauty, the grace of the building that Kyellan had seen from a distance? Now it looked squat and heavy, like a crouching animal. He ran his hand along the outside wall and quickly drew back. It was as smooth as glass, and cold. The cold of the grave, the feel of the flesh of a man long dead. The black did not come off on his hand as it should have from fire-darkened stone.

He glanced back and saw Firelh watching him, the Earl's face unreadable through the night and the distance. It would look foolish if he turned away without going inside. He drew his dagger and went into the gaping hole that might have been a door. The interior was vast, dark, cold, relieved only by a few cracks of moonlight. Not empty. The sense of being watched that he had felt in the priestesses' Great House was here, too, only far stronger.

The short hairs on his arms rose until his skin tingled. Shadows crowded around him, pressing close, and his breath came quickly. He could leave now. He had gone inside, concealed his fear from the lord of Dafir, and now he could leave. But as his eyes adjusted to the blackness, he saw something in the center. A square slab of ebony stone . . . an altar? The place was a temple, then, a house of worship. The discovery was not comforting.

On the flat top of the altar was an urn, a pottery vessel of the everyday sort used to store water or wine. A wide body, a tapered neck, sealed at the top with wax. The patterns on the sides of the urn were not the usual scenes of battles and heroes. They moved and writhed with a life of their own, pulling Kyellan's eyes in to strain to make out their forms. When he finally saw something clearly, bile rose in his throat. His fingers moved in a childhood sign to ward off evil.

The seal of the urn was broken. A crack ran across it, and through the crack he could see dark mists in motion. A muddy color, streaked with crimson, and undeniably something alive. Something very old, very evil, that had been the object of worship perhaps a few weeks before, and probably for centuries before that. Something sealed with wax into a grotesque pottery prison. Now that prison was cracked, but not enough to allow it to escape.

With a great effort, he turned away from the altar to

leave and found himself checked as if by an invisible chain. He could not take another step. Panic rose like a wave in his mind as he fought to free himself. Firelh! He tried to call out to the Ryasan lord, but his voice, too, was frozen. He felt himself being turned to face the altar once more. His legs moved like independent creatures, stiffly, jerkily, until he was touching the stone. The cold numbed his skin.

The hand with the dagger rose and began to chip away the wax seal of the urn. He was trapped inside his own mind, listening with horror as a wail of triumph started low, then grew with each bit of wax that fell until it resounded through the temple like the roll of thunder. As it was freed, the thing freed Kyellan, and he staggered back with a cry. It rose in a mist, dripping the blood of sacrifices. A demon-shape twice the height of a man, with huge, serrated teeth and claws, and crimson eyes that commanded worship.

"*Abarath . . .*" hissed wan voices from the shadows. Doubtless the thing's name. Kyellan held up his dagger like a shield, but the Power of that crimson gaze drove him to his knees. The dagger began to heat with orange fire. He had to drop it, but in the same moment he drew his sword and leaped at the demon with a war cry that sounded puny against the echo of the thing's triumphant wail.

Abarath screamed with rage as the sword sliced deeply into its rotting flesh, releasing a stench that drove Kyellan back. Then it leaped toward him, its jagged mouth open and its long claws ready to tear. Kyellan jumped backward but hit the wall of the temple with a force that dazed him. The demon reached out, grinning. Kyellan screamed as claws gripped him, pulled him from the wall, dug into his back like white-hot knives. But he swung his sword in both hands, driving it into the demon's neck with a desper-

ate strength that half-severed the head. Abarath fell back
but seemed little hurt.

Dizzy and weak, Kyellan had not the strength to lift his
sword again. The demon sensed its victory, coming closer,
its sharklike teeth glittering. It knocked the sword aside
with a contemptuous swing of its five-foot arm and dug
into Kyellan again with its talons. The Guardsman could
not even cry out as the thing's teeth grazed his neck, ready
to close in a tearing bite.

And then it was gone. Kyellan knelt on the ground
beside his smoking sword, breathing in shuddering gasps,
alone in a lifeless, blackened temple that reeked of a rotten
smell. He could still feel the dry, cold scales of the thing
as it had held him, and his back throbbed with overpowering
pain.

Firelh boomed from the doorway, "By all the gods!
What happened, man? You're hurt!" The big Earl hurried
to his side. "I caught a glimpse of the thing, but I couldn't
get inside somehow. Everything was dark. Couldn't see
what was happening. Can you walk?"

The Guardsman nodded faintly and with Firelh's help
stumbled from the temple down the rough path to where
the horses stood. The horses' eyes were rolling, the whites
showing with fear. Kyellan lowered himself gingerly to the
ground and sat cross-legged while Firelh knelt behind him.

"What was it?" the Ryasan asked.

Kyellan shrugged painfully. "I don't know. It was trapped
in an urn, and somehow it made me let it out. A demon, I
guess."

"Managed to ruin a good cloak," Firelh grumbled as he
unfastened the tattered black cloth that hung from Kyellan's
shoulders. Beneath it, the tunic of thick leather had been
ripped up like so much silk. There were two ugly sets of
charred tracks on his skin, bleeding heavily.

"What do you think?" Kyellan asked finally, since Firelh said nothing. The Earl stood up and rummaged in his saddlebag, drawing out another cloak. He fastened it around Kyellan, though it was far too large.

"There will be doctors in Dallynd. Can you ride?"

"Always," Kyellan said dryly, forcing himself to ignore the Earl's unreassuring tone.

Briana awoke trembling with fear after sleeping less than an hour. Her robe was damp with sweat. "Kyellan," she whispered.

"What's wrong?" The Princess Valahtia had been sleeping beside her in the hospital tent. She rose up on her elbows and looked at Briana.

"It's Kyellan . . . the Guard captain, something terrible has happened to him, and I can't tell if he's all right. Either his shields are particularly strong right now, or he's dead."

"Try to reach Firelh, then," Valahtia suggested sleepily.

Briana tried to compose her racing mind, still full of horror at the thing she had contacted. With a minimal prayer, she projected her awareness beyond the camp and down the coast over the twelve miles between them and Dallynd. Nothing. There . . . a slight indication of Firelh's presence, but nothing from his mind. He seemed to be shielded as well as Kyellan usually was. "Maybe Gwydion gave them shields, so they wouldn't be noticed by the wizards," she said with little conviction. "I'll ask him in the morning. Go back to sleep, Princess. There's nothing we can do."

The Dallynd gate guards were understandably suspicious, although Firelh was loudly upset at his treatment. They had expected him, but not in the middle of the night with only one grey-faced, slow-moving Southerner as a guard.

So Kyellan and Firelh were walked under close spears through five circles of the city, past barracks and stables, armories and warehouses, smithies and furnaces. The Sixth Circle held well-kept houses and lawns, the homes of the wealthy of Dallynd. The last was the inner city, the oldest section. Its walls were ancient and worn, showing signs of hasty repair. There were shops and houses, alleys and temples, taverns and bazaars. It was crowded with two-story houses that leaned over the cobbled streets. Open, smelly ditches ran along the way. It felt like home to Kyellan.

The western palace of Ryasa's King Janorwyn was deserted and dark, but the soldiers' quarters near the gate had been converted into a command building for Dallynd's defense. Two guards in impeccable uniforms stood on each side of the door. The soldiers and their captives were waved inside after a muttered exchange of passwords. Kyellan and Firelh moved slowly inside, despite the impatience of the spearmen that surrounded them.

The front room was huge, filled with map tables, models of city walls and fortifications, and shelves of bound books. It was brightly lit. Two men were bent over one of the maps, marking lines with pieces of chalk.

"What's this?" asked one sharply. A thirtyish man, he wore the uniform of a Ryasan battalion commander.

"Waren, is it not?" Firelh said before the guards could speak. "I am Firelh. You were expecting me. And Haval? No words of greeting for an old battle comrade?"

The older man, perhaps in his late forties, was slender and weathered with wiry, muscled arms. He smiled wearily. "Sorry, old friend. I'm glad to see you. But I wish you'd been here two days ago."

"Why?"

Haval dismissed the guards and beckoned Firelh and Kyellan to one of the map tables. It showed a view of the harbor of Dallynd. Small wooden ships were strung across the bay, like the toys of an orderly child.

"A blockade, gentlemen. We've already lost two ships that tried to run it. Their captains were good men. I've forbidden any others to try."

"Blockades have been run. Any good navigator—"

"Not by a fleet the size of this. We've eighty ships in the harbor to carry your men. How many did you gather in the mountains?"

"Twenty-four thousand six hundred and seventy. But I lost men in battle at Yamin Basin with an army of the wizards. How many left, Kyellan?"

He shrugged. "Twenty thousand, more or less. Counting civilians." Kyellan leaned on the map table as if to survey the layout of ships. He was dizzy with pain.

"All badly needed in Altimar," Firelh said.

"I won't risk the ships on such a venture," Haval said irascibly. The two veterans' eyes locked as they scowled like two stubborn old bears. Kyellan glanced at the sharp-faced aide Waren, who smiled slightly.

"We'll go to another port. Come, Kyellan."

"My lord," the Guardsman said, "no other port would have the ships."

"And what good are these ships that can't leave harbor?"

"What would eighteen thousand men do for Dallynd's defenses?" Kyellan asked Haval. "Would they be enough to free up men to take out the blockade?"

"Possibly." The city commander brightened.

"Use my men to defend this doomed city? You have to be joking. They're needed in Altimar."

"Altimar is not under siege!" Haval pounded the table,

scattering the toy ships. "Dallynd is probably the only free city left on the mainland. It must not fall."

"We can't leave until the blockade is gone, and to do that we have to defeat the wizards," Kyellan pointed out.

"Very well. Very well." Firelh glowered at them. "Tomorrow night I'll bring the first part of my army here, with the women and children."

"Good!" Haval embraced his friend warmly. "Waren, you and Firelh's second here arrange to house the people from Dafir. When you return, we'll work on our strategy."

"That will have to wait. Captain Kyellan is wounded. And we all need to sleep," Firelh said.

"He's right, sir," said Waren. "It's late. I'll send the guard for a physician."

"Had some trouble getting through the wizards' lines?" Haval asked as he showed them to rooms opposite his own quarters.

"Not what you'd expect," Firelh said. "A creature in a ruined temple south of Dallynd. We had the luck to encounter it as it was escaping."

Haval stared at them and whistled low. "That thing is loose? I'm surprised you survived at all."

"It's happened before?"

"Not in my lifetime. The King of my father's time, Carywis, forbade that worship under sentence of death, but we suspected it still went on in secret. There are legends in plenty about that place."

"Time was, in a case like this, magic being involved, I'd have sent for a wizard for the healing," said the plump little doctor. Firelh and Haval watched as he applied a thick salve to Kyellan's back. The younger man slept after drinking the physician's drugged wine. "But now there's not one to be found, except for them. It's a shame, my lords, for what's an honest medical man to do in a case of magic?''

"You've done all you can?" Firelh asked.

"All I know to do. If they'd been normal wounds, I'd not have called them serious, but there's a poison at work.''

"Lord Waren will pay your fee." Haval dismissed the physician with a wave. "You'll find him in the map room."

"I have a young wizard with my army," Firelh commented. "They aren't all in the Kharad."

"I'd not trust him. They're a devious race."

"He's been useful, though. We'll see what he can do for the Southerner."

"You mean to bring him inside the walls?" Haval said in distaste.

"At the least, he can heal Kyellan. I'm beginning to value this young Caer." He laughed. "Don't look so dour, Haval. I'm a good judge of men."

"Wizards are not men, Firelh," he said. "I hope you're right about this."

The next evening at dusk, Firelh and two of Haval's guards rode out of Dallynd. They would attempt to bring back part of the Dafir army. Kyellan and Waren rode with them as far as the last walls, to tour the progress on the fortifications. The men on the walls had an exhausted, haunted look. If the wizards' men did not attack soon, they would meet little resistance. The physical and emotional effects of the siege seemed to be overwhelming Dallynd's defenders. Knowing the wizards, Kyellan wondered if some spell might be responsible for the depression that hung over the city. If so, perhaps Gwydion could do something to alleviate it.

The night was more than half gone when Kyellan and

Waren returned to the command center to discuss the deployment of Firelh's troops in the plan for the city's defenses. Kyellan argued for his men to be held in reserve, since they were already exhausted from the battle on the plains. Waren and Haval, however, seemed to think that having experienced men on the First Wall was more important.

"I know you've heard the saying, 'The man who survives five minutes of battle, he is a soldier.' " Haval stared at the lowest point of the outermost walls in the model city on one of the tables. "Most of mine were babes in arms during the Hoabi pirate wars of twenty years ago. Even Waren here had barely reached his teens."

"You were in the Hoabi wars, sir?" Kyellan said. "I've studied those campaigns. Brilliant tactical warfare."

"Your Firelh and I were comrades. He was the rebellious son of an Earl, and I no more than an ambitious young man with a sword. I'm sure he's spoken of those days."

"I haven't been with him long."

"Then I'm surprised you've won his confidence. Usually he's a suspicious man."

Firelh came in not long after, followed by Tobas and Gwydion. They were muddy and tired. "Well, we managed the women and children, and a quarter of the men," the hill lord said cheerfully. "And I'm ready to sleep the day away. Haval, why don't you let Kyellan and Waren do the same? Wouldn't do you any harm, either."

The city commander stood stiffly, staring at Gwydion. "You brought the wizard here?"

"Thought I'd put him and Tobas in with Kyellan, and move my own blankets in with you. If you don't mind. Oh, forgot the introductions. Haval, this is Captain Tobas of the Caerlin Royal Guard, and Gwydion, a very useful young wizard.'' Firelh took Haval's arm and propelled him toward the sleeping rooms, muttering, ''Trust me on this one, will you?'' Waren followed them.

''You're hurt,'' Gwydion said softly as Kyellan showed them to his room. ''Firelh told me, but I guessed it already from the feel of the thing you encountered last night.''

They sat on the narrow cot. ''Let me see the marks,'' the wizard said. ''What possessed you to go near a place like that? I thought you had some sensitivity to danger.''

Kyellan shrugged painfully out of his tunic. ''Curiosity. Or so I thought.''

Gwydion shuddered when he saw the festering, angry claw tracks. ''It must have called you into the building. But it would have had little Power, imprisoned as it was. You could have refused the call.''

''The place fascinated me. Until I got inside.''

''It shouldn't have had that much Power until you were very near it. I don't understand.'' Gwydion searched in his leather pouch. He brought out a bottle of a cloudy, gaseous substance that ranged in color from pale orange to deep red as it shifted in his hands.

''What's that?'' Tobas reached out.

Gwydion pulled it away. ''Something very precious, very powerful. If you know how to use it. Otherwise, it can destroy you.''

Tobas grimaced. ''I'll leave it to you, then.''

''If the demon was powerful enough to project so far, my remedies may not be strong enough for its poison.''

''Encouraging,'' Kyellan said sourly.

''You must be perfectly still once I've got it out, Ky. Or it could get distracted and not obey my commands.''

''It's alive?''

''Actually, it's a relative of your friend in the temple. A household sort of demon.''

"Wait a minute. Are you sure you know what you're doing?"

"Of course. It isn't very closely related to the major demons. The family ties are a little complex. But it's the only way to neutralize the poison of a demon, without killing the patient."

Gwydion chuckled.

"Very funny."

"I'd better leave," Tobas said uncomfortably.

"Stay. There is power in threes."

The wizard sat quietly for several moments, looking at the bottle. The gaseous orange thing began to agitate like a shaken drink. Then Gwydion began a slow, deep chant, a weird, unmusical sound, slurring from note to note, slowly growing in volume and speed. The two listeners shuddered. At the climax of the cadence, he slowly uncorked the bottle. Kyellan sat rigidly still, beginning to sweat. Gwydion upturned the flask and shook its occupant out into the palm of his hand, still chanting.

There was no form to the thing. A shifting, smoky blob, it moved like thin gelatin in Gwydion's hand. The wizard's chant was coming in painful gasps. His hand was bone white under the orange of the thing. Then with a sudden movement, Gwydion tossed it square onto Kyellan's back.

The Guardsman clenched his teeth against the shock. It was colder than the heart of a blizzard, colder than the spaces between the stars, a cold that burned. The hot pain of his wounds lessened, then disappeared, giving way to a numbness that spread with paralyzing speed through his body.

Gwydion suddenly keened a high, wordless note and reached out to gather the thing off Kyellan's back and compress it between his hands into a thin rope. He thrust it back into the bottle and corked it, resuming his chant, slower, until he finally stopped and replaced the bottle in his pouch.

Kyellan shivered uncontrollably with cold. He could feel no sensation in his back now. Gwydion pulled a blanket from the other bed and tossed it around the Guardsman's shoulders, then sank back exhausted. His face was drawn, and his hands were blue with frostbite. His strength and Power drained, he was still for long minutes regaining his breath. Tobas watched in stark amazement.

"Well." Gwydion spoke finally. "That's done. It worked as well as ever. Whatever Power that temple demon had didn't extend to its poison."

"How are your hands?" Tobas asked. The wizard held them up. The blue color was fading visibly.

"Let's see what we've done for you, Ky," Gwydion said briskly. He took the blanket off. The marks that had been festered red wounds were now thin, white, raised scars on the brown skin. "You'll have the scars, but it worked well."

"What's a few more scars?" Kyellan grinned at the young wizard. "Thanks. I wonder, though. Could I have kept that thing in the temple off me if I'd sung to it, instead of swinging a sword?"

"I doubt it. With your voice, you'd only have made it angrier," Tobas answered for Gwydion, relief giving way to mischief on his boyish face.

Only half of Firelh's men had reached the city the morning that an armored herald rode to the east gate of the outermost wall. He carried a brown-and-gold standard with the wizards' device of seven inverted triangles in a star shape. The gate guards kept him waiting, since Haval still slept; finally, in the early afternoon, the city commander rode to meet him with Waren, Kyellan, and Tobas. They walked their horses calmly through the crowded streets until they reached the First Wall.

The herald controlled his horse with difficulty. He did not raise his visored helmet, and his voice rang hollow. "You are in authority here?"

"I am Haval."

The wizards' man declaimed, "Know, citizens of Dallynd, that we the unopposed rulers of this land Ryasa, under the scepter of His Imperial Majesty Belaric, hereby demand that you surrender this city and all its people, lands, and assets to the disposal of our viceroy, the Most High Lord Cosirin. If these demands are not immediately met, without delay or obstacle, we will be compelled to destroy said city without mercy. We await your reply."

Haval was scornful. "The free people of Dallynd, under His Majesty King Janorwyn the Third, will never surrender. Tell your masters that."

"There can be no loyalty to a King who has fled and left his people to face the enemy alone. You doom yourself."

"Dallynd has not fallen in a thousand years," Haval said. "We do not expect this time to be different. Good day." He turned his horse and motioned the others to follow.

"Dallynd has never faced the skill of wizards. We will see if these old stones can withstand magic."

"Leave my city!" The gate guards approached the herald. He wheeled his horse and galloped away. Kyellan sharply checked his own horse, which was restive and bored and would have liked to follow. He looked at Haval. The commander's face was pale, and his hands shook on the reins.

"I wish I was so sure," he whispered. Then he raised his voice to be heard by the men on the walls. "They will attack within the hour! Prepare the city!"

Chapter Eleven

By the time Kyellan and the others reached the Third Circle, the streets were a mass of confusion. Small, harried groups of city guards were trying to herd the anxious women and sobbing children left in the outer circles inward. They seemed to be evacuating entire households, complete with goats and cows, barking dogs, geese and chickens. People carried on their backs such varied items as bags of meal, quilts, rolled tapestries, and one gilded birdcage containing a small, frightened yellow songbird.

Against this tide of panicked people marched grim troops bound for the outer walls. Some were well-ordered companies of city soldiers. Most were clad in ill-fitting, makeshift uniforms. There were corpulent merchants, priests with dark robes under their leather tunics, rough laborers, entertainers and acrobats, and assorted thieves and cutpurses. Many were youths no older than twelve or thirteen years, pleased at being allowed to fight.

The acrid smell of human fear rose from the streets, making the horses prance nervously and shy from movement. It fed Kyellan's growing sense of excitement, of battle readiness, and made him long to turn his horse and ride with the troops to the outer walls to face the first assault. He did not want to be safe behind all of Dallynd's protective circles awaiting news of battle. But Firelh had not yet returned from his latest foray to bring his army, and Kyellan had to take his place with Haval in the command center.

A child ran in front of his horse, shrieking as another chased it. The horse reared and pawed the air. Kyellan cursed it roundly, throwing his weight to one side and dragging the horse's head so it landed a foot or so from the suddenly frozen child. A burdened mother ran to gather up her strayed offspring, glaring at Kyellan venomously and swearing at all soldiers and their monstrous horses.

"She recognizes a creature of Darkness when she sees one." Tobas chuckled, reining in next to him.

"What does that mean?" Kyellan snapped.

"I've been talking to Gemon. She seems to think you're some kind of demon. Or at least in league with the wizards. I can't figure out why she hates you so much."

"She's a priestess." Kyellan shrugged. "They don't like men."

"It's more than that. Pima's a novice, too, and she's half in love with Erlin. Even Briana was really worried about you that night you and Firelh met that temple demon."

A dim roaring came from far behind them. The wizards' army beginning their charge, Kyellan guessed. He fingered his sword hilt. Men and women in the street moved faster, spurred on by fear, and more children began to cry.

Haval halted, and the others followed suit. He looked at them gravely. "I hoped they wouldn't be so prompt. I intended to go over our strategy again, but there's no time. They'll need commanders on the outer wall. Tobas and Waren, I'm sending you back. Dispatch messages every quarter hour with reports to me and Kyellan. The Goddess go with you."

On a weird impulse, Kyellan undid the pouch of luck-stones from his neck and handed them to Tobas. The younger man grinned and tied the thongs around his own neck. They said nothing. Tobas bowed to Haval, saluted Kyellan, and wheeled his horse to follow Waren through the mass of terrified civilians.

"We're faced by a larger force than I expected," Haval began the conference he had called. "Well armed, with at least two wizards, according to Firelh's young one. I won't mislead you. Our chances are not good."

"Your men are fighting for their homes and families," Briana said. "The enemy will weary of a siege against a determined city."

"Unlikely, with the wizards' control over their men. You priestesses and the young wizard, if you trust him—I want you to try to break that control. Kyellan tells me you killed a wizard in Yamin Basin. Since Firelh hasn't returned, the Southerner will assist me here. Dormain and Gawal, my old friends, you must study the harbor to find how best to destroy those enemy ships." The two old men, who had not expected to be consulted, seemed to be eager to begin. Haval paused, his hands clenched on the side of a table. "That's all I wanted to say. The Goddess be with you all."

The others left quickly, until Kyellan and Haval were alone. Kyellan studied the map of the walls. From what he knew of strategy, there should be no way the wizards could succeed. The Dallyndi had plenty of food, and numerous wells within the city. The six walls were built as strong as the Border Hills. Yet magic changed the standard theories. He wished he knew the limitations of the wizards, if there were any.

"You'll regret joining your men with mine," the city commander said morosely. "Many will die. Perhaps all."

"Maybe not. If Firelh can hold his people together, he

can attack the wizards from behind. He could turn the battle for us.''

"We can't count on him.''

"We can't forget him, either. There are nearly ten thousand men with him.''

"You're an optimist, Southerner." Haval lowered himself into a well-stuffed chair, but his back was as straight as when he sat his horse. "But some things you simply have to accept. One is the odds against us. What good is useless hope to my city tonight? It will fall. The only question is when.''

Neither side gained an advantage during the night. The Ryasans made periodic forays outside the wall, through a heavily guarded gate set several hundred yards from the main gate. But every wizards' man they killed was replaced by a fresh one. That could not last much longer, Tobas told himself, leaning wearily on the ramparts. He had led three of the charges, each time driving away the attackers that battered and crashed against the main gate. Each time he was met with renewed force and was obliged to retreat behind the wall again.

The gate was weakening. Tobas and Waren had withdrawn many of the First Circle troops back to the next wall; it would not be long before the first was breached. A foray led by Waren was churning within the enemy ranks gathered around the gate. It was a cacophony of screams and death cries, the shrill of spears and arrows, the clamor of steel on steel. Stranger sounds, too. The familiar clouds of acrid smoke drifted purposefully through the field, concealing demonic shapes like those at Yamin Basin. Men hit by spears would burst into flames, carrying three or four others with them. The catapults of the wizards' forces hurled smoking grey globes over the walls to explode when they hit, maiming and killing men who should have been safe behind the ramparts.

Erlin had been close to one of them, and his left side was blistered. He refused to go down to the busy hospital in the circle, and a doctor had come up to dress the wounds. Standing in his archer's port, he watched the movements of men below, muttering imprecations at the slowness of doctors.

"Tobas!" he suddenly called.

The young captain joined him in the cramped portal. Far from the walls waved the unmistakable red plume of Waren's helmet. He and a few of his men were surrounded by a mass of brown-clad soldiers.

"We can't afford to lose him, my lord," said the young archer as the doctor packed up his salves and left.

"The rest of the officers are on the field or back in the next circle," Tobas muttered. "I'll have to go. You take command here, Erlin. Try to get that ram away from the gate!"

Tobas gathered thirty men. The stablers hurried to them with war-geared horses, and they drove in a wedge out through the close-packed fighting around the side gate. The momentum of fresh horses carried them through groups of foot soldiers until they reached the place Tobas had seen Waren's plume. The Dallynd lord was not among the dead that lay there, but his horse was down. They would have to go further into the melee. Tobas turned to his men.

"The gate, my lord," one whispered, staring white-faced toward the city. "The gate has fallen."

Rising up in his stirrups, Tobas could see the hole in the wall like a dark, leering mouth through which the battle spilled into the First Circle. "Sorry, Waren," he muttered. Some of his men were already racing their horses back toward the breached wall, not wanting to be caught behind enemy lines as the front moved into the circle. He followed them, hacking his way through rows of newly confident wizards' men and disheartened, desperately fighting Ryasans who were rapidly losing ground.

The dead at the gate were piled atop each other, so thick had the defenders been. Tobas lost hope of gaining the Second Wall soon. Wizards' men surrounded the horses and tried to pull off their riders. He was soon fighting for his life and wishing Kyellan was beside him.

Restless and alone, Kyellan paced in the candlelit command center. He had heard no report for an hour. Haval had gone with the two old sailors Dormain and Gawal to look at the harbor. He wished fervently he was in the battle. It was torture to wait, knowing it was going badly, forced to watch for the coming of a messenger before he knew what orders to send.

At last the door to the front room opened, and a boy staggered in bleeding from several small wounds. Kyellan caught him quickly and helped him to a chair, waiting with outward patience as the youngster found his voice.

"The gate has fallen, my lord," he finally gasped. "They are in the First Circle. Lord Wramin is dead, killed by a flaming ball. We have lost so many. . . ."

"Tobas, what of him? And Waren?"

"I don't know, my lord. They were outside the wall when the gate fell. Corporal Erlin sent me; he says to tell you all of the officers are dead. It's as if the wizards knew who to kill. He's commanding the Second Wall now."

"Erlin? Commanding?"

"Yes, my lord. Do you have any orders for him?"

The Guardsman shook his head. "Not for you to take. Have those wounds looked after." The boy started to protest. "No argument."

The messenger left, downhearted and slow-moving. Kyellan changed the battle lines on the map table to the Second Wall. The gate of the First Circle had been the strongest in the city. It would be less difficult for them to breach the next one. He was beginning to understand Haval's pessimism. How many ways were there to defend Dallynd against a force armed with more than military strength?

"Magic," he swore. "I know nothing of it. I wish Gwydion was here."

"Your wish is my command," joked the young wizard, stepping into the room. His smile was taut in a haggard, shadowed face.

Startled, Kyellan took a moment to return the smile. "How did you do that?"

"My incredible perception, of course, and the power of instant travel. Actually, I was coming to report to you."

"You were going to tell me that the gate has fallen, and there is a seventeen-year-old corporal in command on the Second Wall?" Kyellan inquired.

Gwydion nodded, impressed.

"Are you badly needed in your pool of magicians?"

He nodded again. "Chela has more Power, but it's uncontrolled. Briana probably has as much, but it's been suppressed for too long."

"Bring them here, then. At least until Haval returns."

"You're going to the walls?" The wizard's voice was carefully nonjudgmental.

"Those inexperienced city men won't hold them for long." Kyellan buckled on a mail-vest and tied the straps of his old leather helm. "And I have to look for Tobas. The boy said he didn't know what happened to him. Explain to Haval, will you?"

"Luck with you, Captain," said the wizard softly as Kyellan ran from the room.

*   *   *

The streets were dark and deserted in the cold hours before dawn. The horse's hooves echoed loudly on the cobblestones as Kyellan raced through the streets, glad to be moving again and trying hard to convince himself Tobas could not be dead. Gwydion and the priestesses would have known if he had died. Probably he was on the Second Wall by now. Just because it was his first battle without Kyellan at his side did not mean he was defenseless.

A stabler took his horse in the Second Circle. Erlin saw him from the wall and hurried down the curving stone stairway.

"My Captain! I've tried to keep the men together, but I'm no commander, and it's gone badly for us. . . ."

"Where's Tobas?"

"He didn't reach the wall," the youth said reluctantly. "We saw him go down."

Kyellan raced up the steps to the top of the Second Wall. Erlin followed, his usually cheerful face tense and worried.

"Where?" Kyellan demanded.

"I marked the place, sir, but I'm afraid he's dead." Several bodies lay together at the point Erlin had indicated, about halfway into the First Circle, near a fire-gutted smithy. They were too far away for identification.

"He's not dead." Kyellan turned and descended the steps again. He yelled for his horse and saw the same stabler turn back. "Not yet."

"Even if that's true, we can't get to him, sir," Erlin panted as he tried to match the taller man's pace. "He's behind the wizards' lines. You'd only lose more men."

"I won't risk any men," Kyellan said grimly. "I'll go alone. Don't try to stop me, Corporal." He checked the horse's cinch and mounted. "Do you want to tell the Earl of Laenar that we did nothing to rescue his second son?"

A scrawny boy with burns on his face opened the side gate. It was so low he had to lean over his horse's neck to pass through it. A tight knot of Ryasans, fighting in phalanx to hold the enemy from the gate, parted a little for him. His horse shied from the smell of blood and the noise. Ryasan animals were not trained from birth for war as were S'tari horses. But this horse was heavier than a S'tari, better for pushing through lines of grimly battling men, swinging his sword in arcs on either side and protecting himself with a shield wrested from a skewered enemy soldier. Kyellan's concentration was centered on the place his friend had fallen. He would not think of anything else. There was a terrible quality to his face, a deadly sureness to his curved sword, that gave pause even to the madness of the invaders.

He reached the place Erlin had shown him. Keeping a firm hold on the reins of his terrified mount, he leaped off. He searched past bodies of both sides, turning the corpses with one hand, barely noticing them, until he found the curved tip of a Caer sword. Hands still held it, under two dead wizards' men. Kyellan kicked the others aside. It was Tobas. The Earl's son was limp and blood-covered, with a gaping spear wound in his right side; the blood seeping from the wound was bright red, and he was probably still alive. Kyellan could not stop to find out. Wizards' men were converging on him. He slung Tobas across the back of the restive horse, killed one particularly quick enemy soldier, and mounted behind his friend's body.

Now that he had found Tobas, his intense concentration, his confidence, was broken, replaced by a sick fear. The young man was alive, but just barely. He jolted and jerked with the uneven lunges of the horse, and his blood stained the saddle. A brawny wizards' man aimed a blow with an axe at the bobbing head of the unconscious youth. Kyellan blocked it with his shield, which shattered, pieces of it driving into his forearm. The enemy died with a sword wound that cleaved his neck.

A wagon driven by one of the Ryasan children took Tobas up to the Inner Circle in hope that Gwydion could do something for him. The doctor in the field hospital said he was as good as dead, but Kyellan would not give up.

Dawn came sluggishly in the grey, smoke-filled sky. Fires were burning in the First Circle, some of stranger colors than orange or red. The morning light barely filtered through the clouds. Kyellan stood on the Third Wall. Behind him were city factories, shops, and temples. The Second Wall gate had fallen in the early morning hours, breached in spectacular flames of purple and green that killed every man within fifty feet, whether Ryasan or enemy.

Apparently, the wizards had spent their energy in this display. The battle was slower now, man against man, seemingly without the aid of demons or spells. Kyellan hoped the respite would last long enough for his men to regain some of their strength.

Briana leaned wearily against the wall of the command center. Gwydion had gone to attempt to do something for Tobas while the wizards' attack was suspended. There were at least three masters in the field beyond Dallynd, and probably more. The First Priestess had withdrawn from the link after a few hours and seemed barely alive. Gemon had provided a kind of wild strength at the outset, but an attack of violent coughing had possessed her, and now she was curled up asleep under one of the tables.

Pima had little Power they could use. Gwydion was still strong, as was Chela. Briana thought she could last perhaps another day with such a drain, but no more. They had been linked through the night, building elaborate defensive spells only to have them broken like eggshells.

Haval strode into the room, his face set and determined. He stopped, surprised. "What are you doing here?"

"Kyellan went to the walls. They lost their commander. He asked us to stay here." Briana rose with an effort, clutching a table edge for support.

Gwydion returned, shaking his head. "I think he'll live, but I can't be sure. Oh, Haval, Kyellan—"

"Yes, she told me. Who were you talking about?"

"Tobas. He was wounded. Did you find anything in the harbor to help us?"

"Ships," the city commander said. "The ships that were intended to take Firelh's army to Altimar. We can evacuate the people in them. I think the city will fall by tonight."

"Are there enough ships?"

"If we capture the blockade instead of destroying it."

"Is that possible?"

"The wizards aren't seamen. And we lose nothing by trying."

"Form the circle!" Chela suddenly called, leaping to her feet from where she had been resting and taking Gwydion's hand. "They're attacking again."

Briana turned to her, but Haval stopped her with a heavy hand on her shoulder. "I need to know if there are any wizards on the blockade ships."

Half-angry at the touch, she composed herself with difficulty and reached outward. The ships were hard to find. Masses of confused thoughts, wizard-bound men whose minds were half-mad and half-shielded, on nineteen of them. One vessel, however, was fogged and opaque to her probe. She pulled back quickly and stood for a moment trying to calm her shivers of exhaustion.

"Well?" The Dallyndi was rough-voiced and impatient.

"One wizard, I think," she said at last. "I cannot tell how powerful."

"Briana!" Gwydion was insistent.

She sat gracelessly on the floor and reached for the proffered hands.

"Priestess, I'll need one of you people to deal with him. I want those ships."

"All of us are needed here," Gwydion said through teeth clenched with the effort of his defensive spell.

"The commander is right," said Gemon hoarsely, uncurling from her place beneath a table. "The city will fall. We must try to save at least some of its people." She rose unsteadily. "I'll go."

"No." Briana stood again, quivering with weariness. "I'll go with Haval. If the First Priestess agrees . . ." She looked at the blanket-wrapped form beside Pima. The old woman slept.

"The decision is yours," Gwydion said. "But I think it would be futile. That wizard is beyond your Power."

"Perhaps." Briana was dismayed to find she was angry. "But nothing is beyond the Power of the Goddess." Especially if she summoned Rahshaiya. "I'll . . . remain linked with you and Chela. You can help if I find it too hard. Only don't underestimate the Power I serve."

Gwydion bowed slightly. "If you are right, may She be with you today. And with all of us."

Unable to find a trace of mockery in the wizard's words, Briana nodded her thanks and followed Haval out into the smoke-clouded morning.

*　　*　　*

"Captain! Look, sir. What is it?" A young Dallyndi tugged Kyellan to the ramparts of the Third Wall and pointed urgently.

A party of wizards' men was climbing the broken steps of the section of the Second Wall that still stood. It was too far to see them clearly, but they had two captives. One was a corpulent city man in a brown tunic and dark leggings. The other's helm was red-plumed. Waren.

A harsh call sounded from a short, wide-bored horn. The fighting slowed as men of both armies looked up. Kyellan knew what was going to happen, but he could not bring himself to turn away.

"Don't look," he said to the boy who stood eagerly at his side awaiting his orders. The messenger obeyed briefly, but his curiosity was too strong.

Kyellan watched through narrowed eyes as first the city man and then Waren were slowly disemboweled and hacked into small pieces with a great axe. When the last of the screams had stopped echoing, the wizards' men threw the fragments down into the mass of fighting men below. Holes opened in the battle, as men drew back to avoid being hit. Beside Kyellan, the Dallyndi boy was quietly sick.

Below, the wizards' men were pressing their attack on the dazed Ryasans. Kyellan swore. The scene on the Second Wall had been calculated to shock men who had already seen too much death. Now the defenders of Dallynd looked like helpless children on the field. He gave the wall command to Erlin once more and gathered a small force to go outside the Third Wall and rally the troops.

Briana sat dizzily on a cot in the field hospital just beyond the Third Wall. She had come to ask Kyellan for the soldiers Haval needed aboard his ships for the harbor battle. The commander wanted his sailors free to navigate; he required fighters to board the enemy vessels and take them. But Kyellan was leading a foray outwall, and Erlin would not give her any commitment. So she waited, doing her best to help the wounded. At first she had used her Power to hasten their healing, but it drained her, and she would need all the strength she could muster for the wizard in the harbor.

She did not think she would have to summon Rahshaiya. The specter of the Third Face of the Goddess seemed everywhere, as if wars and warriors had become Her chief concern. When Briana had been working with Gwydion and Chela, she had been helping to kill people. It horrified her to find she was good at it. Still more horribly, she'd encountered no resistance from the Goddess as she'd provided strength for wizardly spells that broke off huge slabs of rock from the walls to crush men who swung battering rams, spells that turned men's swords in their hands, spells that drove horses mad and sent them plunging into enemy lines with their riders.

Even this makeshift patching and soothing of wounded men did not seem the Goddess's work. She could not pause at one soldier for long enough to truly heal him, for then another would sicken beyond help. As the doctors did, she found herself ignoring the patients with incurable injuries and devoting all her time to men with minor cuts and easily set limbs. It was insane.

A stabler waited impatiently outside the tent hospital, holding her horse as she had ordered. She had been here almost an hour.

At last she felt the moving blank in her awareness that was Kyellan and the unusually calm and controlled presence of the horse he rode. To her straining ears, the opening of the postern gate was grating and slow. Muttering a short prayer over the wound she had just bandaged, Briana hurried out into the yard.

Kyellan was dismounting slowly from the foam-flecked, heaving horse. Lines of exhaustion etched his face, and two days' growth of beard. His clothes and hair were caked with blood and dirt. The battle was not going well, Briana saw from the grim despair in his eyes. He spoke harshly to the youth who took his mount when the boy pulled it by the bit instead of leading it gently.

Yet when he saw the priestess, he smiled widely and hurried toward her. "Briana! What are you doing here?"

She ignored his use of her given name and the leap of pleasure she felt in hearing it. "Haval sent me, Captain. He's going to try to capture the wizards' ships in the harbor, and he needs men."

Kyellan leaned on a hitching post that had been charred by a wizards' fireball and gazed down the wide city street. "It's too late for anything that ambitious. The wizards will be through this wall in less than an hour, I think. I can't spare anyone."

"You must. The city is sure to fall, you know that as well as Haval."

"Did you just come from the command center? Is Tobas there?"

"He may be all right, Gwydion says. If we capture those ships, we can evacuate at least the women and children, and the men who are with them in the Inner Circle. Isn't that better than everyone dying? Which will happen if the wizards breach the Sixth Wall."

He shook his head, smiling a little. "If I gave you men, they'd still have a naval battle to win, and then to evacuate the city before the wizards reach the last wall . . . if we can hold them that long."

"It can be done."

"Either way, it's a toss with long odds. Very well. We'll go along with the city commander in this. I'll send a third of the men we have left, as soon as I can get them together. I'll try to find some that have shipboard experience, if I can."

"Good." She tried to project a confidence she did not feel. "Haval was in the Hoabi wars, and if anyone can take those ships, he can. Will you come with the men?"

"I'll stay on the walls."

Briana lost the composure proper to a priestess. "You can't! Even if we win in the harbor, you won't make it to the ships in time. You'll be killed."

"I'll stay. We might still carry the day, if Firelh gets here with the rest of his army."

"This isn't your city," she said desperately. "You owe them nothing. And Firelh should have been here long ago."

"They put me in command. I owe them that." His dark eyes held hers. He was very near. The sweat and leather smell of him was overwhelming.

Briana pulled her hood up, shadowing her face. "I understand duty," she said softly. "I will not beg you to come. But we . . . but I . . . will sorely miss you, if you do not."

His hand reached out gently, cupped her chin, and raised her face to meet his, and then he kissed her. For a wild, crushing moment, she yielded, melted, joyed in the feeling. But when he released her, she pulled away, shaking like a frightened deer. Their eyes met again, hers wide and startled, his like moonless night, unfathomable.

Briana ran to the horse being held for her and leaped to its back, disdaining the proffered assistance. She kicked it to a rough gallop. The Fourth Wall gate opened as she clattered toward it, cold with the realization of her transgression. If she had not broken her vows with her body, she had broken them in her heart.

Tears whipped from her eyes with the wind, and she pulled the horse to a slower speed as it stumbled from lack of guidance. Over and over in the Old Tongue she prayed. "Forgive me, Cianya, forgive me. . . . Oh, Goddess, forgive . . ."

Chapter Twelve

From the western tower of the Fourth Wall, Kyellan counted thirty ships leaving harbor, detaching from the assortment of eighty vessels that were moored at the long Dallynd docks. Haval must have decided to try a smaller number of better-armed, better-manned ships against the wizards' blockade. Kyellan knew nothing of naval warfare beyond the bare instructions in strategy he had received as a cadet. The Royal Guard was a cavalry arm of the Caerlin Empire's forces.

The midday sun was straining through the haze that still hung over the city, its light blood red from the wizards' stratagems. The Third Wall had exploded in destruction, much as the Second Wall had before, and an unnatural calm prevailed. Kyellan had wanted to press the attack in this time of the wizards' weakness, but his men had been too exhausted to consider it. There were no reserves left in the circles of the city. Every man was in the battle now.

He had climbed the tower hoping to find something in the field that could be turned to their advantage. The factories, the shops of the Third Circle were burning. As the fighting moved farther into the city, the defenders might gain a little from their knowledge of the streets. Perhaps. The city's armories were in the Third Circle, and

the Dallyndi were left with only the weapons they carried.
And only three walls remained.

Briana prayed softly in the Old Tongue, sitting alone in
an out-of-the-way corner of the leading ship, the *Falisha*.
She could do nothing to help until they engaged the wizard's
vessel. So, like the soldiers, she had to wait and try to
keep out of the sailors' way. She was not certain now that
she could do anything against the wizard even when they
reached him. If Gwydion was right, and the priestesses'
Power was the same sort as the wizards', she would need
to have all the confidence she could muster. And she had
none. The Goddess must surely have deserted her, after
what she had done that morning.

She had tried to convince herself that Kyellan had forced
himself on her. That would be no cause for disgrace, only
for anger. But it was not true. She had showed him her
feelings, and she had half expected it; moreover, she had
enjoyed it. That was worst. What would the First Priestess
say when she knew? Probably that it had been a mistake,
giving too much authority to one so young. Certainly, if she
was not replaced in Fourth Ranking, she could expect no
promotion from Third. She began another penitent prayer
in the Old Tongue, begging the Goddess to at least forgive
her long enough to defeat the wizard she would fight.

Ryasans who passed where she sat avoided looking at
her. The air surrounding the priestess seemed to crackle
with Power. Some whispered, "The Goddess is with us,"
but were not comforted by the thought. It was usual to
pray to the Goddess for a safe voyage and pleasing to say,
"She is with us," but it was very different when She
really seemed to be.

Battle-weary soldiers massed against the sides of the
ship with nests of spears and slings. Some, instructed by

the sailors, readied the lines and hooks they would use for boarding. The ship's catapults were unmanned. They were commanded not to harm the wizards' ships, for those ships needed to be seaworthy enough for the passage to Altimar.

Haval stood wide-legged in the prow, regaining his sea balance, straining his eyes to see the blockade though he knew the man on the masthead would see it first. The points of land between Dallynd harbor and open sea curved in so at their closest there was less than eight miles between them. The wizards' ships would be waiting there, twenty of them, huge Garithian galleys, if reconnaissance could be trusted. They would not maneuver quickly, but they would be strong and swift in straight runs, and they were not under the handicap of trying not to harm their enemies' vessels.

Yet the city commander felt his confidence rise as he rode the choppy waves with the *Falisha*. He was more at home on the sea than ever in Dallynd, despite the position and honor the city had given him. Together with Firelh, he had been the best student of the great strategist Marelen in the Hoabi wars twenty years before. It would all depend on him, and on the Power of the unsmiling young priestess aboard his ship. He hoped neither would fail.

The men of the wizards' army seemed to care little if they died. Four of them were killed for each man of the city, but they were replaced almost as quickly as they fell. Their eyes were glazed as in the madness of battle, but there was more to their madness than the mingled elation and fear felt by all professional soldiers. In the beginning, they must have been ordinary mercenaries of the bragging, brawling sort that frequented the taverns and brothels of Rahan Quarter. Kyellan had counted many such men his friends. Every time he went outside the walls, he feared that one of the wild-eyed faces that went down under his sword would belong to someone whom he had last seen laughing with a girl in some Cavernon dive. Thus far it had not occurred, but it was likely to.

The Fourth Wall shuddered and groaned under the fresh impact of a ram, shaking Kyellan from his thoughts. The last two gates had been breached by magic, not strength, but this one was less well constructed. No enemy had reached it in Dallynd's long history. The ram struck again, then stopped, as one of Gwydion's counterspells burst it asunder. The men who had swung it ran, those who had not been impaled by flying splinters.

The wizards should have still been tired from the destruction of the Third Wall gate, yet Kyellan felt their next magical attack would come soon. The air tingled with a buildup of energy. His skin felt hot, alive, as during a lightning storm in Caerlin's deserts. Perhaps with Briana in the bay with Haval, the resistance was weakened.

"Back from the gate!" he shouted down to the soldiers who had massed behind it, ready to fight if it gave way to the ram. They moved reluctantly. The pillar of fire that had taken the Third Wall had killed twenty men, and Kyellan did not want to lose any more to magic. The men on the wall began to retreat, slowly, climbing down the steps beside the gate. Kyellan followed, hurrying the last man. Across the circle, some would already be taking up positions on the Fifth Wall. Most waited a few streets from the gate for the attack they knew would come.

The men before him on the stairs were moving far too slowly. Shouting at them, Kyellan felt his foreboding grow unbearable. He suddenly leaped from the second landing, down the more than twelve feet that remained, on the side away from the gate. He landed and rolled just as the roaring filled his ears. The light of the explosion blinded him momentarily, and he felt himself pinned by something heavy that fell from above. The flame-wall shot from the Fourth Wall gate down the main street of Dallynd, racing more than man-high, faster than a Khymer sandstorm, until it reached the distant Fifth Wall and exploded that smaller gate with a geyser of flame.

Kyellan struggled under the piece of stone stairway that had crumbled on him. He could smell the odor of charred flesh. All the men who had waited at a safe distance from the gate must have been caught in the river of fire. How had the wizards found enough Power to perform such a feat? If Gwydion's explanations of their Power were correct, they would now be all but unconscious, and would remain so for some time.

Small, strong hands helped him lift the stone that pinned him, then assisted him to his feet. It was the stocky youth Erlin. The corporal's black hair was partly singed away, and there was a blistered burn on his left arm where bits of his tunic were stuck. His face was bloody.

"Are you all right, Captain? We'd better get out of here."

Kyellan nodded. "Nothing broken," he said hopefully, leaning on Erlin for a moment as he checked himself mentally. They started into the carnage of the street, joining the running men that spilled in through the gaping hole of the gate.

"Have I mentioned the commission you're getting when we get back to Cavernon?" Kyellan asked as he drew his battered sword and plucked a blackened shield from the lifeless hands of a Ryasan.

"We're not likely to get back."

"Consider yourself a lieutenant, then." Kyellan paused to run his curved weapon through a brown-clad soldier in the vanguard of the wizards' men, then he ran with Erlin

through the smoldering streets toward the blasted Fifth
Wall.

The flagship of the wizards' armada, proudly bearing
the star device that was their standard, changed its course
immediately upon sighting the *Falisha*. Briana stood on
the forecastle now with Haval, trying to silence her doubts
and gather the confidence she would need. One of the
other Dallyndi ships shadowed the *Falisha*, maneuvering to
the side of the commanding wizard's vessel in an attempt
to force it toward Haval's ship. That seemed to be what
the galley's master had in mind, anyway.

"This should be interesting." The commander smiled,
his hands gripping the railing as if to pull the ship faster by
his own strength.

"One way to look at it, I suppose," said the ship's
master, Nemoth. The curly-bearded Garithian spat over
the side. "You'll be needed at the helm, sir. And you'd be
safer there, Priestess."

Briana shivered, looking at the gap-mouthed rhino's
head that was the oaken tip of their opponent's ram. It could
destroy their light sailing ship with one well-aimed blow.
And Haval was heading the *Falisha* straight for it.

"Come on, Priestess," said the commander. "They'll
be using their catapults on us, and worse, if the wizard is
aboard."

She followed him, trying to keep out of the way of
scurrying men. Most of the sailors were scrambling
belowdecks to the single bank of oars the *Falisha* carried
for docking and warfare. Others worked frantically aloft,
furling sails to slow the ship for close maneuvering. Briana
tied her hood back out of her way and rolled her full
sleeves to the elbows. She found an unoccupied place near

the mainmast and sat cross-legged on the shifting deck to begin her work.

The wizard was certainly aboard the flagship. There were hints of his presence through the shields, and he did not expect her. If she did not engage him in battle soon, he could probably ensure their defeat through illusion or another craft. So she abandoned her long preparations, hoping Gwydion was right that she did not need chants and diagrams to channel the Goddess's Power.

"Wiolai, Cianya, Rahshaiya, attend me here," she invoked quickly, gathering her Power in a concentrated bolt. She visualized it as a heavy, clothyard arrow such as the one Erlin had used in the gorge of the Border Hills. With a rope tied to it, the rope of her continuing strength feeding into it. With luck, she would catch him without defenses. Briana summoned all her will and energy into the sending from the four corners of her body, then shot it from her mind, an arrow of inimical force. It blazed visible through the air, a streak of white fire. She hastily erected her own defenses, then sagged drained to the deck.

She had caught him by surprise. She felt him stagger with the effect of the blow, but he recovered quickly and joined battle with stunning ferocity and Power. It sorely tested her slim defenses. She had learned something of shielding herself against magical attack from Gwydion. It was an art not taught at the Sanctuary. But it was not enough. Her mental walls were eroding like a canyon under a swift mountain river.

"Goddess!" she gasped, her face a few inches from the rough wood of the deck, her back bowed under the wizard's attack. "I call you, who are Wiolai the Maiden; Cianya the Mother; Rahshaiya the Death-Bringer. Rahshaiya. It is . . . it is you I call. Help me take this unbeliever's life. I offer it to you, a sacrifice, a man of Power, a wizard, to feed your Dark strength, blood for blood.''

The smell of smoke and fire grew stronger. She suddenly knew how to fight her enemy. She parried his spells, sending her own, with a speed that allowed for no ritual, no thought. An aura of white flame grew around her, shielding her from sight, not even scorching the dry wood of the deck. The Goddess's Flame, but she had no thoughts of the Goddess now.

Haval was somewhat unnerved by the fire. Its crimson counterpart on the other ship was beginning to arc over the water toward them. But he spoke in a steady stream to the helmsman as Nemoth shouted commands down a speaking tube to the rowers. They were speeding toward the enemy ram. He hoped his helmsman had the skill for the ancient trick he intended; he hoped the opposing captain had too little experience to recognize the danger. At least Briana had the wizard well occupied, so that he would not be reading their minds.

The ships approached each other like fighting bulls, one slim and clean-lined, the other squat and bristling with oars. A few catapult balls from the wizard's ship fell harmlessly between them. White fire and crimson rose over their decks.

''Ready!'' Haval shouted, wiping sweat from his face. ''Oars prepare to ship! Helm prepare to turn on my signal!'' He made a quick Sign of the Goddess and rubbed his hands on his thighs. Soldiers and sailors who were not rowing seized ropes, masts, anything that was attached firmly to the ship. Haval braced himself against the wheel housing, staring at the agitated stretch of water between the opposing prows.

When the enemy was seventy-five feet away, Haval signaled the helm to turn. When it was fifty feet from them, he joined the helmsman at the wheel in a desperate effort. The ship finally veered the few degrees necessary. He hoped the priestess was well braced inside her white fire.

"Ship oars!" he cried. The enemy vessel was close enough for him to see the suddenly understanding faces of its sailors, but it was unable to stop or turn. Nemoth repeated his command again, twice, and the clatter of oars was welcome music.

The impact rocked the *Falisha* violently as the galley scraped along its side. The oars on the right side of the enemy ship snapped like kindling. Their speed slowed by the friction, the vessels moved on, but the galley began to circle ineffectually while the *Falisha* came about smoothly to engage its opponent again. It had worked. Haval thanked the Goddess that the Hoabi wars were twenty years gone. Few of the men who had fought them could still be found on ships of the Northern Sea.

"Prepare to board!" he called, allowing his pleasure to show a little in his voice. The men picked themselves up from the decks where they had been flung by the impact and gathered their weapons and grappling lines. The *Falisha* scraped once again at the side of the galley. The soldiers flung their hooks into the other ship and began to swing hand over hand across the slight gap.

The white-and-crimson fire of Briana's battle with the wizard burned a swath down the center of both ships, from the *Falisha*'s mainmast to the central cabin of the galley. The place where the two flames met had moved from a point near the *Falisha*'s railing to the very door of the wizard's cabin. Neither blaze consumed anything in its path.

"It appears the priestess is winning," Nemoth commented dryly.

The men of the galley were still spell-bound enough that they could not think of surrender. A hail of arrows and spears met the boarders, and several dropped into the sea, but most managed to mount the low railing of the galley's upper deck. Swords were drawn, and the battle was man to man. Haval and the crew of the *Falisha* tied the two ships together, and the fighting spilled across both decks. The combatants all avoided the path of the uncanny fire-wall.

A party of Ryasan soldiers pushed through to the main hatch of the galley, into the hold where the chained slaves of the wizards sat on their triple deck of benches. Some had been injured when their oars had been sheared away, but they moved in an angry mass when they were released, wielding their chains and broken oars as weapons. The wizards had apparently not felt the need to bind them with spells, when chains were compulsion enough. Haval laughed. He was sure of his victory, if only the priestess could manage with the wizard.

"Come on, girl, we haven't that much time," he fretted. As if in response, the white flame suddenly towered high over the decks, then bore down to engulf the crimson with a roaring sound and the smell of pine smoke. Soon both flames vanished. Haval gingerly stepped into their path. It was not even warm. He crossed to the galley cabin. When he opened the door, he choked at the stench. The occupant had been burned beyond recognition.

The wizards' men seemed disoriented. Some still fought, but soon all were either killed or captured. Haval wondered if the death of the wizard had weakened their spell-bindings. The captives did not speak, did not even protest when they were put to the galley's remaining oars, as Haval's prize crew transferred half the unbroken oars to the side where they had been sheared away. Haval left the galley with orders to return to the docks as soon as it was able to move.

He returned to the *Falisha*. The boarding ropes were untied, and the ship began to tack slowly across the harbor to assist the other Dallyndi vessels. Haval was able to turn at last to tend the young priestess.

Briana lay prone inside a fading ring of white flame. Haval carefully stepped over the barrier and knelt beside her. She was only unconscious. He picked her up gently and carried her to Nemoth's cabin.

"If the rest of the blockade ships don't have wizards, we ought to do well," said the ship's master cheerfully as he helped Haval lay Briana in his broad hammock.

Haval's cheerfulness was quickly fading. He was thinking of the city he had commanded for nearly ten years. This would all be for nothing if the Sixth Wall did not hold back the enemy from the Inner Circle long enough for evacuation. The helmsman called out that more ships had been sighted, and the city commander followed Nemoth out onto the wind-sprayed deck once more.

Kyellan and Erlin had fought their way across once manicured lawns and wide parklands for nearly an hour before they finally reached the Sixth Wall. The inner city spread before them. The evacuation had obviously begun, for the streets were lifeless and strewn with discarded possessions. Kyellan hoped one or two ships had been left for the soldiers.

"There you are, lad," a gruff voice said beside the wall. "You don't seem to have done too well with the job I left you."

"Firelh!" Kyellan felt a rush of pleasure. The big man was ragged and blood-covered, but there was no mistaking the hill lord. "What happened to the rest of the army?"

"Gone." Firelh shook his shaggy head. "The night before this madness began. Half the wizards' army fell upon us before we had time to pick up our weapons. I was down the coast waiting for Haval's messenger, and when I got back the camp was utterly destroyed."

"How could they have known you were there?" Kyellan sighed heavily as he sharpened his dulled sword edge on the rock wall.

Firelh unsheathed his own sword, looked at it critically, and joined Kyellan at the wall. "You wouldn't believe the time I had getting here." He laughed harshly.

"Are you wounded, my lord?" Erlin asked. "I'll find a doctor."

"Don't bother. Just a few scratches." He grinned at Kyellan like a tired crocodile. "Don't think we'll be getting out of this one. Eh, boy?"

"Not likely."

Fifty ships waited in the bay for the return of Haval's warships. A few captured wizards' galleys had already come in, loaded, and left the docks again to wait with the others. The vessels were impossibly crowded with women, children, the elderly, and some of the wounded. There were still huge, frightened crowds waiting on the docks.

Gwydion had insisted that Chela and the priestesses get aboard one of the ships. They had taken Tobas with them. He would wait for Haval's flagship to return. Briana had done well in destroying the wizard, but Gwydion did not know how she had done it, for about a third of the way into the battle she had abruptly severed her link with the remainder of the circle. He was afraid she might be badly hurt. He had not been able to contact her.

The explosion that had taken the Fourth Wall and Fifth Wall gates had also shattered Gwydion's defensive spells

so badly that he had been unconscious for more than a
quarter hour. His head still throbbed with the Power that
had attacked. It had been far beyond anything he had
encountered before. It was as if a new, great Power had
suddenly joined the wizards and then as suddenly abandoned them. No traces of it remained in the energy that
probed against his weakened defenses of the last wall.

The harbor battle was going well. Two of Haval's thirty
ships had been sunk, and three of the wizards' ships had
escaped into the ocean. But by the end of three hours the
Ryasan ships escorted seventeen captured galleys back
toward the city docks.

Briana woke when the armada was nearing Dallynd. She
ached in every muscle, and her brain whirled in exhaustion
and confusion. She had done it. She had used every aspect
of her Power, directed every part of her being, toward the
goal of killing a man. It had not been the same when she
had worked with Gwydion; then, she had merely fed him
strength, allowed him to use her Power in his own wizard
rituals. This was different. She had invoked Rahshaiya.
The First Priestess had forbidden her even to consider it.
She was a killer, the same as Kyellan, the same as the
wizards. There was Darkness in her she had never known
before. But was Darkness necessarily from the enemy?
She had not invoked any but the Goddess, albeit the third
aspect of the Goddess, and the flame that had come to her
aid was as white as the flames that had burned at the
Sanctuary. She could not reconcile her thoughts.

And she was proud of this terrible thing she had done.
She had shown Gwydion that the Goddess had more than
enough Power to succeed against the wizards. Such pride
had to be wrong. As unthinkable as calling the Death-Bringer.

"You're awake, Priestess?" Haval's head appeared in the door of the master's cabin. "Good. It was well done."

Briana called weakly to him. "The last wall hasn't fallen. Many people are still on the docks. We must hurry!"

"We're going as fast as we dare," he grumbled, but he went back to Nemoth and requested still more sail.

Kyellan watched morosely from the Sixth Wall as the battered ships came into the docks, loaded quickly with people, and moved away again. One finally remained, only half-loaded. Waiting for them? Like the island of Lorin, he thought, it would probably have disappeared if they ever reached it. It was time for the wizards to attack again. He barked an order to retreat from the wall. This time, the men moved quickly.

"They can't push us much farther," Erlin said, his pleasant dark face frozen into a half smile of tension that Kyellan recognized as the same expression he himself wore. They fully expected to die within the next hour, but they were far from resigned to it.

Perhaps two hundred Ryasans, all who remained behind the wall, were forming a phalanx in the light of a filtered sunset. They waited fifty yards from the gate. They would not give up their city without a last battle. Kyellan thought them fools. There was nothing left in Dallynd to protect.

"There's one last ship in the harbor, idiots!" he shouted furiously at them. "Run for it!"

They stood their ground, hopelessly brave. Kyellan could not bring himself to run to the docks without them. Neither Firelh nor Erlin moved a step. But the dilemma was solved for them. The gate exploded, and through the breach came rank upon rank of wizards' soldiers. Far too many.

"Run!" he screamed again. This time they obeyed,

turning as one man and racing into the narrow streets of
the Inner City. The wizards' men were close behind.
Kyellan, Erlin, and Firelh held the rear, forced to make it
a running fight, astounded by the endurance of the enemy
soldiers who had fought for two days and still could run as
steadily as mail horses.

A group of wizards' men cut them off in a triangular
marketplace, stopping perhaps seventy of the Ryasans while
the rest kept running. Kyellan fought desperately, unsure
whether he fought because he hoped to reach the ship and
escape, or because he had no hope.

Briana stood on the crowded forecastle of the *Falisha* as
the last of the panting soldiers climbed aboard. Kyellan was
not with them. They said a group of their companions had
been detained in battle; among them were Kyellan, Erlin,
and Firelh. A hollowness filled her, and anger followed.
Why should she care if one man, a follower of Rahshaiya
at that, was killed in a battle that had already killed tens of
thousands? He was a commander Altimar could ill afford
to lose, she told herself. But that was not the cause of her
sorrow. It was the memory of the way he had put aside his
anger for Pima's sake when he had saved her from Arel. It
was the memory of the touch of his lips on hers.

"We're overloaded as it is, my lady," Haval said from
behind her. He spoke respectfully to her now. "We must
leave."

"We can't," she cried. "Kyellan and Erlin are still out
there. And your old friend Firelh."

"And fifty others besides." His voice was dead. "We
won't survive a sea voyage with three more men, much
less fifty. And I will not choose." He called to Nemoth
with orders to get under way.

They had gone no more than a half mile when Briana

saw the battling men spill out onto the dock. She tried to get Haval to turn around, but of course he would not. At last, she made her way to the master's cabin, which had been given to the few women on the ship. Once wrapped in her robe, she broke and wept with grief.

The others did not disturb her. Many were crying over husbands and brothers lost. They did not know that Briana had never wept before, not since she was seven years old and became a novice in the Sanctuary. Now she cried for her loss, and in anger at her weakness.

Kyellan and Erlin, separated now from Firelh, had fought their way to the docks only to see the retreating ship. The smoke and haze still in the sky made the early night very dark. Back to back, they cut through the slaughter of their companions and melted into the deserted city.

They discarded helms and belts, with their light-catching metal surfaces. Two dark-skinned, dark-haired men in black uniforms climbed to the rooftops in the poor section of Dallynd near the docks. They crept from roof to roof until they found one with a high stone railing they could crouch unseen behind.

Leaning against a chimney that was still warm, Kyellan tried to quiet his gasping breath. He wished he had Gwydion's cat-slit eyes; surely such pupils could see well in the dark. Until he was sixteen, he had lived in the night with the rest of the underside of Cavernon City. But he had been a day dweller for too long. His night vision was merely better than average.

If wizards could see in the dark . . . he swore softly. He had momentarily forgotten that their enemies were wizards. Such a hiding place as he and Erlin had found would be useless. They would be tracked by the presence of their minds. He envisioned a wizard with jowls hanging like a bloodhound's, sniffing out their lair. Damn.

How many galleys had he seen come in with Haval's fleet? Seventeen, he thought. Three were either sunk or escaped. Most likely escaped, since Haval was not trying to sink them. If those came back to the harbor . . . could they be turned to his advantage? They would do him no good from this rooftop.

He led Erlin back toward the docks. The roofs of Dallynd were no Thieves' Highroad, as were those of Rahan Quarter. Of Northern design, they were sloping and pointed, paved with crumbling, slippery shingles. But finally they reached the area of the docks where so many had died. They perched on a warehouse above the charnel scene until they were certain no wizards' soldiers were around.

"They won't look for us down there among the dead," he said grimly.

Erlin shuddered beside him. They climbed down, shadows against the sea-stained boards, and hid themselves with the bodies. There were forty of them. Firelh was not among them, Kyellan noted; he and the others must have either escaped or been captured.

It was perhaps the hardest thing Kyellan had done, when the wizards' men came to the docks later that night to pillage, to remain still with his eyes closed. They took his battered sword, his knife, his captain's insignia from the Royal Guard, and his boots. One commented on his warmth, but the others laughed and said if he was not dead yet, he soon would be. When they were finished, they threw the bodies into the water of the bay and watched them sink.

Kyellan forced himself to keep stiff and unmoving in the cold salt water until he was more than twenty feet below the surface. Then he frantically kicked toward the dock, his lungs about to burst. He had not dared to take a deep breath when he was thrown in.

When he finally pulled himself up onto the wooden supports below the dock, his labored breathing was loud in the stillness. The wizards' men were gone. Erlin appeared nearby, coughing and sputtering as he pulled seaweed from his wiry hair. They did not speak to each other, but they clasped hands in weary triumph.

Kyellan pulled himself into an intersection of two crossed supports. He dared not sleep, but he leaned against the upright post and allowed his exhausted mind to roam over outlandish plans of action. He still meant to get to Altimar.

Chapter Thirteen

Kyellan woke in the dark hours of early morning, cursing himself for falling asleep. He shivered. His clothing was damp and crusted with salt. Large swells curled around the feet of the beams that held up the dock, agitated by the huge, barnacle-encrusted hull towering out of the water close to where he and Erlin had spent the night. One of the warships was docking. He could hear the sleepy mutter of soldiers above him and felt the jolting vibrations of the dock as the ship scraped against it. The oar holes of the ship's lower two banks were below the pier, and he could faintly hear the mumbling of the exhausted slaves. The holes were not large. A man's head might fit through one, but not his shoulders. A half-plausible idea began to form.

If Firelh and the others had been captured, they would likely be made galley slaves. Perhaps he could rescue them and get to Altimar all in one action. He began to move carefully across the crossed pylons toward the ship but stopped at the sound of many booted feet crossing the pier above. Squirming up one of the vertical posts, he peered through the cracks between the boards. Most of the uniforms were black, shoved along by browns. One especially heavy tread might be Firelh.

He and Erlin would surely be discovered in the dawn light. Kyellan slid down the pillar and climbed over to where Erlin had wedged himself. At his gentle shake, the youth grumbled, half-asleep, and started to roll over. Kyellan grabbed him before he tumbled off into the sea.

"Keep quiet," he whispered. "Remember where we are."

Erlin nodded ruefully, massaging his stiff neck, and moved back to the cleft where he had slept. "I hope we won't be here long."

"We have to get out before sunrise. We'll swim down the coast to the battlefield."

"The battlefield? Why?" The younger man was alert now.

"We need weapons. Lots of them. We're going to take that ship to Altimar." Kyellan pointed toward the hull, which now rocked gently on its moorings less than thirty feet away.

"Two men?" Erlin snorted. "I don't care how many weapons we can get. We can't take a wizards' galley."

"I hope we'll have allies. I doubt the wizards wasted their spells on the galley slaves, when chains serve well enough."

Erlin sighed. "I guess we should try. It's going to be a long swim without breakfast, though."

"Come on."

They climbed down the post into the water, kicked off, and began to swim. The sea was choppy and cold, and near the shore it stank with the refuse of the city. They moved slowly under the high outer wall, expecting to be discovered at any moment by the wizards' night guards. No alarm was raised. Perhaps the conquerors were so sure they held a deserted city that they saw no need to guard it.

The salt water stung in their cuts and bruises and burns, soaking the heavy wool of their tunics and knee trousers until those seemed heavy enough to drag them under. But they would not discard the uniforms. The black material was good camouflage against the night.

By sunrise, they were perhaps halfway around the city. A little farther they found on the bank a large, broken-sided rowboat. They crawled up underneath it and went to sleep, not even bothering to set hours of watch. Kyellan woke once, at midday, with the sun beating down through the slats of the boat. His throat was sore with thirst, but he could not go in search of fresh water. The journey was going to take longer than he had anticipated. He hoped the galley would be there when they got back.

Tobas emerged that evening from the hot nightmare world of fever that had possessed him since the Ryasan ship had left Dallynd harbor the afternoon before. It was pleasant to waken, though he did not know where he was, and the rolling of the ship blended uncomfortably with the memory of his sickness. The last clear memory he had was the quick enemy soldier who had caught him with a spear in his side. He had killed the man somehow. It was the first time he had ever been really wounded; he had thought he was dead.

Tobas pictured his parents' faces when he had told them his decision to join the Royal Guard. They had been proud and relieved that he was not going to follow his older brother Laran to the courts of Cavernon, where packs of wild young noblemen with no responsibilities prowled the streets like tomcats. But they had also feared for him. More so, when they had learned he had attached himself to the reckless young Kyellan, an officer who seemed to court death.

The ceiling over his bunk was low and sea-smelling, and it moved as he watched. Nearby he could hear the groans of other wounded men. Aboard a ship, then. How? Was it a wizards' ship, and he a captive?

"Tobas! My lord, you are awake!" The gentle voice was familiar. It spoke in Caer, welcome to ears that were weary of the harsh Northern languages. The Princess bent over him and wiped the sweat from his face with a dripping freshwater cloth. Her long black hair was tied back severely from her face, which looked tired and drawn. He smiled weakly.

"Are you feeling better? I could have killed that wizard for going in a different ship. He said you'd be all right, but then the fever came after we left harbor. . . ." She sighed and brushed stray curls back from his forehead.

He wondered how this could be the same creature who had tried to have Kyellan assassinate her brother. "How did I get here?" he asked.

She told him, her voice grave.

"You didn't say what happened to Kyellan," he prompted when she seemed to have finished.

He could see exhaustion lying on her like a leaden cloak. "The First Priestess spoke to Briana somehow. Briana's on the last ship. She said he didn't make it to the docks." Valahtia turned away from his pain.

"Does that mean he's dead?"

"I don't know." She turned back, and he could see the true answer in her face. "Will you be all right? You're sure? Then I'll go get some sleep. You should do the same."

Sometime later, he realized that she must have stayed up with him for the night and day he was feverish. How strange. That was not the act of the selfish child he knew. Either Valahtia was changing, or he had never really seen her clearly.

*　　*　　*

By the next sunrise, Kyellan and Erlin had reached the rocky coast a mile from the ship's outer wall. They climbed out of the water and stumbled toward a gutted village. The stream that ran nearby had water pink with blood, but they were too thirsty to care. They drank and found a blackened hut with a partial roof remaining, where they slept the day through.

At nightfall, on the third night since the loss of Dallynd, they ventured out onto the battlefield. The victors had begun the task of burning the bodies, but there were still many intact. The sun had been hot the last few days, and Kyellan was glad he could not see the dead in the dark. The feel of them as he searched for weapons was bad enough, and the smell turned his empty stomach. By the time the sky began to lighten, he and Erlin had gathered a mound of swords and other arms into the corner of the half-sheltered hut. It glittered dangerously. They covered it with cloaks of the dead, and sat three-hour watches that day to guard against wizards' patrols.

Hunger was uppermost in their thoughts. There was no food to be found in the burned-out forests and fields near the city. The wild animals all had fled, and they dared not risk a fire; neither was desperate enough to eat the rats and other vermin raw. They found no rations on the bodies in the field. The Ryasans had been able to retreat into their city to eat, and the men of the Kharad had had supply lines only a few miles from the fighting.

The fourth night was cool and clear, with faint stars. The moon was dark. The followers of the Goddess counted that the unluckiest time of the month, but Kyellan was glad of it. He and Erlin carried the weapons to the coast. There, the night before, they had clumsily patched one of the rowboats the villagers had holed before evacuating to the city. Now they piled the bright weapons into it and covered them with dark cloaks to hide their glitter and protect them from the sea. There was no room in the small boat for either man.

Kyellan pulled the craft from the stony beach with a rope tied to a ring in its prow. Erlin pushed from behind. The sea was calm and smooth as glass, not hindering them, but still it was slow work. The rope tied around his waist, Kyellan struck out at first with a quick overhand stroke but found himself too weakened to continue that for long. He had to take a gentler pace, but even that made him breathe heavily as his stomach began to cramp with his exertion and its emptiness.

His mind wandered over the past week, over the disastrous defense of the city, and he was unable to think of anything that might have been done to prevent it. He found himself thinking of the Priestess Briana. He had been foolish to kiss her. No doubt she hated him for it. Yet the memory brought a smile. He knew women. She had been interested. She had even enjoyed it. It was ironic. Every other woman he had ever wanted, even the Princess, had been flattered by his attentions. And now that he had found one he might really care for, he could not have her.

If his plan did not work, he was unlikely to see any woman again. If the ship had left harbor . . . But he did not allow his imagination to continue. It had to be there. He could not leave Firelh and the others chained to an oar bench; moreover, he intended to reach Altimar. That ship was his only chance.

They would have to make the entire journey back to the docks in one night. There would be no place to hide a loaded boat under the city walls. He tried to will speed and strength into his protesting body and found it responding.

They were halfway around Dallynd when the boat suddenly felt heavier. Kyellan turned to see Erlin floating along with his hands folded on the stern. The youth's teeth gleamed in the darkness in a grin.

"Just taking a rest, Captain. You've been moving so fast with those long legs, I didn't think you'd notice."

Kyellan chuckled and turned over onto his back to float comfortably. "All right, but it'll have to be short."

"Suppose we do get there before sunrise? We aren't going to try to take the ship tonight, are we?"

"No. We'll have to hide the boat somehow, and ourselves as well. I want to talk with the slaves in the ship, and find out what we're facing. We'll move when it reaches full dark tomorrow night."

"What if our people aren't aboard?"

Kyellan stared up into the dark, indifferent sky. "We need this ship. If they aren't there . . . then we can do nothing for them."

The passage through the Venerin Straits was rough. Small islets dotted the path of the fleet, sharp-rocked bits of land that appeared from nowhere to brush the sides of the *Falisha* and the other ships. They could not take the usual path through the Straits, since that led to Keor harbor. Instead, they followed a rough-drawn map that would take them to a small natural harbor on the eastern side of the great island.

Briana found herself busy tending seasick soldiers, with little time to think of other things. Their food was running out. A warship, the *Falisha* had never been intended for long voyages. It was lucky the journey was nearing its end. A day or two at the most, Nemoth had said.

She was beginning to feel a terrible sense of urgency. More and more, she was reluctant to wait until the armies were ready to go to Caerlin. The wizards were there by now, looking for the Seat of the Goddess. If they found it and turned it to their use, there would be no more resistance to their rule. It would be crushed easily.

They must not find it, she thought fiercely. If the armies took too long to get ready for their battling, she would have to get to Caerlin another way. By herself, if it came to that.

The cache of weapons was buried in the sand when the sun rose, and the boat set free to drift as it would. Kyellan and Erlin had found a safer hiding place, on land, under the pier just before it stretched out over the water. The boards of its deck were tight enough there that they could not be seen through cracks. It was cramped, but they were too exhausted to care.

The sun was halfway to zenith, and no soldiers had passed near these docks since the early morning. Kyellan climbed once again into the crossbars, slowed by dizziness, and made his way over to the side of the galley. It was moored close enough for a plank to connect it to the pier, and it required little effort to gain a firm hold on the edge of an oar hole and a more precarious toehold on one of the boards of the ship's overlapping hull. He looked inside.

The interior was dark and close, filled with the stench of unwashed bodies. The slaves were an emaciated lot, sleeping or sitting listlessly on their benches. There was no sign of the Ryasan captives, and no sign of an overseer. Kyellan tried to attract the attention of the slave nearest him by knocking softly on the wood of the oar hole. The slave, a tall, red-bearded Garithian who might have once been a powerful man, finally looked his direction.

"Don't make any loud noises," Kyellan whispered in Garithian.

The slave moved as close as his chains would allow. "Who are you?" His voice was harsh with disuse.

The others began to take notice. Kyellan spoke a little
louder. "I'm looking for some friends. Eighteen men,
more or less, taken in Dallynd a few days ago. Are they
here?"

The Garithian nodded. "They're in the first bank under
the noses of the soldiers. I've not seen them."

Thank the gods. "Are there wizards on this ship?"

"One. I've not seen him, either."

"Two of us escaped the battle," Kyellan said. "We
have enough weapons for you all. We mean to take this
ship, with your help, and go to Altimar to join in the
resistance there."

"You're crazy, Southerner," said the slave. "There is a
wizard to be dealt with."

"We'll all be killed," said another.

"This is no life to regret leaving," Kyellan argued.
"Where's your overseer?"

"He only comes down here to bring us food when we're
in port." The Garithian's voice was low and thoughtful.

"Good. If I give you the weapons, can you hide them?"

"In the corners, under the benches," the slave said.
"No one will see them, not expecting to."

"Are you with me?" Kyellan urged.

The Garithian shrugged eloquently. "As you say, this is
no life. I am Senach, and I was once a soldier of the
Garithian army. It would be good to know your name,
since I'll probably follow you to my death."

"Kyellan, a captain in Caerlin's Royal Guard. What
about the rest of you?"

The other slaves finally agreed. Kyellan and Erlin spent
the rest of the day journeying back and forth from their
weapons cache to the ship, handing the swords through the
oar hold to Senach, who passed them around the room to
be hidden. When the slaves discovered that Kyellan and

Erlin had been without food for four days, they insisted that the two take some of their thin gruel. When they protested, Senach explained that they did not wish to be led into battle by men who were likely to faint from hunger.

By early evening all was ready. Now they waited for darkness. Kyellan lay quietly under the pier, but Erlin moved restlessly, studying the Ryasan broadsword he had kept for himself, shaking his head. Kyellan finally asked him what was wrong.

"This sword," scowled the younger man. "I wish I'd found a better one. The balance is off, with no curve at the tip, and it's far too heavy. How can the Ryasans use it in battle?"

"The Ryasans use two hands," Kyellan said mildly.

"I'll feel like a barbarian. What use are all those hours of fencing, when all you have to do is grab the sword in both hands and swing?"

"You have to swing with someone else swinging back," Kyellan pointed out.

"It's no problem for you," Erlin grumbled. "With your height and reach, you can use one of these like a rapier. Besides, I'm an archer."

"We'll send you up in the rigging, then, and you can shoot down at them in the dark." Kyellan rolled over and pretended to sleep.

The sun set with a brilliant splash of color over the huge bay. Light lingered in the sky for more than an hour afterward; but finally it was dark, and there were only a few lamps glowing on the ship.

"It's time," Kyellan muttered. They crept out of their hiding place and headed for the galley. The side of the ship seemed impossibly high. "Quickly, now." He took a grip on the oar hole, dropped his feet from the last crossbeam of the dock, and found a toehold on one of the planks. "We're lucky this is a Northern ship." They could never have climbed the smooth-sided Caer ship that had brought them to Atolan.

Erlin did not answer. Kyellan grinned. His lieutenant's boyhood training had not included the climbing of walls, and he was not very comfortable clinging to cracks with fingers and toes.

Senach had told them the slaves' second meal was brought after dark. They hoped the pattern would not change. The guard on watch on their side of the ship was bored, not even marginally alert, and they swung over the railing and crept past him without difficulty. The third hatch in the deck was easy to find, and they hid among some canvas-covered baggage to wait.

Soon, a tall, portly overseer came to the hatch, carrying a stack of shallow wooden bowls and a heavy iron pot. He put them down, opened the hatch, and picked up his burden again. They could hear him grumbling as he descended, and they hurried to follow. The steps were dark and steep, shifting with the tethered motion of the galley.

Kyellan drew his knife. The overseer was no wizard. He never had a chance as a hand covered his mouth and a blade thrust up from behind into his heart. He stiffened more in surprise than pain and went down just as Erlin grabbed the pot and bowls to prevent their clattering fall. Kyellan pulled the long knife from the man's back. He regretted having to kill that way.

The slaves were waiting nervously. They murmured in relief when Kyellan and Erlin appeared, the body of the overseer in tow. Erlin took keys from the dead man's belt and began to unlock the slaves' chains. Kyellan, swallowing his distaste, stripped the body of the brown uniform.

The overseer was near his height, but heavier. The boots were far too large. When he was dressed, Kyellan put his own belt over the uniform, pulling in the extra folds of fabric.

"How do I look?"

Erlin was amused. "You could use a better tailor."

"It will have to do." Should he use the dead man's sword and sheath, or the Ryasan broadsword he had taken from the battlefield? The overseer's was an inferior weapon, but the broadsword would not fit in the uniform sheath. He decided on the smaller sword. "Stay here, all of you," he said. "If I'm not back within ten minutes, take your orders from Erlin. I'm going to get rid of that wizard." He moved quickly to the stairs, trying to feel the confidence he had projected. Surely a wizard could die as easily as another man.

Kyellan crept out the hatch and moved quietly across the deck. What was the name of Dallynd's new ruler again? Carigan? Cogisan? No, it was Cosirin. He glanced at the insignia on his tunic; not the ranking system he was familiar with. An overseer could be no more than a second lieutenant, no less than a corporal, but it would have been nice to know his own rank

Soon he had maneuvered over to the gangplank. He turned halfway down and walked back up it, his boots loud on the hollow wood. The guard challenged him. "Halt!" It was not a formidable sound. "What's your business, Sergeant?"

Kyellan caught his smile in time. He saluted. "I've been transferred. Assigned to this ship as of tonight."

The guard seemed curious, but not suspicious. "I didn't know we were getting any more men."

Kyellan grinned sheepishly at him. "Neither did I. Until tonight." He took a confidential tone. "Orders from the

High Lord Cosirin himself. I'm afraid I walked in on His Lordship at the wrong time. I had a message, but he was in no mood for interruptions. There was this girl . . ."

The guard groaned in sympathy. "You were in the High Lord's Guard? I'd give anything . . . they must have found that uniform for you pretty fast." He laughed. "Welcome to galley duty, Southerner. I hope your stay with us is a pleasant one. But I doubt it."

Kyellan said, with unfeigned reluctance, "I'm supposed to report to your Lord here, and tell him what happened. Can you show me where?"

"Sure," said the soldier. "I can be away from this post for a few minutes." He led Kyellan to the central cabin of the large galley and spoke to the equally bored-looking guard at its door. "This man needs to see His Lordship. What was your name, Sergeant?"

"Kylen," he said, giving a boyhood short-name. There was a remote chance the wizards had heard his name from one of the captives.

The door guard went inside and returned immediately. He beckoned Kyellan through the door. The wizard sat at a large, paper-strewn desk. He was middle-aged and rather chubby, with stringy white-blond hair. His yellow eyes gleamed with contempt.

"What is it?" he demanded. "Gawen said you've been assigned to me."

"Yes, Your Lordship," Kyellan said with downcast eyes, wishing he knew the wizard's name. "I was in the High Lord Cosirin's Guard, and I . . . saw something I shouldn't have. He sent me away."

The wizard frowned. "What could you have seen? Perhaps Cosirin with some handsome young soldier; his vice is not widely known." He looked measuringly at Kyellan and grinned like a shark. "Or you were one of his little harem and he tired of you. You're the type he favors."

Better and better. Kyellan wished he knew how to blush. He looked at his feet. The wizard chuckled. "Well. Now I have a man who has been privy to . . . shall we say . . . the High Lord's most intimate secrets? Such a man might be willing to tell me many things, for that knowledge not to become widespread aboard this ship. Eh?"

"I *have* heard conversations, seen reports and diagrams that might interest you, my lord," Kyellan said softly. "I could tell you much, if you promise not to tell the men." Apparently this wizard was not the best of friends with the High Lord Cosirin.

"Well?" said the wizard impatiently.

"I remember a map I saw once," Kyellan mused, "and the markings on it."

"Tell me! What did it say?"

"I'll have to show you. Do you have a map of Ryasa?"

The wizard searched his desk eagerly. Kyellan moved around beside him, amazed that the wizard did not seem to know his thoughts.

"There. Show me," said the wizard greedily.

Kyellan pointed to a spot with his left hand. "You see here, my lord, where the mountains of Ryasa come to a point—" And on that word, Kyellan drove his knife into the wizard's heart with his free right hand.

The yellow eyes filled with disbelief and pain. The wizard did not die quickly. "How could I not have known," he gasped, "that you came to kill me? Cosirin . . . he must have sent you . . . must have . . . must have . . . blocked . . . your . . . mind—" He crumpled into a heap on the desk.

Kyellan withdrew his knife and wiped the blood from it on the dead wizard's clothes. He felt no remorse over this killing. He sheathed the weapon and went out the door, closing it quickly behind him. He gave a huge sigh of relief. The two guards laughed.

The ship was drifting almost imperceptibly. One of the slaves must have cut the mooring rope. A yell came from the other side of the ship. Erlin had begun his attack. He smiled at the confused guards, drew his sword, and took their weapons before they knew what was happening

"Sorry, friends." He herded them into the wizard's cabin. They froze at the sight of the body. "Simple piracy. Stay here and don't do anything foolish, and you may keep your lives." He checked the closets and the desk, found a few more weapons, and confiscated them. A huge ring of keys on the wizard's belt caught his attention, and he took that as well. Then he left the cabin, locking the door from the outside.

The slaves moved in a tight, deadly, bristling circle around a massed group of brown-clad soldiers and sailors. Kyellan leaped up on a pile of crates and shouted, "Lay down your weapons and you won't be harmed."

The slaves were incredulous. "They must die!" some shouted. "Kill them!"

Kyellan called, "No! They were spell-bound. They didn't know what they were doing." The slaves ignored him, circling the wizards' men, brandishing their smuggled weapons.

Senach stepped in front of the enemy soldiers, tall and imposing even in his slave rags. "We're headed for Altimar," he yelled cheerfully to the slaves. "Who will row if we kill them?"

His statement was met with laughter and scattered cheers. The enemy soldiers finally laid down their weapons. Kyellan found the two men who had been overseers for the upper two decks of slaves, who were still chained to their oars.

He took their keys and sent several of the freed men to unlock the rest.

Finally, the captives who had been in his command emerged from one of the deck hatches, stumbling a little. They had been beaten, but they were smiling.

"Where is Lord Firelh?" Erlin asked them when the hillman did not follow.

"I don't know," said a grey-faced city man. "We've not seen him since our capture."

"He was alive then," said a youth.

Kyellan moved to the sullen group of prisoners. "Does anyone know of a man called Firelh? A large man, older than the rest who were captured at Dallynd?"

One stepped forward. "I'm the ship's master, young man," he said. "I don't know if such a man is aboard, but the first deck cabin has been locked and guarded for several days. No one was allowed inside but Lord Magorn."

"Who has the key?"

"The Lord himself."

Kyellan headed for the cabin with the large ring of keys he had taken from the wizard. He tried them one by one, until at last the door opened. Firelh rose from a bunk, grinning like a great bear.

"I should have known who was making all that noise," he said.

The cabin was small but looked confortable. "They seem to have treated you well, my lord," Kyellan said in a slightly accusing tone.

"Have you ever been questioned by a wizard? No? Well, we won't speak of it. They didn't hurt me. They were going to take me to their Emperor, whose name I have forgotten."

"Belaric?" Kyellan recalled Gwydion saying the name.

"That's it." Firelh clapped him on the shoulders, almost knocking him down. "It's good to see you, boy! We all thought you were dead. But you're just a little skinnier. Where's that youngster who was with you on the docks?"

"Erlin's here."

Firelh strode out into the darkness beside Kyellan. "Now that you have a ship, what are you going to do with it?"

"We're going to Altimar." Kyellan smiled wearily. "I think they'll be glad to see us."

Chapter Fourteen

It was a cold morning in Narkham, the crowded, sprawling camp that had been a tiny fishing village a few short weeks before. Briana walked quickly across the yard of the makeshift command building, clutching her cloak around her against the clinging mist, thankful to the Altimari child who had summoned her. The First Priestess had been ill during the crossing from Dallynd and had not been allowed visitors for three days since; this morning would be the first time Briana had seen her in a week.

Sentries opened their ranks for her, bowing and saluting with the almost comic respect they had been showing since she had killed the wizard in Dallynd harbor. The young priestess smiled at them with an effort, not at all sure that what she had done would prompt even approval from the First Priestess. It had been the work of Rahshaiya. Necessary, perhaps, but not praiseworthy.

A mourning-clad Dallyndi woman sat in the entrance to the hospital tent. She rose with clumsy haste and curtsied, holding her coarse black skirts wide. Briana made a Sign of the Goddess for the woman, reflecting that piety had been no help to the husband, brother, son, or all three, that prompted such grief.

"I was called for the First Priestess," she said gently, waving the Dallyndi back to her seat. "May I see her?"

"Of course." The woman clapped her hands, and a burn-scarred Ryasan child appeared from the inner ward of the converted market that was the hospital. "Shael, please take this lady to the First Priestess."

Briana went with the child. The girl was perhaps ten years old, her dark brown face pitted down the left side with shiny yellow scars that pulled her features into a contorted half frown. The First Priestess had a section of the tent curtained off for her alone; doubtless the doing of the woman at the door.

"I'll be back in ten minutes," said the young girl. "Carys says she is very weak."

"Thank you," Briana said as Shael hurried away. She pulled aside the flap of cloth and entered the tiny, dimly lit room.

"Good morning," said the First Priestess from her pillow. Her voice was barely audible. The spidery lines on her face had sunk into deep hollows. The Power in her seemed to mist around the bed like curling steam, no longer able to be contained in the shrinking body.

Mastering her shock, Briana answered. "I am told . . . you are recovering, Mother."

The old woman laughed, a wheezing, painful sound. "No. Do not humor me, child. I am not recovering at all. Still, I am glad to see you. I know you have been wishing to speak to me."

Briana sat on the edge of the bed, a plump and cushioned thing that must have come from the richest house of the village. "You won't be surprised at what I'm going to say. There have been too many delays in the formation of the army. I think we should leave for Caerlin now. Whether they will go with us or not." The First Priestess was silent. "Time grows short! We must find the Seat before the wizards do."

"You are too impatient." The First Priestess spoke softly, but her rebuke was like a lash across Briana's face. "A council has been called for this afternoon, in which I expect a date will be set for the armies' departure. We shall attend the council. If the date is too far, I may reconsider."

Briana bowed her head. "Yes, Mother. I am sorry."

"I did not mean to be harsh with you, child," the old woman said with a slow smile that revealed her long teeth. "You have done well. I do not think I would have dared to battle that wizard even when I was young."

"I called on Rahshaiya." Briana's voice shook.

"Yes. You were disobedient. But I think you were right. If you had not done so, you would be dead, and we would not be safely in Altimar. You will be a worthy successor, when I am Called."

"Successor? To you?" Briana was horrified.

"Surely you must know I have favored you for it."

Briana stood abruptly and turned away, unable to face the sharp falcon's eyes in their wrinkled sockets. "I am unworthy."

"The Goddess will need your strength, your courage. You have Her favor."

"No. . . ." It was a formless sound. "I am unworthy. Didn't you know? Didn't you suspect?" Briana turned back to the First Priestess and said firmly, "I have broken the Goddess's laws."

"You refer to young Kyellan?"

She nodded, her throat catching so she dared not speak.

"We cannot see the Goddess's footsteps on the earth," the old woman quoted. "It was Her will that guided you, child. Think on this: The Goddess is three. Maiden, Mother, and Crone."

"Yes, I know. You have taught me."

"Meditate on it. Perhaps an understanding will come. I cannot explain more fully now." Her hand, which had been gesturing weakly, fell back to the bedclothes, and her breathing grew still more shallow.

"Mother?" Briana bent close, alarmed. "Do you have the strength to go to the council this afternoon? I fear it would be too much."

She nodded finally. A smile appeared, fainter than the glimmer of the Tarnsea from the Sanctuary's southern wall. "Well, if you are to succeed me—which is the Goddess's will—you must learn to make decisions. Go in my place, and decide what we will do. You will make the right choice."

"Lady? Priestess?" The child Shael peered through the opening in the curtains. "Carys says you must leave now."

"A moment," Briana said desperately.

"Trust yourself." The voice was dim. "Decide for us."

The young priestess nodded and bent to kiss the ancient face.

"And do not despair," whispered the old woman inches from her ear, "of the return of your Captain Kyellan. He is a resourceful young man. Good day."

"Good . . . good day, Priestess," Briana stammered, turning to follow the scarred girl with a flustered half bow. She barely acknowledged the deep obeisance of the woman Carys at the hospital entrance or the salutes of the sentries. Her mind in turmoil, she needed to retreat to the tiny room she shared with Pima in the house of a village elder, to sit and think with the Goddess's Flame burning.

Tobas stood apart from the other dock guards to read the note that a messenger had brought. "From a lady," the child had said, and waited now to take his reply.

The note bore Valahtia's small, round script. "My friend," it began. "They said you were back in the village for the council, from training your battalion in the woods. I beg you come talk to me this afternoon after the meeting, if you cannot before. They have me cloistered with the other royalty here until I am ready to die of boredom. One in particular, the Crown Prince of Keris, has been pestering me so that I shall have to be very rude to him very soon if you do not stop me. Yours in desperation, Valahtia."

Tobas grinned, amused by her plight, and turned to the message boy. "Tell her I'll come." The lad scampered away. Tobas crumpled the note and put it in his belt pouch.

"Sir, there's a disturbance in the harbor," said one of his men abruptly.

Thoughts of the Princess left his mind as he ran with his patrol to the end of the long docks. Two Dallyndi ships could dimly be seen at the far mouth of the bay, escorting a hulking vessel.

"They think we're wizards' men," Erlin whispered above the hush that had fallen over the galley at the appearance of the two sailing ships that turned to flank them.

"At least this must be the right place," Kyellan answered. The island was dark with forest and rock, a wild, primeval land, and it had been a long afternoon and night of sailing up and down its coast before he'd found this small opening between cliffs. He still could not see the land across the bay for the mist, but he was certain it was the resistance camp.

"We'll take it slow and careful." Firelh, taking his turn at the helm, guided the galley between its two shadows. The rhythm of the oars, wielded now by the ex-slaves since the wizards' crew had dropped with exhaustion, became a soft lapping in the gentle current. Soon the pier was in view. It was crowded with row upon row of assorted ships, moored to each other in thick clusters. The shadowing vessels herded the galley to the far end of the pier. The ex-slaves went through their well-remembered docking cadence, and on the pier a group of soldiers clad in black and red supervised a mooring crew.

"Let's go." Kyellan helped Firelh secure the wheel as the anchor was winched into the water. With Erlin, they disembarked as the galley's gangplank lowered before them. Ranks of uniformed soldiers closed in. Kyellan did not blame them for their suspicion; all three men, like all aboard the ship, were filthy and unshaven and half-starved from the crossing. No one spoke.

"I have prisoners aboard the ship," he finally ventured. "Wizards' men. You'll need to move them somewhere more secure."

"You're in command?" said a Parahnese youth with evident scorn.

"Captain Kyellan of Caerlin's Royal Guard," he snapped.

"What did he say?" a familiar voice called through the ranks.

"My lord, he claims to be from Caerlin," said the Parahnese.

"Ky?" It was Tobas, shoving his way roughly through his men. "Is that you?" Apparently satisfied that it was, he ran to him and embraced him with enough strength to almost knock him from the pier.

Kyellan grinned like a crazy man, dizzy with relief and the roughness of his friend's clasp. Firelh patted Tobas amiably on the shoulder and pulled him away.

"Careful, lad. You'll take the breath from him."

The other soldiers began to relax. Tobas told them to

take care of the rest of the men on the ship while he took his friends to the command center.

"I'd given up on you," he said softly, propelling Kyellan from the docks with an arm around his shoulder, while Firelh and Erlin walked behind.

"You should have known I'd make it. I never doubted it."

"I didn't have your confidence in yourself," Tobas said. "Besides, we didn't know if you were even alive. The priestesses tried to find out, and Gwydion and Chela, but they couldn't tell."

"Well, here I am. I hope you're taking us to some food."

Tobas laughed. "You look like you could use a couple of meals. We've done a lot of hunting here. The food's good."

A farmer's wagon stood at the end of the village street. Tobas commandeered it, promising the boy watching the horses that it would be returned soon.

"What is this place, anyway?" Kyellan asked, trying to get his exhausted body to sit up straight on the driver's box.

"Narkham, they call it. You won't believe the size of the army, Ky. We may have a chance. I'm in command of a battalion on maneuvers, but I was called in for the council this afternoon, and they put me on the dock guards meanwhile."

"Did the rest make it here?" he said hesitantly.

Tobas nodded. "You'll see some of them at the council. I'm taking you, though you weren't invited. They'll sure be glad to see Firelh."

"Without my army, I'll be less welcome," muttered the hill lord.

Kyellan's attention was arrested by a slight figure on

horseback, who clattered up and down the narrow street past unsafe-looking shacks crowded with women and small children, tilting at straw effigies that had been hung from roof trees. Chickens scurried from the horse's hooves as it galloped in tight circles under flawless control. As he stared, the rider turned and met his eyes, and squealed in recognition.

"Chela!" Erlin called gladly.

She slowed her S'tari horse and vaulted from it into the wagon, hugging Kyellan violently and fighting back tears. The mount trotted beside them like a dog on leash.

"You don't look very good with a beard," she said at last, giggling. "I told them! I told them you wouldn't be dead." She turned to Erlin. "Pima will be glad."

"What were you doing?" Kyellan asked, indicating the swinging straw figure on the nearest shack.

She glared in Tobas's direction. "They won't let me train with the troops. So I have to do it by myself. They won't even let me use the training fields outside of town. But we're getting good, Yhanda and I." She smiled proudly at the horse, which pricked its ears and pranced as if in response.

"It's not that she's female," Tobas explained with a rueful grin. "There are a lot of Parahnese women who insisted on being allowed to fight. But she's too young."

"I'm fourteen, maybe fifteen, I forget," Chela said. "Boys that age fought at Dallynd."

"You're thirteen, according to the army doctor and the priestesses."

She tossed her head, releasing wisps of long red hair from their confines. "What do they know?" Moving to the edge of the wagon, she jumped into the saddle of her S'tari horse. "I'll tell everyone you're here!" She raced away.

Kyellan wondered if Briana would be pleased.

Bathed, shaved, and fed, Kyellan felt like himself for the first time in a long while. The black-and-red captain's uniform Tobas had brought him hung a little loosely, but the new Caer sword that curved at his side felt good. He would have to weight the pommel, though; it had been made for a smaller man.

"We'll get your hair cut later," Tobas said, surveying him critically. "After the council."

Kyellan grinned at himself in the mirror. His black hair curled now almost as much as his young friend's, lying thick around his collar. "We'd better," he said. "I don't want to look like Arel."

"Not a chance." Tobas suddenly looked stricken and dived into his belt pouch to bring out a crumpled piece of paper. "Valahtia! I forgot all about her."

"The Princess? How's she holding up?"

Tobas offered him the note. Kyellan read it and handed it back.

"I'll have to wait until after the council to rescue her." The younger man sighed. "It's time."

Kyellan followed him out into the sunny afternoon. They walked down the muddy streets to the command building, through corridors that still smelled of fish, and to the inner courtyard. The long table was half-full. Firelh was there, his beard combed and freshly braided, dressed in the finery of some local merchant, which bulged at the shoulders and hung in folds over the once mighty stomach that had shrunk during the week and more on the galley. Haval sat next to him. The Dallyndi's face had settled into deep lines which had not been there when Kyellan had seen him last.

Four other grim-looking older men occupied the chairs

near the upper end of the table. The head chair was empty, but at its right hand sat Briana. She glanced up at the newcomers, but when her eyes met Kyellan's she looked down again, with an expression that seemed to combine joy and horror. Kyellan stared at the top of her grey hood for a moment, then shrugged and greeted Haval.

"Good to see you, lad," said the Dallyndi. "Take a seat here with us."

Kyellan shook the man's proffered hand and did as he was told. Tobas sat farther down the table, among a group of younger officers.

"This is the Southerner you told me about, Firelh?" asked a stocky middle-aged warrior from across the table.

"Kyellan, General Orlandin of Hoab," Haval said warily.

The white-braided man looked like an islander. His face was crossed with knife scars. "I fought against these two back in the wars," he said expansively. "But we're against a common enemy now."

He had been a pirate, then. Kyellan liked him immediately.

"The others here are General Haram of Keris, General Maryse of Venerin, and General Diveshi of Parahn," Haval continued. "I think you'll be assigned to them, with the land-based forces."

"We'll arrange a promotion, of course," said the dry-voiced Maryse, a small, quick-looking man. "Though your King will have to make it final when this is over."

Kyellan allowed himself a wistful moment of pleasure but shook his head. "I've gone as far as I can in Caerlin, sir."

"They limit promotions for commoners, I've heard." Diveshi frowned at him. The Parahnese general was mahogany-skinned, and his black hair clustered in tight curls. "Uncommonly effective way of keeping the most able men at the bottom."

"The commander!" Haval whispered. "We'll be getting started."

A tall, fast-striding man with iron-grey hair that still showed traces of red took the head seat beside Briana. Gwydion followed him in and sat at his left. Now the table was full, but the canopied chairs that stood nearby were unoccupied.

"Where are the royalty, Halcira?" asked Orlandin.

The commander looked exasperated. "The servants wouldn't even let me into the house. Said they were having their own private council, and they'd join ours when they finished."

"Can we start without them?"

Halcira banged his fist on the table. "Why not? General Haram, you may begin."

The Kerisian general stood and cleared his throat. He was the oldest man present, his white hair thinning above a wrinkled face, but his body looked lean and hard. "The wizards' forces occupy every mainland Kingdom," he began bluntly. "The last of the rebellion in Parahn has been suppressed. Garith, Keris, and Ryasa seem well subdued; they are crowing their victory at Dallynd, but they suffered great losses. However, in Caerlin, they are having as much trouble with the S'tari as Chaeris had. Their rule extends only to the Maer Cunin in the north and the city of Erinon in the east. The holy city of Khymer is still free."

"No longer," Firelh interjected. "They were going to take me to Belaric, who has made Khymer his capital."

"They've conquered the S'tari?" Haram said in disbelief.

Firelh shook his head. "I don't think so. But they've driven them back."

"You began without us, Halcira?" A fat old man led the glittering group of royalty that entered then. Haval whispered their names to Kyellan: the speaker was the King of Garith, followed by his Queen, the widowed King Janorwyn of Ryasa and his son, the old Queen of Parahn, and the Crown Prince of Keris. Arel and Valahtia completed the array.

"Only the preliminaries, Your Majesty." Halcira bowed. The others at the table rose as the royalty sat themselves in the canopied chairs.

"We have a glad announcement to make," said Janorwyn, a spare, bony man with a hawk's face. He nodded to Arel, who stood with a broad smile and spoke in badly accented Ryasan, which had been designated the language of the conference.

"It gives me great pleasure to announce the engagement of my sister, Valahtia des Ardavan, to the Crown Prince Werlinen of Keris. A match that will benefit all the Kingdoms."

"What?" Tobas half rose from down the table, but an officer beside him pulled him back with a restraining hand. Kyellan saw the look that passed between his friend and Valahtia. The Princess looked like a trapped wildcat, at least in her eyes. Her face was fixed in a strained smile. The Kerisian Prince took her hand and stood with her, beaming; he was perhaps thirty-five, a soft, chubby man with curly brown hair and a pale face. There was polite applause from the assembly. Neither Kyellan nor Tobas joined in.

"We congratulate you," Halcira said, "but if you'll be seated, Your Highnesses, we will continue this council."

"Of course," Werlinen said, pulling Valahtia into the seat beside him. She landed with an ungraceful thump.

Kyellan glared at Arel, who gave him a look of pure hatred. The Prince had no right to betroth his sister. Unless, as was likely, their father was dead and Arel was now as good as King. Even so, he should have considered her wishes.

Haram rose again and continued his report. "Even if Khymer is taken, much of Caerlin is still held by the S'tari. Our decision is to retake that Kingdom, with the help of the desert tribes, as the first action of this army. We hope to occupy the island Syryn as a base of operations. That must be a naval maneuver. I call on my colleague, Orlandin of Hoab."

The ex-pirate stood. He was not a tall man, but he had the presence of one, and his shoulders were as broad as Firelh's. "Before we discuss the Syryn offensive, I'll report on the island Kingdoms. The only representative of the wizards on Altimar is the creature in the harbor of Keor, and our wizard here is working on that. Hoab has been raided, and I think it will fall within the week. Venerin went quickly, eh, Maryse?"

The slight, dark general sighed. "Venerin is a land of peaceful farmers. We've not found it necessary to keep a standing army since the Hoabi stopped raiding, if you'll excuse my saying so, Orlandin."

"Ancient history, friend Maryse. To continue: Barelin was the first to fall, and is not present at this council. I'm told there has always been a colony of wizards in Barena. Takar, they hold with a token force; it will be a good preliminary base, I think. Syryn itself is heavily fortified and full of troops. Some time will be required to take it. And there's always the danger the wizards may send reinforcements from Cavernon. Still, nothing in such a venture is ever sure, eh? We've a good chance, I think."

"Thank you," Halcira said soberly. "That is our situation, my friends. It will be difficult, but we must move before the wizards are secure enough to send a force to Altimar. We'll begin the evacuation of the first fleet within seven days, to take Takar. Meanwhile, we'll be moving the civilians overland to Keor. It's more defensible, and far more comfortable than Narkham. Gwydion will leave tonight, and the monster will be dead by the time we get there.''

Briana cut in. ''If you will take Takar in a week, how long until the army can reach Caerlin?''

''Assuming another week to occupy Syryn and set up a base there''—Halcira frowned—''and time enough to ally with the S'tari . . . perhaps three weeks from today, Priestess.''

''It is too long.''

Halcira sighed but said respectfully, ''We cannot shorten the time, Priestess, and be sure of success.''

''If you lengthen the time, you'll be sure of failure!'' she flared. ''The wizards will find the Goddess's Seat, and our cause will be lost.''

''I have heard you speak of this Goddess's Seat before. What is it?''

''The Focus of Power,'' she said hesitantly. ''An amplifier, but also a Power in itself.''

''Couldn't it defend itself against attack?'' Gwydion suggested. ''Only allow itself to be used in the service of your Goddess?''

''No. The Seat is a tool, a thing of the earth, that channels and strengthens Power. . . . Who wields that Power does not matter. We believe that if the Seat is used for an evil purpose, the user will eventually destroy himself, but before that happens he could do great harm.''

''Enough to threaten an army of this size?'' Halcira was skeptical.

''Yes. Enough to reduce us all to dust, or turn us into willing servants of the wizards. We must find it before they do!''

"What do you suggest?"

"I cannot wait until you have captured Syryn and made an alliance with the S'tari, if that is even possible. I must go to Caerlin now. I would like your help, but I will go without it if need be."

Halcira sat back heavily and looked at her, reading the determination in her young face. "Very well. You have a ship and men."

"Only a few men, besides the ship's crew. Secrecy will be vital. And no one must go against his will. Five will be enough, I think." She began to sound more cheerful. "We'll go with Gwydion to Keor, and help him destroy the monster, then leave on one of the smaller sailing ships."

"I won't need any help." Gwydion grinned. "But you're welcome to be there. You can see how it's done." More seriously, he added, "I wish I could go to Caerlin with you, but I'm needed here."

"He certainly is." Halcira frowned, looking out over the table. "And I don't want any of my officers volunteering for this mission. Every man here has an important role in the army."

"I don't," Kyellan said quietly, not looking at Briana. "I'll go. There's no real need for me here. I know the country . . . I think I could be helpful to you."

He looked up. Briana's eyes met his for a moment. She smiled a little. "I hoped you would say that," she admitted. "Gwydion's ship leaves for Keor an hour before sunset tonight, at the fifteenth pier. Perhaps your Lieutenant Erlin could come, too, if he hasn't yet been assigned."

Kyellan nodded. He wished he could take Tobas, but he doubted it after Halcira's statement. Ideally, the other volunteers should be Caer, but he did not think there were any others from his country in the resistance army.

"If no one else has anything to say," Halcira said sourly, "we will adjourn. You will all receive individual orders tomorrow."

Tobas was one of the first to rise, and he hurried around the table toward the royalty. Kyellan intercepted him. "Where are you going?"

"I have to talk to her," he muttered. Valahtia was being pulled away by Werlinen and Arel. She glanced back once, her expression unreadable, then she was gone.

Kyellan started in the same direction, his hand secure on Tobas's shoulders to keep the younger man from running. "Wasn't the Crown Prince of Keris the one she mentioned in her note? The one who's been 'pestering' her?"

"Yes. She can't have given consent. We have to do something!"

Beginning to agree, Kyellan moved faster. "Maybe they'll let us in to talk to her. We can say we want to offer congratulations or something."

But Arel was the one who answered the door at the merchant's house that had become royal quarters in Narkham. "She will not see you," he said simply, and started to shut the door again.

Kyellan caught his arm roughly. "We want to hear that from her."

Arel shook his head. "A woman who is to be Queen of Keris will not welcome common soldiers into her house."

"I am the son of the Earl of Laenar," Tobas began, but the Prince had pulled away from Kyellan's grasp and shut the door firmly. They heard a bolt draw on the inside.

Kyellan shrugged and stepped back, but he stopped short at the stricken expression on his friend's face. Taking him gently, he walked Tobas back into the street. "You really care for her, don't you?"

"I'm beginning to, yes," he said defensively.

"She can take care of herself. She won't let them marry her off to someone like that."

"Do you really think so?"

Kyellan looked him straight in the eye, put on his most sincere and convincing expression, and lied.

Chapter Fifteen

The slim, torchlit prow of the ship cut through the dark,
choppy water, sailing before a strong wind along the rough
cliff walls of the southern edge of Altimar. The wind was
chill and damp under sullen clouds. Kyellan, feeling as
uneasy and restless as the sea, made apologies to the
cheerful group drinking in the captain's cabin. He went
forward across the sea-sprayed deck, through the long,
ominous shadows cast by the ship's torches, wishing there
were stars.

He and Erlin had made it to the docks just as the ship
was ready to disembark. Three Ryasan volunteers had
joined them, and they had helped some of the ship's small
crew to hoist the frail First Priestess over the side in a
woven chair. The two novices and Briana had immediately
taken the old woman to the deck cabin they would share.
Kyellan had not seen Gwydion or Chela; he assumed they
were on board, probably in the small mate's cabin amidships.

The steps to the forecastle were slippery and wet, and he
had climbed halfway up when he stopped in surprise.
Briana sat there on the rough planks of the crew's bench,
shivering in the cold. She did not notice him. Her gaze
seemed intent on the dark expanse of water in the ship's
path. Her face was shadowed and secret, surrounded by
torchlit red hair like cascading fire that blew free in the

wind. He had never seen her hair unbound. It was unbearably beautiful.

He went up the last few steps and took off his cloak and laid it around her shoulders. Briana looked up, startled, but relaxed when she saw who it was. She pulled the cloak around her tightly against the night chill and smiled faintly.

Kyellan sat beside her, not too close, and said softly, "It's a cold night to be out."

"I couldn't sleep." She stared at the black sea beyond the railing. "I couldn't stay in the cabin. I heard a call . . . very faint, far away, but I think it was the Seat of the Goddess. We have so little time."

"I wish I understood what this thing is that you're searching for," he said. "And I wish I believed it would make a difference against the Kharad."

"You still don't believe in it? Or in the Goddess?"

"I don't think so."

She turned on him. "Then why are you coming? You must think what we're doing is useless."

Because I want to see how your hair will look with the sun of Cavernon shining on it, he wanted to say. Instead, he shrugged. "I had nothing to do in Altimar." Then, more truthfully, "Why? Because you're going to need me there."

"No," she whispered. "No, I won't . . . we won't . . . need you. We don't need anyone. But they wouldn't have let us go by ourselves."

"Briana," he began, then corrected himself. "Priestess, I've been wanting to talk to you. About what happened in Dallynd . . ."

She rose suddenly, turning to descend the stairs. He could not let her go like that. Leaping up, he caught her arm and held her. "Listen to me. Please."

"Let go." Her voice was stiff with rage.

"Don't you trust me? How do you expect us to survive this journey, which is going to take all the skill both of us have just to stay alive, if we don't trust each other?" His anger was building, but he released her and turned to the railing.

"It isn't you," she said painfully. "It is myself. I don't trust myself."

"I don't understand."

"I think you do. Must I say it? I . . . feel something for you . . . that I should not feel. I cannot allow that feeling to continue."

"So you pretend it doesn't exist. Does that make it disappear?"

"No." She avoided his probing gaze. "But it is the only choice. You can see that as well as I." Shivering, she looked up at the sky. "What a cold night. No stars."

"No moon, either. Your Goddess isn't watching."

"The moon isn't the Goddess," Briana said uneasily. "It's only a symbol we use to represent Her Power."

Kyellan sighed. "Briana . . . if you'd rather I didn't go with you, I could stay with Gwydion in Keor. Erlin knows the country well enough."

"No. Of course you must go with us." She shrugged out of his cloak and handed it back. "As . . . as a protector, and as a friend. There is no law of the Order against friendship."

He nodded finally. "You'd better get to bed, Priestess. Good night."

"Good night." She descended the steps to the deck. He watched her go. It was not fair. Why did it have to be her? He could have chosen any other woman and had her at his side forever. Why was this priestess the only one he had ever felt that way about? And why had he not been able to

say it, straight to her, *Briana, I love you?* It was a simple
phrase.

Across the deck, a dim torchlit face turned toward him
briefly, but then he heard the door open to the priestesses'
cabin. Kyellan wrapped his cloak back around, suddenly
realizing he was cold. He stayed in the bow for a long
time, leaning over the railing, watching the black, forest-
clad banks of Altimar glide past in the night.

Gwydion had barely enough room in his tiny cabin for a
cot, but he was grateful for the privacy. He did not want
the others to guess the doubts that assailed him. He feared
the next morning's work. The monster in the harbor of
Keor was not a creature of the earth. It had been created
by wizards who were Gwydion's masters in learning and
experience. He had been reviewing his memory for the
ancient books in the library at Akesh that spoke of such
creations; he could not find a method of destroying one.
The accounts did not even describe how to create them.
They told of wizards' encounters with them or said such
helpful things as "Then through his incantations the great
Hoab Wizard brought forth a creature the like of which is
not found in this realm."

Gwydion gazed at the dark walls of his cramped cell.
He began to sense the presence of the being in the waters
of the distant harbor. And his trained mind rebelled against
its own perceptions. Everything he knew about the laws of
Nature and magic told him that only illusion was possible
in creating a "living" thing. Illusions could be made real
enough for all practical purposes, especially with the help
of demonic forces. But this creature did not feel like an
illusion. It had a mind, small and dim, but clouded with
pervading evil.

Gwydion felt the beginnings of real fear. He had assumed the monster was a creation of the wizards who had sent him from Akesh. Now everything told him it was not. Could they have called something from the depths of the Western Ocean, where no ship had explored? Or was this a being from the Otherworld that even the most powerful wizards barely began to understand?

Gwydion tried to calm himself. The law of summoning stated, "By definition, no wizard may summon from that World a thing which he cannot control. In the summoning is control." If this creature was indeed from the Otherworld, the wizards who called it must have been able to handle it. He should be able to do the same.

There was a knock at the door, jolting him as it broke his contact with the harbor creature. He took a sip from the jug of Venerin wine on the floor, banishing his fears, before he answered.

It was Kyellan, who looked windblown and tired. "Come on in," Gwydion said, glad of the interruption.

"I was thinking about that thing in the harbor," Kyellan began. Gwydion sighed. "Couldn't we use the ship's catapults on it? They work on warships, and a sea monster can't be much tougher."

"That would make my job a lot easier. But this thing is going to be even more difficult than I thought. I don't think the wizards made that creature."

"Where else could it have come from?"

"The Otherworld. They called it. Maybe." He took another drink of wine and offered Kyellan the jug. "If that's the case, I don't know what to do with it. Banish it, I suppose, but I don't know if I have the Power."

"With Chela's help, you should. Where is she, anyway?"

"Back at the camp." Gwydion sighed. "I tricked her. I

told her the wrong time of departure, and blocked myself from her. She'll be furious.''

''Why?''

''This is too dangerous. I don't know what I'm doing. I just wished they'd held off the Kharad for a few more years, so I could have learned more. It had been waiting for a thousand years. Two more wouldn't have made any difference.''

''Maybe they didn't want you to be ready,'' Kyellan suggested. ''Maybe they started it now so you wouldn't be able to oppose them as well.''

Gwydion laughed softly, wondering if it could be true. They would have known from his first few years that he would not join them in a Kharad against the people who had raised him. They would have known that he saw them merely as teachers, not as members of a race to which he owed any loyalty. And if they had not lied, he *was* the best apprentice to come through their school in a long time. They would not have wanted him opposing them with mature, well-educated Power.

''Do you think I'm right?'' Kyellan smiled.

''I think it's possible.'' Gwydion finished the wine, draining the last bitter dregs, wishing it affected him more. Liquor seemed to produce only clearer thought in wizards; he would have liked to be, for once, disgustingly, staggeringly drunk, so he would not have to think at all. He would even welcome a hangover. It could not be as bad as the backlash of this spell would be, if he succeeded in killing the monster. It would lay him flat for days.

Kyellan was yawning, the wine taking effect. ''I'd better go to bed,'' he said. ''Good night, wizard. And good luck tomorrow.''

Gwydion rose and saw him out, then began the tedious

process of composing his mind for brief, deep sleep while not losing the edge of nervousness that would enable him to fight in the morning.

Briana could not sleep at all. She, too, was beginning to feel the evil, mindless presence of the harbor creature, and it set her skin acrawl. Though she could block her mind against that feeling, she could not block her memory of the scene that night with Kyellan. It had been stupid of her to even talk with him. She should have known she would give herself away. Now he knew how she felt, when it was more important than ever not to feel that way. She had as much as told him she loved him.

Her mind echoed with the thought she had heard. *Briana, I love you.* Was it wishful thinking on her part, or a hallucination? Or had Kyellan communicated with her mind to mind? If the last was true, then he did have Power, as she had long suspected from the strength of his mental shields. He did not seem aware of it. A man of his race should not have it, unless he was born a wizard; perhaps, she thought with a humorless laugh, Gemon was right and Kyellan was the Shape-Changer and their enemy.

"Go to sleep, child," said the wraith-thin First Priestess at her side. "Your strength may be needed on the morrow."

Obediently, Briana tried her best to clear her mind. Perhaps she did sleep a little, open-eyed, but the night seemed to last far longer than the hours between sunset and dawn.

The ship was anchored less than half a mile from the mouth of the harbor when Gwydion woke the next morning. He forced himself to go through the rituals that instilled utter confidence in himself, killing all his doubts and fears and imprisoning them deep in his mind. Belief in his own Power would be the best defense against this creature, whose presence he could feel now as surely as if it was in his room. Concentrating intently, Gwydion finally convinced himself he could not lose. When that was achieved, he left his cabin, taking only an ash staff through which to focus his Power. No chemical potions or sympathetic magic would affect a creature from the Otherworld. He would rely on his own raw Power.

The ship's master refused to go any closer. Having anticipated this, Gwydion had brought along a small sailboat no bigger than one of the ship's lifeboats. It was lashed to the deck, and sailors were busy untying it. The man who had owned it claimed it was sturdy and easily handled, built for moderately rough seas. Gwydion hoped it would suffice.

Briana joined him quietly as the boat was being attached to a winch for lowering into the water. "I know enough of the ways of wizards," she said, "to know you're in a state where you won't admit you need help. But it would be foolish to pass up a source of extra Power. At least establish a light link with me. If you want the aid, I'll be there; if you don't I won't interfere. Agreed?"

His rational mind overrode his artificially strong ego, and he nodded. They clasped hands and opened their minds slightly to each other. It was done in a few seconds. The ship's master came forward, nervous and tugging on a forelock of thick pale hair. One of Orlandin's men, he was a gruff old renegade who bore an intense grudge against wizards.

"Yes, Captain?" Gwydion prompted irritably.

"Look, wizard . . . I know what you're doing is important," the Hoabi said. "But I've got my orders. I'll see the priestesses are safe."

"So if anything happens to me or my boat, you won't come to the rescue? I don't expect you to."

"Well, the Goddess go with you," said the shipman hesitantly. "I don't know if you believe in Her, though . . . or if She'd go with you in any case. . . ." He made a hasty retreat, leaving Gwydion highly amused.

"You're sure you won't let me come?" Kyellan asked as he took a place with the sailors on the winch. "Won't you even take a weapon? You left your sword in your cabin."

Gwydion only grinned, climbing into the swinging boat and holding on to the mast for balance. The winch was rusty and squeaked as Kyellan turned it. The small craft lowered jerkily down the side of the hull, clattering against the ship, until it reached the sea. Gwydion unhooked it from the chains, paddled it away from the larger vessel, and raised its single sail. It caught the wind eagerly, as if it knew his own impatience, and moved toward the harbor mouth.

Something was wrong. Briana felt it like a cold breath as she entered the priestesses' cabin. The others had not gone to see the wizard off, and with her mind busy linking with Gwydion, she had not noticed. The First Priestess lay prone on her cot, her skin ashen, transparent, her eyes sunken and closed. A heavy mist filled the small room. Pima and Gemon were huddled beside the old woman, terrified.

"No . . ." Briana breathed. She could not be dying. Not yet. Please, Goddess, not yet.

The First Priestess beckoned weakly. "Briana."

"Do not speak," the young woman admonished. "Save your strength." She sat on the edge of the bunk.

"I must. I must tell you now, with Death so close. I can feel it near, in this room. Do you not feel it?"

"No. We have not found the Goddess's Seat. You told me you would live until we did."

"The Goddess does not always do as we expect, child. Come close to me and listen. The Goddess . . ." Her voice trailed off into a fit of coughing.

Briana felt tears beginning. "She will sustain you until we fulfill our quest. What you feel is only illness. It is not death."

"The Goddess . . . is three. You and the others serve the Maiden, and only the Maiden, for that is your condition. The First Priestess alone may serve the Mother. You, too, must serve Cianya before you become First Priestess."

"Do not tell me," Briana hissed. "You are not dying. It is not time for me to know."

"Open your mind for a moment. You will sense it. Death is here."

Briana fought back her tears and did as she was told. There was, indeed, a presence in the cabin. She shuddered as it noticed her. Dark. Dark and evil, but not Death. She clung to the knowledge like a lifeline. Death was not evil. Only inevitable, peaceful, a gentle calling. Not something that attacked. Oh, Goddess . . .

The Dark thing closed in on her mind, and with her shields down she could not resist it. Horror filled her, Darkness like the caved-in shaft of a mine, despair, the surety of death. She heard herself screaming Kyellan's name, over and over, and fragmentary prayers in the Old Tongue, yet it was like another voice, far away, one she could not control or stop. Her eyes were open, and the others in the room were fear-tinged shadows, featureless and helpless to save her. "Kyellan!" she screamed, feeling her hoarse voice tear at her throat like the Dark thing

was tearing at her mind. She felt her link with Gwydion
lifted by the roots, like a plucked flower, taken from her
into the Darkness.

Then a bright figure rushed into the mist-filled cabin
with a drawn sword. Her screaming was wordless now.
The brightness moved to her and shook her shoulders hard,
and slapped her face, and the Dark thing left. It was gone.
The mists faded, and she filled with outrage at the indig-
nity of the slap, before she collapsed into Kyellan's arms.
Her sobs were painful in her sore throat. She could not
speak. She held on to the Guardsman, not caring what the
others would think.

"That was not Death," she heard the First Priestess say
weakly. "I cannot believe I was so deceived. Truly, my
skill is waning. But what a powerful force, to almost
convince me to die!"

"Briana, are you all right?" Kyellan asked, his voice
shaken.

She nodded, regaining her composure, and allowed him
to lift her to her feet. "I . . . I think so." Leaning on him,
she moved to her cot and sat heavily. "Mother . . . I think
I've met that force once before. In the battle at Dallynd,
when two gates were taken at once, something helped the
wizards and was suddenly gone. Something that powerful."

"I fear it may have been the Shape-Changer," the First
Priestess said. "If a foe that strong finds the Goddess's
Seat, all will be lost. But what of you, Guardsman? It was
when you touched Briana that the thing left her. I believe
you do have Power."

"There has to be another explanation," he said. "If
you're all right, Priestess, I'll go back on deck; I have a
feeling Gwydion may need help." He picked up the sword
he had dropped and hurried out of the cabin.

*   *   *

Traces of the creature were all around; the destruction on the hillsides, the abandoned ships in the port, and most of all the lingering feel of the thing's unintelligent but evil mind. Gwydion could not find it, though. He tried to take Power from his link with Briana but found it severed. That was strange. She had been the one who had insisted on the link.

The morning sun was hot, and a sickly, alien smell seemed to rise with the heat from the calm waters of the bay. Gwydion furled his sail to halt the small boat. Perhaps he could call the creature to him. He sent out a beacon, challenging it with his mind. *Come and fight, coward. At last you have a foe worthy of your strength.* He touched the end of his ash staff to the water, channeling the call through it. The end of the staff was slimy with green stuff when he pulled it back out. It stank. This was a loathsome place, Gwydion thought.

The city of Keor was not large by comparison with Dallynd or Chelm. Its high wall was stained and bowed in a few places, as if by the efforts of a sea-wet ram. The ships moored at the docks were battered and crushed, with fallen masts and great holes through their hulls. Mounds of flotsam were wedged under the piers; enough timber to construct several more ships, if it was not bent and twisted and splintered.

Gwydion turned suddenly as the presence of the creature entered his awareness. The waters roiled in the narrow mouth of the harbor like the wake left by a whale, but wider and faster. It must have been confident enough in its hold on the town to forage in the open sea. Gwydion shivered, feeling his confidence slipping a little at the apparent size of his opponent. His tiny boat rocked in the center of the bay as the thing bore down on him with the speed of twenty racehorses. He clung to the mast with one hand, fearing the boat would capsize before he could engage the battle.

The roiling of the water stopped, however, fifty yards away, and a great head broke the surface. It was a being from nightmare. The space between its gaping jaws was the height of two grown men, studded with teeth like moat spikes. Its colors shifted from green to purple to crimson. The huge head was set on a neck that rose out of the water to the height of a city tower. Its long, sinuous body floated slowly to the surface behind it, stretching from the center of the harbor almost to its edge.

Truly, this was a creature of the Otherworld, related to the demons Gwydion had encountered; of less intelligence, but with the same magnitude of evil. Its malevolent Power compelled his eyes, willing him to be insensible prey. Gwydion belatedly threw his staff before him as a shield from the brilliance of the many-faceted, hypnotic gaze. He poured his Power into the staff until it crackled visibly and stung his hand like captured lightning. Power not to destroy, but to send the monster back where it belonged.

The horrible head drew back, and the creature bellowed defiance. It was not an animal sound. It was more like the shearing off of a mountain in avalanche. Gwydion held up the glowing staff, chanted a short focusing spell, and began to say the slow Words of Power that would banish his opponent. The creature screamed, such a terrible sound that Gwydion wanted desperately to drop his staff and clasp his hands over his ears. The creature's small mind possessed some defenses, but its shields were not strong enough to sustain it. Its obscene form began to shimmer and fade under Gwydion's steady attack.

The wizard grinned in triumph and repeated his spell.

Wouldn't Chela be proud! Why had he feared this encounter so? It was no harder than controlling his little healing demon.

Suddenly a huge hand seemed to shove against Gwydion's chest, and he was thrown flat on his back. His head smashed against the low railing of the sailboat, and his staff was knocked from his hand. Crimson stars danced before his eyes. He rolled half-blind across the narrow deck to grasp the staff before it was lost to the water. The earth-shaking roar of the creature sounded again, as strong and substantial as before; it had come back. And it was being protected by something else. A wall of Power. A force of incredible strength that had negated Gwydion's strongest spell.

The young wizard staggered to his feet, clutching his staff with both hands. The monster regarded him from its immense height, safe behind an invisible wall. Gwydion probed the new defenses; there was no way to get through. He felt like a child beside this Power. If only he was still linked with Briana! Fear rose in him, eroding his Power as he fought to regain his confidence. He tried to channel all his energy into the fading staff. Perhaps if he could actually touch the monster with the staff, he could banish it despite its protector. Whoever or whatever was protecting it.

His muscles were leaden and unresponsive as he tried to raise the sail to catch the sluggish wind. Slowly, the boat began to move toward the creature. Its wall of protection was not physical; Gwydion could smell the nauseating, decayed odor of the creature, and he was very near before the strange force realized what he was doing. The creature suddenly stiffened, a keen light of intelligence in its eyes. To Gwydion's dismay, it arched its neck and plunged deep into the bay.

Waves swelled and broke over the sailboat. Gwydion knew what would happen and could not prevent it. The gargantuan head came up beneath his tiny boat and threw it out of the water to an immense height, catching it in its jaws. Gwydion fell into its mouth. Spars and timbers cracked around him. His eyes and nostrils burned with the stench, and he could feel the acid on the monstrous tongue eating through his clothes. The creature roared, and Gwydion rolled out of the mouth between gnashing spikes. He fell along with pieces of the splintered boat, and as he fell he threw his staff with all his strength back into the monster's mouth. If he had given the staff enough Power . . .

A section of keel landed on him as he hit the water, knocking him insensible, just as the creature blurred and disappeared.

Kyellan paced the wheel deck, ignoring the stream of invective hurled at him by the Hoabi ship's master. The man sat under the spears of the three Ryasans in Kyellan's command. Briana was screaming at them to go faster. The helmsman piloted the ship through the harbor's mouth, under Erlin's watchful guard, as a few sailors added to the canvas. Most of the crew stood sullenly by. The Hoabi had refused to go to Gwydion's aid, even when Briana had insisted that the thing opposing him was the same that had attacked her in her cabin.

Now Briana broke into sobs. "I can't feel his presence anymore!"

His stomach tightening with fear, Kyellan ran forward to the forecastle. The harbor was coming into view between promontories of towering rock. There was no sign of the monster. If it had killed Gwydion, he thought, it would still be there. Unless it had dragged him below.

There was a dark spot in the center of the bay. As they approached, he saw that it was a mass of floating timber. The wreckage of the little craft?

"Lock the helm!" he shouted aft. "Drop anchor!"

Briana joined him in the bow, straining to see across the clear, smooth harbor. "There," she whispered.

He finally discerned the golden hair of Gwydion's floating body. It was facedown, some distance from the wreckage. How long did it take a man to drown? Kyellan did not know. A lifeboat would be far too slow. He pulled off his boots and dove over the forecastle railing.

The water was cold, full of foul-smelling seaweed but apparently devoid of fish. He broke the surface, shivering, and called, "Toss me a rope!" After a moment, a coil fell a short distance from him. The other end was tied to the railing. He pulled the coil over his shoulder and struck out for where he had seen the wizard. It was like swimming in a lake of firewood. None of the pieces of Gwydion's boat were very large.

Finally he reached the wizard. The youth's body was limp and unresponsive as he tied the rope beneath its arms. He signaled the ship, not very hopeful, and supported Gwydion above the water as they were towed back.

Briana took charge on the deck, pumping sea water from Gwydion's lungs and searching for signs of life. Kyellan shivered under a blanket, watching her, not reassured by her expression.

"No breathing," she said despairingly. "No heartbeat."

"Wizards do not drown easily." The First Priestess, supported by Pima and Gemon, was slowly climbing the steps to the crowded forecastle. "If he had time to remember what to do." The old woman knelt beside the bedraggled body and laid her hand on Gwydion's forehead. A soft chant rose from her wrinkled lips, and her face was intent. Then she broke into a weary smile.

"He is still there. Briana, you know how to bring him back."

Briana dropped to the wizard's other side. Pima began to pump Gwydion's chest, counting slowly, as Briana breathed rhythmically into his mouth. The First Priestess kept her hand on his forehead, and her expression was far away and seeking.

Gwydion took a shuddering breath, arching his body, then another, and began to cough painfully. Briana sighed and signaled Pima to stop. Kyellan watched in astonished relief. He had been certain the wizard was dead and was wondering how he could possibly explain to Chela. Gwydion's eyes fluttered for a moment, but the First Priestess frowned and spoke soft words. He closed them again and began to breathe deeply with the regularity of sleep.

"He must still deal with the backlash from his spell," the old woman explained at Briana's questioning look. "Better he sleep for a day or so, before he must suffer through that."

The novices rushed in to help the First Priestess stand. Briana stared at her in awe, and said, "Your skill is waning, you think? I would have given him up for dead, and yet you found him. I think you will be in the Goddess's hands for a long time to come."

Kyellan helped Erlin lift the sleeping wizard and followed the women down the steps from the forecastle. The First Priestess turned and said softly to Briana, "Your time is coming, child. Sooner than you will admit."

The young priestess slowed her pace, and when the old woman was some distance away, she said to herself, "I don't want to be First Priestess. Not yet."

Kyellan had sharp ears. "You don't have to, Briana," he told her gently. "You have a choice."

"I know." She turned and headed for her cabin. Kyellan watched her, wishing he could understand what she was thinking. That was impossible, however, and he turned back to Erlin with a determined smile.

"When we get Gwydion to his cabin, come with me and we'll try to apologize to the ship's master."

"He shouldn't be too angry," Erlin said hopefully. "The monster is gone, isn't it?"

Chapter Sixteen

"Very good," Pima said diplomatically, sampling a slightly rotted fruit that had been presented to her by the Prince of Altimar. He was a boy of no more than fourteen, tongue-tied by the novice's ripe beauty and laughing eyes.

"It's the best we have," he said. "Since the monster came, there have been no ships. . . ."

The Queen smiled fondly, watching the two youngsters, but finally turned back to Kyellan. She was a small, intelligent woman with light blond hair and a pleasant, open face. Like the food she offered them and the room of her palace where they spoke, she had an air of genteel shabbiness.

"I don't know what we can do, young man. You've seen the shape this city is in. We took in the people of the sea-coast villages when the monster came. An army that large . . ."

"The resistance needs this base and this harbor," Kyellan said, trying to hide his impatience. "Can't you make a few sacrifices?"

"Sacrifices?" she said sharply. "Half my people have died in the last three months, from bad nutrition or simply from fear. My husband was killed in the naval assault against the monster." She rose from her chair and paced across the fading carpet, but her anger soon subsided.

267

Looking back at Kyellan, she nodded abruptly. "Very well. I haven't forgotten that the wizards caused our problems. Ironic, isn't it, that one of them was also the solution?" She went over to where Gwydion lay on an overstuffed couch. "When he wakes, my people and I will show our gratitude, believe me."

"Most of the army can camp outside the city," Kyellan offered. "They'll need a command center, though, and barracks for the officers."

"And we can take the civilians in on a family level, I think," she mused. "Yes, it can be done. I'll have my stewards see to it." She settled a hand on her son's shoulder and sighed. "You're sure you have to leave again tonight? Misha and I will be sorry; we don't often see strangers here."

"The priestesses are in a hurry," Kyellan apologized.

"You must forgive us, Your Highness," Pima said softly to the Prince as she rose and curtsied deeply to his mother. She had not forgotten her noble upbringing, and Kyellan was glad of her manners. "Thank you for everything."

The Guardsman bowed low, trying to ignore the sadness that was settling again over the woman's face. He thanked her again and walked with Pima down to where a wagon awaited them, loaded with water and a little dried food for their journey. He wished he could have said good-bye to Gwydion, but whatever the First Priestess had done to make the wizard sleep had been overeffective.

The ship's master had apparently forgiven Kyellan for his brief mutiny. After the ship was under way that night, he invited the two Guardsmen to his cabin for drinks to start off the voyage. They accepted, a little warily, but he seemed in a pleasant mood.

"May as well be friendly," he greeted them, handing

each a mug of Kerisian brandy. "We have a week to travel, more or less. Pity we can't get any more of this. . . ." He took a swig of the brandy. "But I can't lay in at Faren and restock this trip. One more reason to get rid of those wizards, eh?" He raised his mug in a toast.

Kyellan and Erlin joined in the toast, but it seemed Erlin's mind was elsewhere. "Captain," he said to Kyellan after another drink, "do you think they'll kill many of the people in Cavernon, besides the royal family and what's left of the Guard?"

Kyellan leaned back in the heavy wooden chair, considering the question over his mug. "They'll probably leave the civilians alone. You have a big family there, don't you?"

"My parents, and eleven brothers and sisters. I'm worried most about two of my sisters. They're ladies-in-waiting to the Queen. I hope they're all right."

The ship's master took a huge gulp of brandy and grinned. "Don't hope too much, lad. If they're pretty enough to be Queen's ladies, they'll have been taken to the wizards' beds by now. The surest way to a yellow-eyed baby is a wizard father."

Erlin jumped up, his hand on his sword hilt. The ship's master laughed mockingly. "It's the truth, lad."

Kyellan pulled the young soldier away. "Come on." Halfway through the door, he paused and said sardonically over his shoulder, "Thanks for the hospitality."

Erlin broke away from him as he shut the door and went to the railing. "The bastard."

"He's still mad at us for taking over his ship. Don't let it upset you."

"But it's probably true," said the youth miserably. "My sisters are beautiful. . . . I can't keep from thinking what could be happening to them."

Kyellan could offer him no comfort.

Halcira's army entered the city four days after the ship left Keor harbor. Gwydion rode to meet them and found Chela in the vanguard of royalty and officers who were to be housed inside the walls. A long line of civilian women and children followed.

"You did it, love!" the girl called, worming her horse Yhanda out of the press of tired people eager to stop their journey. "I felt the monster leave. But it would have been easier if you had taken me along."

"You're not angry," he said hopefully, pulling her from her patient mount into his arms.

She giggled, sitting facing him in the furry Altimari saddle. "I was at first. But I know you did it because you didn't want me in danger." She kissed him playfully, then drew back in sudden concern. "You've been hurt! I didn't feel that. Why did you block it from me?"

"I'll be all right. It's the backlash from the spell. I'm much better."

"No, you're not. You shouldn't be riding."

He pulled his horse up in front of the low, sprawling children's school that was to be the command center and officers' quarters. Chela's horse had been following them and nuzzled the girl as she dismounted and linked her arm with Gwydion's.

"I wish Briana and Kyellan had waited. We should have gone with them," Chela said soberly. "I've been feeling Caerlin calling me. Whatever they're looking for, it's important."

"I know," he muttered

Tobas saw them from the doorway of the building and hurried to them with Firelh close behind. "Congratulations, wizard! I hear you got rid of the monster. Is Kyellan still here?''

"No. They left that night, as they planned."

Firelh exchanged a sober glance with the Guardsman. "I'd hoped he'd wait. Those three men who went with him didn't ask me for leave; I'm afraid they'll take this as an opportunity to desert. If they do, he'll only have Erlin."

"Damn," Gwydion said softly. "I should have gone."

"You're needed here," Tobas said.

"Not until the battles in Caerlin," he answered thoughtfully. "I could follow their ship, help them find the Goddess's Seat, and rejoin the army when it reaches the South. I wouldn't be missed."

"Nor would I," growled Firelh. "The council formed without me, and it can stay that way. I know Caerlin well."

"Could we really?" Chela said. "I want to go. Caerlin draws me like a lodestone."

"If you can convince Halcira to allow it, Firelh, we should leave tonight." Gwydion spoke eagerly, realizing now that this had been the reason for his restlessness the past several days. He felt the call Chela spoke of. However this ended, it would be decided there.

Tobas watched the ship leave silently and without fanfare from the farthest dock of Keor. Gwydion, Chela, and Firelh were aboard; he wished he was. Halcira had adamantly refused when he had asked. With Firelh gone, General Maryse would be reassigned to the naval forces, and Tobas would become one of the three land commanders. He would be given the rank of colonel, to be confirmed by Arel, though he doubted the Prince would be pleased with the necessity.

They still would not allow him to speak with the Princess.

No one had seen her on the journey overland from Narkham; presumably she had been kept in one of the royal litters, under the watchful eye of her brother or Werlinen. Tobas wished he knew how she felt about the match. He could not be sure she had not given her consent. She was ambitious enough, perhaps, to accept being married to an apparent fool like Werlinen in order to become the Queen of Keris. The Valahtia he had always known would already be gathering the reins of power. The girl he had begun to know in Ryasa and aboard the ship to Narkham, however, would never accept her brother's authority in such a situation. She would never consent to marry a soft, squeaky-voiced man fifteen years her senior.

He only wished they would let him talk to her.

The ship was anchored off the western coast of Syryn, behind a concealing range of forbidding cliffs. They had been traveling for seven weary days and would reach Cavernon City under the cover of darkness early the next morning. Kyellan slept lightly, vaguely aware that Erlin was gone from the cabin, assuming the young lieutenant was with the novice Pima. Those two had been spending a lot of time together. He knew it was bothering Briana, but he thought it was a waste for such a pretty girl to be a priestess. If he had met Briana when she was a novice, she would never have taken vows. Of that he was almost certain.

"Damn them! The Goddess damn them!" Kyellan woke abruptly as the Hoabi ship's master burst into his small cabin shouting at the top of his considerable voice. "I should never have let Orlandin force me to embark on this miserable voyage!"

"What is it?" The Guardsman sat up and glared bleary-eyed at the interruption.

"Those three bastards in your command, that's what it is. They stole one of my lifeboats! Headed for Syryn to betray us to the wizards, I shouldn't wonder."

Fully awake now, and nearly as angry as the Hoabi, Kyellan pulled on his uniform and stamped into his boots. "I didn't know they were going to desert," he snapped. "And I'm no happier about it than you are. Though I doubt they'll go anywhere near the wizards."

"Neither should we," muttered the pirate, harping on a point he had been wearying Kyellan with through the voyage. "I don't see why you have to go to Cavernon City. The wizards will be crawling all over it, and Erinon as well. Why don't you land on the coast a hundred miles from either of them? That thing you're looking for could just as easily be there. You said you don't know where it is."

"There won't be any wizards in Rahan Quarter. Why should there be? There's nothing to interest them. We can get in and out without being noticed, and find out what the situation is."

"I take my orders from the priestesses. Unless I hear it from one of them, I won't go anywhere near the city."

Kyellan pushed past the man and out the door. "Fine. You'll hear it from them."

"I'll be at the helm," said the Hoabi sullenly.

"Come in," Briana called when he knocked. Kyellan entered, still angry, but he waited until she finished spooning something liquid into the First Priestess's mouth before he spoke.

"Will you come tell that fool of a ship's master that we need him to land us near Cavernon City? He says he has to hear it from a priestess."

Briana sighed. "Of course we're going to Cavernon.

The Temple there is one of the oldest in the world, and if there are any records of the Seat in Caerlin, they're in the city."

Gemon was curled up in a corner, feigning sleep, but Kyellan could feel her watching him with her usual hatred. The malice in her expression made him shudder. She opened her eyes and met his gaze. Once more, he wondered what it was about him that made her dislike him so. Trying to be friendly, he asked her, "Where's your friend Pima?"

"With your Guardsman, of course," she answered distastefully.

"I hope you've spoken to Erlin about the value of restraint," Briana said, putting down the bowl and following him out the door.

"No." He grinned, forcing thoughts of Gemon aside. "And I'm not likely to. She's too pretty to be a priestess."

Looking exasperated, Briana moved in front of him and headed for the helm, where the Hoabi waited. "And so are you," he whispered, not meaning for her to hear; she paused, though, before she spoke.

"It is imperative, good sir, that we land as near to Cavernon City as possible tonight. I thought I had already made that plain."

He shrugged. "Whatever you say, my lady, but I still think it's unwise."

"Let me be the judge of that." She turned on her heel and strode back toward the cabin. "An unpleasant man," she remarked to Kyellan when they had gone some distance.

"Our three Ryasans stole one of his boats in the night."

"Whether we have five men or two will not matter. What we'll need is Power. That's why I can't put Pima out of the Order yet for what she's done with Erlin. We need everyone we have. You can tell your lieutenant, though, to be glad she's not under vows. The penalty for seducing a priestess is death." She slammed her cabin door in his face.

Gwydion woke from deep sleep in the middle of the night. Chela was screaming in the cabin next to his. He leaped out of bed, stumbling, grabbed his sword, and burst through the connecting door. She was alone in the room, sitting bolt upright in her bunk with her face contorted in agony and her mouth wide in a continuous shriek. The Dark, powerful presence of their unknown enemy was strong. Gwydion threw down his sword and took her in his arms, trying to expand his mental shield to include her. She paid no attention to him. He could feel the pain in her slim, muscled body. The note of her screaming changed and she struggled with him, her expression mad with fear and hatred, like a wild animal, trying to bite him.

He held her firmly, unable to enter her mind, unable even to engage the Dark thing in battle. The shield he built around her only contained the enemy and was quickly torn down again. Powerless to help her, he could only murmur caressingly, meaningless, comforting words that one would use when a small child had a scraped knee.

Suddenly she began to quiver in his arms, then to sob, and the Darkness was gone. Gwydion crushed her to him, stroking her tangled hair, trying to comfort her with his strength; but he, too, was shaking.

"It's gone now, you're all right," he soothed. "Everything's all right. . . ."

She choked back a sob and tried to speak. "I . . . I couldn't . . . block it . . . couldn't defend . . ."

"Shh. No one could have done any better. It's too strong."

"It kept . . . kept showing me, over and over, my

village being destroyed, and Dael, the boy I was to marry, like a torch in the wizards' fire. . . .''

"It's over now. You're safe."

She shook her head, her blue eyes pleading with him. "No. It's stronger than any of us. I could feel you trying to stop it, like a moth flying around a lamp, and nothing happened."

"Why did it leave, then? I didn't drive it away."

"It only wanted to show me its strength," she said, slowly gaining control again. "And to make me doubt you."

"Doubt me?"

"It showed me Dael burning, again and again, and tried to make me think you were one of the wizards who had done it, that somehow it was terrible for me to love you and not his memory. It doesn't make sense now." She wiped the tears roughly from her eyes. "How will we ever defeat something like that?"

Gwydion sighed heavily. "I just wish I knew who it was."

The night in Cavernon City was hot and dry, soaking the priestesses' robes with sweat as the small group searched the outer wall for the opening Kyellan knew was there. Briana was tired. The ship's captain had deposited them two miles from the city, and they had walked nearly that distance again trying to find Kyellan's gap. Gemon was about to collapse. If this lasted much longer, she would have to insist that Erlin let go of Pima's hand and carry the smaller novice, as Kyellan was carrying the First Priestess.

"Here!" hissed the Guardsman triumphantly. The section of wall was crumbling with age, and the years aided by the work of various smugglers and outlaws had created a hole wide enough for a person to pass through. Briana followed the others through the dark opening, into an ancient cemetery crowded with weathered wooden markers and choked with brush.

"I don't like this place," Pima protested softly.

Kyellan chuckled. "No one does. Except people like us who have to get into the city unseen. Come on. And remember, everyone, speak Caer now. Don't draw attention to yourself."

There were perhaps three hours remaining before dawn, and the quarter-moon was setting. They finally reached the end of the cemetery. The street looked deserted, rundown, neglected. Briana's nose wrinkled at the smells, but she saw no people. It was a desolate place.

"This is the Rahan Quarter you keep talking about?" she said sarcastically.

"The city has drawn in from the walls," Kyellan said. "This is one of the oldest sections. Half a mile inward, and we'll be among the night people of Rahan." He walked quickly, forcing Briana nearly to run to keep up.

"Isn't that dangerous? If there are wizards' men, they'll notice our robes," she pointed out. "And your uniforms."

He grinned. "We won't be down in the streets long enough for anyone to notice anything, Priestess. I know a place that can hide us."

The sounds of the night grew louder. Laughter, hysterical or drunken; slurred, loud singing; screams that could have been death cries or squeals of pleasure. Briana shivered. She had found the crowded streets of Dallynd too much for her senses, which were used to the peace of the Sanctuary. Now she was walking into the most notorious section of the largest city in the Kingdoms, trusting as her guide a man whose smiles grew wider as the noises became more raucous.

A turban-wrapped man stumbled by them, sobbing, clutching a bloodstained robe. Kyellan did not give him a second glance. Briana started toward him, asking if she could help.

"No, Priestess." Kyellan grabbed her roughly.

"But he's hurt!"

"Most likely not. He thought we looked sympathetic. He'd have been far more likely to cut your throat for money than to thank you for your charity."

"But . . . I have no money."

"He didn't know that. And speak Caer!"

Subdued, she followed him into the main streets. Pima and Erlin were behind her, and Gemon followed at a short distance, sullen and exhausted. The crash of breaking chairs came from the first tavern they passed, one with the unprepossessing name The Crawling Toad. A group of cheering men and women were clustered around its smoky door, and Briana could barely make out the forms of shadowy children drifting through the people with furtive speed.

Nearly every other building on the street bore a red-lantern sign. Briana was awed by the number. Prostitution appeared to be a mainstay of the Rahan economy. She had never seen so many people abroad in the middle of the night.

As if reading her thoughts, Kyellan glanced back. "It's almost morning now. You should see it at its peak."

"Sorry to have missed it," she said untruthfully.

He suddenly stopped and turned into a dark alley between two red-lantern buildings. "This way," he said sharply. "Quick." They hurried after him. A dark, weathered door in the side of one house opened to reveal a steep stairway and a sleeping drunk sprawled at its foot. Kyellan nudged the derelict aside with a foot and began to climb. The building had four stories, and they passed more doors, until at last they reached a hatch set in the ceiling. The Guardsman gently put the First Priestess down on the narrow landing and shoved the hatch open, breaking a leather strap that had locked it.

He motioned Erlin to precede him, then passed the First Priestess up before ascending himself. Briana waited for Gemon to complete the climb and made certain the frail girl got through the hatch before she followed and closed it behind her. They were on the roof, a wide, flat expanse of broken stone that was stained with soot and birds' nests.

"The Thieves' Highroad of Rahan," Kyellan said grandly, making a sweep with his arm that took in the surrounding crowd of housetops. "Follow me."

He led them across the flat roofs. The spaces between the houses were narrow, easily jumped, some even connected by makeshift planking that served as a bridge. Breathing hard from the speed of their traverse, Briana waited with Kyellan after they had gone perhaps a mile, as the others caught up.

"It doesn't look like they make much of an effort to hinder the thieves that use this 'road,' " she said.

"No," he agreed, smiling a little. "Rahan is fueled by thieves and their victims; they are its life's blood. I don't know anyone who doesn't profit by theft and fraud." He chuckled. "It's a well-kept secret. The city taxes the taverns and brothels, but those are just here to pull in the marks."

"And to entertain the criminals," Briana said acidly.

"We're almost there. Come on," Kyellan called softly, trotting across the roof with the First Priestess carefully balanced in his arms.

Their destination appeared to be another red-lantern house. It had a tiny half roof reached by a plank bridge, but there was a room with a door and curtained windows where the

rest of the roof would have been. Kyellan handed the First
Priestess to Erlin, motioned them all against the dark
walls, and moved quietly to the door.

He knocked softly, in a peculiar rhythm, and whistled a
short section of a song whose bawdy lyrics Briana had
heard in the street below. Inside the room, through the
thin walls, the priestess heard a muffled curse and a soft,
feminine laugh.

"I'm sorry, lover," said the young voice. "That's all
for tonight." A drunken male voice protested, saying he
had been promised more time, but the woman firmly told
him to leave. A door slammed, and they heard footsteps
stumble down stairs. There was a rustling in the room, and
after a moment the occupant came to the door.

"Who is it?"

"Kyellan," he answered.

The woman gasped. "What? Dhomli, don't tease me
like that. You know I don't like it." She opened the door.
Her mouth dropped open in shock when she saw Kyellan,
and she clutched the door frame for support. Briana could
see her clearly: young and slender, her face showing hard
edges under too much paint, her black hair cut off at her
shoulders. She wore a filmy purple gown.

"Hello, Alaira."

"Ky? Is that you?" Her voice shook. "Gods, it's been
so long! I was sure you were dead." Briana realized with
sudden insight that this sharp-faced child was deeply in
love with Kyellan.

"I need your help," he said gently. "We need to
hide."

"Oh!" She saw the others for the first time; swallowing
hard and blinking rapidly, she gained control of her
emotions. "Come in, then."

The tiny room was dimly lit with a few cheap, scented

candles, and half-filled by a rumpled bed. Alaira looked guilty and tried to smile at Kyellan. "Things haven't been good since the wizards came. A girl has to live." A sudden stricken look crossed her face. "Oh, gods. Dhomli's going to be back soon. How do we explain this? He always hated you, Ky, and he was so glad when the royal ship never came back. He'll be furious to find you here."

Kyellan did not respond. Briana could see anger rising in him like a spring tide. Then, in a tightly controlled voice, he said, "You should have gone to another soldier. You'd have been taken care of."

"It took me a while to decide you were dead. And by that time, there weren't many soldiers left." With a nervous laugh, she ran her hand through her short hair and looked at Briana. "Are you really priestesses?"

Briana nodded, feeling a rush of pity for the young woman. "We're working against the wizards," she said in explanation.

"I should have been a priestess," said Alaira, looking slowly from Briana to Kyellan and back again. "Sometimes I see things . . . but they wouldn't take me. Said I was a criminal, at seven years old."

"I remember how relieved you were." Kyellan laughed, relaxing a little. But he stiffened again as someone began pounding on the door, in the same rhythm he had used. "Dhomli," he muttered.

"Damn him." Alaira trotted to the door. "Coming, love! Ky, you'd better cover him when he comes in. Don't want anyone hurt."

He nodded, drawing his sword and taking a stance beside the door. It opened, and Dhomli entered; a huge man, half a head taller than Kyellan, he had a hard, unintelligent face that was scarred in several places. He stopped when the sword touched his neck, and turned. "You! You were supposed to be dead. She's mine now!"

"He didn't come back for me," Alaira said, glancing at Briana.

"Relax, Dhomli," Kyellan said. "Remember, I was always faster than you."

The scarred man finally nodded. "All right, soldier boy. But I want an explanation. Then I want you out of here."

"They need a hole for a few days," Alaira soothed. "They're working against the wizards, Dhomli, if that means anything to you."

Kyellan sheathed his sword again, watching the big man warily.

"Damn right it does," Dhomli said sullenly. "They take everything worth stealing. Even the richest-looking marks—you roll them, they've got nothing. Just a few pennies to see them through the night." He looked around the room, his brow furrowed with thought. "Against the wizards? Those some kind of uniforms you're wearing? And are these priestesses? You'll have to get some new clothes."

Kyellan grinned. "There's a few hours of darkness left."

Dhomli shrugged. "Come on, then. We'll find you something. You too, small one." Erlin, looking sheepish, followed them out the door.

"Be careful," Briana whispered.

Alaira leaned out after them, smiled, and turned to Briana. "It's a beautiful night, Priestess. Would you like to talk? I won't ask you why you're here, so if the wizards want to know, I won't be able to tell them."

The room was stuffy and close. Briana watched the novices trying to get the First Priestess comfortable on the lopsided bed. She nodded and followed the black-haired girl outside. They shut the door and sat back against it, looking out over the rooftops of Rahan.

"I told you I sometimes see things," Alaira said hesitantly. "Well, it's like there's a line between you and Kyellan. I saw the way he looks at you. . . ." She took a deep breath. "Listen, I know you're a priestess and it's forbidden, but have you ever . . ."

"No. And we won't."

Alaira said bitterly, "Do you know what you're giving up? The chance, Priestess, to be the only person he's ever loved."

"I can't believe that."

"It's true. I know him. I grew up with him. We ran the streets together, after his mother turned him out to fend for himself."

"His mother . . ." Briana was shocked.

The slim girl's eyes measured her. "He hasn't told you, has he. His mother was a pretty tavern girl, and she hated him. He ruined her chances of getting married and out of the profession. She turned him out, and by the time he was six he was one of the best thieves in the Quarter. By the time he was twelve he had killed three grown men in knife fights, and twice they were over me; I was ten, and just getting pretty. Anyway, when he was sixteen he somehow got into the Royal Guard and went to the wars. He came back a lieutenant."

Briana listened, fascinated in spite of herself, as Alaira warmed to her subject. "So there he was, an officer, and so good-looking he could have had any girl he wanted." She giggled, twisting a strand of black hair. "And frequently did. From ladies of the court to people like me. He cared about me . . . he did care . . . but he never loved me. He's never loved anyone. I thought he was incapable of it."

Briana was silent, remembering the words she thought she had heard in her mind. Alaira, not angry anymore, went on. "He loves you, Priestess. You must know that. I'm sorry if you don't want to hear it."

"Don't be sorry," Briana managed to say over the tightness of her throat. She could not meet the girl's dark eyes.

"Well, good night, Priestess," Alaira said awkwardly, and retreated back into the room. Briana stayed out in the night almost until dawn, staring up at the stars, wishing she knew what to do.

Chapter Seventeen

Briana stared numbly at the white stone ruin, brightly lit in the hot morning sun, that had been the Temple in Cavernon. She should have known the wizards would not tolerate the presence of their sworn enemies in the city they had regained after thousands of years. They blamed the priestesses for the deaths of Caerlin's infant wizards; a charge that was not entirely false. The marks of their fire, crimson and orange, stained the jumbled stones. Yet she could feel little death in the place. Perhaps the priestesses had escaped, taking whatever records and chronicles the Temple had housed.

"There's nothing here," Kyellan said impatiently. She looked up at him and once again fought the impulse to giggle. The clothing he, Erlin, and Dhomli had "found" the night before was the garish attire of the Caer petty nobility: flimsy, cheap silks and brocades, overelaborated with ribbons and embroidery, very much out of place on a soldier. Briana felt equally ridiculous, and slightly blasphemous, in a full skirt of brown-and-gold sateen with a laced bodice stitched with flowers.

She did not know why she lingered to gaze at the devastation. Perhaps in the hope of being noticed by another priestess in disguise, who would recognize her kindred calling and take her to where the writings that spoke of the Goddess's Seat had been hidden. Shaking her head at the stretch of her imagination, she turned away, and stopped at Kyellan's hand on her arm. She shivered at the touch. It recalled the disturbing conversation of last night. Then she felt his fear and saw that his other hand had gone to his sword hilt.

A wizard had entered the square and looked at the ruins of the Temple with apparent satisfaction. Though thinner and older, he was uncannily similar to Gwydion. On his arm, pale and exhausted-looking, was a young Garithian woman who would have been pretty had her face not been shadowed by deprivation and fear.

"Melana," Kyellan gasped. "The minstrel from Atolan."

"You know her?" Briana started slowly away from the wizard, risking a glance backward. The red-haired woman stared at Kyellan, wide-eyed, in obvious recognition. Then she turned abruptly and began to tease the wizard, pleading with him to take her to a nearby tavern; he smiled indulgently, and they strolled the other direction.

Kyellan moved quickly from the square, and Briana hurried to stay with him. "I had no claim on her beyond a night. She could have risen in the wizard's favor if she had turned us in."

"His favor? That girl was terrified. Her feelings were all over the square. The wizard must enjoy it, or he'd have blocked her."

"They must have brought her from Garith." Kyellan scowled. "I liked her."

"When we find the Goddess's Seat, we can help her. And all the others."

The fleet was moored together nearly the length of Keor harbor. Tobas felt a surge of satisfaction looking at it. Preparations were complete for the invasion of Syryn; a messenger ship had arrived the day before, saying Takar was taken, and today would be the last council before launch. Events were finally moving toward the confrontation he yearned for. Once in Caerlin, he would command the S'tari contact patrol to negotiate the alliance with the fierce desert warriors. He hoped that Gwydion and Firelh would return before that alliance had to be tested. And Kyellan. And the priestesses. It was probably too much to hope.

It was time to start for the command center. The previous councils had been tiring, argumentative affairs, and this one should be no different. The royalty would watch from their canopied chairs, and if their opinion was asked, Janorwyn of Ryasa would give it in measured tones. Valahtia would not speak or even look his direction. Anger once again flushed through him as he walked, remembering the many times in the last few weeks that he had been denied admittance to the rundown palace of Altimar's Queen. It was a new experience, being considered socially inferior, and Tobas did not like it.

When all had arrived for the council, Halcira began. His usually sober face was lit with suppressed excitement, and his voice was unusually loud. "We launch today to take Syryn!"

There was scattered cheering, but dark-skinned General Diveshi, beside Tobas, muttered, "High time, I'd say."

"General Orlandin?" Halcira relinquished his place to the stocky Hoabi, whose piratical face was creased in a huge grin.

"We'll launch in waves, a rank at a time. The soldiers have already begun their march across the bridge of vessels in the harbor to fill the farthest ships. Each wave will hold approximately ten thousand men, for a total of five waves and fifty thousand."

"Reconnaissance claims the wizards have sixty thousand in Caer alone," Diveshi interrupted. "With the losses we're bound to sustain in Syryn, will we be enough to face them?"

Orlandin shrugged. "I estimate we'll lose between twenty-five hundred and five thousand men at Syryn. The wizards have a large garrison there. But we must have the base from which to operate. And the projected alliance with the S'tari should more than compensate."

Diveshi half rose and said bitterly, "If this council had not seen fit to disregard my counterproposal, we would not face any losses. If we bypassed Syryn entirely, and established our base in S'tari territory, we might be able to match the wizards' numbers."

"We voted to retake Syryn," Halcira admonished, "and that we will do. Continue, Orlandin."

"In five days, with a straight path and fair winds, we'll reach Syryn." The Hoabi glared at the stormy-visaged Parahnese. "The first wave will engage the island with the second in reserve. The other ranks will head immediately to the agreed-upon point on the southern shore of Caerlin, below Erinon, where Diveshi and Tobas will take command. We know little as yet of Syryn's actual fortifications, and our tactics will have to wait until we have better information."

"Thank you, General." Halcira smiled thinly. "Now, General Diveshi, objections to our overall strategy aside, will you please explain the plans for when we reach Caerlin?"

He did not stand. "They're indefinite enough. A reconnaissance party led by Colonel Tobas will penetrate the western desert below the Maer Cunin and attempt to contact the S'tari tribesmen there. They will negotiate an alliance. It may be difficult, since Tobas is the only one among us who has even fought the S'tari, and he does not know their language. He tells me Captain Kyellan can speak it, but you let Kyellan go with the priestesses.''

There was a rustling among the royalty as Valahtia tried to rise and was pulled back by Werlinen. ''I will speak!'' she said loudly enough for the company to hear. ''You cannot keep me from it!''

Tobas met her eyes, which glowed like brown coals. She squirmed angrily and freed herself from the grasp of the Crown Prince, twisting away from the canopied chairs to stand behind Tobas. ''I will speak,'' she repeated, breathing hard.

''What is it, Your Highness?'' Halcira asked courteously.

''I can speak S'tari. Take me to Caerlin with you.''

''You, Princess? With the army? Impossible.''

''My father thought it was important for rulers to know the languages of their subjects. He taught me S'tari. I can interpret for you.''

''Did he also teach your brother?''

''Arel wouldn't learn. He said if a S'tari wanted to talk to him, he had better learn Caer.''

In that language, his face scarlet, the Prince spoke. ''Come back here, Valahtia. You're behaving foolishly.''

''No. I've been foolish, and I've decided to stop.'' Her hand moved to Tobas's shoulder, and her eyes searched his. ''Will you take me? I've learned to care for myself. I won't be a burden.''

He grinned. ''We do need someone who can speak S'tari.''

''You most certainly will not take her,'' Werlinen said with royal authority. ''She is to be my wife. I forbid it.''

''No. You forbid me nothing. I renounce you, and the throne of Keris, and our betrothal. Before witnesses.'' She began to repeat the words in every language of the Kingdoms, as custom required.

"Think of your duties, child!" sputtered the old King Janorwyn. "Your responsibilities! Your brother has made you a match that—"

She interrupted her recital. "I do not care about duties or responsibilities. I will not be married to this overstuffed, pompous idiot." Quietly, she resumed her formal renunciation.

Tobas rose from his chair and seated the Princess with all the formality he could muster from his boyhood training, as she finished her last phrase in a fractured Hoabi dialect that made Orlandin wince. She smiled tentatively, reading the message of pride and reassurance in his eyes.

"Tobas of Laenar!" Arel stood, his fists clenched, barely under control. "You will not take my sister to Caerlin."

"I will."

Valahtia's hand in his was beginning to shake.

"I am your King in all but name. My father is dead by now. If you take her, you will lose both rank and lands when Caerlin is mine."

"What rank and lands?" he said lightly. "I'm a second son, Arel, remember?"

"Where's Dhomli?" Kyellan wondered sleepily, wakening at midday of their second day in Cavernon City. He reached across the empty floorspace and shook the slight figure there. "Alaira?"

She blinked and stretched like a cat. "Gods, Ky, it's the middle of the day. What's wrong?"

"Dhomli's gone."

The girl shook her short hair from her face. "Oh, don't you remember, he set up a meeting with a man he knows who can supply you with horses. I'd know if anything was wrong. . . .'' Her head came up sharply, and she stared at him.

"He's been captured," Gemon said from the corner. "By the wizards."

There was a time when Kyellan would have questioned her certainty. Now he only nodded and began to wake the others.

"The imbecile," Alaira cursed. "They'll probably come up through the house. If you leave by the roof . . ."

"They'll know you helped us," Kyellan pointed out. "You'd better come, too."

"All wizards and their kin be forever damned." She began to search frantically in the floorboards, Kyellan wondered how much could be left of the money and jewels she had been hoarding since childhood for a dowry to the marriage she had always dreamed of.

"They're here," Briana said. Footsteps were suddenly loud across the roof. "They were blocked. By an expert."

Kyellan leaped for his swordbelt and drew his weapon, positioning himself beside the door. Erlin joined him sleepily.

"Put those away! There are twenty of them!"

The wizards' men kicked in the door. Briana was right. There were too many, and they had long iron-shod spears that tipped the balance further. Four circled him, and he reluctantly handed over his sword and allowed himself to be prodded out into the bright noon sun with the others. The brown-uniformed soldiers produced strong leather straps and bound their prisoners' hands behind them. Dhomli, similarly bound, stood at one side of the crowded roof. He glanced at Kyellan.

"I'm sorry. I don't know how they found out about you, but they caught me as I entered the square, and I had to bring them here . . . I had to. . . .''

"It's not your fault. I think I know whose it was, though. That girl Melana. Remember, Priestess?"

"I was so sure she wouldn't. . . ." Briana scowled. "And how could she have known Dhomli was with us? It had to have been someone else."

"Who?"

"Stop talking and start moving," said one of the wizards' men in barely intelligible Caer.

The great Tiranon was still splendid. The walls of marble with inlays of quartz and ivory stood intact; brilliant fountains still played in the courtyards; spring-budding trees, green and full of chattering birds, still stood along the pathways. Kyellan noticed only one thing missing on their hurried walk to the gold-filigree door of the throne room: the beautiful tapestries depicting the exploits of the Ardavan line through the centuries.

The young wizard who had been with Melana in the street sat on the ruby-and-emerald throne of Chaeris Ardavan, in a comfortable, cross-legged sprawl, as a blank-faced Caer girl combed his yellow hair. His eyes, however, were sharp and predatory, like a hawk about to pounce on a rabbit and enjoying the moment beforehand.

"The prisoners, my lord," said the patrol sergeant with a fawning bow. He spoke in Garithian.

"Ah." The wizard shifted forward and smiled. "The First Priestess of the Goddess, not looking at all well. A young Third Ranking, who killed a wizard in the battle of Dallynd harbor, and so must be respected. Two very young novices, one quite pretty; to be given to the soldiers eventually, I shouldn't wonder." He laughed at Erlin's outraged expression and continued his catalog.

"An angry Caer soldier who understood what I just said. And his captain, a man to be reckoned with, who somehow killed another wizard in the same harbor, and led the doomed defense of the walls of Dallynd. A fine group, Freghen. But who are these others? The overweight street fighter and the young lady of the evening?''

''They were hiding the prisoners in Rahan Quarter,'' the sergeant said. ''I understand the lady was once the captain's lover.''

Changing to well-modulated Caer, the wizard addressed Dhomli. ''You must understand the position you've placed yourself in. So you'll not be surprised when I condemn you to death in the dungeons. Take them out, Freghen. Your men may have the girl.'' He waved his hand in airy dismissal.

Alaira bit and scratched at the three soldiers who came for her. They lifted her with little effort and carried her out, grinning in anticipation. Dhomli tried to go bravely, but he was whimpering before he was out the door. Kyellan's anger clouded his vision with red. He wanted to crash through the ring of brown soldiers and somehow, with his hands tied behind his back, kill the wizard. He had known Alaira since she was four years old.

''The captain doesn't like me very much, Gretha,'' observed the wizard to his black-haired, unresponsive companion. ''I can't say I blame him.''

''My lord Hirwen!'' A guard entered and bowed low, then rose and said in urgent Garithian, ''Captain Threl sent me to get the spies. Our Most High Lord Belaric commanded that we bring them with us when we leave this afternoon for Khymer and his presence. The caravan is loaded and ready.''

The wizard drummed his fingers on the swirled, jeweled arm of the throne in annoyance. ''Very well. Take them. I had hoped to have some conversation with them, especially with the captain; our informant claimed he has Power,

against all laws. Give Threl my compliments, and ask him
to put in a few words for me with Belaric. I should be in
Khymer, not stuck here like an exile.''

His informant? Kyellan wished he did have Power, so
he could read the wizard's mind and learn the identity of
their betrayer. It was true Melana could not have known
about Dhomli, and Briana was very sure the minstrel had
not done it. It could have been neither Alaira nor Dhomli,
unless they had been promised other rewards than death or
slavery. He could think of no one else who knew of their
presence in Cavernon.

''Take them!'' Hirwen commanded. The guards herded
the prisoners from the throne room. Kyellan glanced back
at the wizard briefly. Hirwen's hand was tangled in the
Caer girl's hair with indifferent cruelty as tears crept down
her serene face.

Belaric, Gwydion's old master, seemed to have set himself up as some sort of demigod. Kyellan had ridden guard
on many caravans making the journey to Khymer in past
years. It was a hellishly long way, and the last third of it
was straight through the wastes of the northern S'tari
desert. Even on a good horse, his uniform put aside for the
robes and head-wrap of the desert people, he had never
found it an easy road.

''They were here.'' Gwydion cursed, pulling a large
bundle of assorted clothes from beneath the bed. ''Two
soldiers' uniforms, priestess robes. Where's Firelh?''

The hood of his cloak had fallen back, and Chela pulled
it forward again and tied its straps tightly, tucking his
golden hair under it, wishing they could do something about
his eyes.

''He went back down. I guess to ask if anyone saw them
leave.''

The Ryasan hill lord had made himself quite useful when they had reached the break in the walls by the cemetery and found they could follow the trail no farther. Saying he had spent a few years in Cavernon City, more than two decades ago, Firelh had remembered enough of the language and the streets of the sprawling place to find Rahan Quarter.

Once there, Chela thought she sensed their presence and pulled the two men eagerly to this rooftop crib, to find that only cloth remained. She took one of the white novice robes and ran her hand across its rough weave. It felt friendly and smiling, and she knew it was Pima's, but she could find nothing to tell her where the girl had gone.

"Wizards' soldiers took them," Firelh said gravely, blocking the intense sunlight that streamed through the open door.

"You're certain?" Gwydion stood up.

"The day watchman of a costume jewelry stall saw them taken away, in the direction of the palace." The Ryasan smiled a little. "Of course, everything that goes out of Rahan goes toward the Tiranon; still, I think it's likely they will be there."

"We came too late," Chela said angrily.

"If we were here, we'd have been captured, too. As it is, our friends have a better chance since we're free." Gwydion threw the clothing back onto the bed. "Come on."

The prisoners were quick-marched along a way familiar to Kyellan: the corridors and courtyards between the throne room of the Tiranon and the barracks of the Royal Guard. The uniforms of these soldiers were brown, but other than that, the scene was not unusual. Several patrols' worth of men lounged in the shaded doorways of the long stone buildings, watching and commenting on the caravan that was taking shape in the yard. Bored, irritable mules submitted to their loads with kicks and bites, while the slim, lightly harnessed S'tari horses moved restively at the picket line. From the wrappings of the bundles on the mules, Kyellan guessed that the caravan would be carrying flour and other foodstuffs for the garrison in Khymer. It seemed heavily armed and guarded for such a mission. Perhaps the S'tari were still causing trouble.

Upon their arrival, the cavalry soldiers untied their horses and mounted, and the drivers on their riding mules took their places behind rows of pack animals; the prisoners were shoved to a position behind the mules, with three rows of horsemen following. Apparently they were going to walk. Kyellan glanced at the First Priestess, who had somehow found reserves of strength during their two-day rest in Alaira's room. She had been able to walk across the city, but she would not last long overland. Neither, he thought, would the thin child Gemon. The pallor of her face was stark in the bright afternoon sun.

For the moment, in the confusion as the caravan formed, they were not being watched closely. He moved close to Briana.

"Have you thought of anyone yet?"

"Who informed on us, you mean? I think I know." She shrugged slightly, restrained by her bound hands. "But it's not much help. Do you remember the being that attacked me, and later Gwydion, in Keor harbor? Our strongest enemy, strong enough to break through our best shielding. No one else could have found us."

"The Shape-Changer," said the First Priestess firmly. "It has to be."

"Perhaps." Briana frowned. "Meaning it could be anyone."

"But who?" Kyellan said in frustration.

A whiplash suddenly stung his left cheek, making a deep weal; he turned to see a Syryni soldier on horseback scowling at him. "No talking among the prisoners," barked the man, re-coiling the long lash.

"None of that." The commanding voice was familiar. "We've orders to bring them unharmed to Belaric." A soft Kerisian accent and a harsh, grating tone. Kyellan squinted against the glare and looked up as the captain of the wizards' patrol pulled to a halt. Yes, he was familiar. A mercenary named Mharis who had been a pleasant companion when he and Kyellan had roamed the taverns of Cavernon together.

"It's been a long time, Mharis." He felt the blood trickling down his face and wished, annoyed, that his hands were unbound so he could wipe it off.

Confused, the scarred Kerisian peered down at him. "My name is Threl, prisoner. Have we met before?"

"We've known each other for years, man. Since you first came to the city."

Mharis-Threl frowned thoughtfully, then shook his head and spurred his horse away, calling out orders to get the caravan moving. The two leading ranks of soldiers, seven abreast, trotted out, followed by the lines of protesting mules under the long whips of their drivers. The six prisoners went more slowly, but their pace was the swiftest the First Priestess could manage. Though the soldiers behind them chafed and swore at the delay, they could see the cause of it.

They left the palace walls behind and moved through the quiet, palm-shaded streets of the northeastern part of Cavernon. It was an area Kyellan had rarely seen, with the tall, ornately faced city homes of the country's aristocracy. It had always been forbidden for caravans to pass through this section; though the northeastern gate was the departure point for Khymer, they were forced to take a route outside the walls to avoid offending the court. Apparently the wizards had changed the laws. Not surprisingly, there was no evidence the stately homes had been occupied recently. Vines and grasses were beginning to climb onto the smooth stones.

After they passed the quiet, heavily guarded city gate, the order came through to speed their pace. Kyellan felt the lash again, this time a hot stripe on his back that ripped the flimsy material of his stolen shirt. At his lack of response, the whip wielder spurred his horse up beside the Guardsman.

"Move, you dog!"

"The old woman is sick," he growled. "If you make her walk faster, she'll probably die in the heat, and you'll have to explain that to Belaric."

The soldier looked at the First Priestess, who stumbled along doggedly, but who was obviously near collapse. He swore softly and trotted ahead to the front of the column. Soon he returned with the Kerisian captain, Threl.

"We can't burden the mules any more, sir," said the soldier as they came into earshot. "And the men must be free to fight."

"Very well. Untie the captain and have him carry her."

This was done while the caravan moved. Kyellan had a moment to flex his cramped arms before he was obliged to pick up the First Priestess. She was not very heavy, but she certainly would be if he had to carry her all the way to Khymer.

The old woman smiled weakly and whispered, "The day the Goddess deserts me, I will be a burden to you. She is still with me." Then her face grew still as a mountain pool, and after a few minutes it seemed Kyellan was carrying a sack of feathers. She weighed nothing.

"How—" he began, but silenced when the whip man glared at him and fingered his weapon.

The wizards' captain lingered by them, his furrowed face troubled. After a few miles, he spoke. "You say you knew me before, spy. When was that?"

Keeping his voice low, Kyellan answered. "Don't you remember? We've been friends for three years, Mharis. Ever since you chose the side of the Royal Guard in a tavern brawl by the waterfront. Gods, we even shared the same girl for a while." He looked up into the narrowed brown eyes. It seemed as if a mist covered them, a veil, a curtain. Kyellan sharpened his gaze, trying to see through it, and it suddenly parted a little. The First Priestess shifted in his arms and stared at him in thinly disguised surprise.

"Alaira," the mercenary whispered, then broke his eyes away and blinked hard. "I remember. Almost. And you were . . ."

"Kyellan. Of the Royal Guard."

"Yes. Ky." He shuddered. "It seems so long ago. When I was Mharis and not Threl."

"The wizards made you forget?"

"I suppose so." The soldier looked down again, his expression grave. "I'm . . . sorry you're here, but they still hold me. You must not think I can help you. You mustn't trust me. Do you understand?" He jerked his horse through an opening in the mule line and raced to the head of the column, not looking back.

"Damn," Kyellan said softly. "I thought I could break through to him."

"You did." The old woman sighed. "You tore his shields, but they implanted deeper suggestions and bindings in him than can be loosened in one attempt."

''Tore his shields?'' Kyellan frowned.

''Indeed. And they were strong.''

''That sounds like something Briana would do. Or Gwydion.''

Her hooded eyes pierced him. ''Yes. Oh, the wizards are right, swordsman. You do have Power. And you should not.''

He could feel the malevolence of Gemon, walking nearby, like an enemy force across a plain waiting for battle; but he shook his head and said nothing.

''It troubles me.'' The First Priestess turned her face away.

''Names of Power!'' Gwydion swore, momentarily dropping the illusion he had wrapped around himself to make it appear he was a wizard's soldier. ''Firelh, what are you doing?''

The Ryasan lord had reappeared from his mission, wearing the clothing of the enemy and dragging with him a whimpering Garithian girl who struggled vainly against his hand covering her mouth. ''She was running straight for us,'' Firelh said with a grin. ''Now don't call out, lass, and I'll let go.''

The red-haired young woman, emaciated and pale under a robe of silken, expensive weave, nodded jerkily. Released, she gasped for air, her eyes wide and staring at Gwydion. ''A wizard, hiding in the oldest part of the palace? You could be his brother. . . .''

He sighed and relinquished his fading illusion. ''Whose brother?''

''Hirwen's. The Lord's.'' She shuddered. The wildness in her eyes reminded him of the first time he had seen Chela. She was afraid, but not of them nearly as much as of Hirwen. From what he remembered of the older youth,

he was unsurprised. Perhaps Firelh had done well to bring
her, instead of the planned soldier who would have had to
die after answering their questions.

"We're looking for some friends," he began.

"Oh!" she gasped. "I know who you are! You're that
renegade wizard they're all so upset about. The traitor, the
one who is aiding the rebels . . . Kyellan's friend."

So they were upset about him. That was good. They
should be.

"You know Kyellan?" Firelh asked.

"I met him in Atolan, just before everything began. He
was kind to me. They've taken him, and the others with
him, to Belaric." She suddenly clutched Gwydion's arm.
"If you're going to follow them, take me with you! I'm
running away from Hirwen."

Firelh scowled. "Not into the desert."

Gwydion measured her fear and nodded. "The safest
place for her, if Hirwen will be upset at her leaving. Come
on."

Chela would be waiting at the North Bazaar, with the
four horses that were all they could afford; one had been
meant for a packhorse, but it could just as well carry the
Atolani girl. Somehow, Gwydion had not expected to find
his friends in Cavernon. It seemed that all roads led to
Belaric. It would be an interesting meeting, and he
wondered: Who would be the master now?

Chapter Eighteen

Tobas, restless and impatient, stood on a rocky promontory facing the trackless expanse of the Southern Sea. The voyage had taken six days in silent shipping lanes, unexpectedly empty of wizards' patrols, though they had arced far around the more populated South to their makeshift base east of Erinon. The first two waves of the fleet would have arrived in Syryn two days before. There should be word soon of the battle.

Diveshi had been organizing his forces according to the Parahnese methods, relying on his own Special Forces to front the army; he took the rest through elaborate drills and battle formations daily. Tobas had participated in some of this, fascinated by the way the general could create a coherent fighting force from such disparate groups: Hoabi pirates, who fought on land with great axes; Kerisian slingers and pikemen; Garithian scouts and bowmen; Ryasan city dwellers and mountain raiding parties; and, of course, Diveshi's Special Forces, a cavalry unit that wheeled and ran as one beast.

Mostly, however, Tobas had spent his time preparing his small patrol for contact with the S'tari. They could not depart until the news came from Syryn; they had to be able to assure the S'tari of the numbers of their army, and that would depend on the losses at the island. Most of his men were Garithian, sturdy hunters and sheepherders who perhaps would hold up better under desert conditions than men from the more cultured Kingdoms. They were good men, he thought, but all were quite disgusted with the prospect of including the Princess of Caerlin on their mission.

He turned from the sea, thinking of Valahtia—and found her standing there, watching him, an enigmatic smile on her face. She had pulled her hair up austerely behind her head and wore the black uniform of the resistance army, complete with a short sword in her belt and a stiletto in her boot. Like some dark Syryni goddess of war, though she lacked an extra pair of arms, and her eyes were not red but deepest brown.

"Searching for the isle of Lorin, Colonel?" she asked gravely. "It's not known to journey down the Four Rivers from the Tarnsea, I fear, though you might sight it from your father's palace in Laenar."

"Only a ship do I desire," he quoted, equally unsmiling. "Will you watch with me?" He took her slim hand and led her to the edge of the cliff, where they sat with their feet swinging over the rhythmic pounding of waves on rocks.

"The Southern Sea." She shivered a little. "As far as you go there is nothing, only wind on the water. How many men have never come back from it? I prefer the land, my lord. This land, my father's land. It's good to be home, though it's hardly what I left."

He nodded, feeling the same, knowing that her thoughts would be following his to their families' houses and the death that would be there.

"Why wasn't I born a man?" she asked presently. "If we win . . . when we win . . . this land will need healing. Something Arel will not understand. If I had been a man, I could take the throne from him without the council of the Kingdoms protesting more than a token amount. It isn't a law that the eldest son must inherit.''

"A daughter can inherit."

"Only if she has no brothers, or those she has are crippled or idiots. And then only until she bears a male child. She can have no more than regency after that." She grinned suddenly. "If I could have a son, now, they'd be more likely to go along with a coup. What do you think, Tobas?''

"Don't look at me." He chuckled, actually not minding at all.

The scrub fire burned low and fitfully in the hollow of desert sand and stones. Gwydion fed it slowly, miserly, keeping it barely live enough to slow-roast the hare Firelh had brought down earlier in the day. The Ryasan lord, impatient, had ridden on to scout the caravan's trail; it was growing increasingly difficult to follow in the shifting sand. Gwydion, too, felt the urge to press on, but he said nothing in the face of Melana's exhaustion.

The minstrel had been ill-treated by the wizards. Though Gwydion had been giving her more than her share of the rationed food and water, each morning she was more faded. They had been on the trail of their friends for six days. Now she sat huddled in a light cloak, shivering despite the heat the sand radiated still although the sun was going down.

Chela, having given up her chattering efforts to bring Melana out of her miserable prison, now sat combing her thick red hair in the firelight. It had lost some of its luster, since it had not been washed for the past week, but it still glowed enough for Gwydion. Yet he could not admire it properly this evening. His apprehension had grown each day the captives drew closer to Belaric.

The master had ruled his College at Akesh with icy discipline and offhand cruelty; he would not be gentle with prisoners. And knowing Belaric's Power, Gwydion doubted Briana's shields were strong enough. If she broke, not only would the captives be lost, but the army in the South would be met and destroyed before it had a chance to ally with the S'tari. Gwydion gave the fire a last piece of brush and cleared his mind. This would drain him badly, but he did not think he should need to use his Power until they were close to Khymer.

"We're being followed," Briana whispered. The captives were huddled closely on the ground, guarded by a ring of sleepy soldiers who no longer paid any attention to their talk.

"Who?" Kyellan asked in a strained voice. His shoulders were swollen and throbbing against their ropes; apparently the soldiers expected him to attempt some sort of magical escape, and they had kept him tightly bound since the third day, when the First Priestess and Gemon had been transferred to mule-dragged ground litters. The other captives, even Erlin, merely had their hands bound in front of them.

"Gwydion, Chela, Firelh, and another girl. Gwydion warns me of Belaric's Power, and offers, I think, to reinforce our shields."

"The Goddess keeps our minds strong. We don't need wizards' magic," Gemon said.

"Nevertheless, I think it's a good idea. If we can all clear our thoughts for a moment, he can work better."

Kyellan did not find it difficult not to think. He had been in a trance of exhaustion and pain for the last two days, his only desire to keep from falling along the trail as he kept to the horses' pace set by the soldiers. Through the emptiness of his mind, he could feel Gwydion's walls going up, adding to and reinforcing something that was already there. Triple walls, he thought, of iron and seamless stone and tempered sword steel; yet he could not tell which were Gwydion's and which were his own.

"He should not be doing this," the First Priestess said sharply.

"He strengthens us greatly," Briana said.

"He has need of his strength."

Gwydion came back from his sending and reeled with the shock of the attack. Evil, foulest evil, guided by something he had met before . . . His vision slowly cleared, and he leaped out of the way of the thing's claws barely in time. Demonic, armed with nightmare teeth and claws, beating vast dark wings . . . very like what Kyellan had encountered in the temple near Dallynd, if not the same being.

Melana was screaming with her singer's lungs, enough to be heard from the Maer Cunin to Khymer. The thing was bounding toward her. Gwydion tried to shield her with Power, but he had no Power left.

"Chela!" he cried. "Help Melana! I cannot. . . ." Then he saw that his apprentice was on the ground, sprawled senseless from a clip by one of the thing's pinions.

The minstrel beat weakly at the creature's chest as it bent her backward and its mouth reached for her neck. Crippled as he could not remember ever being before, Gwydion drew his short sword and leaped at the demon, hacking at it from behind. It threw Melana to the ground, where she lay with her head at an impossible angle, and turned to him with a roar.

Helpless to fight it effectively, Gwydion could only dodge the blows of the demon's poisoned claws, slashing at it with his sword. Its apelike arms were longer than his hand and sword combined, and it was only angered by his scratchings. He would not be as lucky as Kyellan. It would not simply disappear this time.

Beyond it, Chela was staggering to her feet. He had to keep it from her until she regained her composure and her Power. But the demon, tired of chasing a young wizard who radiated fear and desperation, reached out suddenly and took hold of the sharp end of the sword, wrenching it away from Gwydion. Black, foul-smelling blood spurted from the demon's paw, burning the wizard's face and hands. The thing leaped for him, and he ran.

It did not follow. Chela hit it with a bolt of Power, making it howl with rage and pain and turn for her. Gwydion jumped for his sword again. It advanced like a cavalry charge on Chela, even as she beat at it with blasts of Power. Roaring with agony and madness, it engulfed her in its huge arms and dug its claws into her back. Chela shrieked. Gwydion attacked it from the rear, but it threw him backward with one long arm with such force that he hit the ground near stunned.

He struggled fuzzily to rise, each of Chela's screams a sledgehammer blow. But she was now crying Words of Power with her pain. Storm clouds drew overhead, and lightning flashed dangerously close. The illumination revealed another form, some distance away and cloaked with illusion, a tall, golden-haired figure. But Gwydion could not be certain he saw it at all.

"Abarath!" Chela keened horribly, her voice no longer that of the child-woman he loved. "Abarath Zylnyarmo'ae . . ." And then she spoke a Word so old it bore no relationship to language. Thunder answered, and lightning struck between Gwydion and the struggling pair.

The demon howled. Its form began to quiver and fade as it was forced to return to its own world. Chela fell heavily to the sand, her long red hair mingling with a growing pool of blood at her back. Gwydion stumbled to her as the rain began to flood from the clouds she had created. The deep trenches in her skin revealed sections of her ribs. The wounds were already inflamed with the demon's poison. Ripping off his tunic, Gwydion pressed it ineffectually against the tattered flesh.

Cursing and sobbing, he ran to the terror-stricken horses. Two of them had managed to uproot their picket pins in their efforts to escape the demon; they were gone. His horse remained, thank fortune, but it was mad with fear, and he lacked the Power to calm it. Calming himself was difficult enough. But finally he was able to be quiet, to speak to it softly, to reach close enough to soothe it with familiar hands. The poor beast required more soothing than he had time to give. He fumbled with his saddlebags and finally found his bag of herbs and medicinal spells.

Racing to the blasted sand dune where Chela lay, he paused long enough to be certain Melana was dead. Her neck was broken. As he ran on, he pulled a needle and strong thread from his bag. The wounds would have to be stitched to stop their bleeding, before he could do anything about the demon's poison. If he could do anything about the poison without his Power.

He began to work, praying she would not wake before it was done. After a time, he looked up to see Firelh standing over him, pale, his left arm bloody, carrying a stained, unsheathed sword. The Earl's horse stood placidly nearby.

"What happened, lad?"

Gwydion did not want Firelh to know he had been

crying. "We . . . we were attacked. By a High Demon.
Melana's dead. Chela destroyed it, but she's badly hurt."
He quickly took up the last few stitches, feeling her begin
to rouse under his hands. "What about you?"

"Me? Oh, this. Nothing that needs doctoring. I ran into
a S'tari who didn't understand I was on his side. Had to
kill him."

Chela groaned, and her lips moved. Finally, she mumbled,
"Gone?"

"You banished it, love, with a Word I never taught
you." He felt his throat tighten again.

"What about Melana?" she whispered.

"Dead. It's my fault. I used all my Power reaching
Briana and strengthening their shields. And I came back,
and there it was, and I had no Power. Nothing."

"You had to help them." Her voice quivered. He took
one of her hands, holding tight. "Gods, Gwydion, it
hurts! . . ." she finally blurted, fighting tears.

"I know. Chela, I've got to get the poison out. Remember what I told you about when Kyellan was hurt? To use a
demon to heal a demon's work?"

"You're in no condition for that."

"I have to try. It's too near your heart already." Perhaps the little demon was so used to obeying him that it
would not notice he had no Power this time. The chants
had Power in themselves, he thought, if he could remember the proper notes.

"Link with me, then," Chela said weakly.

"No. You must concentrate anything you have left on
healing yourself. And on shielding yourself from everything but the healing that comes from my bottled imp. Can
you do that?"

Not waiting for her answer, he began the chant. The
opening had to be repeated three times before he had the

volume right. He had at least wakened the orange-red thing, and it strained to escape. Not allowing himself to project anything but absolute confidence, he shook it out onto his palm.

It burned. Like holding live coals from the heart of a star. He did not have the Power to shield himself. Crying out with the pain, somehow making his cries into properly pronounced Words, he continued the chant, but the melody was lost. The thing consuming his hands was beginning to realize what it was dealing with. Then he threw it onto Chela's back.

She winced but made no sound. Her eyes were screwed shut in concentration. The pale color of the demon's fiery coldness spread over her wounds, overcoming the reds and purples of the poison. It was done. Feeling blisters cracking in his palms, Gwydion steeled himself, steadied his chanting voice, and plucked the cloudy creature from Chela's back. It seared his hands. He could see smoke begin to rise and smell the odor of charred flesh.

He could not shake it back to the bottle. It clung to his skin, a small volcano, scorching, blazing, roasting . . . He screamed and screamed again, unable to continue the chant, nauseated from the pain, from the smell. . . .

Chela rose on her elbows and spoke a minor Word of Power, one Gwydion vaguely remembered having taught her. The form of the demon began to waver, insubstantial. Chela reached out and took the bottle from between Gwydion's knees where he had been steadying it. She set it on the ground, chanting in a voice as harsh as a carrion crow's. Then she pulled the demon from Gwydion's hands and stuffed it back into its bottle, corking it firmly.

Gwydion clutched his hands to his stomach, sobbing uncontrollably. He felt Chela's arms around him. She held him until he quieted. Then she rummaged in his bag for salves and bandages, and treated his ravaged hands as quickly as she could. The skin was gone from his palms, and the flesh looked like that of the rabbit that still hung over the rain-doused cooking fire. Gwydion sat gazing at them, numb with pain and shock, until Chela finished bandaging them. She wrapped him in blankets and ordered him to rest.

"Are you . . . all right?" he croaked. "The demon . . . did it work?"

"I'll be fine," Chela whispered. "And you will be, too. Go to sleep."

Khymer rose out of the desert like a pearl from a bed of cracked, discolored oyster shells. Its many temples and palaces shone white in the diamond sun, the richer sparkling with white gold leaf, the poorer making do with whitewash. This isolated, ancient city of the desert had been a holy place for as long as anyone knew. It held the Dawn Temple of the Goddess, the cave where She had made Herself known to the original First Priestess, and contained the largest enclave of priestesses anywhere besides the Sanctuary. In Khymer the martyr of the Nyesin sect had been stoned, and the angry Northern god Ban had walked one stride and carved out the Tarnsea with a blow from his cudgel.

Briana could not contain her excitement at the sight. Few of the women of the Sanctuary ever came to the Dawn Temple, and it was the same from the other direction. She supposed the First Priestess must have seen it before. The wizards would have burned the Temple, but she doubted they could destroy the cave itself. The sacred peace of Khymer might have been disturbed, but it did not rely on altars and worshippers. Its history stood from the beginning of time as a home of Light.

Kyellan looked at her sourly, offended by her obvious happiness. She tried to school her expression into one appropriate for a miserable, exhausted prisoner being taken to face her greatest enemy—which indeed she was, and it frightened her, but the peace of Khymer was much more powerful than her fears. More powerful than the pain of her blood-encrusted feet from which the Cavernon slippers had fallen on the fifth day, than her angry sunburn and knifelike hunger, than her fear that the First Priestess and Gemon might die under Belaric's interrogation. They were horribly weak, both of them, though the First Priestess was worst.

The Ardavan winter palace loomed over the city, graceful and elegant. Belaric had made it his headquarters. The prisoners were not given long to admire the arches and carvings of the facade. They were hustled inside and given to a new group of guards. The First Priestess and Gemon were forced to walk, prodded with spears. The palace was a huge barracks, full of soldiers patrolling or lounging or gambling in the courtyards and halls. The atmosphere of oppression was thick.

"Where are the dancing girls?" Kyellan whispered. "Last time I was here, the place was much more lively."

"You've been here before?" Briana said, to keep her mind from what faced them: a huge pair of arched doors, triple-bolted, guarded by three ranks of impassive soldiers. It would have to be the Great Hall. And Belaric.

"Retook it during the S'tari wars. Made lieutenant afterward for leading the assault." He grinned, but his smile was twisted.

"Fighting in the Holy City got you promoted?" Briana was prepared to get angry, but the doors opened and fear lowered itself upon her like a clammy shroud. She pressed close to Kyellan, unable to help herself, like a child hiding behind its parents' legs. Erlin and Pima walked in ahead of them, both visibly shaken. Briana knew with her reasoning mind that Belaric was manipulating them into fear, that she could resist it by simply concentrating on her shields, but the sensation was powerful. The First Priestess and Gemon seemed little affected behind her as the guards herded them into the hall.

Belaric was middle-aged, with a trim, hard body and an angular, handsome face. But his eyes were not the clear, tawny color of Gwydion's. They were the eyes of a diseased cat, pale yellow and clouded.

Two obscene creatures flanked his throne, their hunger broadcast through the Great Hall. They had eagles' heads and claws, bodies of alligators on long tigers' legs, the tails of scorpions. The slim, delicate chains would not hold them if they wished to go farther. Summonings from the Otherworld, Briana guessed.

"Welcome," said the wizard benignly, his voice soft and low. Briana met his repulsive eyes with hatred and defiance, and he dropped his pretense and said harshly, "It was a great day for the New Empire when you were captured. Your pitiful army, your doomed quest, all is finished now."

"You haven't stopped those things by taking us," Briana said scornfully. "There are others to fulfill your destruction."

Belaric chuckled, an unpleasant sound. "My dear girl, if you mean the traitor Gwydion, he and his pretty apprentice will be joining you soon. We are waiting for them."

Briana tried to hide her shock, but it must have been visible in her eyes. The wizard laughed loudly, mockingly.

"Young Gwydion may yet surprise you," said the First Priestess. She supported herself on Gemon, who looked near collapse herself.

Belaric shrugged. "He may have Power, but he is

inexperienced. We watched him closely at Akesh once we
knew his weakness, and did not teach him many of the
things he should have learned.''

"Is it weakness to follow the Light, wizard?'' The First
Priestess smiled serenely. ''The Dark has always thought
the Light weaker than it, but which has always won in the
end? Answer me that.''

"The last battle between them was long ago,'' Belaric
said angrily. ''The Hoab Wizard was a fool. Old woman,
who are you to speak of the Light? Many innocent children
have been murdered in the name of Ayetra.''

"If that was done in our name, we are at fault in some
measure,'' she acknowledged. ''But the Light does not for-
sake its own for a few mistakes. The Goddess is with us,
Belaric. Can you say the same?''

"She is an ancient Power, unfit for the modern world.
We have no need of Her. She has aided you little, besides.''

"She has not sent us angelic hosts to repel your army of
demons; that is not the way She gives Her aid. But come,
wizard. We need not argue theology. Neither of us will
change our beliefs.''

"Then we will speak of more pressing matters,'' he said
grimly. ''There is information which you possess and I
desire. It is that simple. Be reasonable and you will not be
harmed.''

"Your spies will tell you about the resistance army,''
Kyellan said. ''We have no other information.''

"Do not play the innocent, Captain; the role is ill
suited. I want the Goddess's Seat. Tell me where it is and
I will spare your lives.''

Briana laughed. ''The promise of a wizard is like a
cheap dish: soon broken,'' she quoted, allowing defiance
to overcome her terror of his Power.

"I will wrench the information from you, and leave you

with less than half a mind, and no Power," he said softly. "Tell me where it is, Priestess."

"We have not found it."

"Obviously. For if you had found it, you'd be using it against me. You know where it is, or you would not have come into the danger of Cavernon City."

"You know as much as we do," Gemon said, her voice rasping. "It is somewhere in Caerlin. We had no time to begin a search."

"What of the rest of you? Come, someone, speak. Speak now, and save yourself and your friends from unpleasantness. Where is it? Not in Cavernon City, for you were buying horses to leave the capital. Where, then?"

"We do not know," Briana said. A moment later it had become a lie. She heard a high, distant call, very soft and gentle and far away, and knew it was the beginning of the call of the Goddess's Seat. She looked up and found Belaric frowning thoughtfully at her.

"No?" he said. "We shall see. Take the others to the dungeons," he told the guards. "You may begin to work on the soldiers, but do not touch the women. I'll deal with them one by one until they tell me what I wish to know."

"Well, we wanted to meet them," Tobas said over a thicket of S'tari spears. His hand ached for a sword. These dark young faces with tightly curled black hair falling from beneath their hoods were, to his mind, nothing but the enemy. The desert warriors who had killed so many of his companions in the wars were not to be soft-spoken and diplomatic with. They were to be killed.

"Should I talk to them?" Valahtia inquired, seeming not at all uncomfortable. He nodded. They had been traveling north along the western shore of the Maer Cunin for two days now, but the first sign of habitation they had encountered was this band of youthful, fierce-visaged S'tari who had appeared out of nowhere as they had passed through a stand of gnarled trees.

The leader of the band answered the Princess with reluctance. She bowed slightly and turned back to Tobas. "They'll take us to their lord, a half day's ride. They're disgusted at having to talk through a woman, and they're not impressed by my name." Her laughter was rueful.

They reached the camp by early evening. Large tents of camel hides were set in two even circles, surrounded by picketed camels and free-roaming, sleek horses. Small children ran games of tag between horses' legs and over the backs of the ill-tempered camels. Women in heavy robes and veils balanced buckets of water from a rough stone well. The children crowded curiously around the incoming patrol, staring at Tobas's people and their shaggy Northern horses, until the young patrol members laughingly shooed them away.

After a hurried conversation at the door flap of the largest tent, a burly guard motioned Tobas inside. He entered. Valahtia followed, hoping she would be allowed as an interpreter. The tent was richly furnished, hung with deep-violet-and-blue curtains, scattered with vibrant geometric-designed cushions and subtly woven rugs banded with brilliant color. It hardly seemed a tent at all, the Princess thought. Rather like one of the rooms of her father's palace. One would have to lean against a wall to discover it was not solid.

Five old men sat in a circle, passing an elegant water pipe that smelled intoxicating. They were being served an evening meal of meat gravy over rice, with a large platter of dates in the center.

"Good evening," Tobas ventured. Valahtia quickly translated, addressing herself to the imposing man in the center, whose heavy black beard showed no grey despite his wrinkled face.

"Good evening," that one answered in perfect Caer. "Do you lead the army that is coming from the coast?"

"Colonel Tobas," the Guardsman said with a low bow. "Sharing command with General Diveshi of Parahn's Special Forces."

"That name is known to us," said the S'tari lord, turning and speaking to his companions for a moment. "I am Surleien, leader of the People of the Inland Lake, the Maer Cunin. You are not Parahnese, youngster. Caer, but probably too young to have fought us in the late wars."

"I had that honor, my lord," Tobas said stiffly. Careful, Valahtia urged silently, knowing how much the young Guardsman hated the people he had been sent to negotiate with.

"You fought against us. Now you enter our territory with an armed band, and a woman by your side who claims to be the daughter of our greatest enemy. Why?"

"To propose an alliance. The wizards have already driven people in every Kingdom from their homes, and they intend to do the same to you. Join us in fighting them."

"We fight them now, without the help of Caerlin or any other Kingdom."

"The wizards have at least sixty thousand men in Caerlin. How many can you face them with? We offer you more than forty-five thousand men to help you win back the lands the wizards have taken. If you help us win our Kingdoms again."

"We care little for your Kingdoms," Surleien growled.

"How many men can you have?" Tobas persisted, making an obvious effort to stay calm. "Surely no more than ten thousand."

"Counting the boys whose fathers died fighting for freedom against Caerlin, we have perhaps five thousand warriors. We have lost many to the wizards."

Valahtia sensed Tobas's growing anger. With a glance at his tightly set face, she moved forward and bowed as if to an equal. There were murmurs among the old men. She spoke softly in S'tari. "The freedom you fought for is more sorely endangered now than it has ever been. The wizards have enslaved every Kingdom, killing without mercy. I know they have killed my father." Their reaction was not one of sorrow. She swallowed and continued. "This time it will not be the fathers but the sons who will die, not the warriors but their wives and babies. The wizards believe this will truly enslave a people, to break their spirits and their hearts. And the burden they place on you will be far worse than that which caused you to go to war five times in two centuries against Caerlin. Think on that, Council of Surleien." She bowed again and went back to her place behind Tobas, who turned to question her.

The S'tari lord raised his palm for attention. "We must deliberate long on an alliance with Caerlin. Leave us. You will be shown a tent for the night."

"What did you say?" Tobas demanded as they followed a quiet, veiled girl to a small hide tent where their patrol was billeted.

Pleased with herself, she kissed him lightly on the cheek and grinned mischievously. "I told them you were only a foolish soldier, and a member of the decadent aristocracy, besides being a mere child. They praised my perception to the four winds. Really, my lord, if you would only stop hating these people, you might get to like them."

His anger had been ready to explode, but now he could not help but laugh. Then, suddenly, he swept her off her

feet and kissed her thoroughly, to the astonishment of the
S'tari near the tent.

"I'm certain you were marvelous, Your Highness, whatever you really said. And if you've won a treaty for us, I'll
never refuse you anything. Satisfied?" He smiled, and his
boyish face lit up, a blaze she could warm herself by.

"For now," she conceded, and giggled uncontrollably as
he carried her into the crowded tent.

Chapter Nineteen

"Kyellan. Kyellan." The whisper insinuated itself into his fogged brain, somehow penetrating the mists. "Damn you, Ky, wake up." Why couldn't they leave him alone? He opened his eyes to slits.

"Go away."

"Fool, I'm trying to help. Now be quiet," the voice insisted. A key fought in the stubborn hasp of the chains that suspended Kyellan by his wrists from the ceiling of the small cell. The bands released him, and he fell to the floor, pain clawing steel fingers through his body. His shoulders ached, and his back throbbed angrily where they had whipped him.

Someone knelt beside him. "I can't do more. They'll kill me if they find out."

Kyellan finally recognized the soft accents. "Mharis? What—"

"Shh. I know you're in no condition to escape, but—"

"Escape?" He pulled himself to his hands and knees, shaking his head in an effort to clear it. "From this place? How? I lost track of the steps they brought me down, but we're below ground a long way, with them all between us and the door."

"I can show you a way. But hurry, man."

Kyellan laughed, short and harsh. "Hurry? I don't think I can even walk, Mharis."

"Come," the mercenary said, pulling Kyellan to his feet with an ungentle arm around his shoulders. "You'll thank me for this someday."

"Maybe," the Guardsman gasped. "Right now I'd rather strangle you."

"If you get out, and I ever see you again, you'll have your chance."

He took a few labored steps then stopped. "I can't leave them."

"Your priestesses are in a triple-doored cell with eight guards. Your young lieutenant . . ." He paused, then continued. "He tried to escape, killed two guards. Of course they caught him. He's unguarded now, but I've never seen a man so bloody. They used a rod on his feet. He won't be able to walk."

"Damn." Kyellan looked bleakly at the scarred soldier. "It's not right, Mharis. I can't leave them here like this."

Leading the way through the deserted corridor, Mharis spoke in a bare whisper. "I spoke to the young priestess for a moment, when Belaric was done with her."

"Briana? Is she all right?"

"Weak, but I don't think she was hurt. She told me to tell you this: 'We are lost when the wizards find the Seat of the Goddess. And they will. Find it first, Kyellan. Hold it from them. It's the only chance we have.' That's what she said."

How could she ask him to leave her here? Did she really think he would be able to find her Goddess's Seat before the wizards? Yet he could not disobey her.

"What's between the two of you, Kyellan? She's a priestess."

"Don't you think I know that?" he said irritably. "Take me to this place where I can get out before you're missed."

They descended another flight of stairs and entered a cavelike tunnel with walls of sooty sandstone. Water trickled down in places, but puddles were quickly absorbed by the porous earthen floor. Kyellan stumbled along, following Mharis's brown uniform, barely seeing anything. Gods, he hurt. He didn't think they had gotten anything from him; but then, he hadn't known what they wanted, the location of the Seat. They had beaten him a long time before they had whipped him. He had lost blood and thought he might have a few broken ribs.

They took inexplicable turnings deep into narrow caverns. These could hardly be man-made. Kyellan shivered in the damp. He hated being underground. It seemed he was in the entrails of some giant beast which might at any moment contract and smother him.

"When will we be done with this moles' work?" he complained. "We haven't started climbing yet."

"Not much farther to the outlet." Mharis turned again and exclaimed with satisfaction. There was a dark hole in the low roof of the cave. "We're no longer under the winter palace. This hole will let you out in the anteroom of the temple of the Nyesin sect, who are required by their Order to aid fugitives. I had to use it once myself, long ago, when I was accused of indiscretion with a certain Earl's wife. One of the woman's maids knew of these tunnels. I suppose they were meant for the use of the royal family in case of attack."

Kyellan shuddered. He loathed small enclosed spaces. This was going to be difficult.

"Up with you, and I'll get back to my command," Mharis said with nervous briskness.

He pulled himself slowly and agonizingly into the shaft,

finding handholds cut from the rock of its cylindrical walls, and looked back down at the taut-faced mercenary.

"Come with me. They'll find out you helped me."

"I can't." His eyes were trapped. "I'm not yet free of their Power, old friend. I'll probably go back and betray you. Go quickly. Their part of me screams 'traitor' for bringing you here." He wheeled and ran back down the rock-walled corridor.

Wonderful. Kyellan should never have trusted the spellbound Kerisian, whether or not he answered to the name Mharis now. Yet it was better to be here, barely able to climb this narrow shaft, than to be hanging in chains awaiting the next unpleasantness. He willed himself to think of nothing but reaching for the next handhold, and the next, to ignore the fiery blaze of his shoulders. Twice he nearly fell when his tortured muscles gave way and left him clinging with one hand and scrabbling with his feet for purchase on the stone.

He had been climbing for perhaps an hour when a heavy wooden trapdoor blocked his way. He could not open it. To come all this way and be stuck beneath a trapdoor . . . He hoped the Nyesin priests still harbored fugitives. Pounding with all his strength seemed to produce little effect; he called weakly, ready to drop back through the vertical tunnel as his hands grew numb.

Footsteps thudded on a wooden floor above him. The door was removed with much grunting and effort. An ascetic, disapproving face peered down at him. Kyellan attempted a smile, knowing he hardly looked pleasant. The priest was a dark-skinned man with S'tari blood. "Are you armed?" he asked sharply.

The Guardsman shook his head, pulling himself through the trap with a groan he could not suppress. The priest moved to him with swift concern when he saw his condi-

tion and helped him to the narrow cot which was the only
furniture in the cool, whitewashed room. Kyellan sa▮
gingerly.

"The wizards will be looking for me, Sun-Brother." He
hoped he had remembered the correct address.

The priest nodded. "May He be with us. I fear they d▮
not respect our right to give sanctuary. You will have t▮
leave as soon as possible."

"I will. But I need clothing to cover these rags, an▮
food for a journey in the desert. I'll pay you someday, if ▮
can."

"Of course. Rest, and we will gather what you wil▮
need."

Kyellan could feel his probably broken ribs catching
with each breath. All he needed was for one to puncture ▮
lung. He ripped the remainder of his shredded Cavernor
tunic apart and tied it into a single long strap, which he
wrapped tightly around his lower chest, then over one o▮
his lacerated shoulders to secure it.

The room had begun to spin, dipping slowly as a buoy
lapped by gentle waves. He closed his eyes firmly against the
sensation, but even the cot swayed and rocked unnervingly.
Between pain and hunger and loss of blood, he wondered
if he would be able to rise again.

The soft rustling of woolen robes, and the padding of
sandaled feet, told him the priest had reentered the room.
He opened his eyes. The dark-skinned Nyesin's arms were
full of something. He set it down on the cot and produced
a steaming meat roll and a heavy mug.

Kyellan knew he ate the roll too fast, but he could no▮
help himself. He began on the mug; it was bitter red wine,
spiced with something he could not recognize. He guessed
it contained medicinal herbs from the warm, numbing

feeling that spread from his throat to his stomach and radiated out from there.

"Our hospitality is greatly lacking," said the priest unhappily. "You must forgive us, but the wizards' men are nearly at our doors. Here is what food we could spare, and two waterskins." He handed over a bulky goat-skin bag. "The robes were taken from a S'tari rebel who sought sanctuary with us and was taken by force. You are in no condition to be going out into the desert, I know, but we cannot keep you here."

"I'll be all right. Can I leave without being seen by the wizards' men?"

The priest nodded. "Follow me. Put the robe on quickly. There is a scimitar wrapped in cloths within the folds. We could not let you leave weaponless against the wizards."

Kyellan stopped and gazed at the thin, dark man in surprise. The Nyesin sect was fanatically opposed to violence in all forms. Yet the blade was there. He pulled on the robe and slipped the wicked-looking weapon into its bronze-edged hole on the wide camel-skin belt. It hung bare at his side, curving backward; an aspect of S'tari dress he had never been comfortable with. A double-edged blade, in his opinion, required a sheath. But the weight of it felt marvelous.

"Thank you," he said inadequately. Impatient, the priest pulled him from the room, down a short, bare hallway, and out into the bright sunlight of midday. They hurried along a path in the temple's courtyard garden, between beehive-shaped white buildings, toward a low wall. The unlocked gate opened into a deserted alley of Khymer. The boots of wizards' soldiers clattered in the street not far away. Kyellan pulled the hood of the white homespun robe forward and attached the dustcloth that covered the lower part of the face. He bowed to the priest.

"Go quickly," said his benefactor. "I must return to the gates and let the demons in." He turned and trotted back down the path.

Kyellan ducked into the alley, silent as a S'tari ghost in the worn sandals the priest had given him. He would have to steal a mount somewhere, a S'tari horse or camel, to complete his disguise. He paused at a pile of charred, abandoned wood in a gutter. The blackened end of one of the sticks, rubbed liberally across his olive-skinned face and blended by guesswork, made him even darker than many true desert dwellers. The rough homespun of his robe chafed his torn back, and his ribs pained him with each heartbeat, but he could feel the Nyesin wine taking effect, numbing his discomfort and clearing his mind. He strode through the quiet midday city, trying to affect the free-swinging, graceful walk of a S'tari warrior.

Even in his lawless childhood, he had never stolen a horse from the bazaar. First time for everything, he supposed. It was not difficult to creep around the edge of the white-cobbled square. Merchants napped in their stalls or gamed with each other under canopies. Neither customers nor thieves could be expected in the noonday sun; anyway, Khymer had never been a city of crime. If Kyellan had been his usual self, he would not have worried, but he did not trust his skills in this half-drugged state.

The horses were at the western end of the bazaar. They began to snort and shuffle as he came near. All S'tari animals, though only a few worth his attention. He crooned soft nonsense in their native language, moving with as much grace and confidence as he could muster. They let him approach, nuzzling him with friendly curiosity, the familiar smells of his clothing reassuring them.

One caught his eye, short-coupled, deep-chested, with corded muscles and a long scratch on its left flank. It had to have been a warrior's horse, recently captured at its master's death. Near it on the ground, dusty and bloodstained, lay a goat-fleece S'tari saddle, stirrupless, as was their custom. The horse whickered a welcome as he buckled the worn fleece to its back and untied the halter rope that tethered it. He worked quickly, fastening the end of the rope around the horse's lower jaw in the S'tari manner and bringing the single length of rein to the left side.

Mounting would be difficult, considering his back and shoulders. He led the animal silently away from the bazaar, and when they were well out of sight in a narrow alley, with quite un-S'tari clumsiness he climbed a short distance up someone's roof ladder and slid onto the confused horse's back. It wanted to run. He held it to a trot, promising it a gallop when they were free of the city.

Kyellan fought to keep his back straight and soldierly as he moved down the dusty, unpaved streets of the perimeter of the Holy City. Signs of the wizards' presence were everywhere, in new unpainted buildings of harsh browns and greys, in desecrated temples and defaced idols, in the bitter, fearful faces of the few people he saw.

The detachment at the gates looked surprised to be confronted by a S'tari warrior from within the city. Their orders probably only covered keeping the desert people out.

"Who are you?" demanded a Northern mercenary in badly accented Caer.

"I don't understand," Kyellan said in S'tari.

The guard tried again, in Caer and Garithian, which seemed to be the limit of his education. "Does anyone speak his idiot language?" he finally called.

"I do, a little," said a younger man uncomfortably. "Your name is?" he began in fractured S'tari. "Why you here, tell. . . . Get off camel, come down. . . ."

"Camel?" the Guardsman said in his haughtiest voice. "Dog of a Northman, this is a horse; I do not suppose you would know the difference."

The hapless guard had followed little. "Why you here?"

"My name is K'hreni se Jairanh," he said slowly, as if to a child. "I am an emissary of His Eminence Surleien, leader of the People of the Inland Lake." He hoped the old warrior was still alive.

"We . . . fight the S'tari."

"Yes. I have spoken with Belaric, and return to my people."

Nodding with understanding, the guard waved Kyellan through. "An important spy for Belaric," he told the others. They had heard the wizard's name used and were satisfied.

Gleefully spurring his horse to a gallop, Kyellan thanked any god who would take responsibility for inventing ignorance, apathy, and incompetence.

"Is there a chance he'll succeed, Mother?" Briana whispered out of the darkness of her cell.

The old woman's breathing was harsh and labored in the other cubicle. Pima and Gemon had been taken away early that morning and had not returned. "In finding the Seat, yes. In taking it and holding it, if it is the Goddess's will."

"How could it be possible? He is a man, and does not believe."

"He is more than you know, more than he himself knows. I think Gemon sensed it before I did, before those two days he carried me on the trail."

"He is not evil, as Gemon claims!" she protested.

"But he is dangerous. There is a Power in him I would

not wish unleashed. Yet if he is to hold the Seat, it must be used." The First Priestess sighed heavily.

"I love him." The words were defiant.

"That is unfortunate. It would be better if you could find another for your service to Cianya, before you must become First Priestess."

Briana strained to make out the wizened face through the shadows. Another? Another man, did she mean? And what service to Cianya?

"You are confused, child. I was much the same, when the First Priestess before me died. It is contrary to what you have learned. Come, listen, and understand."

Briana crawled forward toward the straining voice and took the frail, thin hand that reached between the bars of the cell. The First Priestess gripped her hand and spoke. "Hear me before I am Called. To be First Priestess, you must serve the Goddess in all Her aspects. You have been Wiolai, Maiden, all your life. You have been Rahshaiya, bringing death in battle. You have not been Cianya."

"The Mother," she said softly, beginning to see.

"You must find a man, know his love, bear his child. Only then may you be the Voice of the Goddess on this earth." The old woman's grip weakened, and Briana began to smell the battle smoke of Rahshaiya.

"Not yet," she whispered urgently, tightening her own clasp. "Afterward, after the child . . . what? What of the man?"

"You will know of your pregnancy as soon as it is accomplished. Then you must return to the life of the Order, to prepare yourself to become First Priestess. When the child is born, you will take the place I leave empty. Thus has it always been." The old woman had the voice now of a mouse, of a ghost. Rahshaiya was descending. Briana raised the spider-veined hand to touch her face.

"And, child, daughter," breathed the First Priestess, "for the sake of the child you will bear, do not choose Kyellan. Promise me that." And she was gone, her last breath cool in the damp cell.

The young priestess lowered the lifeless hand, feeling tears begin. She keened her grief in the words of the death chants of her Order and wished she had the strength in her body for the Dance. Adding burden to her sorrow was guilt, for she could not promise to honor her Mother's last request.

Afterward Kyellan remembered that journey as a dream-like time, full of shifting images and clouds. The glow of strength and energy that brought him out of Khymer was soon lost, and his pain rose to engulf him until he felt he was a diver, deep under the ocean, who had stayed down too long and could not return. Sometimes he was conscious enough to dismount and give his horse and himself sips of the water provided by the Nyesin priest; most of the time, he slumped in the saddle without thought, rein dragging and the horse picking its own way through the sand.

The second day, he felt the touch of a seeking mind. Soon after, he was attacked by a demonic creature with curling horns and falcon's wings, and a lashing hooked tail that cut deep furrows in the sand. The horse screamed and flailed, and he fell, hacking at the creature with his scimitar; but it was all vague and far away, as if he were a spectator rather than a combatant.

He had fallen on his knees before the demon, helpless, ready for the blow, when something that he did not recognize welled up in him like an artesian spring that had been trapped deep underground. Something that pressed against the confines of his body and exploded from him with shattering force, leaving him gasping on the sand, with the demon gone and a blackened rent in the earth where it had been.

Later that day, mounted again, he realized his horse was walking northwest, away from the S'tari lands, the rebel army, and Tobas. He came out of his tranced state long enough to turn the horse's head. But in another hour, he was in the rocky, barren, windswept terrain that led to the Tarnsea. It was very strange, but he did not have the strength to fight it. He fell asleep instead.

Tobas and Valahtia were summoned to the council tent late that afternoon. They had spent the day in nervous boredom, watching the activities of the camp, riding herd on their men when they grew too admiring of the lithe S'tari girls who set out their weaving in the sun.

"We will need no interpreter," Surleien greeted them. "However, the King's daughter may remain."

"You've decided, then?" Tobas said eagerly.

"We will ally ourselves with you. We have drawn up a treaty. But we have several conditions that must be met."

Valahtia could see the satisfied complacency of the other old men. She smiled inwardly, willing to guess what those terms would be. Arel would be displeased, to put it mildly.

"One. The first action of the army will be to liberate Khymer, the Holy City."

"We already intended that," Tobas said with a smile.

"Two. The S'tari warriors will remain under S'tari command, though integrated into the overall strategy of your generals, if our councils approve of that strategy."

Valahtia enjoyed Tobas's discomfiture. Doubtless he was picturing what Diveshi's reaction would be, but he finally nodded.

"Three. When the wizards are defeated, the Caerlin

ruler will grant freedom to the S'tari lands. From the river Eri in the west to the Maer Cunin to Khymer: all lands east of that line will be ours, as in the time before the Caer Empire. Khymer will remain a holy city, not part of either land. If this is not agreed, we will not join you.''

She had expected it. Nevertheless, it was staggering. All the Caer lives that had been lost to maintain her father's control over this sprawling wasteland . . . to be tossed aside as unimportant? Yes. ''I agree to your terms.'' She took a deep breath. Tobas was watching her. ''Yet my approval is hardly binding. My brother would never honor such an agreement.''

Tobas nodded in sudden dejection. She plunged ahead. ''I have a counterproposal. I believe the S'tari should be their own masters. I know your language and your customs. Help me to achieve the throne of Caerlin and all your desires will be accomplished.'' She repeated her words in their language and met Surleien's speculative eyes with a steady gaze.

''What?'' Tobas finally sputtered. ''Are you out of your mind?''

''No,'' she said. ''I've come to my senses.'' She bowed to Surleien, equal to equal, and after a moment he returned the gesture with great formality, a slow smile lighting his black eyes.

''There is a treaty to be signed,'' said the S'tari lord. He produced a copy in each language from the folds of his robe. He had been sure of their agreement with his terms. Valahtia laughed and took the proffered pen. Surleien had known they had little choice. She signed with a flourish: Valahtia Ardavan, Queen of Caerlin.

''You know damn well you'd rather serve me than my brother,'' she whispered to Tobas, knowing she detected pride and something else behind the shock on his handsome face. "Admit it!"

He nodded slightly.

"I offer you a place by my side, my lord," she pressed.

He answered gravely. "I am with you. But the Goddess help us all."

"Don't you feel it, don't you hear it?" Chela reined the horse to a stop and rose in her stirrups, eliciting a protest from Gwydion, whose bandaged hands were tied around her waist.

"Hear what?" said Firelh sourly, stopping in his turn.

"A call, a call . . . high and sweet, old as the earth. . . ."

"She's babbling, wizard."

"We must go north," she insisted. "Oh, can't you understand? We have to go, we have to follow!"

"I can't hear anything," Gwydion said. "If we turn from the caravan's trail, we'll lose it."

"They'll be following it, too. Don't you see? It's the Seat of the Goddess, the object of their quest. It's calling me!"

"The Goddess's Seat?" Firelh was incredulous. "You can find it?"

"Yes, yes, of course. Before the wizards do. It's calling."

Her dirt-encrusted face was shining. "Why can't I hear it?" Gwydion asked.

"You're a wizard, and a man," she said sadly. "She doesn't call to you. I wish She would. It's so beautiful."

"Come, Gwydion. Don't doubt her word," Firelh growled. "It's what we've all been looking for. Show us, Chela."

"Come on, then! Come on!" She spurred the weary horse to a rocking canter, all it was capable of. Gwydion had to use all his concentration just to keep his seat.

*   *   *

Kyellan shouldered his saddlebag, unable even to feel regret. The horse had fallen, heaving, foundered, in its effort to follow the high, sweet voice that had driven them both these past hours. He started over the rocks at a trot. The cold salt breeze swept up from the choppy waves along the shore, slicing through the loose weave of his S'tari robe. His legs gave way, and his knees fell to the sharp rocks. He gasped for air.

The voice changed, losing its strident urgency, now more of a caressing, gentle pull. It pulled him to his feet, not allowing him to rest, but slowed him to a walk. He plodded on, unable to stop, unable to protest.

What now? Execution, Briana thought. The wizards could surely hear the call of the Seat by now, strong as it was; they would not need the priestesses anymore. The guards prodded her and Gemon up the endless stairway, blinding their eyes with unaccustomed torches. They had not seen Pima since the morning, when the soldiers had thrust Gemon back into the dank cell and roughly removed the husk of the First Priestess.

The sunlight of the yard was painfully bright, slanting in late afternoon fury. The moon would be full that night, a fitting tribute to the passing of the Voice of the Goddess. Briana wished she had her old hooded robe instead of the pitiful rags of stolen Cavernon finery. Her hands were not tied, and she shaded her eyes against the glare. Belaric awaited her in the center of the yard, at the head of a troop of mounted soldiers. Two of the horses bore a litter between them.

Her breath caught angrily. On the litter was Erlin, broken and bloodied but alive, his dark eyes meeting hers from a bruise-swollen face. Pima stood next to him, her head down and her shoulders slumped in defeat. The novice did not meet her gaze.

Belaric chuckled and turned the girl's face so Briana could see her shame. "Bring a horse for our young priestess, and two more for the novices. They shall travel in style to see the end of their quest."

Shattered, Briana mounted the complacent animal she was offered. Pima must have told them, her block forgotten when she was forced to watch them torture Erlin. She did not blame the girl. But all was lost.

The patrol moved out, the three young women in the middle with the litter that bore the silent Guardsman. Pima stared at her hands as Briana fell in beside her.

"I should have let them kill him," she said at last. "I have brought us all to ruin."

"They would have found it eventually anyway," Briana said, knowing nothing she could say would make any difference now.

Chapter Twenty

She stood on a rocky outcropping high above the Tarnsea, smiling down on him, where nothing had been in the moment before. Taller than he, clad in iridescent, flowing robes that reflected the colors of the restless sea, her face pale as a new-won pearl under windblown black hair, eyes like pools of black fire. When Kyellan met those eyes, he was swept into a vortex of night, of age, of memories, of Power. He fought the urge to kneel.

"I never believed in you," he said wearily. "So don't expect anything from me."

"I am not the Goddess, warrior," she said in gentle amusement. "I am called Va'shindi, She-Who-Guides, and I was human once. Or at least as human as you are."

"What are you now?" He was determined not to be awed.

"Very old." She laughed again, musically, and climbed down the rocks with little effort. "As old as the Shape-Changer, but its spirit grows and fathers its successor and dies each generation, while I am unchanging."

"Do you know who the Shape-Changer is?"

"As you should also know, Kyellan of Rahan, he is two, father and son, one choosing to side with Dark and one with Light. Neither shaped as the wizard he is. And the younger sadly ignorant; we must remedy that, if you are to hold and defend the Seat for the Goddess." She passed him, a mosaic of sea color and perfume.

"Wait," he scowled.

"Yes," she said impatiently, looking over her shoulder. "I said you were the younger of our current Shape-Changers, though you are quite different from the others I have encountered. I have never known your spirit not to know who it is. You believe yourself to be human so strongly that no one could discover otherwise. Even your father will be surprised to find you. He has searched long enough."

"My father," Kyellan whispered, absorbing the things she was saying and finding he did not deny them. There was a part of him that had built triple-walled shields in his mind, that had rent the veil of wizard spells from Mharis, that had effectively blasted a demon in the desert.

"You must have had a mother who refused to believe you were a wizard," Va'shindi continued as she walked. "She thought of you as human, and you changed yourself to match her desires and soon believed it yourself." She stopped and waited for him to join her, then said soberly, "It is only the strength of your identification with humanity that brings you here now, on the behalf of Light. If your father had found you and raised you a wizard, you would now be wresting the Seat from me at his side."

"You have to give me time," Kyellan protested. "It's too much all at once." He was barely able to walk now, as each breath shot arrows of pain through his chest; he could not keep pace with She-Who-Guides.

"I know. But there is no time left to give."

Briana averted her face as Belaric reined his horse up beside her. She was walking next to Erlin's litter, trying to splint his broken bones with long sticks from a cart of firewood. Pima and Gemon had both been trying to help, but neither was much assistance: Pima quietly wept the whole time, and Gemon coughed and shook so badly Briana feared she would infect the patient.

"Do you feel it, Priestess?" asked the wizard eagerly.

She ran her hand down Erlin's leg to check the tightness of the rags that bound it. "I no longer need to be told, Priestess," he continued. "I cannot help but know. Such Power, such strength! I can see why you have worshipped Her for so long. But She is beaten now."

Anger flared, and she turned on him. "You'll regret those words. She is more powerful than you can imagine, and She will destroy you."

Belaric only laughed. They were nearing the sea.

The canyon walls rose in a mist around Kyellan, towering cliffs of sheer rock above a barren stone floor that was unnaturally smooth. In the place where the walls met there rose a structure of stones so old and time-worn they seemed living beings, a colony of silent coral from undersea. Together they formed a mighty throne that dwarfed Kyellan and the one called Va'shindi who led him onward. Age sat in that Seat, the birth and death of years, and Power beyond measuring, all silent, all waiting. Smoky fear rose in Kyellan's throat. This was far from his understanding.

Va'shindi turned to him, concern and compassion on her face of terrible beauty. "There is so much more you should be told, and made to comprehend, but they are coming. You must climb the Seat and take what is offered. And heed this warning: Use no more than you must of the Shape-Changer Power within you. For it is a spirit with no allegiance either to the Goddess or to Her enemy, the Unnamed. It can only be guided to serve Light or Dark by the strength and will of your human soul. But beware its seduction, warrior. And may She be with you."

The shifting colors of her gown modulated into the hue of the canyon walls, and the rocks appeared through her woman's body; then she was gone. He stepped forward, unwilling to be left alone in this place, but there was nothing but stone and silence. He was one in the gathering cold, facing a gargantuan monument to Power that stirred something alien in him.

As he gazed at the titanic throne, the desire grew to climb it and sit in that high seat. What might he not see, what might he not learn? He started slowly for it, putting aside the pain each step cost him. His mind whirled with what Va'shindi had told him. He was a wizard, and more, something vast and powerful and inhuman. That spirit leaped within him at the recognition. He could feel it lusting to control him and his actions. The temptation was strong to sink within the identity of the Shape-Changer, to set it free with no constraints.

As he began to climb the human-sized steps that crawled up the sloping front of the Goddess's Seat, he recalled what else Va'shindi had said: his human personality, the exhausted, rather foolish Caer soldier, should retain command. How? The Power that swelled in him had no use for Kyellan.

The stone was supple and yielding under his sandals, humming with strength, coursing up his body in waves. He could feel the bones in his chest begin to knit, the gashes on his back to draw together like joined cloth, the bruises and inflammation to subside. He was getting strong, and his weariness fell from him like a discarded cloak. He reached the last broad steps before the Seat in little time.

Welcome. A whisper brushed his ears.

"I come in peace, sworn to defend," he heard himself say, though he had not known he was going to speak. "Allied in this time and place with you, Cianya."

Most welcome.

He bowed deeply and positioned himself on the lip of the giant throne. His feet dangled over the edge far above the canyon floor, and the back stretched overhead to many times his height. With no need for thought, he drew a complex pattern in the air before him, which grew and rose until it blazed in the darkening sky over the rim of the gorge.

They will know I am here, he thought grimly. Come, lords of the Dark. Come, Shape-Changer, Father, who has betrayed me many times. You will find this place fortified against you in a way Dallynd was not. Your own seed, half your spirit, ranged against you, commanding the Power of this Seat you so desire.

His thoughts ranged, aided by the amplifying quality of the Goddess's Seat, and he saw many images; some were clear, some confused, and he could not say which were real and which illusion. . . .

Tobas and Valahtia, lovers in the darkness of a hide tent, while outside rose the sounds of an army preparing for morning battle. Erlin, twisted and broken in a litter, with Pima nearby, life budding within her. Briana, her beauty drawn and weary, but like a beacon calling him. Chela, alight with the call, the pounding of the sea beside her; close, then. Gwydion, his Power dimmed, full of pain and exhaustion. Firelh, tired but strong, doggedly following the trail Chela led. But where was the Shape-Changer? His enemy, his father? He could not see that which he most sought.

"This is the place," said Belaric, his crisp voice betraying his nervousness to Briana's ears.

So much was obvious. The atmosphere outside the canyon mouth sharpened her senses like the incense that burned during the Dances; evidence enough, without the wheeling symbol of Power that turned slowly above them, blazing with defiance.

"Be sure of what you do, wizard," she warned. "You are not the first to arrive here. The Seat is occupied." And the being she felt who controlled it made her realize what the First Priestess had meant. It was barely recognizable as Kyellan, this presence of Power that broadcast its challenge.

"Yes, I feel it, but it does not matter," said Belaric. "My Power is stronger than all but one other, who is coming, but has not yet arrived."

He ordered his soldiers into the canyon. They went, most reluctantly, only in obedience to his spell-reins over their terrified minds. Erlin's litter remained outside, and Pima would not move from it, but Gemon and Briana were herded along before the wizard.

"You see now, my lady, what I've been trying to tell you," said the thin novice with a hint of satisfaction in her voice. "Every time I went near your Kyellan, *that* is what I felt in him."

"Only Power," Briana defended. "Not evil. He is using it for Light."

"He is using it for himself."

Belaric laughed when he saw who held the Seat from him. "Only the soldier who escaped from my dungeons. A fly to be brushed from the cake; shoot him down."

His archers responded like men in dreams, slowly notching their arrows, slowly drawing back and letting fly. Their aim was good, but the bolts clattered on the stones far below Kyellan. The man on the Seat smiled unpleasantly. Briana was too far behind the ranks of wizards' men to see, but the sinking of her heart told her his eyes were golden now.

"It will not be so easy after all, Belaric," he mocked.

A blaze of red fire arced from the wizard's hands in a lightning bolt of Power that sent Briana reeling backward. It touched the stone where Kyellan sat, retreated, touched it again, and was reflected violently backward. Belaric spoke a sharp word that sent it to dissipate in the air above him, but his handsome face broke into a sudden sweat.

Briana took Gemon's hand and whispered into the novice's ear, "Our chance will come. When he's concentrating on Kyellan, we can attack."

"With my shields this strong, I can't project even a prayer."

"Lower your shields. He's found the Seat; we don't need them as high."

Gemon nodded. Briana calmed herself, following her own advice, and reduced her shielding to simple battle defenses.

Belaric seemed frustrated. Everything he sent against the Seat was simply returned. As yet Kyellan had not attacked. "You have only the Power of the Seat," the wizard called. "Enough to defend against me. But you can have no Power of your own, young warrior, and one is coming who will wrest your puny control as a lion takes a kill from a jackal."

"The Shape-Changer? I don't think he's coming," Kyellan said with confidence. "I can't see him."

"He is here."

The clear, strong voice reverberated through the canyon. Briana whirled. Three people she knew had entered through the gap. There was a cry of betrayal from Chela, a low curse from Gwydion, as the suddenly changing figure of Firelh walked forward into the ranks. The solid, bearlike body of the Ryasan hill lord shifted and flowed, becoming something not even human before it settled into the form of a wizard. Tall, well made, middle-aged, dressed in dark robes with short golden hair and eyes as yellow as two small suns. He had the face of a demigod, handsome and cruel. The soldiers fell back from him as if from a river of fire.

Chela's eyes met Briana's over the gulf of wizards' men; they were full of rage, wild with Power. She launched herself at the back of the Shape-Changer, hammering him with all her raw strength, so intense that he staggered. But he threw her from him bodily, his force such that she careened into one of the sheer walls and fell senseless.

With a wordless growl, Gwydion ran toward the man who had been Firelh. The Shape-Changer stopped, smiling, as the young wizard hurtled against an invisible barrier that knocked him from his feet. He rose and tried again, furiously chanting spells of opening, but Briana could sense their lack of Power. The golden figure that was the object of his anger turned and walked toward the Seat.

Horrified, Briana watched him approach. How could she not have known? To have worked so closely with this man and never suspected his true nature said little for her powers of perception. What would Kyellan be thinking? He had admired Firelh, looked up to him, striven for his approval.

"So much is explained," said the figure on the throne. "The first day we came to your hall, you knew who we were. You escaped the ambush of your army near Dallynd because you planned it. When I found you in that wizard's ship, you were in a cabin instead of chained to an oar. Why didn't I see it?"

The Shape-Changer laughed Firelh's laugh, the sound uncanny coming from those godlike lips. "And was it a coincidence I was with you when you loosed the temple demon? Recall Gwydion saying it should not have had the Power to force you to release it. Though I was rather surprised when it disappeared. I didn't know who you were then. And, of course, it was I who betrayed you in Cavernon City.''

"Thus causing the death of the First Priestess," Briana said bitterly. "What did you do with the true Firelh? You were able to talk to Haval about the Hoabi wars as if you were there.''

"I was. The Firelh of whom you speak died in his cabin at the age of twenty-one. I have been the Earl of Dafir since that time. The identity has served me well; I shall be sorry to set it aside.''

Gemon accosted him in her shrillest voice. "You are the Darkness. You are what we of the Goddess have fought for so many years. But when you are destroyed this time, it will be forever. As Firelh you left no heir to your evil spirit.''

"An heir I have, witchling," he said caustically, and Briana felt the searing edges of the impossibly powerful spell he shot at the novice. Gemon's eyes rolled in her head, and she shook like a reed in a storm. Blood ran from her mouth and nose, and her thin body convulsed again and again. She screamed in agony.

Briana tried to hold her still, to quiet her with all the Power of healing she could summon, but the frail child jerked and writhed in her arms. Oh, Goddess, she is so young! She must not die this way, killed by the offhand malice of a demonic spirit.

Someone knelt beside them; Gwydion. "Help me," she pleaded.

"I couldn't even wake Chela," he said miserably. "I have so little Power left. Can't help you, except to move her out of the canyon, away from the battle.''

Briana assisted him in raising the bone weight of Gemon, noticing his bandaged hands and sensing what was beneath the wrappings. Nothing could heighten her horror now, as Gemon lay still, her breathing harsh and shallow, as the traitorous Shape-Changer claimed Kyellan was his son, as she remembered what the First Priestess had told her and the promise she had refused to make.

"Rouse Chela, Priestess," Gwydion said roughly. "Link with her against Belaric, because when Kyellan and the Shape-Changer begin their duel, you'll have to attack quickly or he'll tip the balance against Kyellan." He strode off toward the canyon mouth, brushing past lines of soldiers frozen with fascination and terror.

Briana ran to the wall where the girl had fallen and began a light call. The Shape-Changer was still speaking slowly, calmly.

"Your shields were strong, Kyellan, even against me. I had thought my son suffered the fate of every wizard child in Caerlin. But I could never father another, which should have told me you lived."

"Claim no kinship with me," said the soldier on the throne. "You abandoned my mother, who could have told you I was alive."

"If not as a father, I will face you as an enemy. Choose."

"Onedon, my lord," said Belaric impatiently, "he keeps the Seat from us. Kill him, and you can have another."

From the corner of her vision, Briana saw Kyellan raise his arms and begin a low, rumbling song. White light wove an intricate basket around him, pulsating with Power. Chela began to moan and raised her head, which bled a little. She looked around frantically before she turned to Briana.

"Where's Gwydion?"

"Outside with Gemon, who may be dying. What happened to him?"

The girl rose unsteadily to her feet. "He was burned, trying to control a healing demon when he had no Power for it. The effort spent the last Power he had. It has not returned."

The clash of opposing forces set Briana's skin crawling. She looked toward the throne. A red sledgehammer of brute strength smashed into Kyellan's defenses, throwing him backward against the high stones. The white-light construction flickered, as if he had momentarily lost consciousness, but it soon blazed strong again. Onedon would attack, Kyellan would respond, and every spell Kyellan used transformed him more. Briana was lost to horror, unaware of Chela's efforts to establish a link with her. Kyellan's eyes were now a brilliant gold; his face was growing subtly more angular, paler, cheekbones shifting under bushy brows. His hair was streaking with tawny yellow.

"Names of Power!" Chela used Gwydion's favorite oath. "He's turning into a wizard. What is it, Briana?"

The priestess spoke with painful softness. "He is the next Shape-Changer. That's what Gemon tried to warn us of. Look, Belaric is trying to ally with Onedon. We mustn't let that happen."

They joined hands and opened their minds to each other, with no time for ritual or formality, and ran through the line of soldiers toward the wizard.

"Yes!" exulted Onedon. "Change! As your true being gains full control, realize how foolish this warfare is. The Seat of the Goddess should be wielded by the strongest, and together you and I will be stronger than any god."

The man on the throne was no longer Kyellan. Briana set up defenses against Belaric; the wizard would attack as soon as he saw the threat she and Chela represented. Yet she could not concentrate on the battle. The raw Power of the inexperienced girl would have to direct their strategy. For the white light about the Seat was fading, and the man who sat there smiled at Onedon, a predatory smile full of ambition and power lust.

"No!" she screamed, breaking the link and leaving Chela to face the imminent attack alone. "Dear Goddess, no!" The one who should have been Kyellan frowned, not recognizing her.

Annoyed, Onedon turned his attention to her. His spell crushed her to the stony floor, squeezing the breath from her lungs. She tried to rebuild her shielding and gasped out her words.

"Kyellan, I love you! Don't let it take you. Change back! Use it to fight, control it, but change back. Oh, please. . . ."

Sobbing under the pressure of the wizard's spell, she could barely lift her head high enough to meet the troubled golden eyes. "I love you," she breathed. "You can't leave me now."

"Shall I finish her, my son?" asked the older wizard harshly.

"Briana . . ." whispered the being on the Goddess's Seat.

Her breath was gone, her lungs deflated and pinned together. She could not move as darkness began to cloud her vision. Then it was as if a giant hand lifted stones from her body, and her back arched as she gulped greedily for air. The alien face high above was growing familiar, soft black clouding the sun-blaze hair. It was a struggle, as the Shape-Changer spirit fought to retain control. Pain contorted the shifting features. But soon the man on the throne was an exhausted Kyellan, who smiled at her with still-golden eyes.

"So be it," muttered the enraged Onedon. "Remember

what you could have been, as you take your first step down the Long Road.'' He drew himself up, Power crackling around him, and lifted his arms in supplication. The Words that came from his distended mouth made Briana want to cower down in the rocks with her hands over her ears. She wondered what he was calling.

The sky rent with a chilling shriek. A hopeless wail rose from the terrified soldiers, and Briana could hear Chela screaming. Chela! She had abandoned her to Belaric's attack. Desperately, she calmed her mind and re-formed the linkage in time to repel a wall of orange flame that had surrounded the younger girl. Chela stumbled toward her in relief.

A nauseating stench filled the canyon, wafting from a coven of winged demons, each of them singly a Power to be feared. They were scaled and horned, drooling venom from foaming, fanged mouths, their dull, dead eyes fixed on Kyellan and the Goddess's Seat. The soldier wavered for a moment, flickering into the wizard, but then his jaw clenched in resolution, and a screen of white flame shot into the air before the demons.

Belaric chose that moment to renew his bombardment of the two women. Briana took control of the partnership, siphoning clear raw Power from Chela and forming it into a ring of aggressive defense. Though she tried to make it white, the Goddess's Flame, it insisted on remaining green. A fresh, strong green like new-budded trees, so full of energy and joy that it sprang on its own volition to chase Belaric's orange shapings. Chela laughed, urging it on to new heights. The ruler of the New Empire blanched.

The battle overhead was well joined. Onedon had all the Power of the unbridled Shape-Changer spirit, and he had the experience and training to use it. Kyellan, though he had blunted the force of his own Power by keeping himself in control, was supported by the Goddess's Seat itself, a strong ally. Vague white forms, amorphous and unrecognizable, did battle with the first rank of demons; fire mingled with fire, and neither was consumed.

A few of the demons, bored or mischievous, broke off from the fighting and swooped down over the soldiers of Belaric like carrion birds. Their terror finally shattered the wizard's hold on their minds, and they ran screaming from the canyon mouth. The demons pursued them with hyena laughter.

Chela's green fire slithered across barren rock, hissing merrily as it drew nearer to Belaric's orange flame. Briana closed her eyes and pulled taut ropes of Power inward from the farthest corners of her being, massing them where her hand joined that of Gwydion's apprentice. She had never felt so strong. Her feet outlined in miniature the Patterning of the Third Cycle Dance, the Dance of Enclosure, and cheerfully the green fire kept pace.

"Now!" Chela shouted, and it pounced. But a demon dove and caught Belaric roughly in its claws just as the ring of living Power moved to engulf him. The wizard cursed them and berated his rescuer in some magical language as it swept him over the canyon rim and away.

"Now to join with Kyellan, and get the other one," said Chela in satisfaction. Apparently the Guardsman heard this, for immediately they felt themselves strengthened by the Power of the Seat itself. Briana shuddered at the contact with the barely restrained Shape-Changer spirit. Each time Kyellan drew upon its Power, it came closer to gaining control.

The screen of white was now crossed and banded with living green. It began to advance, slowly but inexorably, on the demonic army. The first of the creatures were absorbed, and the others fell back with their laughter stilled. Onedon shrieked Words of Power from his cloud of illusion cover, but to no avail. The Goddess's Flame advanced.

"Only a little further," Chela hissed.

Two of the demons descended into Onedon's cloud and reappeared with the Shape-Changer in their grasp. His dark robes flapped in the wind as they rose toward the canyon rim.

"We'll meet again, fool, when you do not have the Seat under you," Onedon promised. "But now there is a battle to be fought in the plains below Khymer. And I do not think you can reach it in time to save your friends." He was gone from sight as some of the demons fled and the rest were consumed. The smoke began to lift from the blasted canyon.

Kyellan slowly descended the silent Goddess's Seat. His face was haggard with pain and exhaustion. His hands shook beneath the white S'tari robe. His eyes were still golden, Briana saw as she stood motionless in the midst of the destruction.

Chela ran to hug Kyellan, then hurried for the mouth of the canyon, doubtless to look for Gwydion. If it were only that simple, Briana thought. She loved him. But what kind of service would it be to Cianya, if she bore the child who was the heir to the Shape-Changer? The First Priestess had known, or had guessed closely, what Kyellan truly was. Yet in the end Briana had not promised.

He stopped a few feet away and smiled tentatively. "Did you mean it, Briana? What you said?"

She had to look away. "Your eyes. They're golden."

She felt, rather than saw, the smile disappear. He stepped closer. "It's not over yet. I have to keep it where I can use it again. So I can kill him next time." The voice was that of the old Kyellan.

"I'm sorry," she managed to say, turning to walk where Chela had gone. She would not meet the hurt in his alien eyes.

He followed with a short laugh. "I'd hoped you'd understand this."

She said nothing, fighting the ache in her throat.

"I had no choice, Briana. . . ."

The priestess walked straight ahead, hearing his footsteps slow behind her. The full moon had pulled itself free of the Tarnsea to light the narrow walls, silhouetted in the stark opening of the stone canyon.

Chapter Twenty-one

"Enter," Tobas said sharply, motioning Valahtia back behind the curtains that divided the tent. He shrugged on his undertunic and began to buckle the straps of his mail-vest.

"Report, my lord Colonel," said the adjutant, a Parahnese. Tobas suspected that Diveshi had ordered the man to keep him in hand. "The order to arm has been given. It's as we expected."

"They're massing in the plains between us and Khymer?"

"They must know we have every man we can muster, for they've called in reserve battalions to nearly the full strength of the wizards' forces in Caerlin. Sixty thousand, my lord."

"Wizards?"

"There are many in the ranks, sir. They intend to make this battle decisive."

"So do we, Lieutenant," he snapped.

"If you . . . encounter the Queen this morning, Colonel," said his aide with a knowing smile, "please remind her she promised to return to the S'tari camp to wait out the fighting."

"Dismissed," Tobas scowled. The Parahnese saluted and left the tent.

"He's not very respectful, my lord," Valahtia said sleepily.

"They think the only reason I'm supporting you against Arel is my personal feelings for you." He bent to lace the tall boots up over his knees.

"Isn't it? Or most of it? You're not the revolutionary type, love."

"At least Diveshi trusts my judgment, and he knows we wouldn't have the S'tari unless we acknowledged you Queen. But Halcira won't be pleased when he hears of it."

"Halcira will never hear of it unless we win this battle, because you and I will not be alive to press my claim. Today's problems are more than enough to worry about. We'll discuss this when it's over." She swept out of the tent, disdaining any curious eyes.

"When it's over," he echoed. Gods, he wished Kyellan was here. And Gwydion had soberly promised to return in time for the battle. He had not appeared; they had no one in their ranks who could withstand wizards' magic.

Gwydion kissed Chela when she hugged him, because it seemed to be what she expected, but he could not feel her joy. The victory had hardly been decisive. Belaric and Onedon had escaped. Gemon lay quietly now, breathing weakly, and he had no Power for healing. Erlin had fainted. Pima had exhausted her gentle skills in keeping him free of pain. Now Briana and Kyellan came out of the canyon, and he was almost glad he could not read their grim faces.

"What next?" Chela asked. He pulled her close, unmindful of the pain of his burned and poisoned hands.

"We have no horses, little one," he said. "And though I might call demons to fly us away, I couldn't make them obey me when they came. Though we have the Power to defeat those two in battle, we can't get to the battle to do it.''

"We can't just sit here," she said reasonably.

"Dear Goddess!" Briana gasped. Gwydion looked to where her eyes were fixed in wide astonishment. A tall figure walked lightly down the jagged rocks into the hollow, a woman in iridescent robes with awe-inspiring beauty. She smiled. Briana hurriedly knelt.

"Va'shindi," Kyellan acknowledged, unsurprised.

"You did well, warrior, holding the Seat." She raised the young priestess from the stones. "Now its control must pass from you into the First-Priestess-to-be."

Gwydion watched, frustrated that he could sense nothing of the exchange, as Briana staggered under a new burden. Kyellan held himself a little straighter. The Guardsman's face flickered dangerously close to changing, but Va'shindi, whoever she was, reached out a steadying hand, and his countenance returned. Not to normal, but to a Caer soldier with uncanny golden eyes.

"It will be harder to maintain control without the Seat to assist you," the strange woman said. "But it can be done. You must keep the Shape-Changer alert enough to use in the battle."

"The demons drove away all the horses," Briana said. "How can we reach the battle?"

Va'shindi smiled and called in a clear, ringing voice. They heard hoofbeats above them, and four of the bolted horses appeared, the whites of their eyes showing with fear and confusion. "They will bear you more swiftly than you think. Under my urging, they may reach the battle by midday."

"Four horses?" Kyellan frowned.

"The two novices and the injured young man will re-

main here. I will keep them safe, until they are well
enough to travel."

"You mean that I can stay?" Pima asked incredulously
from beside the litter.

"By the time your child is born, your Erlin should be
healed."

"My . . . my child?"

"Did you not know?" Va'shindi laughed lightly. "But
the rest of you must leave quickly."

"The Goddess be with you," Briana murmured, kissing
Pima and Gemon on the foreheads. Pima hugged her, and
Gemon managed a wan smile from where she lay. The
priestess mounted her horse. Gwydion had to be assisted
into his saddle by Kyellan, but once there, he found to his
relief that his mount needed no guidance. His hands could
not hold a rein. The horses sprang away up the Tarnsea
cliffs like creatures that were not bound to the earth.

Tobas allowed his fiery S'tari horse to prance its
restlessness, though he held it at the point position of the
triangle. The sun was rising pink and hot over the desert
hills, over the massive lines of the wizards' army below,
glinting on pikes and crossbows, lighting the enemy banners and the faces of spell-bound men. Its rays caught and
reflected the blazing hair of the many wizards in the ranks.
Apparently there were so many that some were to fight
with the soldiers rather than holding back with the magical
councils behind the lines.

The army of the Kingdoms waited in tight formation, as
drilled by Diveshi; three wedge-shaped sections, arced
widely in a half circle with the center closest to the enemy.
Tobas commanded a fourth of the cavalry, men from every
Kingdom with battle experience, and an equally hardened
third of the foot soldiers, each armed with sword, shield,

and thrusting spear. These would bear the weight of the
attack. The wing to their right consisted of the inexperi
enced infantry, archers and slingers, some carrying short
swords; another fourth part of the cavalry was mounted at
each side. On the left wing waited the brunt of the horsemen,
the grim Hoabi axes, and the Garithian hill dwellers
Diveshi led the Parahn Special Forces at its apex.

But the opening sally belonged to the S'tari, who had
argued for it and finally convinced the commanders. Now
at Diveshi's signal, they began their sidelong charge. The
wizards' ranks rustled with anticipation but did not move
forward. Three hundred desert warriors pounded their horses
through the sand, robes and turbans rising like gulls' wings,
shrilling mocking battle cries. They drove their animals
with their knees alone, without stirrups, while their fingers
fitted yard-long arrows to great cypress bows.

Tobas could barely restrain his own horse from joining
them. They wheeled and raced just outside the range of the
wizards' pikes and spears, and sent volley after volley into
the enemy ranks. As the first soldiers fell, the wizards'
crossbowmen stepped forward and began to pick off the
S'tari one by one. The bolts had great power but limited
range, and the attackers managed several more rounds
before the wizards' ranks began to move.

Forward they ran like a living wall. We will dash ourselves against it like waves against the Tarnsea cliffs, and
with as much effect, Tobas thought; yet he raised his hand
that held a red S'tari battle flag. Beside him, the standard-
bearer Roren grinned. A Parahnese, Roren bore the flag of
black with a white flame that the resistance army had
adopted, and in the other hand was a naked sword. He had
vowed not to sheathe it until the wizards were gone from
his homeland.

"Advance!" Tobas shouted, and spurred his horse. The

center triangle detached itself from the formation and pointed for the enemy. Memories of other desert battles haunted Tobas as he drew his sword. At least this time the S'tari were on his side. And his horse was equipped with desert shoes, hard leather wrappings that broadened the base of its hooves by several inches, so it sank no more than a lion would in the shifting dunes. Its gallop was truly a run, not the loping canter that had carried the hapless Royal Guard through so many desert engagements with the swift S'tari.

A line of enemy horsemen had broken through to the front of the wizards' men and charged to meet Tobas's formation with ponderous force. Their horses were Northern animals, bred from plow beasts, far larger than those of the S'tari. The men they carried were equally large, the shock troops of Belaric's army.

"Keep tight," Tobas yelled. "Don't break the wedge. We'll cut through them to the infantry."

His horse screamed, borne back by the weight of the enemy charge. A huge Hoabi mercenary aimed a two-handed greataxe for Tobas, who twisted so the blow glanced obliquely off his shield. If it had hit square, the shield would not have stood. He leaned his little horse in a sideways dance around the axeman, trying to find an opening for his thrusting spear. Another blow descended, and the S'tari horse reared flailing to avoid it. Under his mount's leather-wrapped hooves, Tobas leaned past the Hoabi's shield and shoved his spear home.

"Elandi!" The cry came from behind him, where Roren skewered a brown-clad Kerisian who had been ready to run Tobas through. The standard-bearer fought shieldless, guiding his Parahnese pony with his body; the beast was not even bridled.

"Well struck." Tobas laughed. "But what is Elandi?"

"The mountains of Parahn where I was born. Let's

through this veneer of giants, Colonel, and cut down the crops beyond.''

Together they dodged past the heavy warhorses, their mounts skipping between the blows of broadsword and mace. The wedge behind them was thinning but kept its formation doggedly, forcing the enemy horsemen to part like a river around a sandbar. A few pikemen greeted the wedge as it broke through. Roren reversed the banner pole he carried and killed one with the end of it, which was shod with a wicked forked blade like a halberd. Another fell to Tobas's spear, thrown instead of thrust, and the third lost his balance under the press of his fellows and died beneath flashing hooves.

A terrible shriek tore the sky above them, stopping the men of both armies cold. Shadows swept the plain as two pairs of gigantic winged demons soared over the melee. Each had a wizard in its grasp, who dropped smoking globes onto the field; those immediately burst into exploding fire. None landed near Tobas or Roren, or any of the others within enemy ranks, but they heard the cries of their comrades and turned back. Their horses shied and pranced, unwilling to go any nearer to the smoke.

The enemy foot soldiers began to yell and massed around the two small horses that led the wedge, swinging blades that could not all be parried. Tobas and his standard-bearer looked at each other in dismay. Their horses kicked like mules and flashed their teeth, half-mad with fear. The huge shape of a wizards' man on horseback swung his mace for Tobas's head. The Guardsman barely ducked it as a spear thrust from an infantryman pierced his right leg. He stifled a scream.

''Ride!'' shouted Roren, holing the mace wielder with his reversed banner. ''Get out of here!''

Tobas pressed himself to his horse's mane and shot

through a momentary opening in the press, losing his shield as an axeman hacked it from his arm. Roren was beside him, shoving his horse through with his sword singing. At their insane pace, they were soon back among the final ranks of the central triangle of their own soldiers, where the wizards had not penetrated.

"Get to the field hospital, Colonel," Roren said. "You'll be no help here."

Tending to agree, as the pain of his wound began to make him dizzy, Tobas saluted and reined his horse back toward the hilltop S'tari camp. He glanced once more at the banner Roren carried as he cleared the soldiers; it stood straight from the base of the wedge, obscured a little by the smoke of wizards' fires. The white Goddess's Flame was crimson with blood.

The first offensive should have taken many more of the enemy. Curse the wizards' magic, it was turning the balance. Diveshi had intended to withhold his troops until a far later point, hoping to flank the edges of Belaric's army and drive for the guarded square that held the magic-makers. The option was gone; the battle was bringing itself to him. Already the untried right wing had been swept into fighting. He was proud to see they still held together in a rough wedge, as he had hammered into them in endless drills, and were even advancing a little through the crazed enemy soldiers.

It was time. If he waited any longer, there would be no room to maneuver. With a cry Parahn had used so long no one knew its meaning anymore, he gathered his horse beneath him and sprang. Behind him ran the Special Forces mounts an arm's length apart, the phalanx sharp with spears pointing outward like the quills of the porcupine that was their symbol. Wheeling as one man, they turned

sixty degrees as they charged, crashing into the sides of
the wizards' army with the lancing point of a scalpel.

The field was smothering in acrid smoke that hid the
brown uniforms until they appeared at the point of Diveshi's
blade. He could not see to find the direction he meant to
lead his men. No matter. The enemy was equally blind,
and inward was as good a path as any.

If the sun could have been discerned through the pall of
wizard-spawned darkness, it would have been at zenith
when four wind-swift horses and their riders halted above
the carnage.

"We're going down into that?" Chela shivered.

"We'll let them know we're here first." Briana drew on
a fraction of the Power of the Seat, and four ten-foot-high
flames appeared on the crests of four dunes, enclosing the
battlefield with the Goddess's symbol. She felt the strength
of her link with Chela's green magic and the waiting
presence of Kyellan's tightly bound Shape-Changer spirit.
That spirit would have to be used in the battle, she feared,
and she did not know if the Guardsman could maintain
control. And though she knew the Power of their alliance
would increase greatly if she fully opened her mind to
him, she could not do it. She did not want Kyellan to see
the turmoil of her thoughts; the First Priestess's words, her
expected service to Cianya, her betrayal of her true feelings the night before, all fought within her, and she could
not reconcile them.

She had told him she loved him. Yet she knew he would
not hold her to that, if she changed her mind. The priestess
sighed inaudibly. She tried to wall off her confusion into a
tiny corner of her thoughts and open herself as fully as she
could to the Power Kyellan offered.

"I'll ride down with you," said Gwydion rather forlornly. "Even if I can't add any Power, I can fight as a soldier."

"One more soldier won't make a difference," Kyellan said. "Why don't you go to the field hospital instead, around behind the resistance army? There's bound to be someone there who will remember you from Altimar, or Dallynd."

"Even if you can't add magic to your healing, love, you're far better than most doctors. Go on," Chela urged, bending across from her horse to kiss him. He finally nodded and galloped away.

"Don't waste your energies on the minor wizards," Briana reminded them. "Belaric and Onedon are our opponents. The others will be easy to fell afterward."

Without further talk, the three of them charged their horses down the hill into combat.

The wizards' attention was suddenly elsewhere. Diveshi grinned as the clouds of smoke began to clear and the strange shapes that had been forming in them disappeared. He spurred through suddenly revealed gaps in the enemy lines, followed by his nearest men, hacking his way toward the center with his red-to-the-hilt broadsword.

"General! The camp!" a man cried hoarsely.

He looked up. A flotilla of demonic creatures had appeared in the skies, as tightly disciplined as his own men, soaring in close formation in the direction of the S'tari hilltop camp. The women and children, and the wounded. Diveshi felt sick. He had argued and pleaded with the S'tari to leave their civilians far behind, but the terms of Valahtia's ridiculous treaty had left him no authority.

"Gwydion!" Tobas rose from his seat outside the hospital tent. They had stitched and bound his leg, and he had given up his place inside to the many men more wounded than he. Now to see the wizard riding up, grey-faced and somber, but otherwise himself! Hope began to rise again. "You're late. You promised to be back in time for the battle."

The younger man dismounted awkwardly, sliding from his horse, and Tobas noticed his bandaged hands. "You needn't be so pleased to see me. I won't be any help. But the others are here, Chela and Briana and Kyellan, and they're down in the midst of it trying to find the two most important wizards." Gwydion suddenly silenced, looking beyond the tent, and Tobas turned to follow his gaze.

"Merciful gods," he breathed, seeing the tight wing of demons that had just topped the rise.

"Crossbows," Gwydion muttered. "Where?"

"Behind the hospital tent, the weapons of the wounded," Tobas said, as the first demons swept over a stand of S'tari pavilions, setting them afire. Screaming sounded from within, and veiled women began to run out carrying their small children. The demons harassed and tore at them as another squad flamed the hospital tent.

"Valahtia!" Tobas paused in his run for the weapons pile, staring at the burning tent. Gwydion was shouting, gathering the S'tari women who were unburdened by children to scavenge in the weapons pile for the powerful crossbows. A demon dove for Tobas. He slashed at it with his sword and it rose again in the air. The women knelt in a rough circle, shooting upward. Three demons fell, but the others attacked, clawing the women brutally. Gwydion yelled in some wizards' language; confused, more demons fell to the desperate archers.

Valahtia suddenly rolled from the doorway of the huge, flaming hospital tent. The small fires in her clothing were smothered by the sand. Tobas raced to her, picked her up, and held her close as she coughed from the smoke.

"Things are . . . not going well, my lord?" she asked.

"No. They are not going well."

Sweat coursed down Briana's face. Her body throbbed with the strain of holding shields in place against the battering-ram blows of the wizards. Despite her alliance with the other two, she felt utterly alone as she tried to channel their Power and the strength of the Seat into an attack that retained enough shielding to defend them all. A vortex of howling winds twisted around her, trying to pull her from the horse's back; but within her was a calm place, the eye of the storm, serenity she could only attribute to the Goddess.

Mist parted before her seeking eyes, and she found she could discern the dune where her enemies stood, deep within their soldiers' lines, guarded by thick, motionless walls of men. The wizards' faces leapt into sharp relief, and she thought that if she had only a little more acuity, she might see their thoughts. They recoiled from the touch, then suddenly were strengthened by the more limited Powers of every wizard in their army. Briana recognized among them the young wizard Hirwen who had sat on the throne of Caerlin; none of them were adepts, but in concert they shifted the balance measurably.

She would have to strengthen the link. There was no choice remaining. She would have to open her mind to its fullest extent and allow Chela and Kyellan to see what was there.

"Chela! Your hand!" she shouted through the winds. A horse crowded her leg, and a strong grip met her hand. In a moment, they were one mind and one Power, the

Goddess's Flame and the girl's living earth force twined and woven into the framework of the Seat.

"Now Kyellan," she projected with new intensity. But no answer came. The dust between her horse and his was sucked into a whirlwind, deafening her, and she could not see through it. Their link was severed, as her link with Gwydion had been in the battle of Keor harbor. She urged her terrified horse into the storm and found the Guardsman's riderless mount, but there was no trace of Kyellan.

Her heart sank, but Chela's green ropes of Power turned her head to look at the wizards' hill. Belaric stood alone, one bright beacon of Power amid the childish flickering of countless minor wizards. Onedon was gone. Wherever he was, doubtless Kyellan was as well; now, Briana knew, the balance of the match was tilting in her direction. The vigor of her Power and Chela's could destroy Belaric and his followers, without the obstacle of Onedon. She resolutely put aside her fears for Kyellan and directed an awesome bolt of energy at the hill. Three minor wizards fell, and she sensed Rahshaiya's smoky hands gathering them in. Belaric tightened his shields, but before he did so she glimpsed a thought. The wizard apparently suspected Onedon of betraying him, of going to ally with his son against the Kharad. Briana wished it could be true.

Kyellan stumbled and almost fell as he landed. Tall dunes surrounded him, anchored by sun-dried brush, and the noise of battle was distant. How he had gotten there, he could not say. And facing him was Onedon.

He was alone, without a vestige of the link he had had with the others, without the chance to tap into the Power of the Goddess's Seat. The Shape-Changer trapped within him clamored to be released; and, truly, he did not think he could stand up to the wizard who was his father without freeing it.

"You cannot win," said Onedon. "I have the experience and the training to match my Power, where you have only instinct and the blind memories of an ancient spirit."

Kyellan attacked mentally, his blow clumsy but shaking the Shape-Changer's shields. The Power that Onedon returned sparked visibly in the bright afternoon sunlight and halted a finger's breadth from Kyellan's skin. He could feel its heat searing him and could no longer hold on to his reins over the Dark spirit within him. Nor did he want to. Never before in battle had he discarded a weapon that came to his grasp.

The golden color swept through him, a sun ray scattering the residual shadows of the Goddess's Seat. He felt his Power grow until he understood the arrogance and assurance of the mirror-being who faced him; yet this time, through a desperate effort, his identity remained. He knew himself to be Kyellan, though in wizard form, and he did not respond to Onedon's sudden smile.

"I offer again!" said his father generously. "Join me. It is time that our spirit, the Shape-Changer, ruled this world of its inferiors."

Kyellan grinned sardonically and attacked. Onedon stumbled, recovered, and parried. The Guardsman's mind was like a scimitar, he felt, to be wielded with two-handed strokes. Here the niceties of fencing served no purpose. Yet it was like fencing, against a perfectly matched opponent who could read his moves before he made them. Now that both men were the Shape-Changer, their Powers met and strove in every direction, but were caught in equality.

Neither would win this way. The soldier in Kyellan whispered, and the Shape-Changer obeyed, crouching suddenly and drawing his scythelike S'tari sword. Continuing his mental bombardment, he advanced on Onedon with a very physical weapon. The older wizard retreated, shocked, and clumsily drew his own sword. Kyellan laughed. He sensed that this was a breach of the rules. Timing his sword swings with blows of Power, he battered at his father's shields. The scimitar managed to nick the wizard on the side. Onedon grimaced.

Suddenly the wizard turned sideways and disappeared. Kyellan sprawled in midlunge. He had been winning. That much was clear. It was not over yet. He slipped the scimitar back into its hole in the wide belt and began to walk through the deep sand toward the strangely altered sounds of battle.

The green-and-white fire that radiated from the two young women had cleared a space of fifty yards on either side; soldiers of both armies fought to concentrate on their own battles as the clash of lightning and wind raged between the flame of the Light and an equally great crimson fire from the wizards' dune.

Briana, hidden within the flames unconsumed, felt the weariness flowing away from her as the Goddess's Seat fed her with its strength and healing. Her mind was one with Chela's. Now she drew the younger girl with her into the Patterning of the first of the Great Dances, directing Chela's movement as well as her own, their hands and feet flashing sparks and leaving visible trails of their gestures. The First Cycle Dance, which was identical with the Last Cycle Dance, the Dance of birth and death, of Cianya and Rahshaiya.

They sang as they danced. Briana chanted in the Old Tongue, an ancient song of praise and invocation; if what Chela sang were spells remembered from Gwydion's forbidden book, it did not seem to matter to She who supplied their Power. For the white flame and the earth-budding green grew to a towering height and arched over the field of battle, above the soldiers of the Kharad, to the sand hill where the wizards stood. The wizards called frantically to their demonic aides, but the winged creatures were too occupied with their own battles to heed the summons in time. The crimson flame had consolidated and retreated to form a dome of protection over the dune. Chela and Briana leaped high in the air, their arms stretched upward. The flame of their Power seemed to sing with them as it crashed down upon their enemies. The hill burst asunder and fell into a sudden crack in the earth, leaving only a blackened, smoking hole that echoed with the death screams of Belaric and his followers. The demons in the sky began to fade.

Briana fell to her knees, shaking like an old woman. Chela, laughing and crying in relief and triumph, helped her back to her feet. They clung to each other, scarcely believing what they had done.

Kyellan had taken little time to walk back to the battle. He had cut his way inward, but no one had come near him for some time now, armed as he was with both his scimitar and the Shape-Changer spirit. The wizard aspect of him had voluntarily retreated a little, leaving only his eyes sun gold, pooling its strength for the next encounter with Onedon.

"Kyellan!"

He whirled. The caller was Briana, on foot and carrying a huge unsheathed sword in her left hand. Her face was tired and beautiful.

"I saw your fires." He grinned. "And felt the death of Belaric and the others. But Onedon seems to have disappeared."

"We'll find him." She laughed.

Gods, she was lovely. He longed to take her in his arms, to forget his quest to kill the Shape-Changer. The battle seemed very far away and unimportant.

She was very close when her face suddenly contorted, and she took her sword in two hands and brought it down into Kyellan's right shoulder with a strength she should not have had. He fell in agony as the blade bit deep; felt bone crack and blood spurting over his arm and side. He dropped his sword. Through dimming eyes, he watched Briana's face and form change until Onedon stood over him, laughing.

"I overestimated you," mocked the Shape-Changer. "Now I do not need to overcome you with my Power; you will simply bleed to death."

Kyellan thought he was probably right. Blood was seeping rapidly into the sand. But the Shape-Changer within him noticed that the wizard's shields were down, so certain was he that he had destroyed his opponent. With a huge effort, Kyellan raised to his knees. The world spun. He spoke slowly, clearly, Words only half of him understood.

Onedon wheeled in shock and sudden terror, but it was too late. He could not raise his shields in time, and fell to the earth near Kyellan. The attack continued until the older Shape-Changer had expired, without a wound, his unearthly beauty fading. Even that had been an illusion. Now he was merely an ordinary-looking wizard, shorter than before, and dead.

The earth rocked crazily, echoing with the pain of Kyellan's wound. The fire rose to his mind, and he fell into darkness.

Chapter Twenty-two

Grey walls. A spider dropped into Kyellan's limited range of vision, then rose again, trailing sticky pale thread. He slowly realized he was lying on his left side on an uncomfortable cot, that the walls were camelhide, and that the pain in his shoulder continued down his right side. He could feel nothing in his arm. His sword arm. He tried to flex it in its sling, but the commands of his mind were only obeyed in his back and chest.

The Shape-Changer Power was deeply buried, drained so badly in destroying its counterpart that it would probably take a very long time to recover. Which was just as well; Kyellan did not have the strength to fight it now. Yet some traces of it remained in his awareness. Enough to tell him the muscles and nerves of his arm had been severed at the shoulder, rendering it useless. Something Gwydion at the height of his Powers could not have healed.

He cautiously tested the rest of his body and turned until he lay on his back. The tent was quiet, filled with the hoarse, shallow breathing of wounded men and the soft voices of doctors. Obviously the battle was over, and surely the army of the Kingdoms had won, or he would not be here. He wished he had the energy to call a doctor and ask.

*   *   *

Tobas left Valahtia prattling of coronations and male children, and limped to the fourth hospital tent for the twentieth time in two days. Briana and Chela had used their green healing magic on Kyellan, sealing his wounds and setting his bones, but he had not regained consciousness when Tobas had checked the last time. He had listened to Gwydion's efforts to explain how Kyellan had killed the Shape-Changer Onedon, who seemed to have been Firelh, but the young Guardsman neither understood nor believed three-fourths of it. It all sounded too much unlike his longtime commander and friend. He hoped Kyellan would set him straight.

"He's awake," said the old Veneri doctor who had become a familiar scowling face. "And hungry, both for food and answers."

Feeling suddenly self-conscious about the rank of colonel emblazoned on his sleeve, Tobas tried to minimize his limp as he walked down the aisles of makeshift cots and pallets. Kyellan was sitting propped up, drinking from a bowl held in his left hand.

"Gods, Ky, I thought you were dead," he said; not at all how he had intended to begin the conversation, but his relief was intense at seeing the familiar lanky figure grinning up at him. Familiar, except for the flecks of gold in the dark brown eyes, and a few more scars here and there.

"So did I."

"Diveshi brought you in, just before all the wizards' soldiers surrendered." At his friend's questioning look, he went on. "When the last wizard was killed—Gwydion says you killed him, but I don't understand half of what Gwydion says—the spells that held the soldiers disappeared, and we put them to work burying the dead. Most of the army has left for Khymer, to occupy the winter palace and get provisions for the journey back to Cavernon."

"How long have I been here? The doctors won't tell me anything," Kyellan said. "And all they'll feed me is goat broth and dry bread. With water to drink. Could you pull rank and get me something better?"

"Sorry. It's all anyone has. And you've been here two days." Tobas settled carefully on the end of the cot and took a deep breath, unsure of how to continue. "I guess I should tell you before someone else does . . . Valahtia's deposing her brother. I'm backing her, and Diveshi, and the S'tari, since she's promised them their own Kingdom."

"Where's Arel?" Kyellan asked with great interest.

"Still in Altimar, as far as we know. With the rest of the royalty. They won't accept it easily."

He grinned. "Good for Valahtia. And she didn't even have to kill him for it."

Uncomfortably, Tobas nodded and plunged into what he did not want to say. "I'm the Earl of Laenar now, Ky. My father and brother are dead . . . and Valahtia's offered me the place of her consort. I think I'm going to accept."

"The power behind the throne?" Kyellan chuckled. "Sounds good."

Tobas bristled, before he realized his friend was teasing. "You're not mad?"

"I wish you luck. She's a handful."

The doctor scurried over and took the empty bowl. "Sorry, Colonel, but you'll have to go now. Let him rest. And there are others who'll want to see him."

"That's right." He smiled. "You're the hero of the hour, Ky. Everyone knows you killed the wizard, but I think I'm the only one Gwydion tried to explain it to. Maybe someday you can tell me how you did it."

"Maybe." His voice was quiet, and the gold-flecked eyes were unnerving when Tobas looked full at them.

Maybe there was something to what Gwydion had said. . . . Tobas followed the doctor from the tent, still unsure.

When Briana saw Kyellan, awake and alive and gold-brown-eyed, her confusion resolved. It had been too painful to watch him lying there close to death, and to think of another man fathering her child. Yet she was not sure it would be fair of her to ask, knowing she must leave him and return to the Order as every First Priestess before her had done. There was no longer any choice for her; the temples were burned, priestesses scattered and killed, and it would take long years of work to restore the worship of the Goddess to its rightful place. She could not pass that burden on to another. She would at least do that much of what the First Priestess had wanted.

"Briana!" His greeting was glad, but then his sudden brilliant smile faded. He remembered how their last conversation had gone.

She settled softly to the cot beside him and said in a light voice, "Forget what I said, Kyellan."

"Everything you said?" he asked ruefully. The gold flecks in his eyes were not alien, as she had feared, but warming. They softened his arrogant features.

"Not that I said I loved you. I do. That is our problem."

"That's our problem?" His face flushed with laughter.

"It is, because I must be First Priestess. And so I ask you something I have no right to ask, only because I know you love me, and I do not wish another."

He looked confused. "What do you mean?"

"This: To be First Priestess, I must bear a child, conceived in love, to honor Cianya, the Mother. I could only give you the time until the Goddess told me I had conceived; then I would have to return to my Order."

He looked at her long in silence, then said painfully, "That's all?"

"I know it's a terrible thing I ask." She could not meet his eyes. "It's all I can offer. I don't expect you to understand."

"You're right. I don't understand." He sighed. "But I accept. You leave me no choice, Briana."

Relief flooded through her like well water. She had feared he would be angry, would think she was using his love as a tool that would give her what she needed and be discarded. Indeed, she was doing exactly that, but it hurt her more than she could ever tell him. How simple things would be, if there was another suitable candidate for First Priestess. She would leave the Order and go with him, not fearing the wrath of the Goddess she served. The intensity of her feelings was frightening.

"When they let you out of here," she whispered, "I'll come to you. But it must be known only to us two. This is a thing the dying First Priestess passes on to her successor, and only she and the man she chooses may know of it."

"I'll be waiting." His eyes were troubled and sad, but she could sense no bitterness in him. He had changed from the hard, cynical soldier he had been when they met; she wished he had not, almost. Then neither of them would have been hurt.

With the last remnants of their healing link, Briana and Chela had worked on Gwydion's hands. But they were unable to rebuild what was not there, the flesh that had burned away or been lost to the demon's poison. So now he fought to relearn the use of them, these shriveled, clawlike appendages that hid under the soft leather gloves Chela had made.

She had been marvelous, he thought with affection, watching her sorting the provisions from Khymer with the other women. Patient with his moods, with his bitterness and confusion, with his refusal to remove the gloves even in bed. She claimed she did not find his hands repulsive, since they had gotten that way in saving her life. Fortune had certainly smiled on him that day Tobas had brought her out of the wilderness, small and terrified and radiating that incredible wild Power.

He and Briana had agreed that Chela's Power could never have been tamed in a Temple of the Goddess. It was so unlike any other woman's talent, unlike the white flame, and also different from the wizards' inborn Power. Earth magic, Briana had christened it, and green magic; Chela liked both names and concurred with Briana's contention that her Power was green. Gwydion had never seen the color but could not argue.

His own Power was returning a little, haphazard and nearly unusable. It would provide him with an occasional flash of insight, a moment of control, then leave him attempting the simplest spells with as much result as Tobas might have achieved. When the coronation of Valahtia was over, he and Chela would travel back to the College at Akesh, where he could immerse himself in the library and try to understand what had happened to him.

"Gwydion?" Chela had finished packing a crate and leaned against a tent pole, her blue eyes thoughtful. "Is it true what they say, that there are wizards left?"

"Yes. Remember, there were many of them in control of the other Kingdoms. I imagine they've gone into hiding, though, because singly none of them have anything like the Power Belaric had, and their soldiers have deserted them." He had just been talking to Valahtia about the same subject. He had convinced her to offer amnesty to any wizard who would come forward and pledge his loyalty, and to forbid the killing of the wizard children who would continue to be born. The only problem was, Valahtia had a precarious, barely legal hold on her own throne, so she had no influence over the other rulers to convince them to proclaim similar measures.

"Do you think they'll all be trying to reach the College, too?" Chela asked disconcertingly.

"Possibly." He tried to be unconcerned. "If they get there before us, we'll simply have to ask them to share their books, won't we?"

"I can't," Briana said without preamble, when Valahtia answered her knock on the shield that hung from the tent flap.

The Princess was equally firm. "You must. I have to have the Goddess's blessing, or the council will laugh in my face when I press my claim."

"Your brother already has the blessing for Caerlin; there can't be two at once, and I can't take his away from him."

"Why not? He'd be a terrible King."

"If he commits some crime, or breaks the oaths he made to the First Priestess, then the blessing may be revoked, but it's a long process with many lines of appeal."

"But you'll be First Priestess, and the last authority in an appeal, and you'd rather have me on the throne, wouldn't you?"

Briana sighed, repressing a smile. It was quite true that as First Priestess she would not want to deal with Arel; it was also true that by overtly supporting Valahtia she would antagonize the other royalty. "I can give you this, at least," she offered. "I'll acknowledge your firstborn son as heir, and give him the blessing to rule after you, rather than any children Arel might have.''

The Princess quickly agreed. Briana knew that most of her hopes of gaining the approval of the council of royalty lay in the quick producing of a male heir; doubtless she and Tobas were already busily at work on the problem. Along with the coronation would come a consort ceremony, less than a marriage but more than living together unwed. It was the usual option for a Queen who did not wish the man she loved to become King and therefore her ruler. And Tobas had no desire to be King. At least he had enough royal blood that any children of Valahtia's by him would not have their inheritance questioned.

The night was lit by the pale moon, waning from full, and sentries walked silent, watchful paths around the sleeping camp. But Briana moved as a shadow, her bare feet soundless on the sand, wearing a white S'tari robe that blended with the moonlit dunes. She slipped through the sentry lines and melted into the dry grove of trees that clustered around the inadequate oasis well. She tried not to think that the old First Priestess was watching, saddened and disapproving, but she could not suppress the thought.

The soft call at the rear flap of the tent sounded; though Kyellan had been waiting, he moved in disbelief that she had actually come. Somehow he had never truly thought it would happen. Yet with the flap raised, there she stood, like a bride in white. Her face was pale, shy, half-frightened, and without its priestess's dignity. He had never realized quite how young she was.

Briana smiled tremulously. He took her hand in his and led her inside. Silence filled the small space, echoing off the hide walls; but it was a night for silence. They felt no need for words. He unbound her thick auburn hair from its coils, wishing he had two hands to use, marveling at the heavy, soft glory of it; then he kissed her and thought he had waited all his life for this moment.

It was a night for slow pleasures, for awakening her dancer's body to a need it had never acknowledged. And when it awoke, the need was so strong that Kyellan was swept along with it, a reed at floodtide, into fires and moon darkness and the sweet breath of morning; he had never known he could feel so much, and it frightened him, overwhelmed him, but he had no desire to resist. Love was a wine more potent than he had imagined. He would never feel with any other woman what he felt that night with Briana.

Each time she reached her peak of ecstasy, she cried out to the Goddess in a language he could not understand. She was purest flame, so strong it burned him. She was shadow, and mist, and night stars. He knew less of her, comprehended less, than any other who had ever shared his bed, though he desperately wanted to know everything about her. It tore his soul to think he could never learn. She would not be there to teach him.

Nights passed, and days between like pale dreams, and far too soon came the day when the caravan was to leave for Cavernon City. Briana would go the other direction, to Khymer, to gather what priestesses she could find. She would send them on to Cavernon, except for a few who would be assigned to guard and study the Seat of the Goddess.

She walked with Kyellan far out into the desert where no one could see, numb with pain and the need to explain to him something she could not explain to herself.

"Come with me," he said for the hundredth time.

"No," she answered as always, but this time tears could not be stopped. She clung to him like a child.

He stroked her hair. "Don't cry, Briana. I know you can't. I still don't understand it, but I know."

She had intended to be cheerful, and she blinked back her tears with some of her old strength. "At least I know I'm carrying your child. The Power of the Seat told me that."

"What will happen to it?"

"If it's a girl, she will be raised in the Temple. If a boy . . ." She looked down. "He will be given to some kind family, to be raised in the Light."

Kyellan raised her face to meet his gold-brown eyes. "He'll need more than that, Briana. You knew it when you came to me, that if I gave you a child it would be the next Shape-Changer."

She pulled away. Yes, she had known it, but she had wished to forget. "I . . . I will see that someone is found to train him," she finally said. "He will learn to control it, to use it only for the Light."

"I'd take him," Kyellan said ruefully, "except I don't even know how to control my own Power, much less how to teach a child."

The long call of Tobas's horn drifted over the hills. "It's time," he said thickly. His hard-muscled arm drew her close, and his kiss sought something she could no longer give. "Will I ever see you again?"

"I'll be coming to Cavernon eventually, to rebuild the Temple," she said, allowing herself a moment of hope; then she shook her head. "It would be better not. Go quickly, they will be waiting."

"Your Goddess knows I love you," he whispered, and ran back over the desert toward the crowded oasis.

Briana sank to the sun-baked ground. Yes, the Goddess knew. She had done her service to Cianya, known the love of a man, conceived a child. Now the Goddess told her she was complete. Fulfilled. When the child was born, she would be ready to become Her voice on earth. But it was not enough. And Briana did not think it would ever be.

Tobas rode at Valahtia's side, at the army's head. The Princess, who would be Queen before the day was out, was dressed in the uniform of the resistance army. But S'tari women had piled her ebony hair into an elaborate coronet and had rimmed her eyes with kohl. She was stunning. Bells rang as they entered Cavernon City at the northeast gate. The great houses of the court were empty, but the streets were thronged with people, so many that the army had to go only two abreast. A flower-burdened child with perfumed hair was lifted to the Princess. She took the proffered wreath and, to the delight of the parents, placed the small girl before her in the S'tari saddle to ride to the palace.

"They love me!" Valahtia exulted.

He nodded, grinning sardonically. "They will adore you," he assured her, "until your brother lays siege to the city with the support of the council."

Her smile fell. "Do you think he will? Really?"

"I wouldn't be surprised."

"Well, then, the army and my S'tari will defend us. Kyellan won't let him take my throne."

He did not answer. Kyellan had not yet accepted her offer of the command of her army; Tobas did not think he was going to. His old friend had been bitterly silent for most of the journey. He thought it had something to do with Briana; and also with his loss of the use of his sword arm—though Kyellan was almost equally adept with his left and had been practicing with a left-handed sword Diveshi had presented him in honor of his killing of Onedon.

The Princess looked at him askance. "You don't think they'll crown Arel King in Altimar, do you?"

"It's possible."

"I'll worry about that later," she decided, and began to show the little girl at her saddle bow how to rein a S'tari horse. "Today is my day, and I intend to enjoy it. I suggest, my love, that you do the same."

The Tiranon was sadly empty of the wild gaiety of court life; not that Kyellan missed it much. He held the place of Valahtia's champion in the coronation ceremonies and allowed her to pin a medal on him for his part in the battle, but he politely declined her offer of the command of her armies. She had made another offer then, that she would reestablish the Royal Guard with him at its head. He had refused. The detachments of S'tari Surleien had sent to defend her should suffice as a bodyguard; they looked appropriately fierce, positioned around the throne and through the crowded Audience Hall with turbaned heads and bared scimitars.

"But what will you do?" Tobas asked angrily in the small anteroom where Kyellan was helping him into the ridiculous jeweled robes someone had suggested for the consort ceremony.

"I can't be a soldier with only one arm," Kyellan said firmly, buckling a heavy sapphire-studded belt around the Earl of Laenar's waist and untangling the impractical scabbard from the folds of the robe. "Gwydion and Chela have asked me to come with them to Akesh, and I've decided to go."

"I'd have thought you'd have done enough traveling to last a long time." Tobas thrust his worn Guard sword into the soft padding of the ceremonial scabbard. His eyes, the color Kyellan's had once been, pleaded for sanity. "Damn it, Ky, I want you to stay. So does the Queen. You can find something to do here, something important and worthwhile. We're going to need your advice, your experience, when Arel starts pressing for the throne."

"I'm sorry. I can't stay."

Tobas ran a comb with difficulty through his curly hair, grown long over the past months. "Look," he said stubbornly, "I know a lot happened to you that I don't understand, but you're home now. You kept saying how much you missed the city when we were in Garith . . . now you say you want to go back there. It makes no sense."

Kyellan did not respond. He could not explain to Tobas why he was going; that Gwydion thought the libraries of Akesh might teach him to use his Shape-Changer spirit without the fear of losing command. Perhaps even teach him, for instance, to change his right arm into one that worked.

"I could never argue with you," his young friend said in frustration.

"I have to go," he said gently.

"Then go. But come back. We need you."

The streets of Rahan Quarter were untouched by war or invasion or changes in the ruler at the Tiranon. The people went their timeworn way, stealing and whoring and killing with no thought for laws or the morals of their countless gods. Kyellan walked the night, wearing an old uniform of the Royal Guard, and felt for the first time how truly alien he had become. He had returned, perhaps thinking to lose himself among the mazes of his childhood, to forget wizards and battles and melt into the underside of the city.

But a one-armed thief was worse than a one-armed soldier. And people recognized him now, their awe and respect mingled with fear; they recognized him as the soldier who had killed a wizard, not as the thin, amoral child who had roamed these same streets not so long ago. He was a stranger. They wondered what they could get from him.

He did not notice the slight figure until it reached out and touched his sleeve. "Kylen?" The voice was soft and hoarse, the thin face marred by an ugly scar that ran from nose to jawline.

"Alaira." He breathed the name unbelieving.

"I hardly recognized you." She laughed a little, but it turned into a cough. She was terribly thin, and her hand shook when he took it. "You've changed."

You too, he thought, but did not say aloud. "I thought you would be dead."

"I'm a survivor," she said, shivering in the night warmth.

He looked at her, reading the hunger and misery behind her bright smile. Gods, he remembered that look well enough. "Buy you a drink?" Not waiting for an answer, he propelled her into the nearest tavern, sat her at a quiet corner table, and ordered soup for her and ale for himself.

She did not speak again until she had drunk half the bowl. Then, her smile a little less horrible, she met his gaze. "Your eyes! Different, but I like them. Is it true you killed a wizard, and with magic?"

"It's true."

"And that you're going north again?" Her voice was wistful.

"Yes. Alaira, how badly did they treat you? I really thought you'd be killed." He was surprised at the depth of his concern.

She did not answer until she had had another drink of the meat broth. "It wasn't that bad. The captain took me, after two days. He wasn't much worse than Dhomli." She tossed her short black hair in an old dismissive gesture. "Anyway, it's over."

"Is it? You haven't been eating much."

She took a breath to argue, met his gaze, and sighed. "You're right. It's this scar. No one wants me, since I'm not very pretty anymore. I've been thinking about getting back into our old profession. No one cares what you look like, if you're quick and quiet."

"No. Come with me."

"What?"

"I said come with me," he repeated, surprised at himself. "To Garith. Remember, a long, long time ago, I said I'd show you the world?"

Alaira's dark eyes opened wide. "You're not serious. You mean wild places, and mountains, and riding for days without seeing anything but sheep and rocks?"

"Just what you need." And I can hardly leave you to starve in Rahan Quarter, he added silently.

"But you're going with your friends, the wizard and his girl."

"That's why I need company. They won't see anything but each other." He took her hand firmly and trapped her wide eyes with his own. "Come with me."

She looked away miserably. "I can't offer you much, Ky. Look at me."

"Offer me your friendship," he said roughly. "I'm not asking you along to warm my bed. That wouldn't be fair to either of us. I want my oldest friend at my side."

She cocked her head, for a moment the kittenish twelve-year-old who had been his companion years before. "You really mean that? I don't know whether I should be proud

or insulted.'' Her laughter was rueful. ''What the hell.
Show me the world.''

   ''My lady, it awaits you.'' He bowed over her small
hand and led her from the tavern into the crowded streets.
The new moon's crescent, high above the garish red lamps,
seemed to smile in gentle approval.